THE HOUSE ON THE STRAND

Daughter of the famous actor-manager Sir Gerald du Maurier, Daphne du Maurier was educated at home in London, and then in Paris, before writing her first novel, *The Loving Spirit*, in 1931. Three others, and a frank biography of her father, followed before *Rebecca*, in 1938, made her to her surprise one of the most popular authors of the day. Nearly all her fifteen novels have been best-sellers, and several of her works became successful films, notably *Rebecca*, starring Laurence Olivier, and the short stories *The Birds* and *Don't Look Now*. She also wrote biographies of Branwell Brontë and her own Victorian family, two volumes of autobiography, and *Vanishing Cornwall*, an eloquent evocation of her beloved countryside that is such a strong feature of her fiction.

Daphne du Maurier, who was married to Lieutenant-General Sir Frederick Browning, KCVO, DSO, was made a DBE in 1969. When she died in 1989, Margaret Forster wrote in tribute: 'No other popular writer has so triumphantly defied classification . . . She satisfied all the questionable criteria of popular fiction, and yet satisfied too the exacting requirements of "real literature", something very few novelists ever do.'

By the same author

Rule Britannia
My Cousin Rachel
The King's General
The Progress of Julius
I'll Never Be Young Again
The Scapegoat
The Loving Spirit
Frenchman's Creek
Rebecca
Mary Anne
The Birds and Other Stories
The Rendezvous and Other Stories

Non-Fiction

Golden Lads
The Winding Stair
Myself When Young (Autobiography)
The Rebecca Notebook and other Memories
Vanishing Cornwall
The Infernal World of Branwell Brontë

THE HOUSE ON THE STRAND

Daphne du Maurier

ARROW BOOKS

First published by Arrow in 1992

7 9 10 8

© 1969 by Daphne du Maurier

First published in the United Kingdom in 1969 by
Victor Gollancz Ltd

Arrow Books Limited
Random House, 20 Vauxhall Bridge Road, London SW1V 2SA

Random House Australia (Pty) Limited
20 Alfred Street, Milsons Point, Sydney,
New South Wales 2061, Australia

Random House New Zealand Limited
18 Poland Road, Glenfield
Auckland 10, New Zealand

Random House South Africa (Pty) Limited
PO Box 337, Bergvlei, South Africa

Random House UK Limited Reg. No. 954009

A CIP catalogue record for this book
is available from the British Library

Papers used by Random House UK Limited
are natural, recyclable products made from wood grown in
sustainable forests. The manufacturing processes conform to
the environmental regulations of the country of origin

ISBN 0 09 986570 X

Printed and bound in Great Britain by
Cox & Wyman Ltd, Reading, Berkshire

Acknowledgements

I wish to thank Miss Hawkridge, Senior Assistant Archivist of the County Record Office, Truro; Mr H. L. Douch, MA, Curator of the County Museum, Truro; Mr R. Blewett, MA, of St Day; Mrs St George Saunders; and the Public Record Office, to all of whom I am indebted for information and original documents. Most especially I should like to express my gratitude to Mr J. R. Thomas of the Tywardreath Old Cornwall Society, whose unfailing kindness and generosity in lending me his own notes on the history of the Manor and Priory of Tywardreath first awakened my interest, and set me on the road to blending fact and fiction in this tale of the House on the Strand.

Daphne du Maurier

for
my predecessors
at Kilmarth

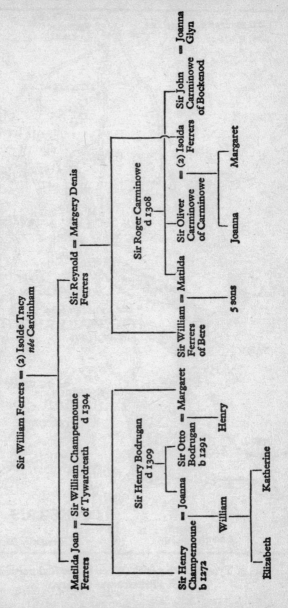

FAMILY TREE OF THE CHAMPERNOUNES, CARMINOWES AND BODRUGANS IN THE 14TH CENTURY

Sir William Ferrers = (2) Isolde Tracy *née* Cardinham

Matilda Joan = Sir William Champernoune of Tywardreath d 1304

Sir Reynold = Margery Denis Ferrers

Sir Henry Champernoune b 1272 = Joanna

Sir Henry Bodrugan d 1309

Sir Otto Bodrugan b 1291 = Margaret

Sir William = Matilda Ferrers of Bere

Sir Roger Carminowe d 1308

Sir Oliver Carminowe of Carminowe = (2) Isolda Ferrers

Sir John Carminowe of Bockenod = Joanna Glyn

Elizabeth   Katherine

William   Henry

5 sons

Joanna   Margaret

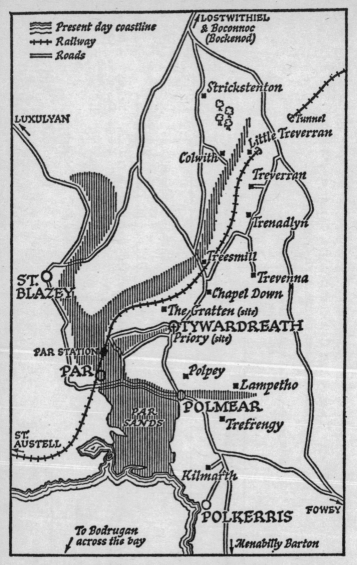

Legend:
- ≋ Present day coastline
- +++ Railway
- ══ Roads

LUXULYAN

LOSTWITHIEL
& Boconnoc
(Bockenod)

Strickstenton

Tunnel

Little Treverran

Colwith

Treverran

Trenadlyn

Treesmill

ST.
BLAZEY

Trevenna

Chapel Down

The Gratten (site)

TYWARDREATH
Priory (site)

PAR STATION

PAR

Polpey

Lampetho

POLMEAR

PAR
SANDS

Trefrengy

ST.
AUSTELL

Kilmarth

FOWEY

POLKERRIS

To Bodrugan
across the bay

Menabilly Barton

Part of Tywardreath parish. When Roger Kylmerth lived,
the shaded area was estuary.

one

The first thing I noticed was the clarity of the air, and then the sharp green colour of the land. There was no softness anywhere. The distant hills did not blend into the sky but stood out like rocks, so close that I could almost touch them, their proximity giving me that shock of surprise and wonder which a child feels looking for the first time through a telescope. Nearer to me, too, each object had the same hard quality, the very grass turning to single blades, springing from a younger, harsher soil than the soil I knew.

I had expected – if I expected anything – a transformation of another kind: a tranquil sense of well-being, the blurred intoxication of a dream, with everything about me misty, ill-defined; not this tremendous impact, a reality more vivid than anything hitherto experienced, sleeping or awake. Now every impression was heightened, every part of me singularly aware: eyesight, hearing, sense of smell, all had been in some way sharpened.

All but the sense of touch: I could not feel the ground beneath my feet. Magnus had warned me of this. He had told me, 'You won't be aware of your body coming into contact with inanimate objects. You will walk, stand, sit, brush against them, but will feel nothing. Don't worry. The very fact that you can move without sensation is half the wonder.'

This, of course, I had taken as a joke, one of the many bribes to goad me to experiment. Now he was proved right. I started to go forward, and the sensation was exhilarating, for I seemed to move without effort, feeling no contact with the ground.

I was walking downhill towards the sea, across those fields of sharp-edged silver grass that glistened under the sun, for the sky – dull, a moment ago, to my ordinary eyes – was now cloudless, a blazing ecstatic blue. I remembered that the tide had been out, the stretches of flat sand exposed, the row of bathing-huts, lined like dentures in an open mouth, forming a solid background to the golden expanse. Now they had gone, and with them the rows of houses fronting the road, the docks, all of Par – chimneys, rooftops, buildings – and the sprawling tentacles of St Austell enveloping the countryside beyond the bay. There was nothing left but grass and scrub, and the high distant hills that seemed so near; while before me the sea rolled into the bay, covering the whole stretch of sand as if a tidal wave had swept over the land, swallowing it in one rapacious draught. To the north-west, the cliffs came down to meet the sea, which, narrowing gradually, formed a wide estuary, the waters sweeping inward, following the curve of the land and so vanishing out of sight.

When I came to the edge of the cliff and looked beneath me, where the road should be, the inn, the café, the almshouses at the base of Polmear hill, I realized that the sea swept inland here as well, forming a creek that cut to the east, into the valley. Road and houses had gone, leaving only a dip between the land which rose on either side of the creek. Here the channel ran narrowly between banks of mud and sand, so that at low tide the water would surely seep away, leaving a marshy track that could be forded, if not on foot, at least by a horseman. I descended the hill and stood beside the creek, trying to pinpoint in my mind the exact course of the road I knew, but already the old sense of orientation had gone: there was nothing to serve as guide except the ground itself, the valley and the hills.

The waters of the narrow channel rippled swift and blue over the sand, leaving on either side a frothy scum. Bubbles formed, expanded and vanished, and all the ordinary timeless waste came drifting with the tide, tresses of dark seaweed, feathers, twigs, the aftermath of some autumnal gale. I knew, in my own time, it was high summer, however dull and overcast the day, but all about me now was the clearer light of approaching winter, surely an early afternoon when the bright sun, already flaming in the west, would turn the sky dark crimson before the night clouds came.

The first live things swam into vision, gulls following the tide, small waders skimming the surface of the stream, while high on the opposite hill, sharply defined against the skyline, a team of oxen ploughed their steady course. I closed my eyes, then opened them again. The team had vanished behind the rise of the field they worked, but the cloud of gulls, screaming in their wake, told me they had been a living presence, no figment of a dream.

I drank deep of the cold air, filling my lungs. Just to breathe was a joy never yet experienced for its own sake, having some quality of magic that I had not sensed before. Impossible to analyse thought, impossible to let my reason play on what I saw: in this new world of perception and delight there was nothing but intensity of feeling to serve as guide.

I might have stood for ever, entranced, content to hover between earth and sky, remote from any life I knew or cared to know; but then I turned my head and saw that I was not alone. The hoofs had made no sound – the pony must have travelled as I had done, across the fields – and now that it trod upon the shingle the clink of stone against metal came to my ears with a sudden shock, and I could smell the warm horse-flesh, sweaty and strong.

Instinct made me back away, startled, for the rider came straight towards me, unconscious of my presence. He checked his pony at the water's edge and looked seaward, measuring the tide. Now, for the first time, I experienced not only excitement but fear as well, for this was no phantom figure but solid, real, the shape of foot in stirrup, hand on rein, all too perilously close for my comfort. I did not fear being ridden down: what jolted me to a sudden sense of panic was the encounter itself, this bridging of centuries between his time and mine. He shifted his gaze from the sea and looked straight at me. Surely he saw me, surely I read, in those deepset eyes, a signal of recognition? He smiled, patted his pony's neck, then, with a swift kick of heel to flank, urged the beast across the ford, straight through the narrow channel, and so to the other side.

He had not seen me, he could not see me; he lived in another time. Why, then, the sudden shift in the saddle, the swing round to look back over his shoulder to where I stood? It was a challenge. 'Follow if you dare!' – compelling, strange. I measured the depth of water across the ford, and, though it had reached the pony's hocks, plunged after him, careless of a wetting, realizing when I reached the other side that I had walked dry-shod, without sensation.

The horseman rode uphill, I following, the track he took muddied and very steep, swinging abruptly to the left when it traversed the higher ground. This, I remembered, pleased with the recognition, was the same course that the lane took today – I had driven up it only that morning. Here resemblance ended, for no hedges banked the track as they did in my own time. Ploughlands lay to right and left, bare to the winds, and patches of scrubby moor with clumps of furze. We came abreast the team of oxen, and for the first time I could see the man who drove them, a small, hooded figure humped over a heavy wooden plough. He raised a hand in greeting to my horseman, shouted something, then plodded on, the gulls crying and wheeling above his head.

This greeting of one man to another seemed natural, and the sense of shock that had been part of me since I first saw the horseman at the ford gave place to wonder, then acceptance. I was reminded of my first journey as a child in France, travelling by sleeper overnight, throwing open the carriage window in the morning to see foreign fields fly by, villages, towns, figures labouring the land humped like the ploughman now, and thinking, with childish wonder, 'Are they alive like me, or just pretending?'

My excuse for wonder was greater now than then. I looked at my horseman and his pony, and moved within touching, smelling distance. Both exhaled a pungency so strong that they seemed of the essence of life itself. The sweat-streaks on the pony's flanks, the shaggy mane, the fleck of froth at the bit's edge; and that broad knee in the stockinged leg, the leather jerkin laced across the tunic, that movement in the saddle, those hands upon the reins, that face itself, lantern-jawed and ruddy, framed in black hair which fell below his ears – this was reality, I the alien presence.

I longed to stretch out my hand and lay it on the pony's flank, but I remembered Magnus's warning. 'If you meet a figure from the past, don't for heaven's sake touch him. Inanimate objects don't matter, but if you try to make contact with living flesh the link breaks, and you'll come to with a very unpleasant jerk. I tried it: I know.'

The track led across the ploughlands and then dipped, and now the whole altered landscape spread itself before my eyes. The village of Tywardreath, as I had seen it a few hours earlier, had utterly changed. The cottages and houses that had formed a jigsaw pattern, spreading north and west from the church, had vanished: there was a hamlet here now, boxed together by a child, like the toy farm I used to play with on my bedroom floor. Small dwellings, thatch-roofed, squat, clustered round a sprawling green on which were pigs, geese, chickens, two or three hobbled ponies, and the inevitable prowling dogs. Smoke rose from these humble dwellings, but not from any chimneys, from some hole in the thatch. Then grace and symmetry took charge again, for below the cluster was the church. But not the church that I had known a few hours earlier. This one was smaller and had no tower, and forming part of it, or so it seemed, ran a long, low building of stone, the whole encompassed by stone walls. Within this enclosure were orchards, gardens, outbuildings, a wooded copse, and beneath the copse the land sloped to a valley, and up that valley came the long arm of the sea.

I would have stood and stared, the setting had such beauty and simplicity, but my horseman travelled on, and compulsion to follow sent me after him. The track descended to the green, and now the village life was all about me; there were women by the well at the near corner of the green, their long skirts caught up round the waist, their heads bound with cloth covering them to the chin, so that nothing showed but eyes and nose. The arrival of my horseman created disturbance. Dogs started barking, more women appeared from the dwellings that now, on closer inspection, proved to be little more than hovels, and there was a calling to and fro across the green, the voices, despite the uncouth clash of consonants, ringing with the unmistakable Cornish burr.

The rider turned left, dismounted before the walled enclosure, flung his reins over a staple in the ground, and entered through a broad, brass-studded doorway. Above the arch there was a carving showing the robed figure of a saint, holding in his right hand the cross of St Andrew. My Catholic training, long forgotten, even mocked, made me cross myself before that door, and as I did so a bell sounded from within, striking so profound a chord in my memory that I hesitated before entering, dreading the old power that might turn me back into the childhood mould.

I need not have worried. The scene that met my eyes was not that of orderly paths and quadrangles, quiet cloisters, the odour of sanctity, the silence born of prayer. The gate opened upon a muddied yard, round which two men were chasing a frightened boy, flicking at his bare thighs with flails. Both, from their dress and tonsure, were monks, and the boy a novice, his skirt secured above his waist to make their sport more piquant.

The horseman watched the pantomime unmoved, but when the boy at last fell, his habit about his ears, his skinny limbs and bare backside exposed, he called, 'Don't bleed him yet. The Prior likes sucking-pig served without sauce. The garnish will come later when the piglet turns tough.' Meanwhile the bell for prayer continued, without effect upon the sportsmen in the yard.

My horseman, his sally applauded, crossed the yard and entered the building that lay before us, turning into a passageway which seemed to divide kitchen from refectory, judging by the smell of rancid fowl, only partly sweetened by turf smoke from the fire. Ignoring the warmth and savour of the kitchen to the right, and the colder comfort of the refectory with its bare benches on his left, he pushed through a centre door and up a flight of steps to a higher level, where the passage was barred by yet another door. He knocked upon it, and without waiting for an answer walked inside.

The room, with timbered roof and plastered walls, had some semblance of comfort, but the scrubbed and polished austerity, a vivid memory of my own childhood, was totally absent. This rush-strewn floor was littered with discarded bones half-chewed by dogs, and the bed in the far corner, with its musty hangings, appeared to serve as a general depository for dumped goods – a rug made from a sheep's coat, a pair of sandals, a rounded cheese on a tin plate, a fishing-rod, with a greyhound scratching itself in the midst of all.

'Greetings, Father Prior,' said my horseman.

Something rose to a sitting posture in the bed, disturbing the greyhound, which leapt to the floor, and the something was an elderly, pink-cheeked monk, startled from his sleep.

'I left orders I was not to be disturbed,' he said.

My horseman shrugged. 'Not even for the Office?' he asked, and put out his hand to the dog, which crept beside him, wagging a bitten tail.

The sarcasm brought no reply. The Prior dragged his coverings closer, humping his knees beneath him. 'I need rest,' he said, 'all the rest possible, to be in a fit state to receive the Bishop. You have heard the news?'

'There are always rumours,' answered the horseman.

'This was not rumour. Sir John sent the message yesterday. The Bishop has already set out from Exeter and will be here on

Monday, expecting hospitality and shelter for the night with us, after leaving Launceston.'

The horseman smiled. 'The Bishop times his visit well. Martinmas, and fresh meat killed for his dinner. He'll sleep with his belly full, you've no cause for worry.'

'No cause for worry?' The Prior's petulant voice touched a higher key. 'You think I can control my unruly mob? What kind of impression will they make upon that new broom of a Bishop, primed as he is to sweep the whole Diocese clean?'

'They'll come to heel if you promise them reward for seemly behaviour. Keep in the good graces of Sir John Carminowe, that's all that matters.'

The Prior moved restlessly beneath his covers. 'Sir John is not easily fooled, and he has his own way to make, with a foot in every camp. Our patron he may be, but he won't stand by me if it doesn't suit his ends.'

The horseman picked up a bone from the rushes, and gave it to the dog. 'Sir Henry, as lord of the manor, will take precedence over Sir John on this occasion,' he said. 'He'll not disgrace you, garbed like a penitent. I warrant he is on his knees in the chapel now.'

The Prior was not amused. 'As the lord's steward you should show more respect for him;' he observed, then added thoughtfully, 'Henry de Champernoune is a more faithful man of God than I.'

The horseman laughed. 'The spirit is willing, Father Prior, but the flesh?' He fondled the greyhound's ear. 'Best not talk about the flesh before the Bishop's visit.' Then he straightened himself and walked towards the bed. 'The French ship is lying off Kylmerth. She'll be there for two more tides if you want to give me letters for her.'

The Prior thrust off his covers and scrambled from the bed. 'Why in the name of blessed Antony did you not say so at once?' he cried, and began to rummage amongst the litter of assorted papers on the bench beside him. He presented a sorry sight in his shift, with spindle legs mottled with varicose veins, and hammer-toed, singularly dirty feet. 'I can find nothing in this jumble,' he complained. 'Why are my papers never in order? Why is Brother Jean never here when I require him?'

He seized a bell from the bench and rang it, exclaiming in

protest at the horseman, who was laughing again. Almost at once a monk entered: from his prompt response he must have been listening at the door. He was young and dark, and possessed a pair of remarkably brilliant eyes.

'At your service, Father,' he said in French, and before he crossed the room to the Prior's side exchanged a wink with the horseman.

'Come, then, don't dally,' fretted the Prior, turning back to the bench.

As the monk passed the horseman he murmured in his ear, 'I'll bring the letters later tonight, and instruct you further in the arts you wish to learn.'

The horseman bowed in mock acknowledgement, and moved towards the door. 'Goodnight, Father Prior. Lose no sleep over the Bishop's visit.'

'Good-night, Roger, good-night. God be with you.'

As we left the room together the horseman sniffed the air with a grimace. The mustiness of the Prior's chamber had now an additional spice, a whiff of perfume from the French monk's habit.

We descended the stairs, but before returning through the passageway the horseman paused a moment, then opened another door and glanced inside. The door gave entrance to the chapel, and the monks who had been playing pantomime with the novice were now at prayer. Or, to describe it more justly, making motion of prayer. Their eyes were downcast, and their lips moved. There were four others present whom I had not seen in the yard, and of these two were fast asleep in their stalls. The novice himself was huddled on his knees, crying silently but bitterly. The only figure with any dignity was that of a middle-aged man, dressed in a long mantle, his grey locks framing a kindly, gracious face. With hands clasped reverently before him, he kept his eyes steadfast on the altar. This, I thought, must be Sir Henry de Champernoune, lord of the manor and my horseman's master, of whose piety the Prior had spoken.

The horseman closed the door and went out into the passage, and so from the building and across the now empty yard to the gate. The green was deserted, for the women had left the well, and there were clouds in the sky, a sense of fading day. The horseman mounted his pony and turned for the track through the upper ploughlands.

I had no idea of time, his time or mine. I was still without sense of touch, and could move beside him without effort. We descended the track to the ford, which he traversed now without wetting his pony's hocks, for the tide had ebbed, and struck upward across the further fields.

When we reached the top of the hill and the fields took on their familiar shape I realized, with growing excitement and surprise, that he was leading me home, for Kilmarth, the house which Magnus had lent me for the summer holidays, lay beyond the little wood ahead of us. Some six or seven ponies were grazing close by, and at sight of the horseman one of them lifted his head and whinnied; then with one accord they swerved, kicked up their heels, and scampered away. He rode on through a clearing in the wood, the track dipped, and there immediately below us in the hollow lay a dwelling, stone-built, thatched, encircled by a yard deep in mud. Piggery and byre formed part of the dwelling, and through a single aperture in the thatch the blue smoke curled. I recognized one thing only, the scoop of land in which the dwelling lay.

The horseman rode down into the yard, dismounted and called, and a boy came out of the adjoining cow-house to take the pony. He was younger, slighter than my horseman, but had the same deep-set eyes, and must have been his brother. He led the pony off, and the horseman passed through the open doorway into the house, which seemed at first sight to consist of one room only. Following close behind, I could distinguish little through the smoke, except that the walls were built of the mixture of clay and straw that they call cob, and the floor was plain earth, without even rushes upon it.

A ladder at the far end led to a loft, only a few feet above the living-space, and looking up I could see straw pallets laid upon the planking. The fire, stacked with turf and furze, lay in a recess let into the wall, and a stew-pot simmered above the smoke, slung between iron bars fixed to the earthen floor. A girl, her lank hair falling below her shoulders, was kneeling by the fire, and as the horseman called a greeting she looked up at him and smiled.

I was close upon his heels, and suddenly he turned, staring straight at me, shoulder to shoulder. I could feel his breath upon my cheek, and I put out one hand, instinctively, to fend him off. I felt a sudden sharp pain on my knuckles and saw that they were bleeding, and at the same time I heard a splintering of glass. He was not there any longer, neither he, nor the girl, nor the smoking fire, and I had driven my right hand through one of the windows of the disused kitchen in Kilmarth's basement, and was standing in the old sunken courtyard beyond.

I stumbled through the open door of the boiler-room, retching violently, not at the sight of blood but because I was seized with an intolerable nausea, rocking me from head to foot. Throbbing in every limb, I leant against the stone wall of the boiler-room, the trickle of blood from my cut hand running down to my wrist.

In the library overhead the telephone began to ring, sounding, in its insistency, like a summons from a lost, unwanted world. I let it ring.

two

It must have taken the best part of ten minutes for the nausea to pass. I sat on a pile of logs in the boiler-room waiting. The worst thing about it was the vertigo: I dared not trust myself to stand. My hand was not badly cut, and I soon staunched the blood with my handkerchief. I could see the splintered window from where I sat, and the fragments of glass on the patio beyond. Later on I might be able to reconstruct the scene, judge where my horseman had been standing, measure the space of that long-vanished house where there were now patio and basement: but not now. Now I was too exhausted.

I wondered what sort of figure I must have cut, if anyone had seen me walking over the fields and across the road at the bottom of the hill, and climbing the lane to Tywardreath. That I had been there I was certain. The state of my shoes, the torn cloth of one trouser leg, and my shirt clammy cold with sweat – this had not come about from a lazy amble on the cliffs.

Presently, the nausea and vertigo having passed, I walked very slowly up the back stairs to the hall above. I went into the lobby where Magnus kept his oilskins and boots and all the rest of his junk, and stared at myself in the looking-glass above the wash-basin. I looked normal enough. A bit white about the gills, nothing worse. I needed a stiff drink more than anything. Then I remembered that Magnus had said: 'Don't touch alcohol for at least three hours after taking the drug, and then go slow.' Tea would be a poor second-best, but it might help, and I went into the kitchen to make myself a cup.

This kitchen had been the family dining-room when Magnus was a boy; he had converted it during recent years. While I waited for the kettle to boil I looked out of the window at the courtyard below. It was a paved enclosure, surrounded by old, moss-encrusted walls. Magnus, in a burst of enthusiasm at some time, had attempted to turn it into a patio, as he called it, where he could flop about nude if a heat-wave ever materialized. His mother, he told me, had never done anything about the enclosure because it led out from what were then the kitchen quarters.

I looked upon it now with different eyes. Impossible to recapture what I had so lately seen – that muddied yard, with the cowhouse adjoining, and the track leading to the wooded grove above. Myself following the horseman through the trees. Was the whole thing hallucination engendered by that hell-brew of a drug? As I wandered, mug in hand, through to the library, the telephone started to ring again. I suspected it might be Magnus, and it was. His voice, clipped and decisive as always, stood me in greater stead than the drink I could not have, or the mug of tea. I flung myself down in a chair and prepared for a session.

'I've been ringing you for hours,' he said. 'Had you forgotten you promised to put through a call at half-past three?'

'I had not forgotten,' I told him. 'The fact is, I was otherwise engaged.'

'So I imagined. Well?'

The moment was one to savour. I wished I could keep him guessing. The thought gave me a pleasing sensation of power, but it was no use, I knew I had to tell him.

'It worked,' I said. 'Success one hundred per cent.'

I realized, from the silence at the other end of the line, that this piece of information was totally unexpected. He had visualized failure. His voice, when it came, was pitched in a lower key, almost as though he were talking to himself.

'I can hardly believe it,' he said. 'How absolutely splendid . . .' And then, taking charge, as always, 'You did exactly as I told you, followed the instructions? Tell me everything, from the beginning . . . Wait, though, are you all right?'

'Yes,' I said, 'I think so', except that I feel bloody tired, and I've cut my hand, and I was nearly sick in the boiler-room.'

'Minor matters, dear boy, minor matters. There's often a feeling of nausea afterwards, it soon passes. Go on.'

His impatience fed my own excitement, and I wished he had been in the room beside me instead of three hundred miles away.

'First of all,' I said, enjoying myself, 'I've seldom seen anything more macabre than your so-called lab. Bluebeard's chamber would be an apter description for it. All those embryos in jars, and that revolting monkey's head . . .'

'Perfectly good specimens and extremely valuable,' he interrupted, 'but don't get side-tracked. I know what they are for: you don't. Tell me what happened.'

I took a sip of my rapidly cooling tea, and put down the mug.

'I found the row of bottles,' I continued, 'all in the locked cupboard. Neatly labelled, A, B, C. I poured exactly three measures from A into the medicine-glass, and that was that. I swallowed it, replaced the bottle and glass, locked the cupboard, locked the lab, and waited for something to happen. Well, nothing did.'

I paused, to let this information sink in. No comment from Magnus.

'So,' I went on, 'I went into the garden. Still no reaction. You told me the time factor varied, that it could be three minutes, five, ten, before anything happened. I expected to feel drowsy, although you hadn't specifically mentioned drowsiness, but as nothing seemed to be happening I thought I would go for a stroll. So I climbed over the wall by the summer-house into the field, and began to walk in the direction of the cliffs.'

'You damn fool,' he said. 'I told you to stay in the house, at any rate for the first experiment.'

'I know you did. But, frankly, I wasn't expecting it to work. I planned to sit down, if it did, and drift off into some delightful dream.'

'Damn fool,' he said again. 'It doesn't happen that way.'

'I know it doesn't, now,' I said.

Then I described my whole experience, from the moment the drug took effect to the smashing of the glass in the basement kitchen. He did not interrupt me at all except to murmur, when I paused for breath and a sip of tea, 'Go on . . . go on . . .'

When I had finished, including the aftermath in the boiler-room, there was complete silence, and I thought we had been cut off. 'Magnus,' I said, 'are you there?'

His voice came back to me, clear and strong, repeating the same words that he had used at the start of our telephone session.

'How splendid,' he said. 'How absolutely splendid.'

Perhaps . . . The truth was that I was completely drained, exhausted, having been through the whole process twice.

He began to talk rapidly, and I could just imagine him sitting at that desk of his in London, one hand holding the receiver, the other reaching out for his inevitable doodling-pad and pencil.

'You realize,' he said, 'that this is the most important thing that has happened since the chemical boys got hold of teonana-catl and ololiuqui? These only push the brain around in different directions – quite chaotic. This is controlled, specific. I knew I was on to something potentially tremendous, but I couldn't be sure, having only tried it on myself, that it wasn't hallucino-genic. If this was so, you and I would have had similar physical reactions – loss of touch, greater intensity of vision, and so on – but not the same experience of altered time. This is the impor-tant thing. The tremendously exciting thing.'

'You mean,' I said, 'that when you tried it on yourself you also went back in time? You saw what I did?'

'Precisely. I didn't expect it any more than you did. No, that's not true, because an experiment I was working on then made it remotely possible. It has to do with DNA, enzyme catalysts, molecular equilibria and the like – above your head, dear boy, I won't elaborate – but the point that interests me at the moment is that you and I apparently went into an identical period of time. Thirteenth or fourteenth century, wouldn't you say, judging from their clothes? I too saw the chap you describe as your horseman – Roger, didn't the Prior call him? – the rather slat-ternly girl by the fire, and someone else as well, a monk, which immediately suggested a tie-up with the mediaeval priory that was once part of Tywardreath. The point is this: does the drug reverse some chemical change in the memory systems of the brain, throwing it back to a particular thermodynamic situation which existed in the past, so that the sensations elsewhere in the brain are repeated? If it does, why does the molecular brew return to that particular moment in time? Why not yesterday, five years ago, or a hundred and twenty years? It could be – and this is the thing that excites me – it could be that there is some very potent link connecting the taker of the drug with the first human image recorded in the brain, while under the drug's influence. In both our cases we saw the horseman. The compulsion to follow him was particularly urgent. You felt it, so did I. What I don't yet know is why he plays Virgil to our Dante in this particular Inferno, but he does, there's no escaping him. I've made the "trip" – to use the students' phraseology – a number of times, and he's invariably there. You'll find the same thing happens on your next adventure. He always takes charge.'

The assumption that I was to continue acting as guinea-pig for Magnus did not surprise me. It was typical of our many years of friendship, both at Cambridge and afterwards. He called the tune, and I danced, in God only knew how many disreputable escapades in our undergraduate life together, and later when we went our separate ways, he to his career as a biophysicist and thence to a professorship at London University, I to the tamer routine of a publisher's office. My marriage to Vita three years ago had made the first break between us, possibly a salutary one for us both. The sudden offer of his house for the summer holidays, which I had accepted gratefully, being between jobs – Vita was urging me to accept a directorship in a flourishing New York publishing firm run by her brother, and I needed time to decide – now appeared to have strings attached. The long, lazy days with which he had baited me, lying about in the garden, sailing across the bay, were beginning to take on another aspect.

'Now look here, Magnus,' I said, 'I did this for you today because I was curious, and also because I was on my own, and whether the drug had any effect or not didn't matter one way or the other. It's quite out of the question to go on. When Vita and her children arrive I shall be tied up with them.'

'When do they come?'

'The boys break up in about a week. Vita's flying back from New York to fetch them from school and bring them down here.'

'That's all right. You can achieve a lot in a week. Look, I must go. I'll ring you at the same time tomorrow. Goodbye.'

He had gone. I was left holding the receiver, with a hundred questions to ask and nothing resolved. How damnably typical of Magnus. He had not even told me if I must expect some side-effect from his hell-brew of synthetic fungus and monkeys' brain-cells, or whatever the solution was that he had extracted from his range of loathsome bottles. The vertigo might seize me again, and the nausea too. I might suddenly go blind, or mad, or both. To hell with Magnus and his freak experiment . . .

I decided to go upstairs and take a bath. It would be a relief to strip off my sweaty shirt, torn trousers, the lot, and relax in a tub of steaming water primed with bath-oil – Magnus was nothing if not fastidious in his tastes. Vita would approve of the bedroom suite he had put at our disposal, his own, in point of fact, bedroom, bathroom, dressing-room, the bedroom with a stunning view across the bay.

I lay back in the bath, letting the water run until it reached my chin, and thought of our last evening in London, when his dubious experiment had been proposed. Previously he had merely suggested that, if I wanted somewhere to go during the boys' school holidays, Kilmarth was mine for the taking. I had tele-phoned Vita in New York, pressing the offer. Vita, not alto-gether enthusiastic, being a hot-house plant like many American women, and usually preferring to take a vacation under a Medi-terranean sky with a casino handy, demurred that it always rained in Cornwall, didn't it, and would the house be warm enough, and what should we do about food? I reassured her on all these points, even to the daily woman who came up every morning from the village, and finally she agreed, chiefly, I think, because I had explained there was a dishwasher and an outsize fridge in the lately converted kitchen. Magnus was much amused when I told him.

'Three years of marriage,' he said, 'and the dishwasher means more to your conjugal life than the double bed I'm throwing in for good measure. I warned you it wouldn't last. The marriage, I mean, not the bed.'

I skated over the somewhat thorny topic of my marriage, which was going through a period of reaction after the first impulsive, passionate twelve months, for if it was thorny this was largely because I wanted to remain in England and Vita wanted me to settle in the States. In any event, neither my marriage nor my future job concerned Magnus, and he passed on to talk about the house, the various changes he had made since his parents had died – I had stayed there several times when we were at Cambridge – and how he had converted the old laundry in the basement to a laboratory, just for the fun of it, so that he could amuse himself with experiments that would have no connection with his work in London.

On this last occasion he had prepared the ground well with an excellent dinner, and I was under the usual spell of his personality, when he suddenly said, 'I've had what I think is a success with one particular piece of research. A combination of plant and chemical into a drug which has an extraordinary effect upon the brain.'

His manner was casual, but Magnus was always casual when he was making some statement that was important to him.

'I thought all the so-called hard drugs had that effect,' I said. 'The people who take them, mescalin, LSD, or whatever, pass into a world of fantasy filled with exotic blooms and imagine they're in Paradise.'

He poured more brandy into my glass. 'There was no fantasy about the world I entered,' he said. 'It was very real indeed.'

This piqued my curiosity. A world other than his own egotistical centre would have to possess some special attraction to draw him into it.

'What sort of world?' I asked.

'The past,' he answered.

I remember laughing as I cupped the brandy glass in my hand. 'All your sins, do you mean? The evil deeds of a misspent youth?'

'No, no,' he shook his head impatiently, 'nothing personal at all. I was merely an observer. No, the fact was . . .' he broke off, and shrugged his shoulders. 'I won't tell you what I saw: it would spoil the experiment for you.'

'Spoil the experiment for me?'

'Yes. I want you to try the drug yourself, and see if it produces the same effect.'

I shook my head. 'Oh, no,' I told him, 'we're not at Cambridge any more. Twenty years ago I might have swallowed one of your concoctions and risked death. Not any longer.'

'I'm not asking you to risk death,' he said impatiently. 'I'm asking you to give up twenty minutes, possibly an hour, of an idle afternoon, before Vita and the children arrive, by trying an experiment on yourself that may change the whole conception of time as we know it at present.'

There was no doubt that he meant every word he said. He was no longer the flippant Magnus of Cambridge days: he was a professor of biophysics, already famous in his particular field, and, although I understood little if anything of his life's work, I realized that if he really had hit upon some remarkable drug he might be mistaken in its importance, but he was not lying about his own evaluation of it.

'Why me?' I asked. 'Why not try it on your disciples in London University under proper conditions?'

'Because it would be premature,' he said, 'and because I'm not prepared to risk telling anyone, not even my disciples, as you choose to call them. You are the only one to know that I'm even thinking along these particular lines, which is way outside the stuff I usually do. I stumbled on this thing by chance, and I've got to find out more about it before I'm even remotely satisfied that it has possibilities. I intend to work on it when I come down to Kilmarth in September. Meanwhile, you're going to be alone in the house. You could at least try it once, and report back. I may be entirely wrong about it. It may have no effect upon you except to turn your hands and feet temporarily numb and make your brain, such as you possess, dear boy, rather more alert than it is at present.'

Of course in the end, after another glass of brandy, he had talked me into it. He gave me detailed instructions about the lab, he gave me the keys to the lab itself and to the cupboard where he kept the drug, and described the sudden effect it might have – no intervening stage, but direct transition from one state to another – and he said something about the after-effects, the possibility of nausea. It was only when I asked him directly what I was likely to see that he became evasive.

'No,' he said, 'it might predispose you, unconsciously, to see what I saw. You've got to make this experiment with an open mind, unprejudiced.'

A few days later I left London and drove to Cornwall. The house was aired and ready – Magnus had briefed Mrs Collins from Polkerris, the small village below Kilmarth – and I found vases filled with flowers, food in the fridge, and fires in the music-room and the library, although it was mid-July; Vita could not have done better herself. I spent the first couple of days enjoying the peace of the place, and the comfort, too, which, if I remembered rightly, had been lacking in former times when Magnus's delightful and somewhat eccentric parents were in command. The father, Commander Lane, had been a retired naval man with a passion for sailing a ten-ton yacht in which we were invariably seasick, the mother a vague, haphazard creature of great charm who pottered about in an enormous broad-brimmed hat whatever the weather, indoors and out, and spent her time snipping the dead heads off roses, which she grew with passion but with singular lack of real success. I laughed at them and loved them, and when they died within twelve months of one another I was almost more distressed than Magnus was himself.

It all seemed a long time ago now. The house was a good deal changed and modernized, yet somehow their engaging presence lingered still, or so I had thought, those first few days. Now, after the experiment, I was not so sure. Unless, having seldom penetrated the basement in those early holidays, I had been unaware that it held other memories.

I got out of the bath and dried myself, put on a change of clothes, lit a cigarette, and went downstairs to the music-room, so called in lieu of the more conventional 'drawing-room' because Magnus's parents excelled at playing and singing duets. I wondered if it was still too soon to pour myself the drink I badly needed. Better be safe than sorry – I would wait another hour.

I switched on the radiogram and picked a record at random from the top of the stack. Bach's Brandenburg Concerto No. 3 might restore my poise and equanimity. Magnus must have mixed up his records the last time he was down, however, for it was not the measured strains of Bach that fell upon my ears, as I lay stretched on the sofa before the log fire, but the insidious, disquieting murmur of Debussy's *La Mer*. Odd choice for Magnus when he had been down at Easter. I thought he eschewed the romantic composers. I must have been mistaken, unless his taste had changed through the years. Or had his dabbling in the unknown awakened a liking for more mystical sounds, the magical conjuring of sea upon the shore? Had Magnus seen the estuary sweeping deep into the land, as I had done this afternoon? Had he seen the green fields sharp and clear, the blue water prodding the valley, the stone walls of the Priory graven against the hill? I did not know: he had not told me. So much unasked on that abortive telephone conversation. So much unsaid.

I let the record play to the end, but far from calming me it had the opposite effect. The house was strangely silent now the music had stopped, and with the rise and fall of *La Mer* still lingering in my head I walked through the hall to the library and looked out of the wide window to the sea. It was slaty grey, whipped darker in places by a westerly wind, yet calm, with little swell. Different from the more turbulent blue sea of afternoon glimpsed in that other world.

There are two staircases descending to the basement at Kilmarth. The first, leading from the hall, goes direct to the cellars and the boiler-room, and thence to the door into the patio. The second is reached by passing through the kitchen, and so down to the back entrance, the old kitchen, scullery, larder and laundry. It was the laundry, reached by the second staircase, that Magnus had converted to a laboratory.

I went down these stairs, turned the key of the door, and entered the laboratory once again. There was nothing clinical about it. The old sink still stood upon the stone-flagged floor beneath a small barred window. Beside it was an open fireplace, with a cloam oven, used in old days for baking bread, cut into the thickness of the wall. In the cobwebbed ceiling were rusty hooks, from which in former times salted meat and hams must have hung.

Magnus had ranged his curious exhibits along the slatted shelves fixed to the walls. Some of them were skeletons, but others were still intact, preserved in a chemical solution, their flesh bleached pale. Most were hard to distinguish – for all I knew they could have been kittens in embryo form, or even rats. The two specimens I recognized were the monkey's head, the smooth skull perfectly preserved, like the bald pate of a tiny unborn child, with eyes closed, and, next to it, a second monkey's head from which the brain had been removed, and which now lay in a jar near by, pickled and brown. There were other jars and other bottles that held fungi, plants and grasses, grotesquely shaped, with spreading tentacles and curling leaves.

I had mocked him, over the telephone, calling the laboratory Bluebeard's chamber. Now, as I looked round it again, the memory of my afternoon still vivid in my mind, the small room seemed to hold a different quality. I was reminded not so much of the bearded potentate in the Eastern fairy-tale as of an engraving, long forgotten, that had scared me as a child. It was called 'The Alchemist'. A figure, naked save for a loincloth, was crouching by a walled oven like the one here in the laundry, kindling a fire with bellows, and to his left stood a hooded monk and an abbot, carrying a cross. A fourth man, in medieval hat and cloak, leant upon a stick conferring with them. There had been bottles, too, upon a table, and open jars containing eggshells, hairs and thread-like worms, and in the centre of the room a tripod with a rounded flask balanced upon it, and in the flask a minute lizard with a dragon's head.

Why only now, after some five-and-thirty years, did the memory of that dread engraving return to haunt me? I turned away, locking the door of Magnus's laboratory, and went upstairs. I could not wait any longer for that much-needed drink.

three

It rained the following day, one of those steady mizzles that accompany a drifting fog from the sea, preventing any enjoyment out of doors. I awoke feeling perfectly normal, having slept surprisingly well, but when I drew back the curtains and saw the state of the weather I went back to bed again, despondent, wondering what I was going to do with myself all day.

This was the Cornish climate about which Vita had expressed her doubts, and I could imagine her reproaches if it happened when the holidays were in full swing, my young stepsons staring aimlessly out of the window, then forced into wellingtons and macs and sent, protesting, to walk along the sands at Par. Vita would wander from music-room to library altering the position of the furniture, saying how much better she could arrange the rooms if they were hers, and when this palled she would telephone one of her many friends from the American Embassy crowd in London, themselves outward bound for Sardinia or Greece. These symptoms of discontent I was spared for a while longer, and the days ahead of me, wet or fine, were at least free, my own time for my own movements.

The obliging Mrs Collins brought me up my breakfast and the morning paper, commiserated with me about the weather, saying that the Professor always found plenty to do in that funny little old room of his down under, and informed me that she would roast one of her own chickens for my lunch. I had no intention of going 'down under', and opened the morning paper and drank my coffee. But the doubtful interest of the sports page soon palled, and my attention wandered back to the all-absorbing question of exactly what had happened to me the previous afternoon.

Had there been some telepathic communication between Magnus and myself? We had tried this at Cambridge, with cards and numbers, but it had never worked, except once or twice by pure coincidence. And we had been more intimate in those days than we were now. I could think of no means, telepathic or otherwise, by which Magnus and I could have undergone the same experience, separated by an interval of some three months – it was Easter, apparently, when he had tried the drug himself – unless that experience was directly connected with previous happenings at Kilmarth. Part of the brain, Magnus had suggested, was susceptible to reversal, restoring conditions, when under the influence of the drug, to an earlier period in its chemical history. Yet why that particular time? Had the horseman planted so indelible a stamp on his surroundings that any previous or later period was blotted out?

I thought back to the days when I had stayed at Kilmarth as an undergraduate. The atmosphere was casual, happy-go-lucky. I remembered asking Mrs Lane once whether the house was haunted. My question was an idle one, for certainly it did not have an haunted atmosphere – I asked simply because it was old. 'Good heavens, no!' she exclaimed. 'We're far too wrapped up in ourselves to encourage ghosts. Poor things, they'd wither away from tedium, unable to draw attention to themselves. Why do you ask?'

'No reason,' I assured her, afraid I might have given offence. 'Only that most old houses like to boast a spook.'

'Well, if there is one at Kilmarth we've never heard it,' she said. 'The house has always seemed such a happy one to us. There's nothing particularly interesting about its history, you know. It belonged to a family called Baker in sixteen hundred and something, and they had it until the Rashleighs rebuilt the place in the eighteenth century. I can't tell you about its origins, but someone told us once that it has fourteenth-century foundations.'

That was the end of the matter, but now her remarks about early fourteenth-century foundations returned to me. I thought about the basement rooms and the courtyard leading out of them, and Magnus's curious choice of the old laundry for his laboratory. Doubtless he had his reasons. It was well away from the lived-in part of the house, and he would not be disturbed by callers or Mrs Collins.

I got up rather late and wrote letters in the library, did justice to Mrs Collins's roast chicken, and tried to keep my thoughts on the future and what I was going to decide about that offer of a New York partnership. It was no use. The whole thing seemed remote. Time enough when Vita arrived and we could discuss it together.

I looked out of the music-room window and watched Mrs Collins walk up the drive on her way home. It was still drizzling, and a long, uninviting afternoon lay ahead. I don't know when it was that the idea came to me. Perhaps I had been harbouring it unconsciously since I awoke. I wanted to prove that there had been no telepathic communication between Magnus and myself when I had taken the drug the day before in the laboratory. He had told me he had made his first experiment there, and so had I. Perhaps some thought process had passed between us at the moment when I actually swallowed the stuff, so influencing my train of ideas and what I saw, or imagined I saw, during the course of the afternoon. If the drug was taken elsewhere, not in that baleful laboratory with its suggestive likeness to an alchemist's cell, might not the effect be different? I should never know unless I tried it out.

There was a small pocket-flask in the pantry cupboard – I had noticed it the evening before – and I got it out now, and rinsed it under the cold tap. This did not commit me to anything one way or another. Then I went downstairs to the basement, and, feeling like the shadow of my boyhood self when I had sneaked a bar of forbidden chocolate during Lent, I turned the key in the door of the laboratory.

It was a simple matter to disregard the specimens in their jars and reach for the neat little row of labelled bottles. As yesterday, I measured the drops from bottle A, but into the pocket flask this time. Then I locked the laboratory door behind me, went across the yard to the stable block, and fetched the car.

I drove slowly up the drive, turned left out of the lane to the main road, and went down Polmear hill, pausing when I reached the bottom to survey the scene. Here, where the almshouses and the inn stood now, had been yesterday's ford. The lie of the land had not altered, despite the modern road, but the valley where the tide had swept inward was now marsh. I took the lane to Tywardreath, thinking, with some misgiving, that if I had in fact taken this same route yesterday, under the influence of the drug, I could have been knocked down by a passing car without hearing it.

I drove down the steep, narrow lane to the village and parked the car a little above the church. There was still a light rain falling, and nobody was about. A van drove up the main Par road and disappeared. A woman came out of the grocer's shop and walked uphill in the same direction. No one else appeared. I got out of the car, opened the iron gates into the churchyard, and stood in the church porch to shelter from the rain. The churchyard itself sloped away in a southerly direction until it terminated at the boundary wall, and beneath it were farm-buildings. Yesterday, in that other world, there were no buildings, only the blue waters of a creek filling the valley with the incoming tide, and the Priory buildings had covered the space the churchyard held today.

I knew the lie of the land better now. If the drug took effect I could leave the car where it was and walk home. There was no one around. Then, like a diver taking a plunge into some arctic pool, I took the flask and swallowed the contents. The instant I had done so panic seized me. This second dose might have a quite different effect. Make me sleep for hours. Should I stay where I was, or should I be better off in the car? The church porch gave me claustrophobia, so I went out and sat down on one of the tombstones, not far from the pathway but out of sight of the road. If I stayed quite still, without moving, perhaps nothing would happen. I began to pray, 'Don't let anything happen. Don't let the drug have any effect.'

I went on sitting for about five minutes, too apprehensive about the possible effects of the drug to mind the rain. Then I heard the church clock strike three, and glanced down at my watch to check the time. It was a few minutes slow, so I altered it, and almost immediately I heard shouting from the village, or cheering, perhaps – a curious mélange of the two – and a creaking sound like wheels. Oh God, what now, I thought, a travelling circus about to descend the village street? I shall have to move the car. I got up and started to walk along the path to the churchyard gate. I never arrived, because the gate had gone, and I was looking through a rounded window set in a stone wall, the window facing a cobbled quadrangle bounded by shingle paths.

The entrance gate at the far end of the quadrangle was open wide, and beyond it I could see a mass of people assembled on the green, men, women, children. The shouting was coming from them, and the creaking sounds were the wheels of an enormous covered wagon drawn by five horses, the second leader and the horse between the shafts carrying riders upon their backs. The wooden canopy surmounting the wagon was painted a rich purple and gold, and as I watched the heavy curtains concealing the front of the vehicle were drawn aside, the shouting and the applause from the crowd increased, and the figure which appeared in the aperture raised his hands in blessing. He was magnificently dressed in ecclesiastical robes, and I remembered that Roger and the Prior had spoken of an imminent visit by the Bishop of Exeter, and how apprehensive the Prior had been – doubtless with reason. This must be His Grace in person.

There was a sudden hush, and everyone went down upon their knees. The light was dazzling, the feeling had gone from my limbs, and nothing seemed to matter any more. I did not care – the drug could work on me as it wished; my only desire was to be part of the world about me.

I watched the bishop descend from his covered vehicle, and the crowd pressed forward. Then he entered the gate into the quadrangle, followed by his train. From some door beneath me I saw the Prior advance to meet him at the head of his flock of monks, and the entrance gates were closed against the crowd.

I looked over my shoulder and saw that I was standing in a vaulted chamber filled with a score or more of people, waiting to be presented, to judge by their hushed sense of expectancy. From their clothes they belonged to the gentry, and so presumably were permitted entrance to the Priory.

'Mark it well,' said the voice in my ear, 'she'll not wear paint on her face on this occasion.'

My horseman, Roger, stood beside me, but his remarks were addressed to a companion, a man of about his own age or somewhat older, who put his hand before his mouth to stifle laughter.

'Painted or plain, Sir John will have her,' he answered, 'and what better moment than the eve of Martinmas, with his own lady safely brought to bed eight miles away at Bockenod?'

'It could be contrived,' agreed the other, 'but with some risk, for she cannot depend upon Sir Henry's absence. He will scarcely sleep at the Priory tonight, with the Bishop in the guest chamber. No, let them wait awhile longer, if only to whet appetite.'

Scandal had not changed much through the centuries, then, and I wondered why this back-chat should intrigue me now, which, if it had been exchanged by my contemporaries at some social event, would have made me yawn. Perhaps, because I was eavesdropping in time and within monastic walls, the gossip held more spice. I followed the direction of their gaze to the small group near to the door, the favoured few, no doubt, to be presented. Which was the gallant Sir John – the same who liked a foot in both camps, if I remembered the Prior's comment rightly – and which the favoured lady of his choice, shorn of her paint?

There were four men, three women and two youths, and the fashion of the women's headgear made it difficult to distinguish their features from a distance, swathed as they were in coif and wimple. I recognized the lord of the manor, Henry de Champernoune, the dignified, elderly man who had been at his prayers in the chapel yesterday. He was dressed more soberly than his friends, who wore tunics of varying colours hanging to mid-calf, with belts slung low beneath the hip, and pouch and dagger in the centre. All of them were bearded and had their hair curled to a frizz, which must have been the prevailing fashion.

Roger and his companion had been joined by a newcomer in clerical dress, a rosary hanging from his belt. His red nose and slurred speech suggested a recent visit to the Prior's buttery.

'What is the order of precedence?' he mumbled. 'As parish priest and chaplain to Sir Henry surely I should form part of his entourage?'

Roger laid a hand on his shoulder and swung him round to face the window. 'Sir Henry can do without your breath, and his Grace the Bishop likewise, unless you wish to forfeit your position.'

The newcomer protested, clinging nevertheless to the protection of the wall, then lowered himself on to the bench beside it. Roger shrugged his shoulder, turning to the companion at his side.

'It surprises me that Otto Bodrugan dares show his face,' said his friend. 'Not two years since he fought for Lancaster against the King. They say he was in London when the mob dragged Bishop Stapledon through the streets.'

'He was not,' replied Roger. 'He was with many hundreds of the Queen's party up at Wallingford.'

'Nevertheless, his position is delicate,' said the other. 'If I were the Bishop I should not look kindly upon the man reputed to have condoned the murder of my predecessor.'

'His Grace has not the time to play politics,' retorted Roger. 'He will have his hands full with the diocese. Past causes are no concern of his. Bodrugan is here today by reason of the demesnes he shares with Champernoune, because his sister Joanna is Sir Henry's lady. Also, out of his obligation to Sir John. The two hundred marks he borrowed are still unpaid.'

Commotion at the door made them move forward for a better view, small fry on the lower rungs of this particular ladder. The Bishop entered, the Prior beside him, sprucer and cleaner than when he had sat up in his tumbled bed with the scratching greyhound. The gentlemen made obeisance, the ladies curtsied, and the Bishop extended his hand for each to kiss, while the Prior, flustered by the ceremonial, presented them in turn. Playing no part in their world I could move about at will, so long as I touched none of them, and I drew closer, curious to discover who was who in the company.

'Sir Henry de Champernoune, lord of the manor of Tyward-reath,' murmured the Prior, 'lately returned from a pilgrimage to Campostella.'

My elderly knight stepped forward, bending low with one knee on the ground, and I was struck once more by his air of dignity and grace, coupled with humility. When he had kissed the extended hand he rose, and turned to the woman at his side.

'My wife Joanna, your Grace,' he said, and she sank to the ground in an endeavour to equal her husband in humility, bring off the gesture well. So this was the lady who would have painted her face but for the Bishop's visitation. I decided she had done well enough to let it alone. The wimple that framed her features was adornment enough, enhancing the charms of any woman, plain or beautiful. She was neither the one nor the other, but it did not surprise me that her fidelity to her conjugal vows had been in question. I had seen eyes like hers in women of my own world, full and sensual: one flick of the male head, and she'd be game.

'My son and heir, William,' continued her husband, and one of the youths came forward to make obeisance.

'Sir Otto Bodrugan,' continued Sir Henry, 'and his lady, my sister Margaret.'

It was evidently a closely knit world, for had not my horse-man Roger remarked that Otto Bodrugan was brother to Joanna, Champernoune's wife, and so doubly connected with the lord of the manor? Margaret was small and pale, and evidently nervous, for she stumbled as she made her curtsy to His Grace, and would have fallen had not her husband caught her. I liked Bodrugan's looks: there was a panache about him, and he would, I thought, be a good ally in a duel or escapade. He must have had a sense of humour, too, for instead of colouring or looking vexed at his wife's gaffe he smiled and reassured her. His eyes, brown like those of his sister Joanna, were less prominent than hers, but I felt that he had his full share of her qualities.

Bodrugan in his turn presented his eldest son Henry, and then stepped back to give way to the next man in the line. He had clearly been itching to put himself forward. Dressed more richly than either Bodrugan or Champernoune, he wore a self-confident smile on his lips.

This time it was the Prior who made the introduction. 'Our

loved and respected patron, Sir John Carminowe of Bockenod,' he announced, 'without whom we in this Priory would have found ourselves hard-pressed for money in these troublous times.'

Here then was the knight with a foot in either camp, one lady in confinement eight miles away, the other present in this chamber but not yet bedded. I was disappointed, expecting a roisterous type with a roving eye. He was none of these, but small and stout, puffed up with self-importance like a turkey-cock. The lady Joanna must be easily pleased.

'Your Grace,' he said in pompous tones, 'we are deeply honoured to have you here amongst us,' and bent over the proffered hand with so much affectation that had I been Otto Bodrugan, who owed him two hundred marks, I would have kicked him on the backside and compounded the debt.

The Bishop, keen-eyed, alert, was missing nothing. He reminded me of a general inspecting a new command and making mental notes about the officers: Champernoune past it, needs replacing; Bodrugan gallant in action but insubordinate, to judge from his recent part in the rebellion against the King; Carminowe ambitious and over-zealous – apt to make trouble. As for the Prior, was that a splash of gravy on his habit? I could swear the Bishop noticed it, as I did; and a moment later his eye travelled across the heads of the lesser fry and fell upon the almost recumbent figure of the parish priest. I hoped, for the sake of the Prior's charges, that the inspection would not be continued later in the Priory kitchen, or, worse still, in the Prior's own chamber.

Sir John had risen from his knees, and was making introductions in his turn.

'My brother, your Grace, Sir Oliver Carminowe, one of His Majesty's Commissioners, and Isolda his lady.' He elbowed forward his brother, who, from his flushed appearance and hazy eye, looked as if he had been passing the hours of waiting in the buttery with the parish priest.

'Your Grace,' he said, and was careful not to bend his knee too low for fear of swaying when he stood upright. He was a better-looking fellow than Sir John, despite the tippling; taller, broader, with a ruthless set about the jaw, not one to fall foul with in an argument.

'She's the one I'd pick if fortune favoured me.'

The whisper in my ear was very near. Roger the horseman was at my side once more; but he was not addressing me but his companion. There was something uncanny in the way he led my thoughts, always at my elbow when I least supposed him there. He was right, though, in his choice, and I wondered if she too was aware of his attention, for she stared straight at us as she rose from her curtsy, and the kissing of the Bishop's hand.

Isolda, wife to Sir Oliver Carminowe, had no wimple to frame her features, but wore her golden hair in looped braids, with a jewelled fillet crowning the small veil upon her head. Nor did she wear a cloak over her dress like the other women, and the dress itself was less wide in the skirt, more closely fitting, the long, tight sleeves reaching beyond her wrist. Possibly, being younger than her companions, not more than twenty-five or twenty-six, fashion played a stronger part in her life; if so, she did not seem conscious of the fact, wearing her clothes with casual grace. I have never seen a face so beautiful or so bored, and she swept us with her eyes – or rather, Roger and his companion – without the faintest show of interest, the slight movement of her mouth a moment later betrayed the fact that she was stifling a yawn.

It is the fate of every man, I suppose, at some time or other to glimpse a face in a crowd and not forget it, or perhaps, by a stroke of luck, to catch up with the owner at a later date, in a restaurant, at a party. To meet often breaks the spell and leads to disenchantment. This was not possible now. I looked across the centuries at what Shakespeare called 'a lass unparalleled', who, alas, would never look at me.

'How long, I wonder,' murmured Roger, 'will she stay content within the walls of Carminowe and keep a guard upon her thoughts from straying?'

I wished I knew. Had I been living in this time I would have handed in my resignation as steward to Sir Henry Champernoune and offered my services to Sir Oliver and his lady.

'One mercy for her,' replied the other, 'she does not have to provide her husband with an heir, with three stout stepsons filling the breach. She can do as she pleases with her time, having produced two daughters whom Sir Oliver can trade and profit by when they reach marriageable age.'

So much for women's value in other days. Goods reared for

purchase, then bought and sold in the market-place, or rather manor. Small wonder that, their duty done, they looked round for consolation, either by taking a lover or by playing an active part in the bargaining over their own daughters and sons.

'I tell you one thing,' said Roger. 'Bodrugan has an eye to her, but while he's under this obligation to Sir John he has to watch where he steps.'

'I lay you five denarii to nought she will not look at him.'

'Taken. And if she does I'll act as go-between. I play the role often enough between my lady and Sir John.'.

As eavesdropper in time my role was passive, without commitment or responsibility. I could move about in their world unwatched, knowing that whatever happened I could do nothing to prevent it – comedy, tragedy, or farce – whereas in my twentieth-century existence I must take my share in shaping my own future and that of my family.

The reception appeared over, but the visit was not yet through, for a bell summoned one and all to vespers and the company divided, the more favoured to the Priory chapel, the lesser ranks to the church, which was at the same time part of the chapel, an arched doorway, with a grille, dividing the one from the other.

I thought I might dispense with vespers, though by standing close to the grille I could have watched Isolda; but my inevitable guide, craning his neck with the same thought in mind, decided that he had been idle long enough, and, signalling to his companion with a quick jerk of the head, made his way out of the Priory building and across the quadrangle to the entrance gate. Someone had flung it open once again and a cluster of people, lay brothers and servants, were standing there, laughing, as they watched the Bishop's attendants struggle to turn the clumsy vehicle towards the Priory yard. The wheels were stuck between muddied road and village green, but this was by no means the only fun to be observed, for the green itself was crowded with men, women and children. Some sort of market seemed to be in progress, for there were little booths and stalls set up, same fellow was beating a drum and another squeaked on a fiddle, while a third nearly split my ears with two horns as long as himself, which he managed by sleight of hand to play simultaneously.

I followed Roger and his friend across the green. They paused every moment to greet acquaintances, and I realized that this was no sudden jollification put on for the Bishop's benefit but some butcher's paradise, for newly slaughtered sheep and pigs, still dripping blood, were hanging upon posts at every booth. The dwellings bordering the green boasted a like display. Each householder, knife in hand, was hard at work stripping the pelt off some old ewe, or slitting a pig's throat, and one or two fellows, higher perhaps on the feudal ladder, brandished the heads of oxen, the wide-spread horns winning shouts of applause and laughter from the crowd. Torches flared as the light faded, slaughterers and strippers taking on a demonic aspect, working fast and furiously to have their task accomplished before night came, and because of it the excitement mounted, and the musician with the horn in either hand, wandering in and out amongst the crowd, lifted his instruments high to make a greater blast upon the air.

'God willing, they'll have their bellies lined this winter,' observed Roger. I had forgotten him in all the tumult, but he was with me still.

'I take it you have every beast counted?' asked his friend.

'Not only counted but inspected before slaughter. Not that Sir Henry would know or care if he was lacking a hundred head of cattle, but my lady would. He's too deep in his prayers to watch his purse, or his belongings.'

'She trusts you, then?'

My horseman laughed. 'Faith! She's obliged to trust me, knowing what I do of her affairs. The more she leans upon my counsel, the sounder she sleeps at night.'

He turned his head as a new commotion fell upon our ears, this time from the Priory stableyard, where the Bishop's equipage had finally been housed, taking the place of smaller vehicles, similarly furnished with wooded canopy and sides, and bearing coats-of-arms. Half-chariot, half-wagonette, they seemed a clumsy method of carrying ladies of rank about the countryside, but this was evidently their purpose, for three of them emerged from the rear premises, creaking and groaning with every turn of the wheel, and stood in line before the Priory entrance.

Vespers was over, and the faithful who had attended were emerging from the church, to mingle with the crowd upon the green. Roger made his way into the quadrangle, and so to the

Priory building itself, where the Prior's guests were gathering before departure. Sir John Carminowe was in the forefront, and beside him Sir Henry's lady, Joanna de Champernoune. As we approached he murmured in her ear, 'Will you be alone if I ride to you tomorrow?'

'Perhaps,' she said. 'Better still, wait until I send word.'

He bent to kiss her hand, then mounted the horse which a groom was holding, and cantered off. Joanna watched him go, then turned to her steward.

'Sir Oliver and Lady Isolda lodge with us tonight,' she said. 'See if you can hasten their departure. And find Sir Henry too. I wish to be away.'

She stood there in the doorway, foot tapping impatiently upon the ground, the full brown eyes surely brooding upon some scheme which would further her own ends. Sir John must be hard-pressed to keep her sweet. Roger entered the Priory, and I followed him. Voices came from the direction of the refectory, and, inquiring from a monk who was standing by, he was told that Sir Oliver Carminowe was taking refreshment with others of the company, but that his lady was in the chapel still.

Roger paused a moment, then turned towards the chapel. I thought at first that it was empty. The candles on the altar had been extinguished, and the light was dim. Two figures stood near to the grille, a man and a woman. As we came closer I saw that they were Otto Bodrugan and Isolda Carminowe. They were speaking low and I could not hear what they said, but the weariness had gone from her face, and the boredom too, and suddenly she looked up at him and smiled.

Roger tapped me on the shoulder. 'It's much too dark to see. Shall I switch on the lights?'

It was not his voice. He had gone, and so had they. I was standing in the southern aisle of the church, and a man wearing a dog-collar under his tweed jacket was by my side.

'I saw you just now in the churchyard,' he said, 'looking as if you couldn't make up your mind whether to come in out of the rain. Well, now you have, let me show you round. I'm the vicar of St Andrew's. It's a fine old church, and we're very proud of it.'

He put his hand on a switch and turned on all the lights. I glanced down at my watch, without nausea, without vertigo. It was exactly half-past three.

four

There had been no perceptible transition. I had passed from one world to the other instantaneously, without the physical side-effects of yesterday. The only difficulty was mental readjustment, requiring an almost intolerable degree of concentration. Luckily the vicar preceded me up the aisle, chatting as we went, and if there was anything strange in my expression he was too polite to comment.

'We get a fair number of visitors in the summer,' he said, 'people staying at Par, or they come over from Fowey. But you must be an enthusiast, hanging about the churchyard in the rain.'

I made a supreme effort to pull myself together. 'In point of fact,' I said, surprised to find that I could even speak, 'it was not really the church itself or the graves that interested me. Some-one told me there had been a Priory here in former days.'

'Ah, yes, the Priory,' he said. 'That's been gone a long time, no trace of it left, unfortunately. The buildings all fell in after the dissolution of the monasteries in 1539. Some say the site was where Newhouse Farm is now, just below us in the valley, and others that it occupied the present churchyard itself, south of the porch, but nobody really knows.'

He led me to the north transept and showed me the tombstone of the last Prior, who had been buried before the altar in 1538, and pointed out the pulpit and some pew-ends, and all that was left of the original rood screen. Nothing of what I observed bore any resemblance to the small church I had so lately seen, with the grille in the wall dividing it from the Priory chapel; nor, as I stood here now beside the vicar, could I reconstruct from memory anything of an older transept, an older aisle.

'Everything's changed,' I said.

'Changed?' he repeated, puzzled. 'Oh, no doubt. The church was largely restored in 1880, possibly not altogether successfully. Are you disappointed?'

'No,' I assured him hastily, 'not at all. It's only that . . . Well, as I was saying, my interest goes back to very early days, long before the dissolution of the monasteries.'

'I understand.' He smiled in sympathy. 'I've often wondered

myself what it all looked like in former times, with the Priory close by. It was a French house, you know, attached to the Benedictine Abbey of St Sergius and Bacchus in Angers, and I believe most of the monks were French. I wish I could tell you more about it, but I've only been here a few years, and I'm afraid I'm no historian.'

'Neither am I,' I told him, and we retraced our steps towards the porch.

'Do you know anything,' I asked, 'about the lords of the manor in early times?'

He paused to switch off the lights. 'Only what I have read in the *Parochial History*,' he said. 'The manor is mentioned in Domesday as Tiwardrai – the House on the Strand – and it belonged to the great family of Cardinham until the last heiress Isolda sold it to the Champernounes, in the thirteenth century, and when they died out it passed to other hands.'

'Isolda?'

'Yes, Isolda de Cardinham. She married someone called William Ferrers of Bere in Devon, but I'm afraid I don't remember the details. You would find out more about it in the St Austell public library than from me.' He smiled again, and we passed through the door to the churchyard. 'Are you staying in the neighbourhood or passing through?' he asked.

'Staying. Professor Lane has lent me his house for the summer.'

'Kilmarth? I know it, of course, but I've never been inside. I don't think Professor Lane gets down very often, and he doesn't come to church.'

'No,' I replied, 'probably not.'

'Well,' he said, as we parted at the gate, 'if you feel like coming, either to a service or just to wander around, it will be nice to see you.'

We shook hands, and I walked up the road to where I had parked the car. I wondered whether I had been impossibly rude. I had not even thanked him for his courtesy, or introduced myself. Doubtless he considered me just another summer visitor, more boorish than usual, and a crank into the bargain. I got into the car, lit a cigarette, and sat there to collect my thoughts. The fact that there had been no physical reaction to the drug whatsoever was an astonishing relief. Not a suspicion of dizziness or nausea, and my limbs did not ache as they had done the day before, nor was I sweating.

I wound down the car window and looked up the street, then back again to the church. None of it fitted. The green where the people had so lately crowded must have covered all the present area, and beyond it too, where the modern road turned uphill. The Priory yard, where the bishop's equipage nearly came to grief, would have been in that hollow below the gents' hair-dresser, boundering the east wall of the churchyard, and the Priory itself, according to one theory mentioned by the vicar, filled the entire space that the southern portion of the churchyard held today. I closed my eyes. I saw the entrance, the quadrangle, the long narrow building forming kitchens and refectory, monks' dormitory, chapter-house, where the reception had been held, and the Prior's chamber above. Then I opened them again, but the pieces did not fit, and the church tower threw my jigsaw puzzle out of balance. It was no good – nothing tallied save the lie of the land.

I threw away my cigarette, started the car, and took the road past the church. A curious feeling of elation came to me as I swept downhill past the valley stream, and so to the low-lying, straggling shops of Par. Not ten minutes since the whole of this had been under water, the sloping Priory lands lapped by the sea. Sand-banks had bordered the wide sweep of the estuary where those bungalows stood now, and houses and shops were all blue channel with a running tide. I stopped the car by the chemists' and bought some toothpaste, the feeling of elation in-creasing as the girl wrapped it up. It seemed to me that she was without substance, the shop as well, and the two other people standing there, and I felt myself smiling furtively because of this, with an urge to say, 'You none of you exist. All this is under water.'

I stood outside the shop, and it had stopped raining. The heavy pall that had been overhead all day had broken at last into a patchwork sky, squares of blue alternating with wisps of smoky cloud. Too soon to go back home. Too early to ring Magnus. One thing I had proved, if nothing else: this time there had been no telepathy between us. He might have had some intuition of my movements the preceding afternoon, but not today. The laboratory in Kilmarth was not a bogey-hole conjuring up ghosts, any more than the porch in St Andrew's church had been filled with phantoms. Magnus must be right in his assumption that some primary chemical process was reversible, the drug inducing this change; and conditions were such that the senses, reacting to the situation as a secondary effect, swung into action, capturing the past.

I had not awakened from some nostalgic dream when the vicar tapped me on the shoulder, but had passed from one living reality to another. Could time be all-dimensional – yesterday, today, tomorrow running concurrently in ceaseless repetition? Perhaps it needed only a change of ingredient, a different enzyme, to show the future, myself a bald-headed buffer in New York with the boys grown-up and married, and Vita dead. The thought was disconcerting. I would rather concern myself with the Champernounes, the Carminowes, and Isolda. No telepathic communication here: Magnus had mentioned none of them, but the vicar had, and only after I had seen them as living persons.

Then I decided what to do: I would drive to St Austell and see if there was some volume in the public library that would give proof of their identity.

The library was perched above the town, and I parked the car and went inside. The girl at the desk was helpful. She advised me to go upstairs to the reference library, and search for pedigrees in a book called *The Visitations of Cornwall.*

I took the fat volume from the shelves and settled myself at one of the tables. First glance in alphabetical order was disappointing. No Bodrugans and no Champernounes. No Carminowes either. And no Cardinhams. I turned to the beginning once again, and then, with quickening interest, realized that I must have muddled the pages the first time, for I came upon the Carminowes of Carminowe. I let my eye travel down the page, and there Sir John was, married to a Joanna into the bargain – he must have found the similarity of name of wife and mistress confusing. He had a great brood of children, and one of his grandsons, Miles, had inherited Boconnoc. Boconnoc . . . Bockenod . . . a change in the spelling, but this was my Sir John without a doubt.

On the succeeding page was his elder brother Sir Oliver Carminowe. By his first wife he had had several children. I glanced along the line and found Isolda his second wife, daughter of one

Reynold Ferrers of Bere in Devon, and below, at the bottom of the page, her daughters, Joanna and Margaret. I'd got her – not the vicar's Devon heiress, Isolda Cardinham, but a descendant.

I pushed the heavy volume aside, and found myself smiling fatuously into the face of a bespectacled man reading the *Daily Telegraph*, who stared at me suspiciously, then hid his face behind his paper. My lass unparalleled was no figure of the imagination, nor a telepathic process of thought between Magnus and myself. She had lived, though the dates were sketchy: it did not state when she was born or when she died.

I put the book back on the shelves and walked downstairs and out of the building, the feeling of elation increased by my discovery. Carminowes, Champernounes, Bodrugans, all dead for six hundred years, yet still alive in my other world of time.

I drove away from St Austell thinking how much I had accomplished in one afternoon, witnessing a ceremony in a Priory long since crumbled, coupled with Martinmas upon the village green. And all through some wizard's brew concocted by Magnus, leaving no side-effect or aftermath, only a sense of well-being and delight. It was as easy as falling off a cliff. I drove up Polmear hill doing a cool sixty, and it was not until I had turned down the drive to Kilmarth, put away the car and let myself into the house that I thought of the simile again. Falling off a cliff ... Was this the side-effect? This sense of exhilaration, that nothing mattered? Yesterday the nausea, the vertigo, because I had broken the rules. Today, moving from one world to another without effort, I was cock-a-hoop.

I went upstairs to the library and dialled the number of Magnus's flat. He answered immediately.

'How was it?' he asked.

'What do you mean, how was it? How was what? It rained all day.'

'Fine in London,' he replied. 'But forget the weather. How was the second trip?'

His certainty that I had made the experiment again irritated me. 'What makes you think I took a second trip?'

'One always does.'

'Well, you're right, as it happens. I didn't intend to, but I wanted to prove something.'

'What did you want to prove?'

'That the experiment was nothing to do with any telepathic communication between us.'

'I could have told you that,' he said.

'Perhaps. But we had both experimented first in Bluebeard's chamber, which might have had an unconscious influence.'

'So ...'

'So, I poured the drops into your drinking-flask – forgive me for making myself at home – drove to the church, and swallowed them in the porch.'

His snort of delight annoyed me even more.

'What's the matter?' I asked. 'Don't tell me you did the same?'

'Precisely. But not in the porch, dear boy, in the churchyard after dark. The point is, what did you see?'

I told him, winding up with my encounter with the vicar, the visit to the public library, and the absence, or so I had thought, of any side-effects. He listened to my saga without interruption, as he had done the day before, and when I had concluded he told me to hang on, he was going to pour himself a drink, but he reminded me not to do likewise. The thought of his gin and tonic added fuel to my small flame of irritation.

'I think you came out of it all very well,' he said, 'and you seem to have met the flower of the county, which is more than I have ever done, in that time or this.'

'You mean you did not have the same experience?'

'Quite the contrary. No chapter-house or village green for me. I found myself in the monks' dormitory, a very different kettle of fish.'

'What went on?' I asked.

'Exactly what you might suppose when a bunch of medieval Frenchmen got together. Use your imagination.'

Now it was my turn to snort. The thought of fastidious Magnus playing peeping Tom amongst that fusty crowd brought my good humour back again.

'You know what I think?' I said. 'I think we found what we deserved. I got His Grace the Bishop and the County, awaking in me all the forgotten snob appeal of Stonyhurst, and you got the sexy deviations you have denied yourself for thirty years.'

'How do you know I've denied them?'

'I don't. I give you credit for good behaviour.'

'Thanks for the compliment. The point is, none of this can be put down to telepathic communication between us. Agreed?'

'Agreed.'

'Therefore we saw what we saw through another channel – the horseman, Roger. He was in the chapter-house and on the green with you, and in the dormitory with me. His is the brain that channels the information to us.'

'Yes, but why?'

'Why? You don't think we are going to discover that in a couple of trips? You have work to do.'

'That's all very well, but it's a bit of a bore having to shadow this chap, or have him shadow me, every time I may decide to make the experiment. I don't find him very sympathetic. Nor do I take to the lady of the manor.'

'The lady of the manor?' He paused a moment, I supposed for reflection. 'She's possibly the one I saw on my third trip. Auburn-haired, brown eyes, rather a bitch?'

'That sounds like her. Joanna Champernoune,' I said.

We both laughed, struck by the folly and the fascination of discussing someone who had been dead for centuries as if we had met her at some party in our own time.

'She was arguing about manor lands,' he said. 'I did not follow it. Incidentally, have you noticed how one gets the sense of the conversation without conscious translation from the medieval French they seem to be speaking? That's the link again, between his brain and ours. If we saw it before us in print, old English or Norman-French or Cornish, we shouldn't understand a word.'

'You're right,' I said. 'It hadn't struck me. Magnus . . .'

'Yes?'

'I'm still a bit bothered about side-effects. What I mean is, thank God I had no nausea or vertigo today, but on the contrary a tremendous sense of elation, and I must have broken the speed-limit several times driving home.'

He did not reply at once, and when he did his tone was guarded. 'That's one of the things,' he said, 'one of the reasons we have to test the drug. It could be addictive.'

'What do you mean exactly, addictive?'

'What I say. Not just the fascination of the experience itself, which we both know nobody else has tried, but the stimulation to the part of the brain affected. And I've warned you before of the possible physical dangers – being run over, that sort of thing. You must appreciate that part of the brain is shut off when you're under the influence of the drug. The functional part still controls your movements, rather as one can drive with a high percentage of alcohol in the blood and not have an accident, but the danger is always present, and there doesn't appear to be a warning system between one part of the brain and another. There may be. There may not. All this is part of what I have to find out.'

'Yes,' I said. 'Yes, I see.' I felt rather deflated. The sense of exhilaration which I had experienced while driving back had certainly been unusual. 'I'd better lay off,' I said, 'give it a miss, unless the circumstances are absolutely right.'

Again he paused before he answered. 'That's up to you,' he said. 'You must judge for yourself. Any more questions? I'm dining out.'

Any more questions . . . A dozen, twenty. But I should think of them all when he had rung off. 'Yes,' I said. 'Did you know before you took your first trip that Roger had once lived here in this house?'

'Absolutely not,' he replied. 'Mother used to talk about the Bakers of the seventeenth century, and Rashleighs who followed them. We knew nothing about their predecessors, although my father had a vague idea that the foundations went back to the fourteenth century; I don't know who told him.'

'Is that why you converted the old laundry into Bluebeard's chamber?'

'No, it just seemed a suitable place, and the cloam oven is rather fun. It retains the heat if you light the fire, and I can keep liquids there at a high temperature while I'm working at something else alongside. Perfect atmosphere. Nothing sinister about it. Don't run away with the idea that this experiment is some sort of a ghost-hunt, dear boy. We're not conjuring spirits from the vasty deep.'

'No, I realize that,' I said.

'To reduce it to its lowest level, if you sit in an armchair watching some old movie on television, the characters don't pop out of the screen to haunt you, although many of the actors are dead. It's not so very different from what you were up to this afternoon. Our guide Roger and his friends were living once, but are well and truly laid today.'

I knew what he meant, but it was not as simple as that. The implications went deeper, and the impact too; the sensation was not so much that of witnessing their world as of taking part in it.

'I wish,' I said, 'we knew more about our guide. I daresay I can dig up the others in the St Austell library – I've found the Carminowes already, as I told you, John, and his brother Oliver, and Oliver's wife Isolda – but a steward called Roger is rather a long shot, and is hardly likely to figure in any pedigree.'

'Probably not, but you can never tell. One of my students has a buddy who works in the Public Record Office and the British Museum, and I've got the business in hand. I haven't told him why I am interested, just that I want a list of taxpayers in the parish of Tywardreath in the fourteenth century. He should be able to find it, I gather, in the Lay Subsidy Roll for 1327, which must be pretty near the period we want. If something turns up I'll let you know. Any news of Vita?'

'None.'

'Pity you didn't arrange to fly the boys over to her in New York,' he said.

'Too damned expensive. Besides, that would have meant I had to go too.'

'Well, keep them all at bay for as long as you can. Say something has gone wrong with the drains – that will daunt her.'

'Nothing daunts Vita,' I told him. 'She'd bring some plumbing expert down from the American Embassy.'

'Well, press on before she arrives. And while I think of it, you know the sample marked B in the lab, alongside the A solution you're using?'

'Yes.'

'Pack it carefully and send it up to me. I want to put it under test.'

'Then you *are* going to try it out in London?'

'Not on myself, on a healthy young monkey. He won't see his medieval forebears, but he might get the staggers. Goodbye.'

Magnus had hung up on me again in his usual brusque fashion, leaving me with the inevitable sense of depletion. It was always so, whenever we met and talked, or spent an evening together. First the stimulation, sparks flying and the moments speeding by, then suddenly he would be gone, hailing a taxi and disappearing – not to be seen again for several weeks – while I wandered aimlessly back to my own flat.

'And how was your Professor?' Vita would ask in the ironic, rather mocking tone she assumed when I had passed an evening in Magnus's company, an emphasis on the 'your' which never failed to sting.

'In the usual form,' I would answer. 'Full of wild ideas I find amusing.'

'Glad you had fun,' was the reaction, but with a biting edge that implied the reverse of pleasure. She told me once, after a somewhat longer session than usual, when I had come home rather high about 2 a.m., that Magnus sapped me, and that when I returned to her I looked like a pricked balloon.

It was one of our first rows, and I did not know how to deal with it. She wandered around the sitting-room punching cushions and emptying her own ashtrays, while I sat on the sofa looking aggrieved. We went to bed without speaking, but the next morning, to my surprise and relief, she behaved as if nothing had happened, and positively glowed with feminine warmth and charm. Magnus was not mentioned again, but I made a mental note not to dine with him again unless she had a date herself elsewhere.

Today I did not feel like a pricked balloon when he rang off – the expression was rather offensive, come to think of it, suggesting the fetid air of somebody's breath exploding – merely denuded of stimulation, and a little uneasy too, because why did he suddenly want a test done on the bottle marked B? Did he want to make certain of his findings on the unfortunate monkey before putting me, the human guinea-pig, to a possibly sharper test? There was still sufficient solution in bottle A to keep me going . . .

I was brought up sharply in my train of thought. Keep me going? It sounded like an alcoholic preparing for a spree, and I remembered what Magnus had said about the possibilities of the drug being addictive. Perhaps this was another reason for trying it out on the monkey. I had a vision of the creature, bleary-eyed, leaping about his cage and panting for the next injection.

I felt in my pocket for the flask, and rinsed it out very thoroughly. I did not replace it on the pantry shelf, however, for Mrs Collins might take it into her head to move it somewhere else, and then if I happened to want it I should have to ask her where it was, which would be a bore. It was too early for supper, but the tray she had laid with ham and salad, fruit and cheese looked tempting, and I decided to carry it into the music-room and have a long evening by the wood fire.

I took a stack of records at random and piled them one on top of the other on the turntable. But, no matter what sounds filled the music-room, I kept returning to the scenes of this afternoon, the reception in the Priory chapter-house, the stripping of carcasses on the village green, the hooded musician with his double horn wandering amongst the children and the barking dogs, and above all that lass with braided hair and jewelled fillet who, one afternoon six hundred years ago, had looked so bored until, because of some remark which I could not catch, spoken by a man in another time, she had lifted her head and smiled.

five

There was an airmail letter from Vita on my breakfast tray next morning. It was written from her brother's house on Long Island. The heat was terrific, she said, they were in the pool all day, and Joe was taking his family to Newport on the yacht he had chartered mid-week. What a pity we had not known his plans earlier on. I could have flown the boys over and we could all have spent the summer vacation together. As things were, it was too late to change anything. She only hoped the Professor's house would turn out to be a success – and how was it, anyway? Did I want her to bring a lot of food down from London? She was flying from New York on Wednesday, and hoped there would be a letter for her at the flat in London.

Today was Wednesday. She was due in at London airport around ten o'clock this evening, and she would not find a letter in the flat because I had not expected her until the weekend.

The thought of Vita arriving in the country within a few hours came as a shock. The days I had thought my own, with complete freedom to plan as I wished, would be upset by telephone calls, demands, questions, the whole paraphernalia of life *en famille*. Somehow, before the first telephone call came through, I must be ready with a delaying device, some scheme to keep her and the boys in London for at least another few days.

Magnus had suggested drains. Drains it well might be, but the trouble was that when Vita finally arrived she would naturally start asking Mrs Collins about it, and Mrs Collins would stare at her in blank surprise. The rooms not ready? This would reflect on Mrs Collins, and bode ill for future relations between the two women. Electricity failure? But it hadn't any more than the drains. Nor could I pretend to be ill, for this would bring Vita down immediately to move me, wrapped in blankets, to hospital back in London; she was suspicious of all medical treatment unless it was top grade. Well, I must think of something, if only for Magnus's sake; it would be letting him down if the experiment was brought to an abrupt conclusion after only two attempts to prove success.

Today was Wednesday. Say experiment on Wednesday, give it a miss on Thursday, then experiment on Friday, a miss on Saturday, experiment on Sunday, and, if Vita was adamant about coming down on Monday, then Monday she must come. This plan allowed for three 'trips' (the LSD phraseology was certainly apt) and, providing nothing went wrong and I chose my moment well, did nothing foolish, the side-effects would be nil, just as they had been yesterday, apart from the sense of exhilaration, which I should immediately recognize and accept as a warning. In any event I felt no exhilaration now; Vita's letter was doubtless the cause of the slight despondency that appeared to be my form today.

Breakfast over, I told Mrs Collins that my wife was arriving in London tonight, and would probably be coming down with her boys next week, on Monday or Tuesday. She immediately produced a list of groceries and other things which would be needed. This gave me an opportunity to drive down to Par to collect them, and at the same time think out the text of a letter to Vita which she would get the following morning.

The first person I saw in the grocer's was the vicar of St Andrew's, who crossed the shop to say good morning. I introduced myself, belatedly, as Richard Young, and told him that I had taken his advice and gone to the county library at St Austell after leaving the church.

'You must be a real enthusiast,' he smiled. 'Did you find what you wanted?'

'In part,' I replied. 'The heiress Isolda de Cardinham proved elusive in the book of pedigrees, although I found a descendant, Isolda Carminowe, whose father was a Reynold Ferrers of Bere in Devon.'

'Reynold Ferrers rings a bell,' he said. 'The son, I believe I'm right in saying, of Sir William Ferrers who married the heiress. Therefore your Isolda would be their granddaughter. I know the heiress sold the manor of Tywardreath to one of the Champernounes in 1269, just before she married William Ferrers, for one hundred pounds. Quite a sum in those days.'

I made a rapid calculation in my head. My Isolda could hardly have been born before 1300. She had not looked more than about twenty-eight at the bishop's reception, which would date that even around 1328.

I followed the vicar round the shop as he made his purchases. 'Do you still celebrate Martinmas at Tywardreath?' I asked.

'Martinmas?' he echoed, looking bewildered – he was hesitating between a choice of biscuits. 'Forgive me, I don't quite follow you. It was a well-known feast in the centuries before the Reformation. We keep St Andrew's Day, of course, and generally hold the church fête in the middle of June.'

'Sorry,' I murmured, 'I've got my dates rather mixed. The truth is, I was brought up a Catholic, and went to school at Stonyhurst, and I seem to remember we used to attach a certain importance to St Martin's Eve . . .'

'You are perfectly right,' he interrupted, smiling. '11 November, Armistice Day, has rather taken its place, hasn't it? Or rather, Armistice Sunday. But now I understand your interest in the Priory, if you're a Catholic.'

'Non-practising,' I admitted, 'but you have a point. Old customs cling. Do you ever have a fair on the village green?'

'I'm afraid not,' he said, plainly puzzled, 'and to the best of my knowledge there has never been a village green at Tywardreath. Excuse me . . .'

He leant forward to receive the purchases dropped in his basket, and the assistant turned his attention to me. I consulted the list given me by Mrs Collins, and the vicar, with a cheery good morning, went his way. I wondered if he thought me mad, or merely one of Professor Lane's more eccentric friends. I had forgotten St Martin's Eve was 11 November. An odd coincidence of dates. Slaughter of oxen, pigs and sheep, and in the world of today a commemoration of uncounted numbers slain in battle. I must remember to tell Magnus.

I carried my load of groceries outside, dumped them in the boot of the car, and drove out of Par by the church road to Tywardreath. But instead of parking outside the gents' hairdressers, as I had done the day before, I drove slowly up the hill through the centre of the village, trying to reconstruct that non-existent village green. It was hopeless. There were houses to right and left of me, and at the top of the hill the road branched right to Fowey, while to the left the signpost said 'To Treesmill'. Somewhere, from the top of this hill, the Bishop and his cortège had driven yesterday, and the covered wagonettes of Carminowes, Champernounes and Bodrugans, their coats-of-arms emblazoned on the side. Sir John Carminowe would have taken the right-hand fork – if it existed – to Lostwithiel and his demesne of Bockenod, where his lady awaited her confinement. Today Bockenod was Boconnoc, a vast estate a few miles from Lostwithiel; I had passed one of the lodge gates on my drive down from London. Where, then, did the lord of the manor, Sir Henry Champernoune, have his demesne? His wife Joanna had told her steward, my horseman Roger, 'The Bodrugans lodge with us tonight.' Where would the manorhouse have stood?

I stopped the car at the top of the hill and looked about me. There was no house of any great size in the village of Tywardreath itself; some of the cottages could be late eighteenth century, but none belonged to an earlier period. Reason told me that manor houses were seldom destroyed, unless by fire, and even if they were burnt to the ground, or the walls crumbled, the site would be put to another purpose within a few years, and a farmhouse erected on the spot to serve the one-time manor lands. Somewhere, within a radius of a mile or two of Priory and church, the Champernounes would have built their own dwelling, or the original manor-house would have awaited them when the first Isolda, the Cardinham heiress, sold them the manor lands in 1269. Somewhere – down that left-hand fork, perhaps, where the signpost read 'To Treesmill' – the foot-tapping Joanna, impatient to be home, had driven in her painted wagonette from the Priory reception, accompanied by her sad-faced lord Sir Henry, and their son William, and followed by her brother Otto Bodrugan and his wife Margaret.

I glanced at my watch. It was past twelve, and Mrs Collins would be waiting to put away the groceries and cook my lunch. Also I had to write to Vita.

I settled to the letter after lunch. It took an hour or so to compose, nor was I satisfied with the result, but it would have to serve.

'Darling,' I said, 'I had not realized, until your letter came this morning, that you were actually flying back today, so you won't get this before tomorrow. If I've muddled things, forgive me. The fact is there has been a tremendous amount to do here to get the place straight for you and the boys, and I've been hard at it ever since I arrived. Mrs Collins, Magnus's daily, has been wonderful, but you know what a bachelor household is, and Magnus himself has not been down since Easter, so things were a bit sketchy. Also, and this is the real crux, Magnus asked me to go through a lot of his papers, and so on – he keeps a mass of scientific stuff in his laboratory which must not be touched – and all this has to be put away safely. He asked me to see to it as a personal favour, and I can't let him down, because after all we are getting the house rent-free, and it's some sort of return. I ought to be clear of this chore by Monday, but want the next few days free to get on with it, and the weekend too. Incidentally, the weather has been foul. It rained without ceasing all yesterday, so you aren't missing anything, but the locals say it will improve next week.

'Don't worry about food, Mrs C has everything under control, and she's a very good cook, so you won't have to worry on that score. Anyway, I'm sure you can occupy the boys until Monday, there must be museums and things they haven't seen, and you will want to meet people, so, darling, I suggest we plan for next week, and by then there should be no problems.

'I'm so glad you enjoyed yourself with Joe and family. Yes – perhaps, in retrospect, it might have been a good idea to have flown the boys out to New York, but it's easy to be wise after the event. I hope you're not too tired, darling, after the flight. Ring me when you get this.

'Your loving Dick.'

I read the letter through twice. It seemed better the second time: it rang true. And I did have to sort things for Magnus. When I lie I like to base the lie on a foundation of fact, for it appeases not only conscience but a sense of justice. I stamped the envelope and put it in my pocket, and then I remembered that Magnus wanted bottle B from the laboratory sent up to him in London. I rummaged about, found a small box, paper and string, and went down to the lab. I compared bottle B with bottle A, but there seemed to be no difference between the two. I was still carrying the flask of yesterday in my jacket pocket, and it was a simple matter to measure a second dose from A into the flask. I could use my judgement when, and if, I decided to take it.

Then I locked the lab and went upstairs, and had a look at the weather through the library window. It was not raining, and the sky was clearing out to sea. I packed up bottle B with great care, then drove down to Par to register it and to drop Vita's letter in the box, wondering, not so much what she would say when she read it, as how the monkey would react to his first trip into the unknown. My mission accomplished, I drove up through Tywardreath and took the left-hand fork to Treesmill.

The narrow road, with fields on either side of it, ran steeply to a valley, and before the final descent sloped sharply to a humped-backed bridge beneath which the main railway line ran between Par and Plymouth. I braked by the bridge and heard the hoot of the diesel express as it emerged from the tunnel out of sight to my right, and in a few moments the train itself came rattling down the line, passed under the bridge, and curved its way through the valley down to Par. Memories of undergraduate days came back to me. Magnus and I had always travelled down by train, and directly the train came out of the tunnel between Lostwithiel and Par we used to reach for our suitcases. I had been aware, then, of steep fields to the left of the carriage window and a valley to the right, full of reeds and stumpy willows, and suddenly the train would be at the station, the large black board with the white lettering announcing 'Par Change For Newquay', and we should have arrived.

Now, watching the express disappear round the bend in the valley, I observed the terrain from another angle, and realized how the coming of the railway over a hundred years ago must have altered the sloping fields, the line literally dug out of the hillside. There had been other disturbers of the peace besides the railway. Quarries had scarred the opposite side of the valley on the high ground where the tin and copper mines had flourished a century ago – I remembered Commander Lane telling us once at dinner how hundreds of men had been employed in the mines in Victorian days, and when the slump came, chimneys and engine-houses were left to crumble into decay, the miners emigrating, or seeking work in the newer industry of china clay.

This afternoon, the train out of sight and the rattle spent, all was quiet once again, and nothing moved in the valley except a few cows grazing in the swampy meadow at the base of the hill. I let the car descend gently to the end of the road before it rose sharply again to climb the opposite hill out of the valley. A sluggish stream ran through the meadow where the cows were grazing, spanned by a low bridge, and above the stream, to the right of the road, were old farm-buildings. I lowered the window of the car and looked about me. A dog ran from the farm, barking, followed by a man carrying a pail. I leant out of the window and asked him if this was Treesmill.

'Yes,' he said. 'If you continue straight on you'll come to the main road from Lostwithiel to St Blazey.'

'In point of fact,' I answered, 'I was looking for the mill itself.'

'Nothing left of it,' he said. 'This building here was the old mill-house, and all that's left of the stream is what you see. The main stream was diverted many years ago, before my time. They tell me that before they built this bridge there was a ford here. The stream ran right across this road, and most of the valley was under water.'

'Yes,' I said, 'yes, that's very possible.'

He pointed to a cottage the other side of the bridge. 'That used to be a pub in old days,' he said, 'when they were working the mines up at Lanescot and Carrogett. It would be full of miners on a Saturday night, so they tell me. Not many people alive who know much about the old days now.'

'Do you know,' I asked him, 'if there is any farmhouse here in the valley that might have been a manor-house in days gone by?'

He considered a moment before replying. 'Well,' he said, 'there's Trevenna up back behind us, on the Stonybridge road,

59

but I've never heard it was old, and Trenadlyn beyond that, and of course Treverran up the valley nearer the railway tunnel. That's an old house all right, fine old place, built hundreds of years ago.'

'How long ago?' I inquired, interest rising.

He considered again. 'There was a piece about Treverran in the paper once,' he said. 'Some gentleman from Oxford went to look at it. I believe it was 1705 they said it was built.'

My interest ebbed. Queen Anne houses, tin and copper mines, the pub across the road, all these were centuries later than my time. I felt as an archaeologist must feel who discovers a late Roman villa instead of a Bronze Age camp.

'Well, thanks very much,' I said, 'good day to you,' and turned the car and drove back up the hill. If the Champernounes had descended this road in 1328, their covered wagonettes would have been baulked by the mill-stream at the bottom, unless an older bridge than the one I had seen once forded it. Halfway up the hill I turned left into a side-lane, and presently saw the three farmsteads the man had mentioned. I reached for my road map. This side-road that I was on would join the main road at the top of the hill – the long tunnel must run deep underground beneath the road, a fine feat of engineering – and yes, the farm on my right was Trevenna, the one in front of me Trenadlyn, and the third, near to the railway line itself, would be Treverran. So what, I asked myself? Drive to each in turn, knock upon the door, and say, 'Do you mind if I sit down for half an hour, give myself what the drug-addicts call "a fix" and see what happens?'

Archaeologists had the best of it. Someone to finance their digs, enthusiastic company, and no risk of a lunatic asylum at the end of the day. I turned, drove back along my side-road, and up the steep hill towards Tywardreath. A car, towing a caravan, was trying to edge its way into the entrance of a bungalow halfway up the hill, effectively blocking my passage. I braked, almost in the ditch, and let the driver proceed with his manoeuvres. He shouted his apologies, and finally succeeded in getting both car and caravan parked beside the bungalow.

He climbed out of his car and walked towards me, apologizing once again. 'I think you can get past now,' he said. 'I'm sorry for the hold-up.'

'That's OK,' I told him, 'I'm in no hurry. You did a fine job getting your caravan clear of the road.'

'Oh well, I'm used to it,' he said. 'I live here, and the caravan gives us extra room when we have summer visitors.'

I glanced at the name on the gate. 'Chapel Down,' I said. 'That's unusual.'

He grinned. 'That's what we thought when we built the bungalow,' he said. 'We decided to keep the name of the actual plot of ground. It's been Chapel Down for centuries, and the fields across the road are both called Chapel Park.'

'Anything to do with the old priory?' I asked.

He did not register. 'There were a couple of cottages here once,' he said, 'some sort of a Methodist meeting-house, I believe. But the field names go back a lot further than that.'

His wife came out of the bungalow with a couple of children, and I started up the car. 'All clear ahead,' he called, and I pulled away from the ditch and drove up the hill until the curve in the road·hid the bungalow from sight. Then I pulled across to a lay-by on the right, where there was a pile of stones and timber.

I had reached the summit of the hill, and beyond the lay-by the road curved down to Tywardreath, the first houses already in sight. Chapel Down . . . Chapel Park . . . Could there have been a chapel here in former days, long since demolished, either on the site of the caravan-owner's bungalow or near the lay-by, where a modern house fronted the road?

Below the house a gate led into a field, and I climbed over it, circuiting the field and keeping close to the hedge until the sloping ground hid me from sight. This was the field the caravan-owner said was Chapel Park. It had no distinctive feature that I could see. Cows were grazing at the far end. I scrambled through the hedge at the bottom, and found myself on the precipitous grassland a few hundred feet above the railway, looking straight into the valley.

I lit a cigarette and surveyed the scene. No chapels tucked away, but what a view, Treesmill Farm away to my right, the other farms beyond, all sheltered from prevailing wind and weather, immediately below me the railway, and beyond it the strange sweep of the valley, no pattern of fields, nothing but a tapestry of willow, birch and alder. A paradise, surely, for birds in spring, and a good place for boys to hide from the parental eye – but boys never went bird's-nesting nowadays, at least my stepsons didn't,

I sat down against the hedge to finish my cigarette, and as I did so became aware of the flask in my breast pocket. I took it out and looked at it. It was a handy size, and I wondered if it had belonged to Magnus's father; it would have been just right for a nip of rum in his sailing days, when the breeze freshened. If only Vita had disliked flying and had chosen to come by sea it would have given me several more days . . . A rattle beneath me made me look down to the valley. A solitary diesel engine was coming up the line, going hell for leather without its load of carriages, and I watched it worm its way, like a fat, swift-moving slug, above the willows and the birches, pass under the bridge above Treesmill, and disappear finally into the gaping jaws of the tunnel a mile distant. I unscrewed the flask and downed its contents.

All right, I told myself, so what? I'm bloody-minded. And Vita's still in mid-Atlantic. I closed my eyes.

six

This time, sitting motionless with my back against the hedge and my eyes shut, I would try to pinpoint the moment of transition. On the previous occasions I had been walking, the first time across fields, the second up the churchyard path, when the vision altered. Now it would surely happen otherwise, because I was concentrating on the moment of impact. The sense of well-being would come, like a burden being lifted, and with it the sensation of lightness as feeling went from my body. No panic today, and no dismal falling rain. It was even warm, and the sun must be breaking through the clouds – I could sense the brightness through my closed eyelids. I took a last pull at the fag-end of my cigarette and let it drop.

If this drowsy content lasted much longer I might even fall asleep. Even the birds were rejoicing in the burst of sunshine; I could hear the blackbird singing in the hedge somewhere behind me, and more delightfully still a cuckoo called from the valley, distant at first, then near at hand. I listened to the call, a favourite sound, connected in my mind with every sort of carefree boyhood ramble thirty years ago. There, he called again, immediately overhead.

I opened my eyes and watched him wing his strange, unsteady flight across the sky, and as he did so I remembered that it was late July. The cuckoo's brief English summer ceased in June, along with the blackbird's song, and the primroses that were blooming in the bank beside me would have withered by mid-May. This warmth and brightness belonged to another world, an earlier spring. It had happened, despite concentration, in a moment of time that had not registered in my brain. All the sharp green colour of that first day was spread about me on the sloping hill below, and the valley with its tapestry of birch and willow lay submerged beneath a sheet of water, part of a great winding estuary that cut into the land, bordered by sandbanks where the water shallowed. I stood up, and saw how the river narrowed to mingle with the tumbling mill-stream below Treesmill, the farmhouse altered in shape, narrow, thatched, the hills opposite thickly forested with oak, the foliage young and tender because of spring.

Immediately beneath me, where the field had shelved precipitously to the railway cutting, the ground took on a gentler slope, in the midst of which a broad track ran to the estuary, the track terminating in a quay beside which boats were anchored, the channel there being deep, forming a natural pool. A larger vessel was moored in mid-stream, her sail partly stowed. I could hear the voices of the men aboard her singing, and as I watched a smaller boat alongside pushed off to ferry someone ashore, and the voices were suddenly hushed, as the passenger in the small boat lifted his hand for silence. Now I looked around me, and the hedge had gone, the hill behind me was thickly wooded like the hills opposite, and to my left, where there had been scrub and gorse, a long stone wall encircled a dwelling-house; I could see the rooftop above the surrounding trees. The path from the quay led straight uphill to the house.

I drew nearer, watching the man below descend from the boat at the quay, then proceed to climb the road towards me. As he did so the cuckoo called again, flying overhead, and the man looked up to watch it, pausing for breath as he climbed, his action so ordinary, so natural, that it endeared him to me for no reason except that he lived, and I was a ghost in time. A time, moreover, that was not constant, for yesterday it had been Martinmas, and now, by the cuckoo's call and the primroses in flower, it must be spring.

He came close, breasting the hill, and as I recognized him, though his expression was graver, more solemn than that of the preceding day, the analogy came to me that these faces were like the diamonds, hearts and spades in some well-thumbed pack of cards shuffled by a patience-player; however they were sorted, they still formed themselves into a combination that the player could not guess at. I did not know, nor they, how the game would go.

It was Otto Bodrugan climbing the hill, followed by his son Henry, and, when he raised his hand in greeting, so instinctive was the gesture that I raised mine in answer, and even smiled; but I should have known the futility of my action, for father and son brushed past me towards the entrance gate of the house, and Roger the steward came forward to greet them. He must have been standing there watching them approach, but I had not seen him. Gone was the festive air of yesterday, the mocking smile of the would-be go-between; he wore a dark tunic, as did Bodrugan and his son, and his manner was as grave as theirs.

'What news?' asked Bodrugan.

Roger shook his head. 'He is sinking fast,' he said. 'There is little hope for him. My lady Joanna is within, and all the family. Sir William Ferrers is already come from Bere, accompanied by the lady Matilda. Sir Henry does not suffer, we have seen to that – or, to speak more plainly, Brother Jean has done so, for he has been at the bedside night and day.'

'And the cause?'

'Nothing but the general weakness of which you know, and a sudden chill with that late frost we had. He wanders in his mind, speaking of his grievous faults and asking pardon. The parish priest heard his confession, but, not content with that, he begged to be shriven by Brother Jean as well, and has received the last rites.'

Roger stood aside to let Bodrugan and his son pass through the entrance gates, and now the extent of the building came into view, stone-walled with tiled roof, fronting upon a court, an outside staircase leading to an upper chamber, the steps similar to those serving a farmhouse granary today. There were stables at the rear, and beyond the walls the track wound uphill towards Tywardreath, the thatched cottages of the serfs who tilled the surrounding lands scattered on either side of it.

Dogs ran barking across the court at our approach, crouching low, ears flat, as Roger shouted at them, and a scared-faced servant emerged from a corner of the building to drive them off. Bodrugan and his son Henry crossed the threshold, with Roger in attendance, and I his shadow close behind. We had entered a long, narrow hall, extending the full width of the house, small casement windows giving upon the court on the eastern side and looking down to the estuary on the west. There was an open hearth at the far end, the banked turf barely smoking, and across the width of the room was a trestle table, with benches alongside. The hall was dark, partly because of the small windows and the smoke that lingered in the atmosphere, partly because the walls were plastered a deep vermilion, giving the whole a rich and sombre air.

There were three youngsters straddling the benches, two boys and a girl, their sprawling atttitude of dejection suggesting a numb bewilderment at the approach of death rather than actual sorrow. I recognized the eldest, William Champernoune, who had been presented to the Bishop; he was the first to rise now and come forward to greet his uncle and cousin, while the younger two, after momentary hesitation, followed his example. Otto Bodrugan bent to embrace all three, and then, as children will at the sudden entrance of adults in a moment of stress, they seized the opportunity to escape from the room, taking their cousin Henry with them.

Now I had leisure to observe the other occupants of the room. Two of them I had not seen before – a man and a woman, the man light-haired, bearded, the woman stout, with a sharp expression which boded ill for those who crossed her. She was already dressed in black, ready for calamity when it came, her white coif contrasting with her dark gown. This must be Sir William Ferrers, who, so Roger had said, had come post-haste from Devon, and his wife Matilda. The third occupant of the room, who was sitting on a low stool, was no stranger; it was my girl Isolda. She had made her own gesture to impending mourning by wearing lilac; but the silver sheen of the dress glistened, and a lilac ribbon, looping her braided hair away from her face, had been placed there with care. The prevailing mood seemed to be one of tension, and Matilda Ferrers wore an expression of high dudgeon which spoke of trouble.

'We expected you long since,' was her immediate reproof to the new arrival, Otto Bodrugan, as he advanced towards her chair. 'Does it take so many hours to sail across the bay, or did you delay purposely that your men might amuse themselves fishing?'

He kissed her hand, ignoring the reproach, and exchanged a glance with the man behind her chair. 'How are you, William?' he said. 'One hour from my anchorage to this, which was fair going, with the wind abeam. It would have taken longer had we ridden.'

William nodded, with an imperceptible shrug, used to his lady's temper. 'I thought as much,' he murmured. 'You could not have come sooner, and in any event there is nothing you can do.'

'Nothing he can do?' echoed Matilda. 'Except support us all when the moment comes, and add his voice to ours. Dismiss the French monk from the bedside and that drunken parish priest from the kitchen. If he cannot use a brother's authority and persuade Joanna to listen to reason, nobody can.'

Bodrugan turned to Isolda. He barely brushed her hand in greeting, nor did she look up at him and smile. The constraint between them surely was due to caution: one word of too great intimacy would draw comment.

November . . . May . . . Six months must have passed, in my leap through time, since the reception at the Priory for the Bishop's visitation.

'Where is Joanna?' asked Bodrugan.

'In the chamber above,' replied William, and now I saw the family likeness to Isolda. This was William Ferrers, her brother, but at least ten, perhaps fifteen, years older, his face lined, his light hair turning grey. 'You are aware of the trouble,' he continued. 'Henry will have no one near him but the French monk Jean, receives no treatment but from his hands, and refuses the surgeon who came with us from Devon and stands in high repute. Now, the treatment having failed, he is fallen into a coma and the end is near, probably within a few hours.'

'If such is Henry's wish and he is not suffering, what is there to complain of?' asked Bodrugan.

'Because it is ill done!' exclaimed Matilda. 'Henry has even expressed a wish to be buried in the Priory chapel, which should be withstood on every account. We all know the reputation of the Priory, the lax behaviour of the Prior, the lack of discipline amongst the monks. Such a resting-place for someone of Henry's standing would make fools of all of us in the eyes of the world.'

'Whose world?' asked Bodrugan. 'Does yours embrace the whole of England or only Devon?'

Matilda crimsoned. 'We know well enough where your allegiance lay seven years past,' she said, 'supporting an adulterous Queen against her son, the lawful King. Doubtless all things French have your attachment, from invading forces, should they cross the Channel, to dissolute monks serving a foreign Order.'

Her husband William laid a restraining hand upon her shoulder. 'We gain nothing by opening old wounds,' he said. 'Otto's part in that rebellion does not concern us now. However . . .' he glanced at Bodrugan, 'Matilda has a point. It might not be politic for a Champernoune to be interred amongst French monks. It would be more fitting if you would let him lie at Bodrugan, seeing that Joanna holds much of your manor fee as her marriage portion. Or I should be most happy for him to be buried at Bere, where we are rebuilding the church at the present time. After all, Henry is my cousin: the connection is almost as close as your own.'

'Oh, for the love of God,' Isolda broke in impatiently, 'let Henry lie where he will. Must we conduct ourselves like butchers haggling over a sheep's carcass before the beast is slain?'

It was the first time I had heard her voice. She spoke in French, like the rest, with the same nasal intonation, but perhaps because she was younger than they, and I was prejudiced, I found the quality more musical, holding a ring of clarity theirs did not possess. Matilda at once burst into tears, to the consternation of her husband, while Bodrugan strode over to the window and stared moodily at the view beyond. As for Isolda, who had caused the commotion, she tapped her foot impatiently, an expression of disdain upon her face.

I glanced at Roger standing beside me. He was making a supreme effort to conceal a smile. Then he stepped forward, his attitude one of respect towards all present, and observed to no one in particular, but I suspected to catch Isolda's eye, 'If you wish, I will tell my lady of Sir Otto's arrival.'

Nobody answered, and Roger, taking silence for acquiescence, bowed and withdrew. He climbed the stairway to the upper chamber, I following close upon his heels as if some thread bound us together. He entered without knocking, pushing aside the heavy hangings that masked the entrance to the room, which was half the size of the hall beneath, most of the space taken up by a draped bed at the further end. The small, paneless windows gave little light, the aperture tight closed by oiled parchment, while the lighted candles standing on the trestle table at the bed's foot threw monstrous shadows on ochre-coloured walls.

There were three people in the room, Joanna, a monk, and the dying man. Henry de Champernoune was propped up in the bed by a great bolster that thrust him forward, forcing his chin upon his breast, and a white cloth was bound round his head turban fashion, giving him an incongruous likeness to an Arab sheik. His eyes were closed, and judging by the pallor of his face he was on the point of death. The monk was bending to stir something in a bowl on the trestle table, and he lifted his head as we entered. It was the young man with the brilliant eyes who had served the Prior as secretary or clerk on my first visit to the Priory. He said nothing but continued stirring, and Roger turned to Joanna, who was seated at the other end of the room. She was perfectly composed, without a sign of grief on her face, and was engaged in drawing threads of coloured silk through a frame to form a pattern.

'Are they all here?' she asked, without turning her eyes from the frame.

'Those who were bidden,' answered the steward, 'and already at odds with one another. Lady Ferrers first scolded the children for speaking too loud, and has now fallen out with Sir Otto, while Lady Carminowe, by her looks, wishes herself elsewhere. Sir John has not yet come.'

'Nor likely to,' replied Joanna. 'I left the matter to his discretion. If he is premature in condolence it might be thought over-zealous on his part, and his sister Lady Ferrers will be the first to make mischief out of it.'

'She is making mischief already,' replied the steward.

'I'm aware of it. The sooner the business is over the better for all of us.'

Roger crossed to the foot of the bed and looked down upon the helpless occupant. 'How long now?' he asked the monk.

'He will not wake again. You may touch him if you will, he cannot feel it. We are only waiting for the heart to cease, and then my lady can announce his death.'

Roger shifted his gaze from the bed to the small bowls on the trestle table. 'What did you give him?'

'The same as before, meconium, the juice of the whole plant, in equal parts with henbane to the strength of a dram.'

Roger looked at Joanna. 'It would be as well if I removed these, lest there should be discussion as to the treatment. Lady Ferrers spoke of her own surgeon. They hardly dare go against your wishes, but there could be trouble.'

Joanna, still employing herself with her skeins of silk, shrugged her shoulders.

'Take the ingredients if you will,' she said, 'though we have disposed of the liquids down the drain. The vessels you may remove if you consider it safer, but I hardly think Brother Jean has anything to fear. His discretion has been absolute.'

She smiled at the young monk, who responded with one glance from his expressive eyes, and I wondered if he too, like the absent Sir John, had found favour during the weeks of her husband's illness. Between them, Roger and the monk, they made a package of the bowls, wrapping them in sacking, and all the while I could hear the murmur of voices from the hall below, suggesting that Lady Ferrers had recovered from her fit of crying and was in full spate again.

'How is my brother Otto taking it?' asked Joanna.

'He made no comment when Sir William suggested that interment in Bodrugan chapel would be preferable to the Priory. I think he is hardly likely to interfere. Sir William proposed his own church at Bere as an alternative.'

'To what purpose?'

'For self-aggrandisement, perhaps – who knows? I would not recommend it. Once they had Sir Henry's body in their hands there could be meddling. Whereas in the Priory chapel . . .'

'All would be well. Sir Henry's wishes observed, and ourselves at peace. I look to you to see there is no trouble with the tenants, Roger. The people have no great love of the Priory.'

'There'll be no trouble if they are treated well at the funeral feast,' he answered. 'A promise of mitigation of fines at the next court and a pardon for all misdemeanours. That should content them.'

'Let us hope so.' She pushed aside her frame and, rising from her chair, went to the bed. 'Is he living still?' she asked.

The monk took the lifeless wrist in his hand and felt the pulse, then lowered his head to listen to his patient's heart,

'Barely,' he answered. 'You may light the candles if you will, and by the time the family has been summoned he will have gone.'

They might have been talking of some wornout piece of furniture that had lost its use, instead of a woman's husband on the point of death. Joanna returned to her chair, took up a piece of black veiling, and began to drape it round her head and shoulders. Then she seized a looking-glass made of silver from the table near at hand.

'Should I wear it thus,' she asked the steward, 'or covering my face?'

'More fitting to be covered,' he told her, 'unless you can weep at will.'

'I have not wept since my wedding-day,' she answered.

The monk Jean crossed the dying man's hands upon his breast and fastened a linen bandage about his jaw. He stood back to observe his work, and as a finishing touch placed a crucifix between the folded hands.

Meanwhile Roger was rearranging the trestle table. 'How many candles do you require?' he asked.

'Five on the day of death,' replied the monk, 'in honour of the five wounds of Our Lord Jesus Christ. Have you a black coverlet for the bed?'

'In the chest yonder,' said Joanna, and while monk and steward draped the bed with its black pall she looked in the mirror for the last time, before covering her face with the veil.

'If I may presume,' murmured the monk, 'it would make the better impression if my lady knelt beside the bed and I stationed myself at the foot. Then when the family comes into the chamber I can recite the Prayers for the Dead. Unless you prefer the parish priest to do so.'

'He is too drunk to mount the stairs,' said Roger. 'If Lady Ferrers has one glimpse of him it will be his finish.'

'Then leave him alone,' said Joanna, 'and let us proceed. Roger, will you descend and summon them? William first, for he is the heir.'

She knelt beside the bed, head bowed in grief, but raised it before we left the room, saying over her shoulder to the steward, 'It cost my brother Sir Otto near on fifty marks at Bodrugan when my father died, not counting the beasts that were slaughtered for the funeral feast. We must not be outdone. Spare no expense.'

Roger drew aside the hangings by the door, and I followed him on to the steps outside. The contrast between the bright day without and the murky atmosphere within must have struck him as forcibly as it did me, for he paused at the top of the steps and looked down over the surrounding walls to the gleaming waters of the estuary below. The sails of Bodrugan's ship were furled loosely on the yard as she lay at anchor, and a fellow in a small boat astern skulled to and fro in search of fish. The youngsters from the house had wandered down the hillside to stare at their uncle's boat. Henry, Bodrugan's son, was pointing out something to his cousin William, and the dogs leapt about them, barking once again.

I realized at that moment, more strongly than hitherto, how fantastic, even macabre, was my presence amongst them, unseen, unborn, a freak in time, witness to events that had happened centuries past, unremembered, unrecorded; and I wondered how it was that standing here on the steps, watching yet invisible, I could so feel myself involved, troubled, by these loves and deaths. The man who was dying might have been a relative from my own lost world of youth – my father, even, who had died in spring when I was about the age of young William down there in the field. The cable from the Far East – he had been killed fighting the Japanese – arrived just as my mother and I had finished lunch, staying in an hotel in Wales for the Easter holidays. She went up to her bedroom and shut the door, and I hung about the hotel drive, aware of loss but unable to cry, dreading the sympathetic glance of the girl at the reception desk if I went indoors.

Roger, carrying the piece of sacking containing the bowls

stained by herb-juices, descended to the court, and went through an archway at the further end leading to a stableyard. What servants made up the household seemed to be gathered there, but at the steward's approach they broke up their gossip and scattered, all but one lad whom I had seen that first day and recognized, by his likeness to the horseman, as Roger's brother. Roger summoned him to his side with a jerk of his head.

'It is over,' he said. 'Ride to the Priory at once and inform the Prior, that he may give orders for tolling the bell. Work will cease when the men hear the summons, and they will start to come in from the fields, and assemble on the green. Directly you have delivered your message to the Prior ride on home and place this package in the cellar, then wait for my return. I have much to do, and may not be back tonight.'

The boy nodded, and disappeared into the stables. Roger passed through the archway into the court once more. Otto Bodrugan was standing at the entrance to the house. Roger hesitated a moment, then crossed the court to him.

'My lady asks you to go to her,' he said, 'with Sir William and Lady Ferrers and the lady Isolda. I will call William and the children.'

'Is Sir Henry worse?' asked Bodrugan.

'He is dead, Sir Otto. Not five minutes since, without recovering consciousness, peacefully, in his sleep.'

'I am sorry,' said Bodrugan, 'but it is better so. I pray God we may both go as peacefully when our time comes though undeservedly.' Both men crossed themselves. Automatically I did the same. 'I will tell the others,' he continued. 'Lady Ferrers may go into hysterics, but no matter. How is my sister?'

'Calm, Sir Otto.'

'I expected it.'

Bodrugan paused before turning into the house. 'You are aware,' he said, and there was something hesitant in his manner, 'that William, being a minor, will forfeit his lands to the King until he attains his majority?'

'I am, Sir Otto.'

'The confiscation would be little more than a formality in ordinary circumstances,' Bodrugan went on. 'As William's uncle by marriage, and therefore his legal guardian, I should be empowered to administer his estates, with the King as overlord.

But the circumstances are not ordinary, owing to the part I took in the so-called rebellion.' The steward maintained discreet silence, his face inscrutable. 'Therefore,' said Bodrugan, 'the escheator acting for the minor and the King is likely to be one held in greater esteem than myself – his cousin Sir John Carminowe, in all probability. In that event, I don't doubt he will arrange matters smoothly for my sister.'

The irony in his voice was unmistakable.

Roger inclined his head without replying, and Bodrugan went into the house. The steward's slow smile of satisfaction was instantly suppressed as the young Champernounes, with their cousin Henry, entered the court, laughing and chatting, having momentarily forgotten the imminence of death. Henry, the eldest of the party, was the first to sense, intuitively, what must have happened. He called the younger pair to silence, and motioned William to come forward. I saw the expression on the boy's face change from carefree laughter to apprehension, and I guessed how sudden dread must have turned his stomach sick.

'Is it my father?' he asked.

Roger nodded. 'Take your brother and sister with you,' he said, 'and go to your mother. Remember, you are the eldest; she will look to you for support in the days to come.'

The boy clutched at the steward's arm. 'You will remain with us, will you not?' he asked. 'And my uncle Otto too?'

'We shall see,' answered Roger. 'But you are the head of the family now.'

William made a supreme effort at self-control. He turned and faced his younger brother and sister and said, 'Our father is dead. Please follow me,' and walked into the house, head erect, but very pale. The children, startled, did as they were told, taking their cousin Henry's hand, and glancing at Roger I saw, for the first time, something of compassion on his face, and pride as well; the boy he must have known from cradle days had not disgraced himself. He waited a few moments, then followed them.

The hall appeared deserted. A tapestry hanging at the far end near the hearth had been drawn aside, showing a small stairway to the upper room, by which Otto Bodrugan and the Ferrers must have ascended, and the children too. I could hear the shuffle of feet overhead, then silence, followed by the low murmur of the monk's voice, *'Requiem aeternam dona eis, Domine, et lux perpetua luceat eis.'*

I said the hall appeared deserted, and so it was, but for the slender figure in lilac: Isolda was the only member of the group who had not gone to the room above. At sight of her Roger paused on the threshold, before moving forward with deference.

'Lady Carminowe does not wish to pay tribute with the rest of the family?' he asked.

Isolda had not noticed him standing there by the entrance, but now she turned her head and looked at him direct, and there was so much coldness in her eyes that standing where I was, beside the steward, they seemed to sweep me with the same contempt as they did him.

'It is not my practice to make a mockery of death,' she said.

If Roger was surprised he gave no sign of it, but made the same deferential gesture as before. 'Sir Henry would be grateful for your prayers,' he said.

'He has had them with regularity for many years,' she answered, 'and with increasing fervour these past weeks.'

The edge in her voice was evident to me, and must have been doubly so to the steward. 'Sir Henry has ailed ever since making the pilgrimage to Campostella,' he replied. 'They say Sir Ralph de Beaupré suffers today from the same sickness. It is a wasting fever, there is no cure for it. Sir Henry had so little regard for his own person that it was hard to treat him. I can assure you that everything possible was done.'

'I understand Sir Ralph Beaupré retains full possession of his faculties despite his fever,' Isolda replied. 'My cousin did not. He recognized none of us for a month or more, yet his brow was cool, the fever was not high.'

'No two men are alike in sickness,' Roger answered. 'What will save the one will trouble the other. If Sir Henry wandered in his mind it was his misfortune.'

'Made the more effective by the potions given him,' she said. 'My grandmother, Isolda de Cardinham, had a treatise on herbs, written by a learned doctor who went to the Crusades, and she bequeathed it to me when she died, because I was her namesake. I am no stranger to the seeds of the black poppy and the white, water hemlock, mandragora, and the sleep they can induce.'

Roger, startled out of his attitude of deference, did not answer her at once. Then he said. 'These herbs are used by all apothecaries for easing pain. The monk, Jean de Meral, was trained in the parent-house at Angers and is especially skilled. Sir Henry himself had implicit faith in him.'

'I don't doubt Sir Henry's faith, the monk's skill, or his zeal in employing that skill, but a healing plant can turn malign if the dose is increased,' replied Isolda.

She had made her challenge, and he knew it. I remembered that trestle table at the foot of the bed, and the bowls upon it, now carefully wrapped in sacking and carried away.

'This is a house of mourning,' said Roger, 'and will continue so for several days. I advise you to speak of this matter to my lady, not to me. It is none of my business.'

'Nor mine either,' replied Isolda. 'I speak through attachment to my cousin, and because I am not easily fooled. You might remember it.'

One of the children started crying overhead, and there was a sudden lull in the murmur of prayers, the sound of movement, and the scurrying of footsteps down the stairs. The daughter of the house – she could not have been more than ten – came running into the room, and flung herself into Isolda's arms.

'They say he is dead,' she said, 'yet he opened his eyes and looked at me, just once, before closing them again. No one else saw, they were too busy with their prayers. Did he mean that I must follow him to the grave?'

Isolda held the child to her protectively, staring over her shoulder at Roger all the while, and suddenly she said, 'If anything evil has been done this day or yesterday, you will be held responsible, with others, when the time comes. Not in this world, where we lack proof, but in the next, before God.'

Roger moved forward, with some impulse, I think, to silence her or take the child from her, and I stepped into his path to prevent him, but stumbled, catching my foot in a loose stone. And there was nothing about me but great mounds of earth and hillocks of grass, gorse-bushes and the root of a dead tree, and behind me a large pit, circular in shape like a quarry, full of old tins and fallen slate. I caught hold of a twisted stem of withered gorse, retching violently, and in the distance I could hear the hoot of a diesel engine as it rattled below me in the valley.

seven

The quarry was steep, carved out of the hillside, spread about with holly and clumps of ivy, the debris of years scattered amongst the earth and stones, and the path leading out of it ran into a small pit, and then another, and yet a third, all heaped about with banks and ditches and knolls of tufted grass. The gorse was everywhere, masking the view, and because of my vertigo I could not see but kept stumbling against the banks, with one thought paramount in my mind – that I must get out of this wasteland and find the car. It was imperative to find the car.

I caught hold of a thorn tree and held on to it to steady myself, and there were more old cans at my feet, a broken bedstead, a tyre, and still more clumps of ivy and holly. Feeling had returned to my limbs, but as I staggered up the mound above me the dizziness increased, the nausea too, and I slithered down into another pit and lay there panting, my stomach heaving. I was violently sick, which gave momentary relief, and I got up again and climbed another mound. Now I saw that I was only a few hundred yards from the original hedge where I had smoked my cigarette – the mounds and the quarry beyond had been hidden from me then by a sloping bank and a broken gate. I looked down once more into the valley, and saw the tail-end of the train disappearing round the corner to Par station. Then I climbed through a gap in the hedge and began to walk uphill across the field and back to the car.

I reached the lay-by just as another violent attack of nausea came upon me. I staggered sideways amongst the heap of cement and planks and was violently sick again, while ground and sky revolved around me. The vertigo I had experienced that first day in the patio was nothing to this, and as I crouched on the heap of cement waiting for it to pass I kept saying to myself, 'Never again . . . never again . . .' with all the fervour and weak anger of someone coming round from an anaesthetic, the revulsion beyond control.

Before I collapsed I had been aware, dimly, that there was another car in the lay-by besides my own, and after what seemed an eternity, when the nausea and the vertigo ceased, and I was coughing and blowing my nose, I heard the door of the other car slam, and realized that the owner had come across and was staring down at me.

'Are you all right now?' he asked.

'Yes,' I said, 'yes, I think so.'

I rose unsteadily to my feet, and he put out a hand to help me. He was about my own age, early forties, with a pleasant face and a remarkably strong grip.

'Got your keys?'

'Keys . . .' I fumbled in my pocket for the car keys. Christ! What if I had dropped them in the quarry or amongst those mounds – I should never find them again. They were in my top pocket, with the flask; the relief was so tremendous that I felt steadier at once, and walked without assistance to the car. Another fumble, though: I could not fit the key into the lock.

'Give it to me, I'll do it,' said my Samaritan.

'It's extremely kind of you. I do apologize,' I said.

'All in a day's work,' he answered. 'I happen to be a doctor.'

I felt my face stiffen, then quickly stretch into a smile intended to disarm. Casual courtesy from a passing motorist was one thing; professional attention from a medico another. As it was he was staring at me with interest, and small blame to him. I wondered what he was thinking.

'The fact is,' I said, 'I must have walked up the hill a bit too fast. I felt giddy when I reached the top, and then was sick. Couldn't stop myself.'

'Oh, well,' he said, 'it's been done before. I suppose a lay-by is as good a place as any to throw up in. You'd be surprised what they find down here in the tourist season.'

He was not fooled, though. His eyes were particularly penetrating. I wondered if he could see the shape of the flask bulging the top pocket of my jacket.

'Have you far to go?' he asked.

'No,' I said, 'a couple of miles or so, no more.'

'In that case,' he suggested, 'wouldn't it be more sensible if you left your car here and let me drive you home? You could always send for it later.'

'It's very kind of you,' I said, 'but I assure you I'm perfectly all right now. It was just one of those passing things.'

'H'm,' he said, 'rather violent while it lasted.'

'Honestly,' I said, 'there's nothing wrong. Perhaps it was something I had for lunch, and then walking uphill . . .'

'Look,' he interrupted, 'you're not a patient of mine, I'm not trying to prescribe. I'm only warning you that it might be dangerous to drive.'

'Yes,' I said, 'it's very good of you and I'm grateful for your advice.' The thing was, he could be right. Yesterday I had driven to St Austell and back home with the greatest ease. Today it might be different. The vertigo might seize me once again. He must have seen my hesitation, for he said, 'If you like I'll follow you, just to see you're OK.'

I could hardly refuse – to have done so would have made him the more suspicious. 'That's very decent of you,' I told him. 'I only have to go to the top of Polmear hill.'

'All on the way home,' he smiled. 'I live in Fowey.'

I climbed rather gingerly into my car and turned out of the lay-by. He followed close behind, and I thought to myself that if I drove into the hedge I was done for. But I navigated the narrow lane without difficulty, and heaved a sigh of relief as I emerged on to the main road and shot up Polmear hill. When I turned right, to go to Kilmarth, I thought he might follow me to the house, but he waved his hand and continued along the road to Fowey. It showed discretion, at any rate. Perhaps he thought I was staying in Polkerris or one of the nearby farms. I passed through the gate and down the drive, put the car away in the garage, and let myself into the house. Then I was sick again.

The first thing I did when I recovered, still feeling pretty shaky, was to rinse out the flask. Then I went down to the laboratory and stood it in the sink to soak. It was safer there than in the pantry. It was not until I went upstairs once more, and flung myself into an armchair in the music-room, exhausted, that I remembered the bowls wrapped in sacking. Had I left them in the car?

I was about to get up and go down to the garage to look for them, because they must be cleansed even more thoroughly than the flask and put away under lock and key, when I realized with a sudden wave of apprehension, just as though something were being vomited from my brain as well as my stomach, that I had been on the point of confusing the present with the past. The bowls had been given to Roger's brother, not to me.

I sat very still, my heart thumping in my chest. There had been no confusion before. The two worlds had been distinct. Was it because the nausea and the vertigo had been so great that the past and the present had run together in my mind? Or had I miscounted the drops, making the draught more potent? No way of telling. I clutched the sides of the armchair. They were solid, real. Everything about me was real. The drive home, the doctor, the quarry full of old cans and crumbling stones, they were real. Not the house above the estuary, nor the people in it, nor the dying man, nor the monk, nor the bowls in sacking – they were all products of the drug, a drug that turned a clear brain sick.

I began to be angry, not so much with myself, the willing guinea-pig, as with Magnus. He was unsure of his findings. He did not know what he had done. No wonder he had asked me to send up bottle B to try out the contents on the laboratory monkey. He had suspected something was wrong, and now I could tell him what it was. Neither exhilaration nor depression, but confusion of thought. The merging of two worlds. Well, that was enough. I had had my lot. Magnus could make his experiments on a dozen monkeys, but not on me.

The telephone started ringing, and, startled out of my chair, I went across to the library to answer it. Damn his telepathic powers. He would tell me he knew where I had been, that the house above the estuary was familiar ground, there was no need to worry, it was all perfectly safe providing I touched no one; if I felt ill or confused it was a side-effect of no consequence. I would put him right.

I seized the telephone and someone said, 'Hold on a moment, please, I have a call for you,' and I heard the click as Magnus took over.

'Damn and blast you,' I said. 'This is the last time I behave like a performing seal.'

There was a little gasp at the other end, and then a laugh. 'Thanks for the welcome home, darling.'

It was Vita. I stood stupefied, holding on to the receiver. Was her voice part of the confusion?

'Darling?' she repeated. 'Are you there? Is something wrong?'

'No,' I said, 'nothing's wrong, but what's happened? Where are you speaking from?'

'London airport,' she answered. 'I caught an earlier plane, that's all. Bill and Diana are collecting me and taking me out to dinner. I thought you might call the flat later tonight and wonder why I didn't answer. Sorry if I took you by surprise.'

'Well, you did,' I said, 'but forget it. How are you?'

'Fine,' she said, 'just fine. What about you? Who did you think I was when you answered me just now? You didn't sound too pleased.'

'In point of fact,' I told her, 'I thought it was Magnus. I had to do a chore for him . . . I've written you all about it in my letter, which you won't get until tomorrow morning.'

She laughed. I knew the sound, with the slight 'I thought as much' inflection. 'So your Professor has been putting you to work,' she said. 'That doesn't surprise me. What's he been making you do that has turned you into a performing seal?'

'Oh, endless things, sorting out junk, I'll explain when I see you. When do the boys get back?'

'Tomorrow,' she said. 'Their train arrives at a hideous hour in the morning. Then I thought I'd pack them in the car and come on down. How long will it take?'

'Wait,' I said, 'that's just it. I'm not ready for you. I've told you so in my letter. Leave it until after the weekend.'

There was silence the other end. I had dropped the usual clanger.

'Not ready?' she repeated. 'But you must have been there all of five days? I thought you'd fixed up with some woman to come in and cook and clean, make beds and so on. Has she let us down?'

'No, it's not that,' I told her. 'She's first-rate, couldn't be better. Look, darling, I can't explain over the telephone, it's all in my letter, but, frankly, we weren't expecting you until Monday at the earliest.'

'We?' she said. 'You don't mean the Professor is there too?'

'No, no . . .' I could feel irritation rising in both of us. 'I meant Mrs Collins and myself. She only comes in the morning, she has to bicycle up from Polkerris, the little village at the bottom of the hill, and the beds aren't aired or anything. She'll be terribly put out if everything isn't absolutely straight, and you know what you are, you'll take a dislike to the place if it isn't shining.'

'What absolute nonsense,' she said. 'I'm fully prepared to

picnic, and so are the boys. We can bring food with us, if that's worrying you. And blankets too. Are there enough blankets?'

'Masses of blankets,' I said, 'masses of food. Oh, darling, don't be obstructive. If you come down right away it won't be convenient, and that's the plain truth of it. I'm sorry.'

'OK.' The lilt in the 'K' had the typical upward ring of Vita temporarily defeated in argument but determined to win the final battle. 'You'd better find yourself an apron and a broom,' she added as a parting shot. 'I'll tell Bill and Diana you've turned domestic and are going to spend the evening on your hands and knees. They'll love it.'

'It's not that I don't want to see you, darling,' I began, but her 'Bye', still with the upward inflection, told me I had done my worst, and she had hung up on me and was now making her way to the airport restaurant to order a Scotch on the rocks and smoke three cigarettes in quick succession before the arrival of her friends.

Well, that was that. . . . What now? My anger against Magnus had been deflected to Vita, but how could I know she was going to catch an earlier plane and ring me unexpectedly? Anyone in the same situation would have been caught on the wrong foot. But that was the rub. My situation was not the same as anyone else's: it was unique. Less than an hour ago I had been living in another world, another time, or had imagined myself to be doing so, through the effect of the drug.

I began to walk from the library through the small dining-room across the hall to the music-room and back again, like someone pacing the deck of a ship, and it seemed to me that I was not sure of anything any more. Neither of myself, nor of Magnus, nor of Vita, nor of my own immediate world, for who was to say where I belonged – here in this borrowed house, in the London flat, in the office I had left when quitting my job, or in that singularly vivid house of mourning which lay buried beneath centuries of rubble? Why, if I was determined not to see that house again, had I dissuaded Vita from coming down tomorrow? The excuses had been immediate, a reflex action. Nausea and vertigo had gone. Accepted. They might strike again. Accepted also. The drug was dangerous, its implications and its side-effects unknown. This, too, accepted. I loved Vita, but I did not want her with me. Why?

I seized the telephone once more and dialled Magnus. No answer. No answer, either, to my self-imposed question. That doctor with his intelligent eyes might have given me one. What would he have told me? That a hallucinatory drug could play curious tricks with the unconscious, bringing the suppressions of a lifetime to the surface, so let it alone? A practical answer, but it did not suffice. I had not been moving amongst childhood ghosts. The people I had seen were not shadows from my own past. Roger the steward was not my alter-ego, nor Isolda a dream-fantasy, a might-have-been. Or were they?

I tried Magnus two or three times later, but there was never a reply, and I spent a restless evening, unable to settle to newspapers, book, records or TV. Finally, fed up with myself and the whole problem, to which there seemed no solution, I went early to bed, and slept, to my astonishment when I awoke next morning, amazingly well.

The first thing I did was to ring the flat, and I caught Vita just as she was tearing off to meet the boys.

'Darling, I'm sorry about yesterday . . .' I began, but there was no time to go into it, she told me, she was late already.

'Well, when shall I ring you?' I asked.

'I can't give you a time,' she answered. 'It depends upon the boys, what they want to do, whether there'll be a mass of shopping. They'll probably need jeans, swimming-trunks, I don't know. Thanks for your letter, by the way. Your Professor certainly keeps you employed.'

'Never mind Magnus . . . How was your dinner with Bill and Diana?'

'Fun. Lots of scandal. Now I must go, or I'll keep the boys hanging about at Waterloo Station.'

'Give them my love,' I shouted, but she had gone. Oh well, she sounded happy enough. The evening with her friends and a good night's rest must have changed her ideas, and my letter too, which she seemed to have accepted. What a relief . . . Now I could relax once more. Mrs Collins knocked on the door and came in with my breakfast tray.

'You're spoiling me,' I said. 'I ought to have been up an hour ago.'

'You're on holiday,' she said. 'There's nothing to get up for, is there?'

I thought about this as I drank my coffee. A revealing remark. Nothing to get up for . . . No more hopping into the underground from West Kensington to Covent Garden, the familiar office window, the inevitable routine, discussions about publicity, jackets, new authors, old authors. All finished, through my resignation. Nothing to get up for. But Vita wanted it to start all over again on her side of the Atlantic. Darting down the subway, elbowing strangers on sidewalks, an office building thirty stories high, the inevitable routine, discussions about publicity, jackets, new authors, old authors. Something to get up for. . . .

There were two letters on my breakfast tray. One was from my mother in Shropshire saying how lovely it must be in Cornwall and she envied me, I must be getting so much sun. Her arthritis had been bad again and poor old Dobsie was getting very deaf. (Dobsie was my stepfather, and I didn't wonder he was deaf; it was probably a defence mechanism, for my mother never drew breath.) And so on and so on, her large looped handwriting covering about eight pages. Pangs of conscience, for I had not seen her for a year, but to give her her due she never reproached me, was delighted when I married Vita, and always remembered the boys at Christmas with what I considered an unnecessarily thumping tip.

The other envelope was long and slim, and contained a couple of typewritten documents and a note scribbled by Magnus.

'Dear Dick,' it read, 'my disciple's long-haired friend who spends his time browsing around the BM and the PRO had produced the enclosed when I arrived at my desk this morning. The copy of the Lay Subsidy Roll is quite informative, and the other, mentioning your lord of the manor, Champernoune, and the to-do about removing his body may amuse you.

'I shall think about you this afternoon and wonder if Virgil is leading Dante astray. Do remember not to *touch* him; reaction can be progressively unpleasant. Keep your distance and all will be well. I suggest you stay put on the premises for your next trip.

'Yours, Magnus'

I turned to the documents. The research student had scribbled at the top of the first, 'From Bishop Grandisson of Exeter. Original in Latin. Excuse my translation.' It read as follows:

'Grandisson. AD 1329. Tywardreath Priory.

'John, etc., to his beloved sons men of a religious order, the Lords, the Prior and Convent of Tywardreath, greetings, etc. By the laws of the sacred Canons it is known that we are warned that the bodies of the Faithful, once delivered for burial by the Church, may not be exhumed except by those same laws. It has lately come to our ears that the body of the Lord Henry of Champernoune, Knight, rests buried in your consecrated church. Certain men, however, directing their mind's eyes in worldly fashion upon the transitory pomps of this life rather than on the welfare of the said Knight's soul and the discharging of due rites, are busying themselves about the exhumation of the said body, in circumstances not permitted by our laws, and about removing it to another place without our licence. Wherefore strictly enjoining upon you the virtue of obedience we give orders that you, in resistance to such reckless daring, must not allow the exhumation of the said body or its removal to be undertaken in any way, when we have not been consulted, nor have the reasons for such exhumation or removal, if there were any, been examined, discussed, or approved; even as you wish to escape divine retribution or that of ourselves. While we for our part lay an inhibition on all and each of our subjects, and no less upon others through whom it is hoped apparently to perpetrate a crime of this kind, so that they should not, under pain of excommunication, afford any help, counsel or favour for such an exhumation or removal of this kind which is in question. Given at Paignton on 27th August.'

Magnus had added a footnote. 'I like Bishop Grandisson's forthright style. But what is it all about? A family squabble, or something more sinister, of which the Bishop himself was ignorant?'

The second document was a list of names, headed 'Lay Subsidy Roll, 1327, Paroch Tiwardrayd. Subsidy of a twentieth of all moveable goods . . . upon all the Commons who possess goods of the value of ten shillings or upwards.' There were forty names in all, and Henry de Champernoune headed the list. I ran my eye down the rest. Number twenty-three was Roger Kylmerth. So it wasn't hallucination – he had really lived.

eight

When I had dressed I went to the garage and fetched the car, and skirting Tywardreath took the road to Treesmill. I purposely avoided the lay-by and drove down the hill into the valley, but not before the fellow at the bungalow Chapel Down, who was busy washing his caravan, waved a hand in greeting. The same thing happened when I stopped the car below the bridge near Treesmill Farm. The farmer of yesterday morning was driving his cows across the road, and paused to speak to me. I thanked my stars neither of them had been at the lay-by later in the day.

'Found your manor-house yet?' he asked.

'I'm not sure,' I told him. 'I thought I'd take another look round. That's a curious sort of place halfway up the field there, covered in gorse-bushes. Has it got a name?'

I could not see the site from the bridge, but pointed roughly in the direction of the quarry where yesterday, in another century, I had followed Roger into the house where Sir Henry Champernoune lay dying.

'You mean up Gratten?' he said. 'I don't think you'll find anything up there except old slate and rubble. Fine place for slate, or was. Mostly rubbish now. They say when the houses were built in Tywardreath in the last century they took most of the stones and slates from that place. It may be true.'

'Why Gratten?' I asked.

'I don't know exactly. The ploughed field at the back is the Gratten, part of Mount Bennett farm. The name has something to do with burning, I believe. There's a path opposite the turning to Stonybridge will lead you to it. But you'll find nothing to interest you.'

'I don't suppose I shall,' I answered, 'except the view.'

'Mostly trains,' he laughed, 'and not so many of them these days.'

I parked the car halfway up the hill, opposite the lane, as he suggested, then struck across the field towards the Gratten. The railway and the valley were beneath me, to my right, the ground descending very steeply to a high embankment beside the railway, then sloping away more gradually to swamp and thicket. Yesterday, in that other world, there had been a quayside midway between the two, and in the centre of the wooded valley, where trees and bush were thickest, Otto Bodrugan had anchored his craft mid-channel, the bows of the boat swinging to meet the tide.

I passed the spot below the hedge where I had sat and smoked my cigarette. Then I went through the broken gate, and stood once more amongst the hillocks and the mounds. Today, without vertigo or nausea, I could see more clearly that these knolls were not the natural formation of uneven ground, but must have been walls that had been covered for centuries by vegetation, and the hollows which I had thought, in my dizziness, to be pits were simply the enclosures that long ago had been rooms within a house.

The people who had come to gather slates and stones for their cottages had done so for good reason. Digging into the soil that must have covered the foundations of a building long vanished would have given them much of the material they needed for their own use, and the quarry at the back was part of this same excavation. Now, the quest ended, the quarry remained a tip for useless junk, the discarded tins rusted with age and winter rains.

Their quest had ended, while mine had just begun, but, as the farmer down at Treesmill had warned me, I should find nothing. I knew only that yesterday, in another time, I had stood in the vaulted hall that formed the central feature of this long-buried house, had mounted the outer stairway to the room above, had seen the owner of the dwelling die. No courtyard now, no walls, no hall, no stable-quarters in the rear; nothing but grassy banks and a little muddy path running between them.

There was a patch of even ground, smooth and green, fronting the site, that might have been part of the courtyard once, and I sat down there looking into the valley below as Bodrugan had done from the small window in the hall. Tiwardrai, the House on the Strand. . . . I thought how, when the tide ebbed in early centuries, the twisting channel would stay blue, revealing sandy flats on either side of it, these flats a burnished gold under the sun. If the channel was deep enough, Bodrugan could have raised anchor and made for sea later that night; if not, he would have returned on board to sleep amongst his men, and at daybreak, perhaps, come out on deck to stretch himself and stare up at the house of mourning.

I had put the documents that had come by post this morning into my pocket, and now I drew them out and read them through again.

Bishop Grandisson's order to the Prior was dated August 1329. Sir Henry Champernoune had died in late April or early May. The Ferrers pair were doubtless behind the attempt to remove him from his Priory tomb, with Matilda Ferrers the more pressing of the two. I wondered who had carried the rumour to the Bishop's ears, so playing on ecclesiastical pride, and ensuring that the body would escape investigation? Sir John Carminowe, in all probability, acting hand in glove with Joanna – whom he had, no doubt, long since successfully taken to bed.

I turned to the Lay Subsidy Roll, and glanced once again through the list of names, ticking off those that corresponded to the place-names on the road map I had brought from the car. Ric Trevynor, Ric Trewiryan, Ric Trenathelon, Julian Polpey, John Polorman, Geoffrey Lampetho . . . all, with slight variations in the spelling, were farms marked on the road-map beside me. The men who dwelt in them then, dead for over six hundred years, had bequeathed their names to posterity; only Henry Champernoune, lord of the manor, had left a heap of mounds as legacy, to be stumbled upon by myself, a trespasser in time. All dead for nearly seven centuries, Roger Kylmerth and Isolda Carminowe amongst them. What they had dreamt of, schemed for, accomplished, no longer mattered, it was all forgotten.

I got up and tried to find, amongst the mounds, the hall where Isolda had sat yesterday, accusing Roger of complicity in crime. Nothing fitted. Nature had done her work too well, here on the hillside and below me in the valley, where the estuary once ran. The sea had withdrawn from the land, the grass had covered the walls, the men and women who had walked here once, looking down upon blue water, had long since crumbled into dust.

I turned away, retracing my steps across the field, low-spirited, reason telling me that this was the end of the adventure. Emotion was in conflict with reason, however, destroying peace of mind, and for better, for worse, I knew myself involved. I could not forget that I had only to turn the key of that laboratory door for it to happen once again. The choice, perhaps, put to Man from the beginning, whether or not to eat of the Tree of Knowledge. I got into the car and drove back to Kilmarth.

I spent the afternoon writing a full account of yesterday to Magnus, and told him also that Vita was in London. Then I drove to Fowey to post the letter, and arranged to hire a sailing boat after the weekend, when Vita and the boys were down. She would not experience the flat calm of Long Island sound, or the luxury of her brother Joe's chartered yacht, but the gesture showed my will to please, and the boys would enjoy it.

I rang nobody that evening, and nobody rang me, with the result that I slept badly, continually waking and listening to silence. I kept thinking of Roger Kylmerth in his sleeping-quarters over the kitchen of the original farmstead, and wondering whether his brother had thoroughly scoured out the bowls six hundred and forty years ago. He must have done so, for Henry Champernoune to lie undisturbed in the Priory chapel until that chapel had crumbled into dust as well.

No breakfast in bed the following morning, for I was too restless. I was drinking my coffee on the steps outside the french window of the library when the telephone rang. It was Magnus.

'How are you feeling?' he asked at once.

'Jaded,' I told him. 'I slept badly.'

'You can make up for it later. You can sleep all afternoon in the patio. There are several lilos in the boiler-room, and I envy you. London is sweltering in a heatwave.'

'Cornwall isn't,' I replied, 'and the patio gives me claustrophobia. Did you get my letter?'

'I did,' he said. 'That's why I rang. Congratulations on your third trip. Don't worry about the aftermath. It was your own fault, after all.'

'It may have been,' I said, 'but the confusion was not.'

'I know,' he agreed. 'The confusion fascinated me. Also the jump in time. Six months or more between the second and third trips. You know what? I've a good mind to get away in a week or so and join you so that we can go on a trip together.'

My first reaction was one of excitement. The second, a zoom to earth. 'It's out of the question. Vita will be here with the boys.'

'We can get rid of them. Pack them off to the Scillies, or for a long day at the Land's End, scattering banana skins. That'll give us time.'

'I don't think so,' I said. 'I don't think so at all.' He did not know Vita well. I could imagine the complications.

'Well, it's not urgent,' he said, 'but it could be a lot of fun. Besides, I'd like to take a look at Isolda Carminowe.'

His flippant voice restored my jagged nerves. I even smiled. 'She's Bodrugan's girl, not ours,' I told him.

'Yes, but for how long?' he queried. 'They were always changing partners in those days. I still don't see where she fits in amongst the rest.'

'She and William Ferrers seem to be cousins to the Champernounes,' I explained.

'And Isolda's husband Oliver Carminowe, absent at yesterday's death-bed, is brother to Matilda and Sir John?'

'Apparently.'

'I must write all this down and get my slave to check for further details. I say, I was right about Joanna being a bitch.' Then abruptly changing his tone, 'So you're satisfied now that the drug works, and what you saw was not hallucination?'

'Almost,' I replied, with caution.

'Almost? Don't the documents prove it, if nothing else?'

'The documents help to prove it,' I countered, 'but don't forget you read them before I did. So there is still the possibility that you were exercising some kind of telepathic influence. Anyway, how's the monkey?'

'The monkey.' He paused a moment. 'The monkey's dead.'

'Thanks very much,' I said.

'Oh, don't worry – it wasn't the drug. I killed him on purpose; I have work to do on his brain cells. It will take some time, so don't get impatient.'

'I'm not in the least impatient,' I replied, 'merely appalled at the risk you appear to be taking with *my* brain.'

'Your brain's different,' he said. 'You can take a lot more punishment yet. Besides, think of Isolda. Such a splendid antidote to Vita. You might even find that . . .'

I cut him short. I knew exactly what he had been going to say. 'Leave my love life out of this,' I said. 'It doesn't concern you.'

'I was only about to suggest, dear boy, that moving between two worlds can act as a stimulant. It happens every day, without drugs, when a man keeps a mistress round the corner and a wife at home . . . That was a major find on your part, by the way, landing on the quarry above Treesmill valley. I'll put my arch-aeological friends on to digging the site when you and I have finished with it.'

It struck me, as he spoke, how our attitude to the experiment differed. His was scientific, unemotional, it did not really concern him who was broken in the process so long as what he was attempting to prove was proved successfully; whereas I was already caught up in the mesh of history: the people who to him were puppets of a bygone age were alive for me. I had a sudden vision of that long-buried house reconstructed on concrete blocks, admission two shillings, car park at Chapel Down. . . .

'Then Roger never led you there?' I asked.

'To Treesmill valley? No,' he answered. 'I strayed from Kil-marth once only, and that was to the Priory, as I told you. I preferred to remain on my own ground. I'll tell you all about it when I come down. I'm off to Cambridge for the weekend, but remember you have all Saturday and Sunday for self-indulgence. Increase the dose a little – it won't hurt you.'

He rang off before I could ask him for his telephone number, should I want it over the weekend. I had hardly put down the receiver before the telephone rang again. This time it was Vita.

'You were engaged a long while,' she said. 'I suppose it was your Professor?'

'As a matter of fact it was,' I told her.

'Loading you up with weekend chores? Don't exhaust your-self, darling.' Acidity, then, was the morning mood. She must blow it off on the boys, I could not cope.

'What are you planning for today?' I asked, ignoring her previous remark.

'Well, the boys are going swimming at Bill's club. That's a must. We've a heatwave here in London. How's it with you?'

'Overcast,' I said without glancing at the window. 'A trough of low pressure crossing the Atlantic will reach Cornwall by mid-night.'

'It sounds delightful. I hope your Mrs Collins is getting on with airing the beds.'

'Everything's under control,' I told her, 'and I've hired a sailing-boat for next week, quite a big one, with a chap in charge. The boys will love it.'

'What about Mom?'

'Mom will love it too, if she takes enough seasick pills. There's also a beach below the cliffs here, only a couple of fields to cross. No bulls.'

'Darling,' – the acidity had turned sweet, or at any rate mellow – 'I believe you are looking forward to our coming after all.'

'Of course I am,' I said. 'Why should you think otherwise?'

'I never know what to think when your Professor's been at you. There's some sort of hoodoo between us when he's around. . . . Here are the boys,' she went on, her voice changing. 'They want to say hello.'

My stepsons' voices, like their appearance, were identical, though Teddy was twelve and Micky ten. They were said to resemble their father, killed in an air crash a couple of years before I met Vita. Judging by the photograph they carried round with them, this was true. He had, they had, the typical Teuton head, hair cropped close, of many American young. Blue eyes, innocent, set in a broad face. They were nice kids. But I could have done without them.

'Hi, Dick,' they said, one after the other.

'Hi,' I repeated, the phrase as alien to my tongue as if I had been speaking Tongalese.

'How are you both?' I asked.

'We're fine,' they said.

There was a long pause. They couldn't think of anything more to say. Neither could I. 'Looking forward to seeing you next week,' I told them.

I heard a lot of whispering, and then Vita was back on the line again. 'They're raging to swim. I shall have to go. Take care of yourself, darling, and don't overdo it with your pail and broom.'

I went and sat in the little summer-house that Magnus's mother had erected years ago, and looked down across the bay. It was a happy spot, peaceful, sheltered from all winds except a south-westerly blow. I could see myself spending a lot of time here during the holidays, if only to get out of bowling to the boys; they were sure to bring cricket stumps with them, and a bat, and a ball which they would continually hit over the wall into the field beyond.

'Your turn to get it!'

'No, it's not, it's yours!'

Then Vita's voice chiming in from behind the hydrangea bushes. 'Now, now, if you're going to quarrel there won't be any cricket at all, and I mean it,' with a final appeal to me— 'Do something, darling, you're the only adult male.'

But at least today, in the summer-house, looking up the bay as a ray of sun touched the horizon, there was peace at Kylmerth. Kylmerth . . . I had pronounced the word in thought as originally spelt, and quite unconsciously. Confusion of thought becoming habit? Too tired for introspection, I got up again and wandered aimlessly about the grounds, clipping at hedges with an old hook I found in the boiler-house. Magnus had been right about the lilos. There were three of them, the kind you inflate with a pump. I'd set to work on them in the afternoon, if I had the energy.

'Lost your appetite?' asked Mrs Collins, when I had laboured through my lunch and asked for coffee.

'Sorry,' I said, 'no reflection on your cooking. I'm a bit out of sorts.'

'I thought you looked tired. It's the weather. Turned very close.'

It was not the weather. It was my own inability to settle, a sort of restlessness that drove me to physical action, however futile. I strolled down across the fields to the sea, but it looked exactly the same as it had from the summer-house, flat and grey, and then I had all the effort of walking up again. The day dragged on. I wrote a letter to my mother, describing the house in boring detail just to fill the pages, reminding me of the duty letters I used to write from school: 'I'm in another dormitory this term. It holds fifteen.' Finally, physically and mentally exhausted, I went upstairs at half-past seven, threw myself fully clothed upon the bed, and was asleep within minutes.

The rain awoke me. Nothing much, just a pattering sound on the open window, with the curtain blowing about. It was quite dark. I switched on the light; it was four-thirty. I had slept a solid nine hours. My exhaustion had vanished and I felt ravenous, having had no supper.

Here was the pay-off for living alone: I could eat and sleep entirely as and when I pleased. I went downstairs to the kitchen, cooked myself sausages, eggs and bacon, and brewed a pot of tea. I felt fighting fit to begin a new day, but what could I possibly do at five o'clock in this grey, cheerless dawn? One thing, and one thing only. Then take the weekend to recover, if recovery was needed . . .

I went down the backstairs to the basement, switching on all the lights and whistling. It looked better lit up, much more cheerful. Even the laboratory had lost its alchemistic air, and measuring the drops into the medicine-glass was as simple as cleaning my teeth.

'Come on, Roger,' I said, 'show yourself. Let's make it a tête-à-tête.'

I sat on the edge of the sink and waited. I waited a long time. The thing was, nothing happened. I just went on staring at the embryos in the bottles as it grew gradually lighter outside the barred window. I must have sat there for about half-an-hour. What a frightful swindle! Then I remembered that Magnus had suggested increasing the dose. I took the dropper, very cautiously let two or three more drops fall on to my tongue, and swallowed them. Was it imagination, or was there a taste to it this time – bitter, a little sour?

I locked the door of the laboratory behind me, and went down the passage into the old kitchen. I switched off the light, for it was already grey, with the first dawn in the patio outside. Then I heard the back door creak – it had a habit of grating on the stone flag beneath – and it blew wide open in the sudden draught. There was the sound of footsteps and a man's voice.

'God!' I thought. 'Mrs Collins has turned up early – she said something about her husband coming to mow the grass.'

The man pushed past the door, dragging a boy behind him, and it was not Mrs Collins's husband, it was Roger Kylmerth, and he was followed by five other men, carrying flares, and there was no longer any dawn light coming from the patio, only the dark night.

nine

I had been standing against the old kitchen dresser, but there was no dresser behind me now, only the stone wall, and the kitchen itself had become the living-quarters of the original house, with the hearth at one end and the ladder leading to the sleeping-room beside it. The girl I had seen kneeling by the hearth that first day came running down the ladder at the sound of the men's footsteps, and at sight of her Roger shouted, 'Go back out of it! What we have to say and do does not concern you.'

She hesitated, and the boy, the brother, was there too, looking over her shoulder. 'Out of it,' shouted Roger, 'the pair of you,' and they backed away again, up the ladder, but from where I stood I could see them crouching there, out of sight of the group of men, who entered the kitchen behind the steward.

Roger set his flare upon a bench, lighting the room, and I recognized the boy he was holding – it was the young novice I had seen on my first visit to the Priory, the lad who had been forced to run round the stableyard to make sport for his fellow-monks, and later had wept at his prayers in the Priory chapel.

'I'll make him talk,' said Roger, 'if the rest of you cannot. It will loosen his tongue to have a taste of Purgatory to come.'

Slowly he rolled up his sleeves, taking his time, his eyes upon the novice all the while, and the boy backed away from the bench, seeking shelter amongst the other men, who thrust him forward, laughing. He had grown taller since I had seen him last, but it was the same lad, there was no mistaking him, and the look of terror in his eyes suggested that the rough handling he dreaded this time was not sport.

Roger seized him by his habit and pushed him on to his knees beside the bench. 'Tell us all you know,' he said, 'or I'll singe the hair off your head.'

'I know nothing,' cried the novice. 'I swear by the Mother of God . . .'

'No blasphemy,' said Roger, 'or I'll set fire to your habit too. You've played spy long enough, and we want the truth.'

He took hold of the flare and brought it within an inch or so of the boy's head. The boy crouched lower and began to scream.

Roger hit him across the mouth. 'Come on, out with it,' he said.

The girl and her brother were staring from the ladder, fascinated, and the five men drew nearer to the bench, one of them touching the boy's ear with his knife. 'Shall I prick him and draw blood,' he suggested, 'then singe his pate afterwards where the flesh is tender?'

The novice held up his hands for mercy. 'I'll tell all I know,' he cried, 'but it's nothing, nothing . . . only what I overheard Master Bloyou, the Bishop's emissary, say to the Prior.'

Roger withdrew the flare, and set it back upon the bench. 'And what did he say?'

The terrified novice glanced first at Roger and then at his companions. 'That the Bishop was displeased with the conduct of some of the brethren, Brother Jean in particular. That he, with others, acts against the Prior's will, and squanders the property of the monastery in dissolute living. That they are a scandal to the whole Order, and a pernicious example to many outside it. And that the Bishop cannot close his eyes to the situation any longer, and has given Master Bloyou all power to enforce the canon law, with the aid of Sir John Carminowe.'

He paused for breath, seeking reassurance in their faces, and one of the men, not the fellow with the knife, moved away from the group.

'By the faith, it's true,' he muttered, 'and who are we to deny it? We know well enough that the Priory, and all within it, are a scandal. If the French monks went back where they belong, we'd be well rid of them.'

A murmur of agreement rose from the others, and the man with the knife, a great hulking chap, losing interest in the novice, turned to Roger.

'Trefrengy has a point,' he said sullenly. 'It stands to reason we valley men this side of Tywardreath would stand to gain if the Priory closed its doors. We'd have a claim to the surrounding land, on which they grow fat, instead of being pushed to graze our cattle amongst reeds.'

Roger folded his arms, spurning the still frightened novice with his foot. 'Who speaks of closing the Priory doors?' he asked. 'Not the Bishop up in Exeter, he speaks for the Diocese only, and can recommend the Prior to discipline the monks, but nothing further. The King is overlord, as you are perfectly aware, and every one of us who are tenants under Champernoune has had fair treatment, and received benefits from the Priory into the bargain. More than that. None of you have held back from trading with the French ships when they cast anchor in the bay. Is there anyone amongst you who has not had his cellars filled because of them?'

Nobody answered. The novice, believing himself safe, began to crawl away, but Roger caught at him once again and held him.

'Not so fast,' he said, 'I haven't finished with you. What else did Master Henry Bloyou tell the Prior?'

'No more than I have said,' stammered the boy.

'Nothing concerning the safety of the realm itself?'

Roger made as though to seize the flare from the bench, and the novice, trembling, put up his hands in self-defence.

'He spoke of rumours from the north,' he faltered, 'that trouble is still brewing between the King and his mother Queen Isabella, and might break out into open strife before long. If so, he wondered who in the west would be loyal to the young King, and who would declare for the Queen and her lover Mortimer.'

'I thought as much,' said Roger. 'Now crawl into a corner and stay mute. If you blab a word of this outside these walls I'll slit your tongue for you.'

He turned and faced the five men, who stared back at him uncertainly, this latest information having shocked them into silence.

'Well?' asked Roger. 'What do you make of it? Are you all dumb?'

The fellow called Trefrengy shook his head. 'It's none of our business,' he said. 'The King can quarrel with his mother if he wants. It does not concern us.'

'You think not?' queried Roger. 'Not even if the Queen and Mortimer should keep the power within their own hands still? I know of some in these parts who would prefer it so, and would be recompensed for declaring for the Queen when the battle was done. Yes, and pay liberally if others would do the same.'

'Not young Champernoune,' said the man with the knife. 'He's under-age and tied to his mother's apron-strings. As for you, Roger, you'd never risk rebellion against a crowned king – not holding your position.'

He laughed derisively and the others joined in, but the steward, looking at each in turn, remained unmoved.

'Victory is assured if action is swift and power seized overnight,' he said. 'If that is what the Queen and Mortimer intend, we shall all of us be on the winning side if we keep sweet with their friends. There could be some division of manor lands, who knows? And instead of grazing your cattle amongst reeds, Geoffrey Lampetho, you might have the advantage of the hills above.'

The man with the knife shrugged his shoulders. 'Easy said,' he observed, 'but who are these friends, so ready with their promises? I know of none.'

'Sir Otto Bodrugan, for one,' said Roger quietly.

A murmur rose amongst the men, the name Bodrugan was repeated, and Henry Trefrengy, who had spoken against the French monks, shook his head once more.

'He's a fine man, none better,' he said, 'but the last time he rebelled against the Crown, in 1322, he lost, and was fined a thousand marks for his pains.'

'He was recompensed four years later when the Queen made him Governor of Lundy island,' replied Roger. 'The lea of Lundy makes good anchorage for vessels carrying arms, and men as well, who can lie in safety there until they're needed on the mainland. Bodrugan is no fool. What is easier for him, holding lands in Cornwall and in Devon, and Governor of Lundy into the bargain, than to raise the men and ships that the Queen needs?'

His argument, smooth, persuasive, seemed to make impact, especially upon Lampetho. 'If there's profit in it for us I'd wish him well,' he said, 'and rally to his side when the deed is done. But I won't cross the Tamar for any man, Bodrugan or another, and you can tell him so.'

'You may tell him yourself,' said Roger. 'His vessel lies below, and he knows I await him here. I tell you, friends, Queen Isabella will show her gratitude to him, and to others, who knew which side to favour.'

He went to the foot of the ladder. 'Come down, Robbie,' he called. 'Take a light across the field and see if Sir Otto is on his way,' and turning to the others, 'I'm ready to strike a blow for him if you are not.'

His brother came down the ladder, and, seizing one of the flares, ran out into the yard beyond the kitchen.

Henry Trefrengy, more cautious than his companions, stroked his chin. 'What lies in it for you, Roger, by siding with Bodrugan? Will the lady Joanna join forces with her brother against the King?'

'My lady has no part in any of it,' replied Roger shortly. 'She is away from home, at her other property of Trelawn, with her own children and Bodrugan's wife and family. None of them have any knowledge of what is at stake.'

'She won't thank you when she hears of it,' replied Trefrengy, 'nor Sir John Carminowe either. It is common knowledge they only wait for Sir John's lady to die so that they can marry.'

'Sir John's lady is healthy and likely to continue so,' answered Roger, 'and when the Queen makes Bodrugan Keeper of Restormel Castle and overseer of all the Duchy lands, my lady may lose her interest in Sir John and look upon her brother with more affection than she does now. I don't doubt I shall be recompensed by Bodrugan, and forgiven by my lady.' He smiled, and scratched his ear.

'By the faith,' said Lampetho, 'we all know you lay your plans to suit yourself. Whoever wins the day will find you at his elbow. Bodrugan or Sir John at Restormel Castle, and you will be standing at the drawbridge, holding a well-lined purse.'

'I don't deny it,' said Roger, smiling still. 'If you possessed the same ability for thought you would do like wise.'

Footsteps sounded from the yard beyond, and he crossed to the door and flung it open. Otto Bodrugan stood on the threshold, with young Robbie behind him.

'Enter, sir, and welcome. We are all friends,' said Roger, and Bodrugan came into the kitchen, looking sharply about him, surprised, I think, to see the little group of men who, embarrassed by his sudden arrival, drew back against the wall. His tunic was laced to the throat, with a padded leather jerkin over all, belted with purse and dagger, and a travelling cloak, fur-trimmed, hung from his shoulders. He made a contrast to the others in their homespun cloth and hoods, and it was evident from his air of confidence that he was used to commanding men.

'I am very glad to see you,' he said at once, advancing to each in turn. 'Henry Trefrengy, isn't it? And Martin Penhelek. John Beddyng I know too – your uncle rode north with me in '22. The others I have not met before.'

'Geoffrey Lampetho, sir, and his brother Philip,' said Roger. 'They farm the valley adjoining Julian Polpey's land, beneath the Priory manor.'

'Is Julian not here, then?'

'He awaits us at Polpey.'

Bodrugan's eye fell upon the novice, still crouching beside the bench. 'What is the monk doing here amongst you?'

'He brought us information, sir,' said Roger. 'There has been some trouble at the Priory, a matter of discipline in the house amongst the brothers, of no concern to us, but disturbing in that the Bishop has lately sent Master Bloyou from Exeter to inquire into the business.'

'Henry Bloyou? A close friend to Sir John Carminowe and Sir William Ferrers. Is he still at the Priory?'

The novice, anxious to please, touched Bodrugan's knee. 'No, sir, he has gone. He left yesterday for Exeter, but promised to return shortly.'

'Well, get to your feet, lad, no harm shall come to you.' Bodrugan turned to the steward. 'Have you been threatening him?'

'Not a hair of his head,' protested Roger. 'He is only frightened that the Prior might learn of his presence here, despite my promise to the contrary.'

Roger signalled to Robbie to take the novice to the upper room, and the pair of them disappeared up the ladder, the novice in as much hurry to be gone as a kicked dog. When the two had gone Bodrugan, standing before the hearth, his hands on his belt, looked keenly at each one of the men.

'What Roger has been telling you about our chances I do not know,' he said, 'but I can promise you a better life when the King is in custody.' No one answered. 'Has Roger informed you that most of the country will declare for Queen Isabella in a few days' time?' he asked them.

Henry Trefrengy, who seemed to be spokesman, was bold enough to speak. 'He has told us so, yes,' he said, 'but little detail of it.'

'It is a question of the timing,' replied Bodrugan. 'Parliament now sits at Nottingham, and it is planned to seize the King –

with all care for his safety, naturally – until he comes of age. In the meantime Queen Isabella will continue as Regent, with Mortimer to aid her. He may lack popularity with some, but he is a strong man, and capable, and a very good friend of many Cornishmen. I am proud to count myself amongst them.'

Silence again. Then Geoffrey Lampetho stepped forward. 'What would you have us do?' he asked.

'Come north with me, if you will,' answered Bodrugan, 'but if not, and God knows I cannot make you, then promise to swear allegiance to Queen Isabella when word comes from Nottingham that we hold the King.'

'That's spoken fairly,' said Roger. 'For my part I say yes, and gladly, and will ride with you.'

'And so will I,' said another, the man called Penhelek.

'And I too,' cried the third, John Beddyng.

Only the Lampetho brothers and Trefrengy were reluctant.

'We'll swear allegiance when the moment comes,' said Geoffrey Lampetho, 'but we'll swear it at home, not across the Tamar.'

'Also fairly spoken,' said Bodrugan. 'If the King had the power himself we should be at war with France within ten years, fighting across the Channel. By supporting the Queen now we strike a blow for peace. I have the promise of at least a hundred men from my own lands, from Bodrugan, from Tregrehan and further west, and from Devon too. Shall we go and see how Julian Polpey stands?'

There was a general stir amongst the men as they made towards the door.

'The tide is flooding across the ford,' said Roger. 'We must cross the valley by Trefrengy and Lampetho. I have a pony for you, sir. Robbie?' He called his brother from the room above. 'Have you the pony saddled for Sir Otto? And mine as well? Make haste, then . . .' And as the boy came down the ladder he whispered in his ear, 'Brother Jean will send for the novice later. Keep him until then. As for myself, I cannot say when I shall return.'

We found ourselves in the stableyard, a huddle of ponies and men, and I knew I must go too, for Roger was mounting his pony beside Bodrugan, and wherever he went I was compelled to follow. The clouds were racing across the sky, the wind was blowing, and the stamping of ponies and the jingle of harness rang in my ear. Never before, neither in my own world nor on the previous occasions when I had strayed into the other, had I felt such a sense of unity. I was one of them, and they did not know it. I belonged amongst them, and they did not know it. This, I think, was the essence of what it meant to me. To be bound, yet free; to be alone, yet in their company; to be born in my own time yet living, unknown, in theirs.

They rode up the track through the little copse bordering Kilmarth, and at the top of the hill, instead of following the route of the modern road I knew, they struck across the summit and then plunged steeply towards the valley. The track was rough, making the ponies stumble from time to time, and twisting too. The descent seemed almost as sharp as a cliff-face, but, disembodied as I felt myself to be, I was no judge of height or depth, and my only guides were the men upon their ponies. Then, through the darkness, I saw the gleam of water, and presently we plumbed the valley's depth and reached a wooden bridge bordering a stream, across which the ponies walked dryshod in single file, and the path wound to the left, following the water's course, until the stream itself widened to a broad creek that opened out in the far distance to the sea itself. I knew I must be on the opposite side of the valley from Polmear hill, but because I was abroad in their world and it was night, the judging of distance was impossible; I could only follow the ponies, my eyes firmly fixed on Roger and Bodrugan.

The path led us past farm-buildings, where the Lampetho brothers dismounted, the elder, Geoffrey, shouting that he would follow later, and we went on again, the track rising to higher ground but still bordering the creek. There were further farm-buildings ahead above the sand-dunes where the river met the sea; even in the darkness I could see the gleam of the white rollers as they broke in the distance and then ran upon the shore. Someone came to meet us, there were barking dogs and flares, and we were in yet another stableyard, similar to the one at Kilmarth, with outbuildings surrounding it. As the men dismounted from their ponies the door of the main building opened, and I recognized the man who came forward to greet us. It was Roger's companion on the day of the Bishop's reception at the Priory, the same who had walked with him afterwards on the village green.

Roger, the first to dismount, was the first at his friend's side, and even in the dim light of the lantern by the house door I could see his expression change as the man whispered hurriedly in his ear, pointing to the further side of the farm-buildings.

Bodrugan saw this too, for jumping off his pony he called out, 'What's amiss, Julian? Has your opinion changed since I saw you last?'

Roger turned swiftly. 'Bad tidings, sir. For your ear only.'

Bodrugan hesitated for a moment, then quickly said, 'As you will,' and put out his hand to the owner of the house. 'I had hoped,' he said, 'we would muster arms and men at Polpey, Julian. My ship is anchored below Kylmerth, you must have seen her. There are several aboard, ready to disembark.'

Julian Polpey shook his head. 'I am sorry, Sir Otto, they will not be needed, nor yourself either. Word came not ten minutes ago that the whole scheme has been defeated before it took final shape. A very special messenger has brought you the news herself, disregarding, if I may say so, her own safety.'

I could hear Roger, over my shoulder, telling the men to mount their ponies and ride back to Lampetho, where he would presently join them. Then, handing his pony's reins to the servant standing by, he joined Polpey and Bodrugan as they made their way past the outbuildings to the further side of the house.

'It is Lady Carminowe,' said Bodrugan to Roger, his glad confidence vanished, his face sharp with anxiety. 'She has brought bad news.'

'Lady Carminowe?' exclaimed Roger, incredulous, then with sudden understanding, and lowering his voice, 'you mean the lady Isolda?'

'She is on her way to Carminowe,' said Bodrugan, 'and, guessing my movements, has broken her journey here at Polpey.'

We came to the other side of the house, which fronted upon the lane leading to Tywardreath. A covered vehicle was drawn up outside the gate, similar to the wagonettes I had seen at the Priory at Martinmas, but this was smaller, drawn by two horses only.

As we approached the curtain was held aside from the small window, and Isolda leant from it, the dark hood that covered her head falling back upon her shoulders.

'Thank God I am in time,' she said. 'I come straight from Bockenod. Both John and Oliver are there, and believe me halfway to Carminowe to rejoin the children. The worst has happened for your cause, and what I feared. News came before I left that the Queen and Mortimer have been seized at Nottingham Castle and are prisoners. The King is in full command, and Mortimer is to be taken to London for trial. Here is an end, Otto, to all your dreams.'

Roger exchanged a glance with Julian Polpey, and as the latter, from discretion, moved away into the shadows I could see the conflict of emotion on Roger's face. I guessed what he was thinking. Ambition had led him astray, and he had backed a losing cause. It now remained for him to urge Bodrugan to return to his ship, disband his men and speed Isolda on her journey, while he himself, having explained his volte-face to Lampetho, Trefrengy and the rest as best he could, reinstated himself as Joanna Champernoune's trusted steward.

'You have risked discovery in coming here,' said Bodrugan to Isolda. Nothing in his face betrayed how much he had lost.

'If I have done so,' she replied, 'you know the reason why.'

I saw her look at him, and he at her. We were the only witnesses, Roger and I. Bodrugan bent forward to kiss her hand, and as he did so I heard the sound of wheels from the lane, and I thought, 'She came too late to warn him after all. Oliver, the husband, and Sir John have followed her.'

I wondered that neither of them heard the wheels, and then I saw they were not with me any longer. The wagonette had gone, and the mail van from Par had come up the lane and stopped beside the gate.

It was morning. I was standing inside the drive leading to a small house across the valley from Polmear hill. I tried to hide myself in the bushes bordering the drive, but the postman had already got out of his van and was opening the gate. His stare combined recognition and astonishment, and I followed the direction of his eyes down to my legs. I was soaking wet from crutch to foot: I must have waded through bog and marsh. My shoes were water-logged and both trouser legs were torn. I summoned a painful smile.

He looked embarrassed. 'You're in a proper mess,' he said. 'It's the gentleman living up Kilmarth, isn't it?'

'Yes,' I replied.

'Well, this is Polpey, Mr Graham's house. But I doubt if

they're up yet, it's only just turned seven. Were you intending to call on Mr Graham?'

'Good heavens, no! I got up early, went for a walk, and somehow lost my way.'

It was a thumping lie, and sounded like one. He seemed to accept it, though.

'I have to deliver these letters, and then I'll be going up the hill to your place,' he said. 'Would you care to get in the van? It would save you a walk.'

'Thanks a lot,' I said. 'I'd be most grateful.'

He disappeared down the drive and I climbed into his van. I looked at my watch. He was right, it was five past seven. Mrs Collins was not due for at least another hour and a half, and I should have plenty of time for a bath and a change.

I tried to think where I had been. I must have crossed the main road at the top of the hill, then walked downhill across country and through the marshy ground at the bottom of the valley. I had not even known that this house was called Polpey.

No nausea, though, thank God, no vertigo. As I sat there, waiting for him to return, I realized that the rest of me was wet as well, jacket, head, for it was raining – it had probably been raining when I left Kilmarth almost an hour and a half ago. I wondered whether I should enlarge upon my story to the postman or let it go. Better let it go . . .

He came back and climbed into the van. 'Not much of a morning for your walk. It's been raining hard since midnight.'

I remembered then that it had been the rain which woke me up originally, blowing the curtain at the bedroom window.

'I don't mind the rain,' I told him. 'I get short of exercise in London.'

'Same as me,' he said cheerfully, 'driving this van. But I'd rather be snug in my bed this weather than take a walk across the marsh. Still, there it is, it wouldn't do if we were all the same.'

He called at the Ship Inn at the bottom of the hill and at one of the cottages near by, and as the van raced up the main road I looked leftward over my shoulder to the valley, but the high hedge hid it from view. God only knew what swampy meadowland and marsh I must have traversed. My shoes were oozing water on the floor of the van.

We left the main road and turned right down the drive to Kilmarth.

'You're not the only early bird,' he said as the sweep in front of the house came into sight. 'Either Mrs Collins has had a lift up from Polkerris or you have visitors.'

I saw the large open boot of the Buick packed tight with luggage. The horn was blowing continuously, and the two children, with macs held over their heads to protect them from the rain, were running up the steps through the front garden to the house.

The shock of disbelief turned to the dull certainty of impending doom.

'It's not Mrs Collins,' I said, 'it's my wife and family. They must have driven down from London through the night.'

ten

There was no question of driving past the garage to the back entrance. The postman, grinning, stopped his van and opened the door for me to get out, and anyway the children had already seen me, and were waving.

'Thanks for the lift,' I said to him, 'but I could do without the reception,' and I took the letter that he held out to me and advanced to meet my fate.

'Hi, Dick,' called the boys, tearing back down the steps. 'We rang and rang, but we couldn't make you hear. Mom's mad at you.'

'I'm mad at her,' I told them. 'I didn't expect you.'

'It's a surprise,' said Teddy. 'Mom thought it would be more fun. Micky slept in the back of the car, but I didn't. I read the map.'

The blowing of the horn had ceased. Vita emerged from the Buick, immaculate as always, wearing just the right sort of clothes for Piping Rock on Long Island. She had a new hair-do, more wave in it, or something; it looked all right but it made her face too full.

Attack is the best form of defence, I thought. Let's get it over.

'Well, for God's sake,' I said, 'you might have warned me.'

'The boys gave me no peace,' she said. 'Blame it on them.'

We kissed, then both stood back, eyeing each other warily like sparring partners before a shadow feint.

'How long have you been here?' I asked.

'About half an hour,' she said. 'We've been all round, but we couldn't get in. The boys even tried throwing earth at the windows, after they'd rung the bell. What's happened? You're soaked to the skin.'

'I was up very early,' I said. 'I went for a walk.'

'What, in all this rain? You must be crazy. Look, your trousers are torn, and there's a great rent in your jacket.'

She seized hold of my arm and the boys crowded round me, gaping. Vita began to laugh. 'Where on earth did you go to get in a state like this?' she asked.

I shook myself clear. 'Look,' I said, 'we'd better unload. It's no good doing it here – the front door is locked. Hop in the car and we'll go round to the back.'

I led the way with the boys, and she followed in the car. When we reached the back entrance I remembered that it was locked too from the inside – I had left the house by the patio.

'Wait here,' I said, 'I'll open the door for you,' and with the boys in close attendance I went round to the patio. The boiler-house door was ajar – I must have passed through it when I followed Roger and the rest of the conspirators. I kept telling myself to keep calm, not to get confused; if confusion started in my mind it would be fatal.

'What a funny old place. What's it for?' asked Micky.

'To sit in,' I said, 'and sunbathe. When there is any sun.'

'If I were Professor Lane I'd turn it into a swimming-pool,' said Teddy. They trooped after me into the house, and through the old kitchen to the back door. I unlocked it, and found Vita waiting impatiently outside.

'Get in out of the rain,' I said, 'while the boys and I fetch in the suitcases.'

'Show us round first,' she said plaintively. 'The luggage can wait. I want to see everything. Don't tell me *that* is the kitchen through there?'

'Of course it isn't,' I said. 'It's an old basement kitchen. We don't use any of this.'

The thing was, I had never intended to show them the house from this angle. It was the wrong way round. If they had arrived on Monday I should have been waiting for them on the steps by the porch, with the curtains drawn back, the windows open, everything ready. The boys, excited, were already scampering up the stairs.

'Which is our room?' they shouted. 'Where are we to sleep?'

Oh God, I thought, give me patience. I turned to Vita, who was watching me with a smile.

'I'm sorry, darling,' I said, 'but honestly . . .'

'Honestly what?' she said. 'I'm as excited as they are. What are you fussing about?'

What indeed! I thought, with total inconsequence, how much better organized this would have been if Roger Kylmerth, as steward, had been showing Isolda Carminowe the lay-out of some manor house.

'Nothing,' I said, 'come on . . .'

The first thing Vita noticed when we reached the modern kitchen on the first floor was the debris of my supper on the table. The remains of fried eggs and sausages, the frying-pan not cleaned, standing on one corner of the table, the electric light still on.

'Heavens!' she exclaimed. 'Did you have a cooked breakfast before your walk? That's new for you!'

'I was hungry,' I said. 'Ignore the mess, Mrs Collins will clear all that. Come through to the front.'

I hurried past her to the music-room, drawing curtains, throwing back shutters, and then across the hall to the small dining-room and the library beyond. The *pièce de résistance*, the view from the end window, was blotted out by the mizzling rain.

'It looks different,' I said, 'on a fine day.'

'It's lovely,' said Vita. 'I didn't think your Professor had such taste. It would be better with that divan against the wall and cushions on the window-seat, but that's easily done.'

'Well, this completes the ground floor,' I said. 'Come upstairs.'

I felt like a house-agent trying to flog a difficult let, as the boys raced ahead up the stairs, calling to each other from the rooms, while Vita and I followed. Everything had already changed, the silence and the peace had gone, henceforth it would be only this, the take-over of something I had shared, as it were, in secret, not only with Magnus and his dead parents in the immediate past, but with Roger Kylmerth six hundred years ago.

The tour of the first floor finished, the sweat of unloading all the luggage began, and it was nearly half-past eight when the job was done, and Mrs Collins arrived on her bicycle to take charge of the situation, greeting Vita and the boys with genuine delight. Everyone disappeared into the kitchen. I went upstairs and ran the bath, wishing I could lie in it and drown.

It must have been half an hour later that Vita wandered into the bedroom. 'Well, thank God for her,' she said. 'I shan't have to do a thing, she's extremely efficient. And must be sixty at least. I can relax.'

'What do you mean, relax?' I called from the bathroom.

'I imagined something young and skittish, when you tried to put me off from coming down,' she said. She came into the bathroom as I was rubbing myself with the towel. 'I don't trust your Professor an inch, but at least I'm satisfied on that account. Now you're all cleaned up you can kiss me again, and then run me a bath. I've been driving for seven hours and I'm dead to the world.'

So was I, but in another sense. I was dead to her world. I might move about in it, mechanically, listening with half an ear as she peeled off her clothes and flung them on the bed, put on a wrapper, spread her lotions and creams on the dressing-table, chatting all the while about the drive down, the day in London, happenings in New York, her brother's business affairs, a dozen things that formed the pattern of her life, our life; but none of them concerned me. It was like hearing background music on the radio. I wanted to recapture the lost night and the darkness, the wind blowing down the valley, the sound of the sea breaking on the shore below Polpey farm, and the expression in Isolda's eyes as she looked out of that painted wagon at Bodrugan.

'. . . And if they do amalgamate it wouldn't be before the fall anyway, nor would it affect your job.'

'No.'

Response was automatic to the rise and fall of her voice, and suddenly she wheeled round, her face a mask of cream under the turban she always wore in the bath, and said, 'You haven't been listening to a word I said!'

The change of tone shocked me to attention. 'Yes, I have,' I told her.

'What, then? What have I been talking about?' she challenged.

I was clearing my things out of the wardrobe in the bedroom, so that she could take over. 'You were saying something about Joe's firm,' I answered, 'a merger of some sort. Sorry, darling, I'll be out of your way in a minute.'

She seized the hanger bearing a flannel suit, my best, out of my hand, and hurled it on the floor.

'I don't want you out of the way,' she said, her voice rising to a pitch I dreaded. 'I want you here and now, giving me your full attention, instead of standing there like a tailor's dummy. What on earth's the matter with you? I might be talking to someone in another world.'

She was so right. I knew it was no use counter-attacking; I must grovel, and let her tide of perfectly justifiable irritation pass over my head.

'Darling,' I said, sitting down on the bed and pulling her beside me, 'let's not start the day wrong. You're tired, I'm tired; if we start arguing we'll wear ourselves out and spoil things for the boys. If I am vague and inattentive, you must blame it on exhaustion. I took that walk in the rain because I couldn't sleep, and instead of pulling me together it seems to have slowed me up.'

'Of all the idiotic things to do . . . You might have known . . . And anyway, why couldn't you sleep?'

'Forget it, forget it, forget it.'

I rose from the bed, seized armfuls of clothes and bore them through to the dressing-room, kicking the door to with my foot. She did not follow me. I heard her turn the taps off and get into the bath, slopping the water so that some of it ran into the overflow.

The morning drifted on. Vita did not appear. I opened the bedroom door very softly just before one, and she was fast asleep on the bed, so I closed it again and lunched downstairs alone with the boys. They chatted away, perfectly content with a 'yes' or 'perhaps' from me, invariably undemanding when Vita was absent. It continued to rain steadily, and there was no question of cricket or the beach, so I drove them into Fowey and let them loose to buy ice-creams, peppermint rock, western paperbacks and jigsaw puzzles.

The rain petered out about four, giving place to a lustreless sky and a pallid, constipated sun, but this was enough for the boys, who rushed on to the Town Quay and demanded to be water-born. Anything to please, and postpone the moment of return, so I hired a small boat, powered by an outboard engine, and we chug-chugged up and down the harbour, the boys snatching at passing flotsam as we bobbed about, all of us soaked to the skin.

We arrived home about six o'clock, and the children rushed to sit down to the enormous spread of tea that the thoughtful Mrs Collins had provided for them. I staggered into the library to pour myself a stiff whisky, only to find a revitalized Vita in possession, smiling, the furniture all moved around, the morning mood, thank heaven, a thing of the past.

'You know, darling,' she said, 'I think I'm going to like it here. Already it's beginning to look like home.'

I collapsed into an armchair, drink in hand, and watched through half-closed eyes as she pottered about the room re-arranging Mrs Collins' brave efforts with the hydrangeas. My strategy henceforth would be to applaud everything, or, when occasion demanded silence, to stay mute, play each moment as it came by ear.

I was on my second whisky, and off my guard, when the boys burst into the library.

'Hi, Dick,' shouted Teddy, 'what's this horrible thing?'

He had got the embryo monkey in its jar. I leapt to my feet. 'Christ!' I said. 'What the hell have you been up to?' I seized the jar from his hand and made for the door. I remembered only that when I had gone out from the lab in the small hours, after taking my second dose, I hadn't pocketed the key but had left it in the lock.

'We weren't doing anything,' said Teddy, aggrieved, 'we were only looking through the empty rooms below.' He turned to Vita. 'There's a little dark room full of bottles, just like the stinks lab at school. Come and look, Mom, quick – there's something else in one of the jars like a dead kitten . . .'

I was out of the library in a flash, and down the small stairway in the hall leading to the basement. The door of the lab was wide open, and the light was on. I looked quickly around. Nothing had been touched except the jar holding the monkey. I switched off the light and stepped into the passage, locking the door behind me and pocketing the key. As I did so the boys came running through the old kitchen, Vita at their heels. She looked concerned.

'What did they do?' she asked. 'Have they broken something?'

'Luckily, no,' I said. 'It was my fault for leaving the door unlocked.'

She was peering over my shoulder down the passage. 'What is through there anyway?' she asked. 'That object Teddy brought up looked perfectly ghastly.'

'I dare say,' I answered. 'It happens that this house belongs to a professor of biophysics, and he uses the small room behind there as a laboratory. If I ever catch either of the boys near that room again there'll be murder!'

They stalked off, muttering, and Vita turned to me. 'I must say,' she said, 'I think it's rather extraordinary of the Professor to keep a room like that, with all sorts of scientific things in it, and not make certain it's kept properly locked.'

'Now don't you start,' I said. 'I am responsible to Magnus, and I can assure you it won't happen again. If you had only come next week instead of turning up this morning at an unearthly hour, when nobody expected you, it would never have happened.'

She stared at me, startled. 'Why, you're shaking!' she said. 'Anyone would think there were explosives in there.'

'Perhaps there are,' I said. 'Anyway, let's hope those kids have learnt their lesson.'

I switched off the basement lights and walked upstairs. I was shaking, and small wonder. A nightmare of possibilities crowded my mind. They might have opened the bottles containing the drug, they might have poured the contents into the medicine-glass, they might even have emptied the bottles into the sink. I must never again let that key out of my sight. I kept touching it in my pocket. Perhaps I could get an impression made of it, and keep both; it would be safer. I went into the music-room and stood there, staring at nothing, thrusting my fingertip into the little hole in the key.

Vita had gone upstairs to the bedroom. Presently, I heard the tell-tale click of the telephone from the bell in the hall. It meant she was speaking from the extension upstairs. I went and washed my hands in the downstairs lavatory, and then wandered into the library. I could still hear Vita talking from the bedroom overhead. Listening to conversations on the telephone is not a habit of mine, but now some furtive instinct made me cross to the instrument in the library and pick up the receiver.

'. . . So I just don't know what to make of it,' Vita was saying. 'I've never heard him speak sharply to the boys before. They're quite upset. He doesn't look awfully well. Very hollow-eyed. He says he's been sleeping badly.'

'High time you got down there,' came the answer. I recognized the drawl; it was her friend Diana. 'A husband on the loose is a husband on the prowl, I've told you so before. I've had experience with Bill.'

'Oh, Bill,' said Vita. 'We all know Bill can't be trusted out of your sight. Well, I don't know . . . Let's hope it will be fine and we can all be out a lot. I believe he's arranged to hire some boat.'

'That sounds healthy enough.'

'Yes . . . Well, let's hope that Professor of his hasn't been putting Dick up to something. I don't trust that man. Never have, and never will. And I know he dislikes me.'

'I can guess why that is,' laughed Diana.

'Oh, don't be idiotic. He may be like that, but Dick certainly isn't. Very much the reverse.'

'Maybe that's his attraction for the Professor,' said Diana.

I replaced the receiver very gently. The trouble was, with women, they had one-track minds, and to their narrow view everything male, be it man, dog, fish or slug, pursued but a single course, and that the dreary road to copulation. I sometimes wondered if they ever thought of anything else.

Vita and her friend Diana nattered on for at least another fifteen minutes, and when she came downstairs, fortified by feminine advice, she made no reference to my scene in the basement, but, humming gaily and wearing an apron of bizarre design – it looked as if it had apples and serpents all over it – set about cooking us steaks for supper heaped about with parsley butter.

'Early bed for all,' she announced as the boys, heavy-eyed and silent, yawned their way through the meal – the seven-hour journey in the car and the jaunt in the harbour was catching up with them. After supper she installed herself on the sofa in the library, and set about mending the rents in my trousers torn in the valley. I sat down at Magnus's desk murmuring something about unpaid bills, but in reality looking once again through the Lay Subsidy Roll for Tywardreath Parish for 1327. Julian Polpey was there, Henry Trefrengy, Geoffrey Lampetho. The names had meant nothing when I first read through the list, but they could have registered unconsciously in my mind. The figures might still be phantom figures that I had followed to the valley, passing the farms that still bore their names today.

I noticed an unopened letter on my desk. It was the one the postman had given me that morning; in my flurry at the family's arrival I had laid it down. It was just a scrap, typewritten, from the research student in London.

'Professor Lane thought you might like this note on Sir John Carminowe,' it read. 'He was the second son of Sir Roger Carminowe of Carminowe. Enrolled in the military 1323. Became a knight 1324. Summoned to attend Great Council at Westminster. Appointed Keeper of Tremerton and Restormel castles 27 April 1331, and on October 12th of the same year keeper of the King's forests, parks, woods and warrens, etc., and of the King's game in the county of Cornwall, so that he had to answer yearly for the profit of the pannage and herbage within the said forests, parks and woods, by the hand of the steward there, and deputy keepers under him.'

The student had written in brackets, 'Copied from Calendar of Fine Rolls 5th year Edward III'. He had added a further note beneath, '24 October. Patent Rolls, for same year (1331), mentions a licence for Joanna, late wife of Henry de Champernoune, tenant-in-chief, to marry whomsoever she will of the King's allegiance. Pay fine of 10 marks.'

So . . . Sir John had got what he wanted and Otto Bodrugan had lost, while Joanna, in anticipation of Sir John's wife dying, had a marriage licence handy in some bottom drawer. I filed the paper with the Lay Subsidy Roll, and getting up from the desk went to the bookshelves, where I remembered seeing the numerous volumes of the *Encyclopaedia Britannica*, legacy of Commander Lane. I pulled out Volume 8, and turned to Edward III.

Vita stretched herself on the sofa, yawning, her repeated sighs following one another in swift succession. 'Well, I don't know about you,' she said, 'but I'm off to bed.'

'I'll be up in a moment,' I told her.

'Still hard at work for your Professor?' she asked. 'Take that volume to the light, you'll ruin your eyes.'

I did not answer.

'Edward III (1312–1377), king of England, eldest son of Edward II and Isabella of France, was born at Windsor on 13 November 1312. . . . On 13 January 1327 parliament recognized him as king, and he was crowned on the 29th of the same month. For the next four years Isabella and her paramour Mortimer governed in his name, though nominally his guardian was Henry, Earl of Lancaster. In the summer of 1327 he took part in an abortive campaign against the Scots, and was married to Philippa at York on 24 January 1328. On 15 June 1330 his eldest child, Edward the Black Prince, was born.'

Nothing there about a rebellion. But here was the clue.

'Soon after, Edward made a successful effort to throw off his degrading dependence on his mother and Mortimer. In October 1330 he entered Nottingham Castle by night, through a subterranean passage, and took Mortimer prisoner. On 29 November the execution of the favourite at Tyburn completed the young king's emancipation. Edward discreetly drew a veil over his mother's relations with Mortimer, and treated her with every respect. There is no truth in the stories that henceforth he kept her in honourable confinement, but her political influence was at an end.'

Bodrugan's too, what he possessed in Cornwall. Sir John, only a year later appointed Keeper of Tremerton and Restormel castles, a good King's man, was in command, with Roger, playing it safe, imposing silence on his valley friends, the October night forgotten. I wondered what had happened after that meeting at Polpey's farm when Isolda risked so much to warn her lover; whether Bodrugan, brooding on what might-have-been, returned to his estates and thought about his love, and whether she, when her husband Oliver was absent, met him perhaps in secret. I had been standing beside them both less than twenty-four hours ago. Six centuries ago . . .

I put the volume back on the shelf, switched off the lights and went upstairs. Vita was already in bed, the curtains pulled back so that when she sat up she could look through the wide windows to the sea.

'This room is heaven,' she said. 'Imagine what it will be like with a full moon. Darling, I'm going to love it here, I promise you, and it's so wonderful to be together again.'

I stood for a moment at the window, staring out across the bay. Roger, from his sleeping-quarters above the original kitchen, had the same dark expanse of sea and sky for company, and as I turned away, towards the bed, I remembered Magnus's mocking remark on the telephone the day before, 'I was only about to suggest, dear boy, that moving between two worlds can act as stimulant.' It was not true – in fact, the contrary.

eleven

The next day being Sunday, Vita announced her intention over breakfast of taking the boys to church. She did this sort of thing from time to time during the holidays. Two or three weeks would go by with never a mention of devotional duty, and then suddenly, without giving any reason, and generally when they were otherwise happily employed, she would burst into their room saying, 'Come on, now, I'll give you just five minutes to get ready.'

'Ready? What for?' they would query, looking up from fitting together a model aeroplane or something momentarily engrossing their attention.

'Church, of course,' she would answer, sweeping from the room again, deaf to their wails of protestation. It was always a let-out for me. Pleading my Catholic upbringing, I would lie late in bed, reading the Sunday papers. Today, despite sunshine flooding our room as we awoke, and the beaming smile of Mrs Collins as she bore in our tray of toast and coffee, Vita looked preoccupied, and said she had had a restless night. I at once felt guilty, having slept like a log myself, and I thought how this thing of how well or how badly one had slept was really the great test of marital relationship; if one partner came off poorly during the night hours the other was immediately to blame, and the following day would come apart in consequence.

This particular Sunday was to be no exception to the rule, and when the boys came into the bedroom to say good morning dressed in jeans and T-shirts, she immediately exploded.

'Off with those things at once and into your flannel suits!' she said. 'Have you forgotten it's Sunday? We're going to church.'

'Oh, Mom . . . No!'

I admit, I felt for them. Sunshine, blue sky, the sea below the fields. They must have had one thought in mind, to get down to it and swim.

'No arguing now,' she said, getting out of bed. 'Go off and do as I say.' She turned to me. 'I take it there is a church somewhere in the vicinity, and you can at least drive us there?'

'You have a choice of churches,' I said, 'either Fowey or Tywardreath. It would be easier to take you to Tywardreath.' As I said the word I smiled, for the very name had a special significance, but to me alone, and continued casually, 'As a matter of fact, it's quite interesting historically. There used to be a priory where the churchyard is today.'

'You hear that, Teddy?' said Vita. 'There used to be a priory where we are going to church. You always say you like history. Now hurry along.'

I have seldom seen a sulkier pair of figures. Shoulders hunched, mouths drooping. 'I'll take you swimming later,' I shouted as they left the room.

It suited me to drive the party to Tywardreath. Morning service would be at least an hour, and I could drop them off at the church, and then park the car above Treesmill and stroll across the field to Gratten. I did not know when I might get another chance to revisit the site, and the quarry with its surrounding grassy banks held a compulsive fascination.

As I drove Vita and the reluctant boys, dressed in their Sunday suits, down Polmear hill I glanced over to the right at Polpey, wondering what would have happened if the present owners had discovered me lurking in the bushes instead of the postman, or, worse, what might well have happened had Julian Polpey bidden Roger and his guests inside. Should I have been found attempting to break into the downstairs rooms? This struck me as amusing, and I laughed aloud.

'What's so funny?' asked Vita.

'Only the life I lead,' I answered. 'Driving you all to church today, and yesterday taking that early morning walk. You see the marsh down there? That's where I got so wet.'

'I'm not surprised,' she said. 'What an extraordinary place to choose for walking. What did you think you were going to find?'

'Find?' I echoed. 'Oh, I don't know. A damsel in distress, perhaps. You never know your luck.'

I shot up the lane to Tywardreath elated, the very fact that she knew nothing of the truth filling me with a ridiculous sense of delight, like hoodwinking my mother in the past. It was a basic instinct fundamental to all males. The boys possessed it too, which was the reason I backed them up in those petty crimes of which Vita disapproved, eating snacks between meals, talking in bed after lights out.

I dropped them at the church gate, the boys still wearing their hard-done-by expressions.

'What are you going to do while we are in church?' Vita asked.

'Just walk around,' I said.

She shrugged her shoulders, and turned through the gate into the churchyard. I knew that shrug; it implied that my easygoing morning mood was not in tune with hers. I hoped Matins would bring consolation.

I drove off to Treesmill, parked the car, and struck off across the field to the Gratten. The morning was superb. Warm sunshine filled the valley. A lark soared overhead bursting his heart in song. I wished I had brought sandwiches and could have had the whole long day ahead of me instead of one stolen hour.

I did not enter the quarry with its trailing ivy and old tin cans, but stretched myself full-length on a grassy bank in one of the small hollows, wondering how the place would look by night when the sky was full of stars, or rather how it had looked once, when water filled the valley below. Lorenzo's scene with Jessica came to my mind.

> 'In such a night,
> Troilus methinks mounted the Trojan walls,
> And sighed his soul towards the Grecian tents
> Where Cressid lay that night . . .

> 'In such a night
> Stood Dido with a willow in her hand
> Upon the wild sea-banks, and wav'd her love
> To come again to Carthage.

'In such a night,
Medea gather'd the enchanted herbs
That did renew old Aeson . . .'

Enchanted herbs was apt. The point was that, when Vita and
the boys were getting ready for church, I had gone down to the
lab and poured four measures into the flask. The flask was in
my pocket. God knew when I should get the chance again . . .

It happened very quickly. But it was not night, it was day, and
a day in summer, too, though late afternoon, judging from the
western sky, which I could see from the casement window in the
hall. I was leaning against a bench at the far end, with a view of
the entrance court with its surrounding walls. I recognized it at
once – I was in the manor-house. Two children were playing in
the courtyard, girls, aged around eight and ten possibly – it was
difficult to tell, with the close-fitting bodices and ankle-length
skirts – but the long golden hair falling down their backs, and
the small clear-cut features so much alike, proclaimed them
miniature editions of their mother. No one but Isolda could
have produced such a pair, and I remembered Roger saying to
his companion Julian Polpey at the Bishop's reception that she
had grown stepsons amongst the first wife's brood, but only two
daughters of her own.

They were playing some chequer game upon the flags, on a
square marked out for them, with pieces like ninepins dotted
about, and as they moved the pieces shrill arguments broke out
between them as to whose turn was next. The younger reached
forward to seize a wooden pin and hide it in her skirt, and this
in turn led to cries and slaps and the pulling of hair. Roger
emerged into the court suddenly, from the hall where he had
been standing watching them, and thrusting himself between
them squatted on his haunches, taking the hand of each in turn.

'You know what comes about when women scold?' he said to
them. 'Their tongues turn black and curl into their throats,
choking them. It happened to my sister once, and she would
have died had I not reached her side in time to pluck it back.
Open your mouths.'

The children, startled, opened their mouths wide, thrusting
out their tongues. Roger touched each in turn with his fingertip, and waggled it.

'Pray God that does the trick,' he said, 'but it may not last unless you let your tempers cool. There now, shut your mouths, and only open them for your next meal, or to let kind words fly. Joanna, you're the elder, you should teach Margaret better manners than to hide a man under her skirt.' He pulled out the ninepin from the younger girl's dress and set it down upon the flags. 'Come now,' he said, 'proceed. I'll see that you play fair.'

He stood up, legs wide apart, and let them move their pieces round him, which they did at first with some hesitation, then with greater confidence, and soon with peals of delighted laughter as he rocked sideways, stumbling, knocking the pieces down, so that all had to be set straight once more with Roger helping. Presently a woman – their nurse, I supposed – called them from a second doorway beyond the hall, and the pieces were taken up and given solemnly to Roger, who as he took them, promising to play again next day, winked at the nurse, advising her to examine both their tongues later, and let him know if they showed signs of turning black.

He put the pieces down near the entrance and came into the hall, while the children disappeared into the back regions with their nurse; and it seemed to me for the first time that he had showed some human quality. His steward's role, calculating, cool, very possibly corrupt, had been momentarily put aside, and with it the irony, the cruel detachment I associated with all his actions hitherto.

He stood in the hall, listening. There was no one there but our two selves, and looking about me I sensed that the place had somehow changed since that day in May when Henry Champernoune had died; it no longer had the feeling of permanent occupancy, but more of a house where the owners came and went, leaving it empty in their absence. There was no sound of barking dogs, no sign of servants, other than the children's nurse, and it came to me suddenly that the lady of the house herself, Joanna Champernoune, must be away from home with her own brood of sons and daughter, perhaps in that other manor of Trelawn, which the steward had mentioned to Lampetho and Trefrengy in the Kilmarth kitchen on the night of the abortive rebellion. Roger must be in charge, and Isolda's children and their nurse were here to break their journey between one house and another.

He crossed over to the window, through which the late sunlight came, and looked out. Almost at once he flattened himself against the wall as though someone from outside might catch sight of him, and he preferred to remain unseen. Intrigued, I also ventured to the window, and immediately guessed the reason for his manoeuvre. There was a bench beneath the window, with two people sitting on it, Isolda and Otto Bodrugan, and because of the angle of the wall, which jutted outward, giving the bench shelter, anyone who sat there would have privacy unless he was spied upon from this one window.

The grass beneath the bench sloped to a low wall, and beyond the wall the fields descended to the river where Bodrugan's ship was anchored. I could see the mast-head, but not the deck. The tide was low, the channel narrow, and on either side of the blue ribbon of water were sand-flats, crowded with every sort of wading bird, dipping and bobbing around the pools where the tide had ebbed. Bodrugan held Isolda's hands in his, examining the fingers, and in a foolish sort of love-play bit each one of them in turn, or rather made pretence of biting them, grimacing as he did so as though they tasted sour.

I stood by the window watching them, oddly disturbed, not because I, like the steward, was playing spy, but because I sensed in some fashion that the relationship between these two, however passionate it might be at other times, was at this moment innocent, without guile and altogether blessed, and it was the kind of relationship that I myself would never know. Then suddenly he released both hands, letting them drop on to her lap.

'Let me stay another night and not sleep aboard,' he said. 'In any event the tide may serve me ill, and I may find myself hard aground if I make sail.'

'Not if you choose your moment,' she replied. 'The longer you remain here the more dangerous for us both. You know how gossip travels. To come here anyway was madness, with the vessel well known.'

'There's nothing to that,' he said. 'I come frequently to the bay and to this river, either on business or for my own pleasure, fishing between here and Chapel Point. It was pure chance that brought you here as well.'

'It was not,' she said, 'and you know it very well. The steward brought you my letter telling you I should be here.'

'Roger is a trusty messenger,' he answered. 'My wife and children are at Trelawn, and so is my sister Joanna. The risk was worth the taking.'

'Worth taking, yes, this once, but not for two nights in succession. Nor do I trust the steward as you do, and you know my reasons.'

'Henry's death, you mean?' He frowned. 'I still think you judged unfairly there. Henry was a dying man. We all knew it. If those potions made him sleep the sooner, free from pain and with Joanna's knowledge, why should we shake our heads?'

'Too easy done,' she said, 'and with intent. I'm sorry for it, Otto, but I cannot forgive Joanna, even if she is your sister. As for the steward, doubtless she paid him well, and his monk accomplice.'

I glanced at Roger. He had not moved from his shadowed corner by the window, but he could hear them as well as I did, and judging by the expression in his eyes he hardly relished what she said.

'As to the monk,' added Isolda, 'he is still at the Priory, and adds something to his influence every day. The Prior is wax in his hands, and his flock do as they are bidden by Brother Jean, who comes and goes as he pleases.'

'If he does so,' said Bodrugan, 'it is no concern of mine.'

'It could become so,' she told him, 'if Margaret comes to have as much faith in his herbal knowledge as Joanna. You know he has treated your family lately?'

'I know nothing of the sort,' he answered. 'I have been at Lundy, as you know, and Margaret finds both the island and Bodrugan too exposed, and prefers Trelawn.' He rose from the bench and began pacing up and down the grass walk in front of her. Love-making was over, with the problems of domestic life upon them once again. They had my sympathy. 'Margaret is too much a Champernoune, like poor Henry,' he said. 'A priest or a monk could persuade her to abstinence or perpetual prayer if he had the mind to do so. I shall look into it.'

Isolda also rose from the bench, and standing close to Bodrugan looked up at him, with her hands upon his shoulders. I could have touched them both had I leant from the window. How small they were, inches below adult height today, yet he was broadly-built and strong, with a fine head and a most likeable smile, and she as delicately formed as a porcelain shepherdess, hardly taller than her own daughters. They held each other, kissing, and once again I felt this strange disturbance, a sense of loss, utterly unlike anything I might experience in my own time, had I seen two lovers from a window . . . Intense involvement, and intense compassion too. Yes, that was the word, compassion. And I had no way of explaining my sense of participation in all they did, unless it was that stepping backwards, out of my time to theirs, I felt them vulnerable, and more certainly doomed to die than I was myself, knowing indeed that they had both been dust for more than six centuries.

'Have a care for Joanna, too,' said Isolda. 'She is no nearer being married to John now than she was two years ago, and has altered for the worse in consequence. She might even serve his wife as she served her husband.'

'She would not dare, nor John,' answered Bodrugan.

'She would dare anything if it suited her. Harm you likewise, if you stood in her way. She has one thought in mind, to see John Keeper of Restormel and Sheriff of Cornwall, and herself his wife, queening it over all the crown lands as Lady Carminowe.'

'If it should come about I can't prevent it,' protested Bodrugan.

'As her brother you could try,' said Isolda, 'and at least prevent that monk from trailing at her heels with his poisonous draughts.'

'Joanna was always headstrong,' replied her lover. 'She has always done as she pleased. I cannot be on watch continually. I might say a word to Roger.'

'To the steward? He is as thick with the monk as she,' said Isolda scornfully. 'I warn you again, don't trust him, Otto. Neither on her account, nor on ours. He keeps our few meetings secret for the time because it pleases him.'

Once again I glanced at Roger, and saw the shadow on his face. I wished someone would call him from the room so that he could no longer play eavesdropper. It would put him against her to hear his faults so plainly stated and with such dislike.

'He stood by me last October and will do so again,' said Bodrugan.

'He stood by you then because he reckoned he had much to gain,' replied Isolda. 'Now you can do little for him, why should he risk losing his position? One word to Joanna, and thence to John, and thence to Oliver, and we'd be lost.'

'Oliver is in London.'

'London today, perhaps. But malice travels with every wind that blows. Tomorrow Bere or Bockenod. The next day Tregest or Carminowe. Oliver cares not a jot if I live or die, he has women wherever he goes, but his pride would never brook a faithless wife. And that I know.'

A cloud had come between them, and in the sky too, gathering above the hills beyond the valley. All the brightness of the summer day had gone. Innocence had vanished, and with it the serenity of their world. Mine too. Separated by centuries, I somehow shared their guilt.

'How late is it?' she asked.

'Near six, by the sun,' he answered. 'Does it matter?'

'The children should be away with Alice,' she said. 'They may come running to find me, and they must not see you here.'

'Roger is with them,' he told her, 'he will take care they leave us alone.'

'Nevertheless, I must bid them good-night, or they will never mount their ponies.'

She began to move away along the grass, and as she did so the steward also slipped from his dark corner and crossed the hall. I followed, puzzled. They could not be staying in the house after all but somewhere else, at Bockenod, perhaps. But the Boconnoc I knew was a longish ride for children on ponies in late afternoon; they would hardly reach it before dusk.

We went through the hall way to the open court beyond, and through the archway to the stables. Roger's brother Robbie was there, saddling the ponies, helping the little girls to mount, laughing and joking with the nurse who, propped high on her own steed, had some trouble in making it stand still.

'He'll go quietly enough with two of you on his back,' called Roger. 'Robbie shall sit on the pony with you and keep you warm. Before you or behind you, state your preference. It's all the same to him, isn't it, Robbie?'

The nurse, a country girl with flaming cheeks, gawked delightedly, protesting she would ride very well alone, and there was further giggling, instantly silenced with a frown from Roger as Isolda came into the stableyard. He moved to her side, head bent in deference.

'The children will be safe enough with Robbie,' he said, 'but I can escort them if you prefer it.'

'I do prefer it,' she said briefly. 'Thank you.'

He bowed, and she crossed the yard to the children, who were already mounted, managing their ponies with the greatest ease.

'I shall stay here awhile,' she told them, kissing each in turn, 'and return later. No whipping of the ponies on the road, mind, to make them go the faster. And do as Alice bids you.'

'We'll do as *he* bids,' said the youngest, pointing her small whip at Roger, 'or he'll twist our tongues to see if they turn black.'

'I don't doubt it,' answered Isolda, 'that, or some other method of enforcing silence.'

The steward smiled in some confusion, but she did not look at him and he went forward, seizing the children's bridles in either hand, and began to lead the ponies towards the archway, jerking his head to Robbie to do likewise with the nurse's mount. Isolda came with us as far as the entrance gate, and then I was torn between compulsion and desire. Compulsion to follow the little party led by Roger, desire to look at Isolda as she stood alone, waving to her children, unconscious that I stood beside her.

I knew I must not touch her. I knew if I did it would have no more effect upon her than a draught of air – not even that, for in her world I never had existed, nor ever could exist, for she was living and I a ghost without shape or form. If I gave myself the sudden useless pleasure of brushing her cheek there would be no contact, she would instantly dissolve, and I should be left with all the agony of vertigo, nausea and inevitable remorse. Luckily I was spared the choice. She waved her hand once more, looking straight into my eyes and through me, then turned and crossed the court back to the house.

I followed the riding party down the field. Isolda and Bodrugan would be alone for a few more hours. Perhaps they would make love. I hoped, with a sort of desperate sympathy, that they would. I had the feeling time was running out for them, and for me as well.

The track led downwards to the ford where the mill-stream, coursing through the valley, met the salt-water from the creek. Now, the tide low, the ford was passable, and when the children came to it Roger released the bridles, and clapping his hand on the hindquarters of either pony set them to gallop through the splash, the children screaming with delight. He did the same to the third pony, bearing Robbie and the nurse, who let out a shriek that must have been heard on either side of the valley. The blacksmith from the forge across the stream – the fire's glow and the anvil beside it, and a couple of horses waiting to be shod showed that this must be the smithy – came out from his shed grinning, and seizing a pair of bellows from the lad at his side pointed them at the nurse, so that the blast caught her petticoats, already spattered with the mill-stream.

'Take the poker red from the fire to warm her up,' shouted Roger, and the blacksmith made pretence of brandishing an iron bar, sparks flying in all directions, while Robbie, half-strangled by the hysterical nurse and doubled up with laughter, dug his heels into the pony's side to make him jump the more. The spectacle brought out the miller and his mate from the mill this side of the stream. I saw that they were monks, and there was a cart drawn up in the yard beside the building, tended by two others, who were filling it with grain. They paused in their work, grinning like the blacksmith, and one of them put his two hands to his mouth and hooted in imitation of an owl, while his companion flapped his arms rapidly above his head as wings.

'Make your choice, Alice,' called Roger. 'Fire and wind from Rob Rosgof in the forge, or shall the brothers tie you by your kirtle to the water-wheel?'

'The water-wheel, the water-wheel,' screamed the children from the further side of the ford, believing, in their excitement, that Alice was to be dowsed. Then suddenly, as swiftly as it had started, the sport was over. Roger waded through the splash with the water mid-thigh, and, seizing the children's ponies once again, took the right-hand track up the valley, with Robbie and the nurse in close pursuit.

I was preparing to follow him across the ford when one of the labouring monks in the millyard let out another shout – at least, I took it to be the monk, and turned to see what he was about, but instead a small car, with an irate driver at the wheel, had braked sharply behind me.

'Why don't you buy yourself a deaf-aid?' he yelled, swerving past me, almost plunging into the ditch as he did so. I stood blinking after the car as it shot away, and the people in the back seat, three abreast, dolled for a Sunday outing, stared through the rear window in shocked surprise.

Time had done its trick, too swift, too soon. There was no running mill-stream and no water-splash, no forge the further side; I was standing in the middle of the Treesmill road at the bottom of the valley.

I leant against the low bridge spanning the marsh. A near-miss; it might have landed the whole party in the ditch, and myself as well. I couldn't apologize, for the car had already disappeared up the opposite hill. I sat still for a while waiting for any reaction, but none came. My heart was beating rather faster than usual, but that was natural, due to the shock of the car. I was lucky to escape. No blame to the driver, all my fault.

I began to walk up the hill to the turning where I had parked my own car, and sat in the driving seat for another short spell, fearing confusion. I must not turn up at the church unless my mind was perfectly clear. The image of Roger escorting the children on their ponies up the track through the valley was still vivid, but I knew it for what it was, part of the other world already vanished. The house above the sandflats had reverted to the Gratten quarry, grass-covered, empty, except for the gorse bushes and the tin cans. Bodrugan and Isolda were no longer making love. Present reality was with me once again.

I looked at my watch, and stared in disbelief. The hands showed half-past one. Matins at St Andrew's had been over for an hour and a half, possibly longer.

I started up the car, guilt-stricken. The drug had played me false, spinning out the time in some incredible way. I couldn't have been more than half an hour at most up at the house, with another ten minutes, possibly, following Roger and the children to the ford. The whole episode had passed swiftly and I had done nothing but listen at the window, watch the children mount their ponies, and go away. As I drove up the hill I was more bothered about the action of the drug than the prospect of meeting Vita with another trumped-up excuse about walking and losing my way. Why the time-lag, I asked myself? I remembered then that when I went into the past I never looked at my watch – the impulse to do so never came; therefore there was no means of knowing how time passed: their sun was not my sun, nor their sky mine. There was no check, no possibility of measuring the time-limit of the drug. As always, when the thing went wrong, I blamed Magnus. He should have warned me.

I drew up at the church, but of course nobody was there. Vita must have waited with the boys, fuming with rage, then begged a lift home from someone, or else found a taxi.

I drove to Kilmarth trying to think of some better excuse than losing my way and my watch having stopped. Petrol. Could I have run out of petrol? A puncture. What about a puncture? Oh, bloody hell, I thought . . .

I rattled down the drive and swerved to a standstill before the house, then walked through the front garden, up the steps and into the hall. The dining-room door was closed. Mrs Collins, with an anxious face, emerged from the passage to the kitchen.

'I think they've finished,' she said apologetically, 'but I've kept yours hot. It won't be spoilt. Did you have a breakdown?'

'Yes,' I said, with gratitude.

I opened the door of the dining-room. The boys were clearing away, but Vita was still seated at the table, drinking coffee.

'God damn that blasted car . . .' I began, and the boys turned round, staring, uncertain whether to giggle or slink away. Teddy showed sudden tact, and with a glance at Micky they hurriedly left the room, Teddy bearing out the laden tray.

'Darling,' I went on, 'I'm most frightfully sorry. I wouldn't have had this happen for the world. You've no idea . . .'

'I've a very good idea,' she said. 'I'm afraid we've rather spoilt your Sunday.'

Her irony was lost on me. I hesitated, wondering whether to continue or not with my brilliant story of a breakdown on the road.

'The vicar was extremely kind,' she went on. 'His son drove us back in their car. And when we arrived Mrs Collins gave me this.' She pointed to a telegram beside her plate. 'It arrived just after we left for church, she said. Thinking it must be important, I opened it. From your Professor, naturally.'

She handed me the telegram. It had been wired from Cambridge.

'Have a good trip this weekend,' it read. 'Hope your girl turns up. Shall be thinking of you. Greetings. Magnus.'

I read it twice, then looked at Vita, but she had already turned towards the library, blowing clouds of cigarette smoke over her shoulder, as Mrs Collins came into the dining-room bringing me an enormous plate of hot roast beef.

twelve

If Magnus had wanted to drop a deliberate brick it could not have been better timed, but I absolved him. He believed Vita to be in London and myself alone. Nevertheless, the wording was unfortunate, to say the least. Catastrophic would be more apt. It must have conjured an instant vision to Vita of my sneaking off with shaving-kit and toothbrush to meet some floozie in the Scilly Isles. My innocence would be difficult to prove. I followed her into the library.

'Now, listen,' I said, firmly shutting the folding doors between the two rooms in case Mrs Collins overheard me, 'that telegram is a complete joke – a leg-pull on the part of Magnus. Don't make an absolute idiot of yourself by taking it seriously.'

She turned round and faced me, her posture the classical one of outraged wife, one hand on hip, the other brandishing her cigarette held at an angle, eyes narrowed in a frozen face.

'I'm not interested in the Professor or his jokes,' she said. 'You share so many of them, and keep me out, that I'm past caring. If that telegram was a joke good luck to you both. I repeat, I'm sorry I spoilt the weekend. Now you had better go and eat your lunch before it gets cold.'

She picked up a Sunday paper and pretended to look at it. I snatched it away. 'Oh no, you don't,' I said, 'you just pay attention to me.' Taking her cigarette I squashed it in the ashtray. Then I seized both her wrists and swung her round.

'You know perfectly well that Magnus is my oldest friend,' I said. 'What's more he's lent us this house rent-free, and thrown Mrs Collins in for good measure. In return for this I've been doing bits and pieces of research for him in connection with his work. The telegram was just his way of wishing me luck.'

My words made no impression. Her face was frozen stiff.

'You're not a scientist,' she said. 'What sort of research can you possibly do? And where were you going?'

I dropped her wrists and sighed, as one whose patience is becoming rapidly exhausted by a wilfully misunderstanding child.

'I wasn't going anywhere,' I insisted, emphasis on the anywhere. 'I had vaguely planned to drive along the coast and visit one or two sites he happens to be interested in.'

'How extremely plausible,' she said. 'I can't think why the Professor doesn't have a teach-in here, with you as his chief assistant. Why don't you suggest it? I'd be in the way, of course, and would make myself scarce. But he'd probably like to keep the boys.'

'Oh, for God's sake,' I said, opening the door to the dining-room, 'you're behaving like every well-worn joke about wives I've ever heard. The simplest thing to do will be to ring up Magnus first thing tomorrow morning and tell him you're filing a divorce suit because you suspect me of wanting to meet up with some scrubber at Land's End. He'll howl his head off.'

I went into the dining-room and sat down at the table. The gravy was beginning to congeal, but no matter. I filled a tankard with beer to wash down the beef and two veg before tackling apple tart. Mrs Collins, tactfully silent, brought in coffee and stood it on the hot-plate, then disappeared. The boys, at a loose end, were kicking the gravel on the path in front of the house. I got up, and called to them from the window.

'I'll take you swimming later,' I shouted. They brightened visibly, and came running up the steps to the porch. 'Later,' I said. 'Let me have my coffee first, and see what Vita wants to do.' Their faces fell. Mom would be a non-starter, and possibly throw cold water on the plan. 'Don't worry,' I said. 'I promise I'll take you.'

Then I went into the library. Vita was lying on the sofa, her eyes closed. I knelt beside her, and kissed her. 'Stop being bloody-minded,' I said. 'There's only one girl in this world for me, and you know it. I'm not going to take you upstairs to prove it because I've told the boys I'd take them swimming, and you don't want to spoil their day for them, do you?'

She opened one eye. 'You've succeeded in spoiling mine,' she said.

'Balls!' I told her. 'And what about my lost weekend with that floozie? Shall I tell you what I'd planned to do with her? A strip-tease show at Newquay. Now shut up.' I kissed her again with vigour. Response was negligible, but she did not push me away.

'I wish I understood you,' she said.

'Thank God you don't,' I said. 'Husbands loathe wives who understand them. It makes for monotony. Come and swim. There's a perfectly good empty beach below the cliffs. It's blazing hot, and it isn't going to rain.'

She opened both eyes. 'What were you actually doing this morning while we were in church?' she asked.

'Mooching about in a derelict quarry,' I told her, 'less than a mile from the village. It has connections with the old Priory, and Magnus and I happen to be interested in the site. Then I couldn't start the car, which I'd parked rather awkwardly in a ditch.'

'It's news to me that your Professor is an historian as well as a scientist,' she said.

'Good news, don't you think? Makes a change from all those embryos in bottles. I encourage it.'

'You encourage him in everything,' she said, 'that's why he makes use of you.'

'I'm adaptable by nature, always have been. Come on, those boys are itching to be off. Go and make yourself beautiful in a bikini, but put something over it, or you'll startle the cows.'

'Cows?' she almost shrieked. 'I'm not going in any field with cows, thank you very much.'

'They're tame ones,' I said, 'fed on a certain sort of grass so that they can't move out of a slow amble. Cornwall's famous for them.'

I think she believed me. Whether she believed my story about the quarry was another matter. She was pacified, for the moment. Let it rest . . .

We spent a long, lazy afternoon on the beach. Everybody swam, and afterwards, while the boys scrambled about in pools hunting for non-existent prawns, Vita and I stretched ourselves full-length on a spit of yellow sand, letting it trickle through our fingers. Peace reigned.

'Have you thought about the future at all?' she asked suddenly.

'The future?' I repeated. In point of fact, I was staring across the bay wondering if Bodrugan had made it that night with a rising tide, after he and Isolda had said goodbye. He had mentioned Chapel Point. In old days, Commander Lane had taken us sailing across the bay from Fowey to Mevagissey, and had pointed out Chapel Point jutting out on the port side before we entered Mevagissey harbour. Bodrugan's house must have lain somewhere close at hand. Perhaps the name existed still. I could find it on the road map if it was still there.

'Yes,' I said, 'I have. If it's fine tomorrow we'll go sailing. You couldn't possibly be seasick if it's as calm as it is today. We'll sail right across the bay and anchor off that headland over there. Take lunch, and go ashore.'

'Very nice,' she agreed, 'but I didn't mean the immediate future. I meant the long-term one.'

'Oh, that,' I said. 'No, darling, frankly I have not. So much to do getting settled in here. Don't let's be premature.'

'That's all very well,' she said, 'but Joe can't wait for ever. I think he was hoping to hear from you fairly soon.'

'I know that. But I've got to be absolutely sure. It's all right for you, it's your country. It isn't mine. Pulling up roots won't be easy.'

'You've pulled them up already, chucking that London job. To be blunt, you have no roots. So there's no argument,' she said.

She was right, for all practical purposes.

'You'll have to do something,' she went on, 'whether it's in England or the States. And to turn down Joe's offer when no one has offered you anything comparable in this country seems utterly crazy. I admit I'm prejudiced,' she added, putting her hand in mine, 'and would adore to settle back home. But only if you want it too.'

I did not want it, that was the crux. Nor did I want a similar job, literary agency or publishing, in London. It was the end of the road, the end, temporarily, of a particular moment in time, my time. And I could not plan ahead, not yet.

'Don't go on about it now, darling,' I said. 'Let's take each moment as it comes. Today, tomorrow . . . I'll think constructively about the whole thing soon, I promise you.'

She sighed, and let go of my hand, reaching in the pocket of her towelling wrap for a cigarette. 'As you say,' she said, the upward inflection on the 'say' proclaiming her origins on the western Atlantic seaboard. 'But don't blame me if you find yourself left high and dry by brother Joe.'

The boys came running across the beach with various trophies to show us, star-fish, mussels, and an oversize, long-dead crab that stank to heaven. The moment of truth had passed. It was time to gather up our things and face the trek uphill back to Kilmarth. As I brought up the rear I looked over my shoulder across the bay. The coast was clearly defined, and the white houses on the edge of Chapel Point, some eight miles distant, were caught by the western sun.

'In such a night
Otto methinks mounted Bodrugan walls,
And sighed his soul towards the Treesmill creek
Where Isold lay that night . . .'

But did she? Surely she must have followed the children later, after Otto sailed. But where to? Bockenod, where her husband's brother, the self-important Sir John, lived? Too far. Something was missing. She had mentioned another name. Treg something. I must look on the map. The trouble was that every other farmhouse in Cornwall began with Tre. It had not been Trevenna, Treverran or Trenadlyn. So where was it that Isolda and her two children had lain their heads that night?

'I don't see myself doing this often,' complained Vita. 'My heaven, what a hill! It's like the ski slopes in Vermont. Let me take your arm.'

The thing was, they had crossed the water-splash below the mill and taken a track to the right. And then I had not seen them any more, because of that car coming up behind me. They could have gone in any direction. And Roger was on foot. When the tide came in the ford would be fully covered. I tried to remember if there was a boat beneath the blacksmith's forge to ferry him back.

'After all this exercise and air I ought to sleep tonight,' said Vita.

'Yes,' I replied.

There had been a boat. High and dry on the edge of the creek. At high water this would be used for carrying passengers to and fro between the blacksmith's forge and Treesmill.

'You couldn't care less, could you,' she asked, 'what sort of a night I have, and whether I'm dead on my feet right now?'

I stopped and stared at her. 'I'm sorry, darling,' I said, 'of course I care.' Why revert suddenly to that business of a sleepless night?

'You were miles away in thought – I can always tell,' she said.

'Four miles at the most,' I told her. 'If you really want to know, I was thinking about a couple of children riding ponies I saw this morning. I wondered where they were going.'

'Ponies?' We continued walking, Vita a dead weight on my arm. 'Well, that's the most sensible thought you've had yet,' she said. 'The boys love riding. Maybe the ponies were let out on hire?'

'I doubt it,' I said. 'I imagine they came from some farm.'

'Well, you could always make inquiries. Nice-looking children?'

'Enchanting. Two little girls, and a youngish woman who looked as if she might be their nurse, and a couple of men.'

'All riding ponies?'

'One man was walking, holding the children's bridles.'

'Then it must be a riding-school,' she said. 'Do find out. It would make something for the boys to do other than swimming or sailing.'

'Yes,' I said.

How convenient it would be if I could summon Roger from the past and bid him saddle two of the Kilmarth ponies for Teddy and Micky, then send them off with Robbie for a gallop on Par sands! Roger would handle Vita to perfection. Her slightest whim obeyed. Juice of henbane whistled up from Brother Jean at the Priory to induce a restful night, and if that failed . . . I smiled.

'What's the joke?'

'No joke.' I pointed to the fading foxgloves, a purple mass thrusting tall stems through the hedge encircling the paddocks below Kilmarth. 'If you have a heart attack, no problem. Digitalis comes from foxgloves. You've only to say the word and I'll crush the seeds.'

'Thanks a lot. No doubt your Professor's laboratory is full of them, along with other poisonous seeds and goodness knows what sinister mixtures.'

How right she was. An error, though, to let her dwell on Magnus. 'Here we are,' I said. 'Through that gate and into the garden. I'll mix you a long, cool drink, and the boys as well. Then I'll cope with the supper. Plenty of cold beef and salad.'

Let cheerfulness prevail. Memories of my misspent morning fade into an urge to please. Attentive husband, smiling step-father; keep the whole thing going to bedtime and beyond.

As it turned out, beyond took care of itself. The swim, the long climb and the soporific Cornish air had done their trick. Vita, yawning her head off at a television play, was in bed by ten, and fast asleep when I crept in stealthily beside her an hour later. Tomorrow would be fine, judging by the sky, and we would sail to Chapel Point. Bodrugan existed still. I had found it on the road map after supper.

There was just enough breeze to take us out of Fowey harbour. Our skipper, Tom, a stalwart fellow with a ready smile, busied himself with the sails, aided or hindered by the boys, while I stationed myself at the tiller. I knew just enough about it not to bring the boat up into the wind and set the sails flapping, but neither Vita nor the boys knew this, and were suitably impressed by my air of efficiency. Soon we had mackerel lines astern, the boys hauling them in with shouts of excitement as soon as they felt the slightest tug, caused by the ripple of tide or a piece of weed, while Vita stretched herself at my side. Her jeans became her – like all Americans, she had a stunning figure – and so did her scarlet sweater.

'This is heaven,' she said, snuggling close and leaning her head against my shoulder. 'So clever of you to arrange it, I give you full marks for once. The water couldn't be smoother.'

The trouble was, it didn't stay heaven for long. I remembered of old, after passing the Cannis buoy and the Gribbin Head, a westerly wind met the tide with a smacking force, increasing the boat's speed – always a joy to the helmsman with his heart in his job, like Commander Lane – but causing the craft to heel over, so that the passenger sitting on the leeward side found himself within a few inches of the sea. In this case the passenger was Vita.

'Hadn't you better let the man steer?' she said nervously, after the boat had curtsied three times like a rocking-horse – my fault, too close to the wind – then lay firmly on her side with the lea rail awash.

'Not a bit of it,' I said cheerfully. 'Crawl under the boom and sit on the weather side.'

She groped to her feet, and caught her head an almighty tonk on the boom. As I bent to help her unravel a rope from her ankle, which took my eye off my work as helmsman, I shipped a short sea across the bows, thus drenching the whole party, myself included.

'A drop of salt-water hurts nobody,' I shouted, but the boys, clinging to the weather rail, were not so sure, and with their mother made a dive for the shelter of the small cabin, which, lacking headroom, forced them to crouch like hunchbacks on the tiny locker seat, where they rose and fell with every curtsey of the over-lively craft.

'Nice fresh breeze,' said our skipper Tom, grinning all over his face. 'We'll be at Mevagissey in no time at all.'

I bared my teeth in imitation of his confidence, but the three white faces upturned to me in the cockpit lacked enthusiasm, and I had the impression that none of them shared the skipper's opinion about the breeze.

He offered me a cigarette, but it proved an error after three puffs, and I let it fall over the side when he was not looking, while he proceeded to light up a particularly noxious pipe. Some of the smoke found its way down to the cabin and circled there in rings.

'The lady would feel the motion less if she sat in the cockpit,' suggested Tom, 'and the lads as well.'

I looked at the boys. The boat was steady enough now, but penned in the dark cabin they felt every thump, and an ominous yawn appeared on Micky's face. Vita, her eyes glazed, appeared hypnotized by Tom's oilskin, which was hanging on a hook by the cabin door, swaying to and fro with the boat's motion like a hanging man.

Tom and I exchanged glances, seized by a sudden freemasonry, and while he took over the tiller and knocked out his pipe I pulled the family up into the cockpit, where Vita and her youngest were promptly sick. Teddy survived, possibly because he kept his head averted.

'We'll soon be under the lea of Black Head,' said Tom. 'They won't feel any motion in there.'

His touch on the tiller was like magic. Or perhaps it was pure chance. The rocking-horse motion moved to a gentle lilt, the white faces lost their pallor, teeth ceased their chattering, and the pasties baked by Mrs Collins were torn from their napkins in the basket and fallen upon by all of us, even Vita, with the ferocity of carrion crows. We passed Mevagissey and came to anchor on the western side of Chapel Point. There was not a tremor in sea or sky, and the sun blazed down.

'Rather extraordinary,' observed Vita, now stripped of her sweater, which she bunched under her head as a pillow, 'that as soon as Tom took charge of the boat it scarcely moved at all and the wind dropped.'

'Not really,' I said. 'We were coming closer to the land, that's all.'

'I know one thing,' she said, 'and that is that he's going to steer the boat home.'

Tom was helping the boys into the dinghy. They had bathing-shorts and towels under their arms. Tom had fishing-lines, baited with worm.

'If you want to stay aboard with the lady, I'll see the lads come to no harm,' he said. 'This beach is quite safe for bathing.'

I did not want to stay aboard with the lady. I wanted to climb up through the fields and find Bodrugan.

Vita sat up, and removing her dark glasses looked around her. It was half-tide and the beach looked tempting, but I saw, with delight, that it was temporarily in the possession of half a dozen cows, who were mooning about aimlessly, spattering the sand in the inevitable fashion.

'I'll stay aboard,' said Vita firmly, 'and if I want to swim I'll swim from the boat.'

I yawned, my immediate reaction when feeling guilty. 'I'll go ashore and stretch my legs,' I said. 'It's too early to swim anyway, after a pasty lunch.'

'Do as you like,' she said. 'It's perfect here. Those white houses on the point look enchanting. We might be in Italy.'

I let her think it, and climbed into the dinghy with the others. 'Land me over there, in the left-hand corner,' I said to Tom.

'What are you going to do?' asked Teddy.

'Walk,' I said firmly.

'Can't we stay in the dinghy and fish for pollack?'

'Of course you can. Much the best plan,' I told him. I sprang ashore amongst the cows, free of encumbrance. The boys were equally glad to be rid of me. I stood for a moment, watching them pull away. Vita waved a languid hand from the anchored boat. Then I turned, and struck uphill.

The path ran parallel with a stream and curved, passing a cottage on the right-hand side, and then the sea was out of sight. The track continued up the hill, leading to a gate between old walls, and on the left-hand side what appeared to be the ruins of a mill. I ventured through the gate, and Bodrugan farm was all about me, a big pond to my left that must have fed the mill-stream, and to my right the gracious, slate-hung farmhouse of today, early eighteenth century, perhaps, curiously like Magnus's Kilmarth, and beside it and beyond great stone-walled barns of a much earlier date that surely must have stood upon the site of Otto's fourteenth-century home. Two children were playing under the windows of the farmhouse, but they took no notice of me and I ventured on, crossing the wide sweep where cows were grazing, and stepped inside the high-roofed barn the further side.

This served as a granary today, and must have done for centuries, but six hundred years ago perhaps a dining-hall stood here, and other rooms, while the long, low barn across the way could have been the chapel. The whole demesne was vast, far larger than the space covered by those mounds and banks that once had formed the home of the Champernounes, below the Gratten; and I realized now why Joanna, born and bred a Bodrugan in this place, may have thought the house above the Treesmill creek a poor exchange when she married Henry Champernoune.

I came out of the barn and followed the low stone walls surrounding the entire farm, then, striking off to the hills on the opposite slope, came once more in sight of the sea. Here, on top of the high field, was a mound that must once have formed a keep or outpost, commanding the bay, and I wondered how often Otto rode here from his house, and looked out from the keep past Black Head to the cliffs in the far distance that gradually descended to Tywardreath bay and to the winding estuary with its narrow arms, the first running to the Lampetho valley, the second to the Priory walls, the third to Treesmill and the Champernoune demesne. He would have seen all of this on a clear day, even perhaps the humped dwelling of Kylmerth, and the little straggling copse beyond.

This would have been the moment to have the flask in my pocket, and have seen Otto leaning from the round tower of his keep, and beneath him, in the sheltered cove where the boys fished today, his ship at anchor, ready to make sail. Or travel even further back in time and watch him ride away to that first rebellion against Edward the Second in 1322, younger and hot-headed, to be fined a thousand marks when the rebellion failed. Champion of lost causes, seeker after forbidden fruit; how often, I wondered, did he steal across that bay, leaving his dim-faced wife Margaret, Henry Champernoune's sister, snugly secure inside Bodrugan house, or in their other property of Trelawn, wherever that might be, in which the Champernounes also seemed to have rights?

I clumped back to the beach, hot and curiously tired. It was odd, but it seemed more of an effort to face the family now, without having swallowed the drug and moved in the other world, than it would had I actually taken a trip in time. I felt thwarted, drained of energy, and filled with a strange sense of apprehension. Imagination was not enough; I craved the living experience which had been denied me, and which I could have possessed had I taken a few drops from the flask safely locked away in the old laundry at Kilmarth. I might have witnessed scenes, on that old site above the cliff, or by the farmstead itself, that now I should never know; and the frustration was absolute.

The cows had gone from the beach. The boys had returned to the anchored boat and were sitting in the cockpit having tea, their swimming trunks strung up on the mast to dry. Vita was standing in the bows taking snapshots. A contented party, everybody happy, myself the odd man out.

I wore bathing trunks under my trousers, and stripping off my clothes I entered the water. It struck chill, after the walk, and seaweed floated on the surface like tresses from the drowned Ophelia's hair. I turned over on my back and stared at the sky, still filled with this strange feeling of despondency, almost of doom. It would need a tremendous effort to respond to the family greeting, join in the general chatter, smile and joke.

Tom had seen me, and was bringing the dinghy ashore to fetch my clothes. I swam out to the boat and managed somehow to clamber aboard, with the aid of a rope's end and the willing hands of Vita and the boys.

'Look, three pollack,' shouted Micky. 'Mom says she'll cook them for supper. And we've found a lot of shells.'

Vita came forward with the remains of the tea from the thermos jug. 'You look all in,' she said. 'Did you walk far?'

'No,' I said, 'only across the fields. There was a castle of sorts there once, but nothing's left of it.'

'You should have stayed on the boat,' she said. 'The bathing was heaven. Here, rub yourself down with this towel, you're shivering. I hope you haven't taken a chill. Such a mistake to plunge into cold water when you've been perspiring.'

Micky thrust a damp doughnut into my hand tasting of cotton wool, and I swallowed the lukewarm tea. Then Tom climbed aboard, bearing my clothes, and before long it was up anchor and away, with Tom at the tiller. I put on another jersey and went and sat up in the bows, where Vita presently joined me.

The little popple in mid-bay sent her back to the cockpit, to wrap herself in Tom's oilskin, and I stared ahead towards the distant prospect of Kilmarth, screened by its belt of trees. In old days, sailing nearer to the coast, Bodrugan would have had a closer view, as he steered his ship towards the estuary that covered Par sands then, and Roger, had he been watching from the fields, could have signalled to him that all was well. I wondered whose fever was the greater, Bodrugan's as he rounded the sloping headland to the channel, knowing she waited for him in that empty house behind the low stone walls, or Isolda's, when she sighted the masthead and saw the first flutter of the dark sail. Now, with the sun astern, we passed the Cannis buoy and made for Fowey, entering the harbour, to the great excitement of the boys, just as a large vessel, her decks white with china-clay and escorted by two tugs, left it outward bound.

'Can we come again tomorrow?' they clamoured, as I paid off Tom and thanked him for our sail.

'We'll see,' I said, uttering the inevitable adult formula that must be so infuriating to the young. See what, they might have asked? If the mood suits and there is harmony in the grown-up world? The success or failure of their day depended upon the state of truce between their mother and myself.

My immediate problem, when we got back to Kilmarth, was to telephone Magnus before he telephoned me, which he was bound to do, now the weekend was over. I hung about the library furtively, waiting for a good moment, and then the boys came in and switched on the TV, so I had to go upstairs to the bedroom. Vita was downstairs in the kitchen seeing about supper: it was now or never. I dialled his number and he answered immediately.

'Look,' I said quickly, 'I can't talk long. The worst has happened. Vita and the boys arrived unexpectedly on Saturday morning. They caught me almost in *flagrant délit*. You understand? And your telegram was an equal calamity. Vita opened it. Since when the situation has been decidedly tricky, and that's putting it mildly.'

'Oh, dear . . .' said Magnus, in the tone of an elderly maiden aunt confronted with a mild household problem.

'It's not "Oh dear" at all, it's hell and damnation,' I exploded, 'and the end of the road, as far as any more trips are concerned. You realize that, don't you?'

'Keep calm, dear boy, keep calm. You say she arrived and actually caught you en route?'

'No, I was returning from one. Seven in the morning. I won't go into it now.'

'Was it valuable?' he asked.

'I don't know what you call valuable,' I said. 'It concerned a near rebellion against the Crown. Otto Bodrugan was there, and Roger, of course. I'll write you fully about it tomorrow, and Sunday's trip as well.'

'So you *did* risk it again, despite the family? How splendid.'

'Only because they went to church, and I was able to slip off to the Gratten. And there is a time problem, Magnus; I can't account for it. The trip seemed to last half an hour to forty minutes at the most, but in actual fact I was "out" for about two and a half hours.'

'How much did you take?'

'The same as Friday night – a few more drops than on the first two or three trips.'

'Yes, I see.'

He was silent a minute, considering what I had told him.

'Well?' I asked. 'What's the significance?'

'I'm not sure,' he said. 'I'll have to work on it. Don't worry, it won't be serious, at this stage. How are you feeling in yourself?'

'Well . . . healthy enough physically, we've been sailing all day. But it's a hell of a strain, Magnus.'

'I'll see how the week goes and then try to get down. I shall have some results from the lab up here in a few days and we can discuss them. Meanwhile, go easy on the trips.'

'Magnus . . .'

He had rung off, which was as well. I thought I could hear Vita coming up the stairs. In a sense, I was relieved this time at the thought of seeing him, even if it meant difficulties with Vita. He would adopt his special brand of charm and smooth them away, and the responsibility would be his, not mine. Besides, I was worried about the drug. This sense of depression, of foreboding, might be a side-effect.

I looked in the shaving mirror in the bathroom. There was something odd about my right eye, it looked bloodshot, and there was a faint red streak across the white. A bloodvessel burst, perhaps, which was nothing, but I did not remember it having happened before. I hoped Vita would not notice it.

Supper passed off all right, with the boys chatting happily about their day and enjoying the pollack they had caught (the most tasteless of all fish, to my mind, but I did not damp their ardour). Just as we were clearing away the telephone rang.

'I'll get it,' said Vita quickly, 'it could be for me.'

At least it would not be Magnus. The boys and I loaded the dishwasher and had set it going when Vita came back into the kitchen. She had on a face I knew. Determined, rather defiant.

'That was Bill and Diana,' she said.

'Oh, yes?'

The boys disappeared to the library to watch TV. I poured out coffee for us both.

'They're flying to Dublin from Exeter,' she said. 'They're in Exeter now.' Then, before I could make some adequate reply, she said hurriedly, 'They're just crazy to see the house, so I suggested they put off their flight for forty-eight hours or so, and came down to us for lunch tomorrow and to stay the night. They jumped at the idea.'

I put down my cup of coffee untasted, and slumped in the kitchen chair.

'Oh, my God!' I said.

thirteen

There are few strains more intolerable in life than waiting for the arrival of unwelcome guests. I had said no more in protest after my first groan of despair, but we had spent the hours until bedtime in separate rooms, Vita in the library watching television with the boys, myself in the music-room listening to Sibelius.

Now, the next morning, Vita was sitting on what she liked to call the terrace, outside the french windows of the music-room, listening for the blare of their horn, while I paced up and down inside, primed with my first gin and tonic, my eye on the clock, wondering which state was the worse – this of anticipating the dire moment of a car coming down the drive, or the full flush of their having settled in, cardigans strewn on chairs, cameras clicking, voices loud and long, the smell of Bill's inevitable cigar. The second, perhaps, was better, the heat of battle rather than the bugle's call.

'Here they come,' yelled the boys, tearing down the steps, and I advanced through the french window like one facing up to mortar-shells.

Vita, as a hostess, was magnificent: Kilmarth was transformed instantly into some American embassy overseas, lacking only a flagstaff bearing the Stars and Stripes. Food borne in by the willing and triumphant Mrs Collins graced the dining-room table. Liquor flowed, cigarette smoke filled the air, we lunched at two and rose at half-past three. The boys, fobbed off with the promise of swimming later, vanished to play cricket in the orchard. The girls, disguised in uniform dark glasses, dragged lilos out of earshot to indulge in gossip. Bill and I installed ourselves on the patio intending, or so I hoped, to sleep, but sleep was intermittent; like all diplomats, he enjoyed hearing his own voice. He held forth on world policy and policy nearer home, and then, with elaborate unconcern and obviously briefed by Diana, touched on my future plans.

'I hear you're going into partnership with Joe,' he said. 'That's wonderful.'

'It's not settled,' I replied. 'There's a lot still to be discussed.'

'Oh, naturally,' he said. 'You can't just decide on a flick of a coin, but what an opportunity! His firm is on the crest of the wave right now, and you'd never regret it. Especially as I gather you've nothing really to lose this side. No special ties.' I did not answer. I was determined not to be led into a lengthy discussion. 'Of course, Vita would make a home anywhere,' he went on. 'She has the knack. And with an apartment in New York and a weekend place in the country, you'd lead a very full life together, with plenty of opportunities for travel thrown in.'

I grunted, and tilted an old panama hat of Commander Lane's over my right eye, which was still bloodshot. Unremarked, so far, by Vita.

'Don't think I'm butting in,' he said, lowering his voice, 'but you know how the girls talk. You've got Vita worried. She told Diana you've blown cool over the idea of coming to the States, and she can't figure out why. Women always think the worst.' He then launched into a long, and to my mind loaded, story about a girl he had met in Madrid when Diana was in the Bahamas with her parents. 'She was only nineteen,' he said. 'I was crazy about her. But of course we both knew it couldn't last. She had a job in the Embassy there, and Diana was due back in London when her vacation was over. I was so wild about that kid I felt like cutting my throat when we said goodbye. However, I survived and so did she, and I haven't seen her since.'

I lit a cigarette to counteract the clouds of smoke from his blasted cigar. 'If you think,' I said, 'that I've got a girl round the corner you couldn't be more wrong.'

'Well, that's fine,' he said, 'just fine. I wouldn't blame you if you had, as long as you kept it quiet from Vita.'

There was a long pause while he tried, I suppose, to think of another tactic, but he must have decided that discretion was the better part of valour, for he went on abruptly, 'Didn't those boys say something about wanting to swim?'

We wandered off to find our wives. Their session was apparently still in full swing. Diana was one of those overripe blondes who are said to be grand fun at a party and a tigress in the home. I had no desire to try her out in either capacity. Vita told me she was the loyalest of friends, and I believed her. The session ceased immediately we appeared, and Diana changed down into second gear, her invariable custom at the approach of masculine company.

'You've got a tan, Dick,' she said. 'It suits you. Bill turns lobster red at the first touch of the sun.'

'Sea air,' I told her. 'Not synthetic like your own.'

She had a bottle of sun oil beside her with which she had been lubricating her lily-white legs.

'We're going down to the beach to swim,' said Bill. 'Rouse yourself, pug-face, it will take off some of that surplus fat.'

The usual badinage ensued, the interplay of married couples before their kind. Lovers never did this, I thought; the game was played in silence, and was in consequence the more delightful.

Carrying towels and snorkels, we made the long trek to the beach. The tide was low, and to enter the water the intending swimmer had to pick his way over seaweed and uneven slabs of rock. It was an experience new to our guests, but they took it in good part, splashing about like dolphins in the shallows, proving my favourite maxim that it is always easier to entertain, albeit unwillingly, out of doors.

The evening to come would be the real test of hospitality, and so it proved. Bill had brought his own bottle of bourbon (a gift to the house), and I cleared the fridge of ice so that he could consume it on the rocks. The muscadet which we drank with supper, on top of the bourbon, made too rich a mixture, and with the dishwasher throbbing away in the kitchen we staggered into the music-room after dinner considerably the worse for wear. I did not have to worry about my bloodshot eye. Both Bill's looked as if he had been stung by bees, while our wives had the high flush of barmaids lounging in some disreputable sailors' joint.

I went over to the gramophone and put on a stack of records – the choice did not matter, so long as the sound served the purpose of keeping the party quiet. Vita was a moderate drinker as a general rule, but when she had had one too many I found her embarrassing. Her voice took on a strident tone, or alternatively turned silky sweet. Tonight the sweetness was for Bill, who, nothing loath, lolled beside her on one sofa, while Diana, patting the empty place next to her on the second, pulled me to it with a meaning smile.

I realized, with distaste, that these manoeuvres had been worked out by the two women earlier on, and we were set for one of those frightful evenings of swapping partners, not for the ultimate act itself, but as a preliminary try-out, like a curtain-raiser before a two-act play. I could not have been more bored. The only thing I wanted to do was to go to bed, and, by God, to go alone.

'Talk to me, Dick,' said Diana, so close that I had to turn my head sideways like a ventriloquist's doll. 'I want to know all about your brilliant friend Professor Lane.'

'A detailed account of his work?' I asked. 'There was a very informative article about certain aspects of it in the *Biochemical Journal* a few years ago. I've probably got a copy in the flat in London. You must read it some time.'

'Don't be idiotic. You know perfectly well I wouldn't understand a word. I want to know what he's like as a man. What are his hobbies, who are his friends?'

Hobbies . . . I considered the word. It conjured a vision of an absent-minded buffer chasing butterflies.

'I don't think he has any hobbies,' I told her, 'beyond his work. He's fond of music, particularly church music, Gregorian chants and plainsong.'

'Is that what you have in common, a liking for music?'

'It started that way. We happened to meet in the same pew one evening at King's College when a carol service was in progress.'

In point of fact we had not gone for the carols but to stare at one particular choir-boy with a golden aureole of hair like the infant Samuel. But though the meeting was accidental it was the first of many. Not that my tastes inclined to choir-boys, but the combination of holy innocence with adeste fideles and a halo of curls was so aesthetically pleasing to our twenty years that we were subsequently enraptured for several days.

'Teddy told me there was a room locked up in the basement here full of monkeys' heads,' she said. 'How deliciously creepy.'

'One monkey's head, to be exact,' I replied, 'and a number of other specimens in jars. Highly toxic, and not to be disturbed.'

'You hear that, Bill?' said Vita from the opposite sofa. I noticed, with aversion, that he had his arm round her and her head was on his shoulder. 'This house is built on dynamite. One false movement, and we'd be blown skyhigh.'

'Any movement?' queried Bill, with an offensive wink at me. 'What happens if we get a little closer? If dynamite sends us both up to the floor above it's OK by me, but I'd best ask Dick's permission first.'

'Dick's staying right here,' said Diana, 'and should the monkey's head explode you two can rise, and Dick and I'll descend. That way we'll all be happy, but in different worlds. Isn't that so, Dick?'

'Oh, absolutely,' I agreed. 'And in any event I've had enough of this particular world. So if you three like to triple-up on one piece of furniture, go ahead and enjoy yourselves. There's a quarter of bourbon left in the bottle, and it's all yours. I'm for bed.'

I got up and left the room. Now that I had had broken up the foursome the petting party would automatically stop, and they would all three sit for another hour or more solemnly discussing the various facets of my character, how I had or had not changed, what could be done about me, what the future held.

I undressed, plunged my head into cold water, flung the curtains wide, climbed into bed and fell instantly asleep.

The moon awakened me. It came through a chink of the curtains, which Vita had drawn, and sent a shaft of light on to my pillow. She lay on her own side of the bed and was snoring, a thing she rarely did, and with her mouth wide open. It must have been that last quarter of bourbon. I glanced at my watch: it was half-past three. I got out of bed, went through to the dressing-room, and pulled on a pair of jeans and a sweater.

I stood at the head of the stairs and listened at the guest-room door. Not a sound. Silence, too, along the passage where the boys slept. I went downstairs, down the back way to the basement, and so to the lab. I was perfectly sober, cool and collected, neither elated nor depressed; I have never felt more normal in my life. I was determined to take a trip, and that was that. Pour four measures in the flask, get the car out of the garage, coast downhill to Treesmill valley, park the car, and walk to the Gratten. The moon was bright, and when it paled in the western sky the dawn would come. If time played tricks with me and the trip lasted until breakfast, what did it matter? I would return when I was ready to return. And Vita and her friends could lump it.

On such a night . . . a rendezvous with whom? The world of today asleep, and my world not awakened, or not as yet, until the drug possessed me. Tywardreath was a ghost village as I skirted it, but in my secret time I knew I traversed the green, and the Priory stood conspicuous though aloof behind stone walls. I crept down the Treesmill road and the moonlight flooded the valley, shining on the grey-lidded hutches of the mink-farm on the further side. I parked the car close to the ditch, and climbed the gate across the field. Then I made my way to the pit near the quarry which I knew formed the site of part of the original hall, and in the darkness there, close to a tree-stump, in a square patch of moonlight, swallowed the contents of the flask. Nothing happened at first, except a humming in my ears which I had not experienced before. I leant against the bank and waited.

Something stirred, a rabbit, perhaps, in the hedge, and the humming in my ears increased. A piece of corrugated iron behind me in the quarry rattled and fell. The humming became universal, part of the world around me, changing from the sound in my own ears to the rattle of the casement in the great hall, and the roaring of the wind without. The rain was teeming down from a grey sky, falling slantwise across the parchment panes, and moving forward I looked out and saw that the water in the estuary below was turbulent and high, short-crested seas racing with the tide. What trees there were on the opposite slopes bent in unison, the autumn leaves scattering with the force of the wind, and a flock of starlings flying north formed into a clamouring mass and disappeared. I was not alone. Roger was by my side, peering down into the creek also, his face concerned, and when a greater draught of wind rattled the casement he fastened it tight, shaking his head and murmuring, 'Pray God he does not venture here in this.'

I glanced round, and saw that a curtain had been drawn across the hall, dividing it in two, and voices came from behind it. I followed Roger as he crossed the hall and drew the curtain aside. I thought for a moment that time had played another trick, taking me into a past I had witnessed already, for there was a pallet bed against one wall, with someone lying on it, while Joanna Champernoune was seated at the foot, and the monk Jean close to the pillow. But drawing closer I saw that the sick man was not her husband but his namesake, Henry Bodrugan, Otto's eldest son and her own nephew, and standing well withdrawn, with his handkerchief covering his mouth, was Sir John Carminowe. The young man, evidently in a high fever, kept trying to raise himself, calling for his father, as the monk wiped the sweat from his forehead and tried to ease him back on to his pillow.

'Impossible to leave him here, with the servants at Trelawn and no one to care for him,' said Joanna. 'And even if we tried to move him there we could not do so before nightfall, in such a gale. Whereas we could have him beneath your own roof, at Bockenod, within an hour.'

'I dare not risk it,' said Sir John. 'If it should prove to be smallpox, as the monk fears, none of my family have had it. There is no other course but to leave him here in Roger's care.'

He looked at the steward, his eyes apprehensive above the handkerchief, and I thought what a poor figure he must cut before Joanna, showing such fear that he might catch the disease himself. Gone was the cocksure bearing I had seen at the Bishop's reception. He had increased in weight, and his hair was turning grey. Roger, respectful as ever before his masters, inclined his head, but I noticed a look of scorn in his lowered eyes.

'I am willing to do whatever my lady commands me,' he said. 'I had smallpox as a child, my father died of it. My lady's nephew is young and strong, he should recover. Nor can we be certain yet of the disease. Many a fever starts in the same fashion. In twenty-four hours he could be himself once more.'

Joanna rose from her chair and approached the bed. She still wore her widow's headdress, and I remembered the note scribbled by the student at the Public Record Office from the Patent Rolls dated October 1331: 'Licence for Joan late the wife of Henry de Champernoune to marry whomsoever she will of the King's allegiance.' If Sir John was still her choice of suitor, then the marriage had not yet taken place. . . .

'We can only hope so,' she said slowly, 'but I am of the monk's opinion. I have seen smallpox before. I too had the disease as a child, and Otto with me. If it were possible to send word to Bodrugan, Otto himself would come and fetch him home.' She turned to Roger. 'How is the tide?' she asked. 'Is the ford covered?'

'It has been covered for an hour or more, my lady,' he replied, 'and the tide is still flooding. There is no possibility of traversing the ford before the water ebbs, or I would ride to Bodrugan myself and tell Sir Otto.'

'Then there is nothing for it but to leave Henry in your care,' said Joanna, 'despite the lack of servants in the house.' She turned to Sir John. 'I will come with you to Bockenod, and proceed to Trelawn at daybreak and warn Margaret. She is the one who should be at her son's bedside.'

The monk, despite his preoccupation with young Henry, had been listening to every word. 'There is another course open to us, my lady,' he said. 'The guest chamber at the Priory is vacant, and neither I nor my fellow brethren fear smallpox. Henry Bodrugan would fare better under our roof than here, and I would make it my business to watch him night and day.'

I say the expression of relief on Sir John's face, and on Joanna's too. Whatever happened they would be quit of responsibility.

'We should have decided upon this sooner,' said Joanna, 'then we could all have been on our way hours since, before this gale. What do you say, John? Is not this the only remedy?'

'It would seem so,' he said hastily, 'that is, if the steward can arrange for his removal to the Priory. We dare not take him in your chariot for fear of infection.'

'Infection for whom?' laughed Joanna. 'You mean for yourself? You can ride as escort, surely, with your handkerchief over your face as you have it now? Come, we have delayed long enough.'

The decision taken, she had no further thought for her nephew but went to the door of the great hall, escorted by Sir John, who flung it open, only to stagger back with the force of the wind.

'You'd be well advised,' she said with irony, 'to travel in comfort at my side, despite that sick boy, rather than feel the wind on your back when we reach high ground.'

'I have no fear for myself,' he began, and then, seeing the steward close behind him, added, 'You understand, my wife is delicate, and my sons also. The risk would be too great.'

'Too great indeed, Sir John. You show prudence.'

Prudence my arse, I thought, and so did Roger, judging from his expression, and Joanna's too.

The lumbering chariot was drawn up outside the further gate, and crossing the court in the blustering wind we escorted the widow to it, whilst Sir John mounted his horse. Then we returned once more to the hall. The monk was piling covers about the half-conscious Henry.

'They are ready and waiting,' said Roger. 'We can bear the mattress between us. Now we are alone, what hope have you of his recovery?'

The monk shrugged. 'As you said yourself, he is young and strong, but I have seen weaklings live and stalwarts die. Let him remain at the Priory under my care, and I will try certain remedies.'

'Watch your skill on this occasion,' said Roger. 'If you should fail you would have to answer for it to his father, and in that event the Prior himself could not protect you.'

The monk smiled. 'From what I understand, Sir Otto Bodrugan will have trouble enough protecting himself,' he answered. 'You know Sir Oliver Carminowe lay at Bockenod last night and left at dawn, telling none of the servants of his destination? If he has ridden in secret along the coast it would be for one thing only, to seek out his lady's lover and destroy him.'

'Let him try,' scoffed Roger. 'Bodrugan is the better swordsman.'

Once again the monk shrugged. 'Possibly,' he said, 'but Oliver Carminowe used other methods when he fought his enemies in Scotland. I would not give much for Bodrugan's chances should he be caught in ambush.'

The steward signalled him to silence as young Henry opened his eyes. 'Where is my father?' he asked. 'Where are you taking me?'

'Your father is home, sir,' said Roger. 'We are sending for him, he will come to you in the morning. This night you are to rest at the Priory in the care of brother Jean. Then, if you feel stronger and as your father so decides, you can be moved either to Bodrugan or to Trelawn.'

The young man looked from one to the other in bewilderment. 'I have no wish to stay at the Priory,' he said. 'I would rather go home tonight.'

'It is not possible, sir,' replied Roger gently. 'It is blowing a full gale and the horses cannot travel far. My lady is waiting for you in the chariot, and will take you to the Priory. You will be safely in bed in the guest-chamber there within half an hour.'

They bore him on the mattress, still protesting weakly, through the hall and across the court, to the waiting vehicle, stretching him full-length at his aunt's feet. Then the monk climbed in beside him. Joanna looked at her steward through the open window. The veil had blown back from her face, and I noticed how her features had coarsened since I saw her last. Her mouth was slacker, and there were pouches under her full eyes.

She leant close to the window, so that her nephew could not hear. 'There have been rumours,' she said softly, 'of possible trouble between Sir Oliver and my brother. Whether Sir Oliver is in the neighbourhood or not I cannot say. But it is one of the reasons I want to be away, and quickly.'

'As you will, my lady,' answered the steward.

'Neither Sir John nor I wish to take part in the dispute,' she said. 'It is not our quarrel. If they come to blows my brother can take care of himself. My strict charge upon you is that you side with neither, but concern yourself solely with my affairs. Is that understood?'

'Perfectly, my lady.'

She nodded briefly, then turned her attention to young Henry at her feet. Roger signalled to the driver, and the heavy vehicle pursued its course up the muddied road towards the Priory, followed by Sir John on horseback and an attendant servant, both riders bent low on their saddles, lashed by the wind and rain. As soon as they had topped the brow and disappeared, Roger walked swiftly through the archway into the stableyard and called for Robbie. His brother came at once, leading a pony, his mat of unruly hair falling over his face.

'Ride like the devil to Tregest,' Roger said, 'and warn Lady Isolda to stay within doors. Bodrugan was to have sailed here to the creek tonight, but he will never venture in this gale. Whether Sir Oliver is with her or not – and I doubt it – she must get my message without fail.'

The boy leapt on to the pony's back and was away, streaking

across the field, but in an easterly direction, our side of the valley, and I remembered that Roger had said the ford was impassable because of the tide. He would have to cross the stream higher up the valley, if the place called Tregest lay the other side. The name conveyed nothing. I knew there was no Tregest on the ordnance map today.

Roger made his way across the court and through the gate in the wall to the sloping hill above the creek. Here the strength of the wind nearly blew him off his feet, but he continued downhill towards the river, into the driving rain, taking the rough track that led to the quayside at the bottom. His expression was anxious, even haggard, quite different from his usual air of self-possession, and as he walked, or rather ran, he kept looking towards the river mouth where it entered the wide Par estuary. The sense of foreboding that had been mine when I returned from the expedition across the bay was with me once again, and I felt that it was with him too, that somehow we shared a common bond of anxiety and fear.

There was some shelter when we came to the quay because of the hill behind us, but the river itself was in turmoil, the wavelets short and steep, bearing upon their crests every sort of autumn debris, floating branches, logs and seaweed, which, as they were driven towards the quay or passed it in mid-channel, were skimmed by a flock of screaming gulls endeavouring with outstretched wings to stem the wind.

We must have seen the ship simultaneously, our eyes turned seaward, but not the brave craft I had admired at anchor on a summer's afternoon. She staggered like a drunken thing, her mast broken, the yards upon it hanging halfway to the deck, and the sails dropping around the yards like shrouds. The rudder must have gone too, for she was out of control, at the mercy of both wind and tide that bore her forward but broadside on, her bows turned towards the shallower sands where the seas broke shortest. I could not see how many were on board, but there were three at least, and they were endeavouring to launch from the deck a little boat that was caught up in the tangle of sail and fallen yards. Roger cupped his hands to his mouth and shouted, but they could not hear him, because of the wind. He sprang on to the quay wall and waved his arms, and one of those aboard – it must have been Otto Bodrugan – saw him and waved in answer, pointing to the opposite shore.

'This side the channel,' shouted Roger, 'this side the channel,' but his voice was lost in the wind. They did not hear him, for they were still working hard to launch the boat from the ship's side.

Doubtless Bodrugan knew the channel well, and if they launched the smaller boat they would have little difficulty in getting ashore, despite the short seas breaking above the sandflats on either side. It was not like open sea, rock-bound and dangerous, and, although the river was broadest where the craft drifted, she could at worst only run aground and wait for the falling tide.

Then I saw the reason for Roger's fear, and why he strove to attract Bodrugan and his sailors to the quay. A line of horsemen was riding on the opposite hill, some dozen of them, in single file. Because of the contours of the land the men aboard were not aware of their presence, the clump of trees masking them from the vessel.

Roger continued to shout and wave, but those on board took it as encouragement for the successful launching of the small boat, and replied in like fashion. Then, as the vessel drifted on up-channel, they managed to lower the boat over the side, all three men dropping into it a moment afterwards. They had a hawser fastened from the ship's bows to the stern of the small boat, and while two of the men bent to the oars and pulled towards the opposite shore the third, Bodrugan, crouched in the stern, holding fast to the hawser in an attempt to turn the vessel in the same direction as themselves.

They were too intent upon their task to pay further attention to Roger, and as they drew slowly nearer to the opposite shore I saw the horsemen on the hill dismount by the belt of trees. Taking advantage of the cover they crept down towards the creek, where the land dipped suddenly to the water's edge, forming a spit of sand. Roger shouted for the last time, waving his arms in desperation, and forgetting my phantom status I did the same, without sound, more powerless as an ally than any spectator at a football game cheering a losing side, and as the small boat drew nearer to the shore so their enemies, screened by the belt of trees, came closer to the spit of sand.

Suddenly the hawser parted as the larger vessel ran aground, and Bodrugan, flung off his feet, tumbled amongst his men and the small boat upset, throwing all three of them into the water.

They were already so close to the opposite shore that the river had no great depth where they received their ducking, and Bodrugan was the first to stand, the water up to his chest, while the others floundered beside him, and Bodrugan answered Roger's final warning yell with a triumphant cry.

It was his last. The band of men were upon him and his companions before they had time to turn their heads or defend themselves, a dozen against three, and before the driving rain that burst upon us, heavier than ever, blotted them from view I saw, with sick revulsion, that instead of dragging their victims up the spit of sand to finish them there, by sword or dagger, they were thrusting them face-downwards in the water. One was already still, the other struggling, but it took eight men to hold Bodrugan down. Roger started to run along the river's edge towards the mill, cursing, gasping, and I knew it was useless, that we ran in vain, for long before he could summon help it would be over.

We came to the ford below the mill, and, just as he had told Joanna earlier, the water ran swiftly here, and deep, almost to the door of the forge itself. Once again Roger put his hands to his mouth.

'Rob Rosgof,' he yelled, 'Rob Rosgof,' and the frightened figure of the blacksmith appeared at the door, with his wife beside him.

Roger pointed downstream, but the man gestured with both his hands in denial, shaking his head, then jerked his thumb up the hill behind him, this play without words suggesting he had known of the ambush and could do nothing, and he dragged his wife with him inside the forge and barred the door. Roger turned in despair to the mill, and the three monks I had seen there on the Sunday morning, when Isolda's children crossed the ford, came through the yard to meet him.

'Bodrugan and his men have been driven ashore,' cried Roger. 'His vessel's aground, and an ambush lay in wait to destroy them. They are dead men, all three, against a dozen fully armed.'

I hardly know which showed the more strongly upon his face, his anger, or his grief, or his powerlessness to help.

'Where is Lady Champernoune?' asked one of the monks. 'And Sir John Carminowe? We saw the carriage at the house all afternoon.'

'Her nephew, Bodrugan's son, is sick,' answered Roger. 'They have taken him to the Priory, and they themselves are now on the road to Bockenod. I have sent Robbie to Tregest to warn the household there, and I pray God none of them ventures forth, or their lives could be in danger too.'

We stood there, below the millyard, uncertain whether to go or stay, and all the time straining our eyes towards the river, where the curving banks above the creek hid the stranded vessel and the murderous scene on the spit of sand.

'Who led the ambush?' asked the monk. 'Bodrugan had enemies once, but that is long past, with the King firmly established on the throne.'

'Sir Oliver Carminowe, who else?' answered Roger. 'They fought on opposing sides in the rebellion of '22, and today he does murder in another cause.'

No sound but the wind, and the turmoil of the river as it coursed between the narrowing banks, with the gulls skimming the surface, screaming. Then one of the monks pointed to the bend in the creek and cried. 'They've launched the boat, they're coming up with the tide!'

It was not a boat, at least not the whole of it, but what seemed in the distance to be part of the planking stripped from its side, and set afloat upstream as jetsam, circling slowly as it drifted with the current. Something was lashed to it that now and again bobbed to the surface, then disappeared, only to reappear again. Roger looked at the monks and I at him, and with one accord we ran down to the edge of the creek where the eddy carried the driftwood and the scum, and all the while, as we waited, the planking rose and fell with the force of the tide, and the thing that was lashed upon it rose as well. Then there was shouting from the opposite bank, and through the belt of trees rode the horsemen, their leader ahead. They cantered down to the road by the forge, and the shouting ceased, and they stood there watching in silence.

We plunged into the river to drag the plank ashore, the monks with us, and as we did so the leading horseman shouted, 'A birthday package for my wife, Roger Kylmerth. See that she receives it with my compliments, and when she has done with it tell her that I await her at Carminowe.'

He burst out laughing, and his men with him, and then they turned their horses up the hill and rode away.

Roger and the first monk drew the plank ashore. The others

crossed themselves and began to pray, and one of them went down upon his knees at the water's edge. There was no knife wound upon Bodrugan, no sign of violence. The water streamed from his mouth and his eyes were open. They had drowned him before they lashed him to the plank.

Roger untied the hawser strands and bore him in his arms, with the water dripping from his hair, towards the mill. 'Merciful God,' he said, 'how am I to tell her?'

There was no need. As we turned towards the mill we saw the ponies, Robbie upon his own, Isolda mounted on a second, her hair loose upon her shoulders, wet and lank, her cloak billowing out behind her like a cloud. Robbie at a glance saw what had happened, and put out his hand to seize her bridle and turn her pony back, but in a moment she had dismounted and came running down the hill towards us.

'Oh, my love,' she said, 'oh, no . . . oh, no . . . oh, no . . .' her voice, that had started clear and strong, trailing off into a single cry.

Roger laid his burden on the ground and ran towards her, and so did I. As we took hold of her outstretched hands she slipped out of our grasp and fell, and instead of holding on to her cloak I was scrambling amongst bales of straw piled against a corrugated tin shed across the road from Treesmill farm.

fourteen

I lay there waiting for the nausea and the vertigo to pass. I knew it had to be endured, and the quieter I remained the quicker it would go. It was already light, and I had sense enough to glance at my watch. It was twenty-past five. If I gave myself a quarter of an hour, without moving, all should be well. Even if the people at Treesmill farm were already astir no one was likely to cross the road and come to the shed, which was hard against the wall of an old valley orchard, the stream a few yards away from where I lay, all that remained of the tidal creek.

My heart was thumping, but it gradually eased, and the

dreaded vertigo was not as bad as that previous time when I had come to at the Gratten, and had the encounter with the doctor at the lay-by at the top of the hill.

Five minutes, ten, fifteen . . . then I struggled to my feet, and slipping from the orchard walked very slowly up the hill. So far so good. I climbed into the car and sat another five minutes, then started the engine and drove equally carefully back to Kilmarth. Plenty of time to put away the car and lock up the flask in the lab, then the wisest thing to do would be to go straight to bed and try to get some rest.

There was nothing more I could do, I told myself. Roger would take Isolda back to that Tregest place, wherever it was, and poor Bodrugan's body would be safe in the care of those monks. Someone would have to carry the news to Joanna at Bockenod. Roger would take care of that, I felt sure. I now had a regard, even an affection for him, he was so obviously moved by Bodrugan's appalling death, and we had shared the horror of it together. I was right to have had that sense of foreboding on the beach below Chapel Point before sailing back to Fowey with Vita and the boys. Vita and the boys . . .

I drove into the garage just as I remembered them, and with the memory came full understanding. I had driven home in one world with my brain still in the other. I had driven home, part of my brain completely sensible to the fact that I had the wheel in my hands and belonged to the present, while the rest of me was still in the past, believing Roger on the way to Tregest with Isolda.

I began to sweat all over. I sat quite still in the car, my hands trembling. It must not happen again. I must take a grip on myself. It was just on six o'clock in the morning. Vita and the boys, and those damned guests of ours, were all asleep upstairs, and Roger and Isolda and Bodrugan had been dead for more than six centuries. I was in my own time . . .

I let myself in at the back door and put the flask away. It was fully light by now, but the house was silent still. I crept upstairs and into the kitchen, and put on the electric kettle to make myself a cup of tea. Tea was the answer, a steaming cup. The purr of the kettle was oddly comforting, and I sat down at the table, remembering suddenly how much we had all had to drink the night before. The kitchen still smelt of the lobster we had eaten, and I got up and opened the window.

I was in the middle of my second cup when I heard a creak on the stairs, and I was about to streak down to the basement and remain *perdu* when the door opened and Bill came into the room. He grinned sheepishly.

'Hello,' he said. 'Two minds with but a single thought. I woke up, thought I heard a car, and suddenly had the most fearful thirst. Is that tea you're drinking?'

'Yes,' I said. 'Have a cup. Is Diana awake?'

'No,' he replied, 'and if I know my wife after a binge, not likely to, either. We were all pretty well stoned, weren't we? I say, no hard feelings?'

'No, none,' I told him.

I poured him out a cup of tea, and he sat down at the table. He looked a mess, and his pyjamas, a livid pink, did not tone with his grey complexion.

'You're dressed,' he said. 'Have you been up long?'

'Yes,' I said. 'I've been out, as a matter of fact – I couldn't sleep.'

'Then it was your car I heard coming down the drive?'

'It must have been,' I said.

The tea was doing me good, but it was making me sweat as well. I could feel the sweat pouring down my face.

'You look a bit off,' he said critically. 'Are you all right?'

I took my handkerchief out of my coat pocket and wiped my forehead. My heart had started thumping again. Must be something to do with the tea.

'As a matter of fact,' I said slowly, and I could hear myself slurring my words, as if the tea had been a strong dose of alcohol that had temporarily knocked me off balance, 'I was an unseen witness to an appalling crime. I just can't forget it.'

He put down his cup and stared at me. 'What on earth?' he began.

'I felt I needed some air,' I said, speaking very fast, 'so I took the car down to a place I know, about three miles from here, near the estuary, and a boat went aground. It was blowing damned hard, and the chap aboard with his crew had to take to the dinghy. They made the opposite shore all right and then this appalling thing happened . . .' I poured myself another cup of tea, despite my trembling hands. 'These thugs,' I said, 'these bloody thugs on the opposite shore – the chap from the boat didn't have a chance. They didn't knife him or anything, they forced his head under water and let him drown.'

'My God!' said Bill. 'My God, how terrible. Are you sure?'

'Yes, I said, 'I saw it. I saw the poor devil drown . . .' I got up from the table and began walking up and down the kitchen.

'Well, what are you going to do?' he asked. 'Hadn't you better ring the police?'

'Police?' I said. 'It's not a job for the police. It's this chap's son I'm thinking of. He's ill, and someone will have to tell him, and the other relatives.'

'But, good God, Dick, it's your duty to inform the police! I can see you don't want to be involved, but this is murder, surely? And you say you know the chap who was drowned, and his son?'

I stared at him. Then I pushed aside my cup of tea. It had happened, oh, sweet Christ, it had happened. The confusion. The confusion between worlds . . . The sweat was running down the whole of my body.

'No,' I said, 'I don't know him personally. I've seen him about, he keeps a yacht the other side of the bay, I've heard people talk about the family. You're right, I *don't* want to be involved. And anyway I wasn't the only witness. There was another chap watching, and he saw the whole thing. I'm pretty sure he will report it – in fact, he's probably done so already.'

'Did you speak to him?' asked Bill.

'No,' I said, 'no, he didn't see me.'

'Well, I don't know,' said Bill. 'I still think you ought to telephone the police. Would you like me to do it for you?'

'No, on no account. And, Bill, not a word of this to Diana or Vita. Swear it.'

He looked very troubled. 'I understand that,' he said. 'It would upset them terribly. My God, you must have had one hell of a shock.'

'I'm all right,' I told him, 'I'm all right.' I sat down again at the kitchen table.

'Here, have some more tea?' he suggested.

'No,' I said, 'no, I don't want anything.'

'It just goes to prove what I'm always saying, Dick. The crime figures are mounting steadily, in every civilized country in the world. The authorities have just got to take things in hand. I mean, who would believe it happening here, off the map, down in Cornwall? A set of thugs, you say? Any idea where they came from? Were they local men?'

I shook my head. 'No,' I said, 'I don't think so. I've no idea who they were.'

'And you're quite certain this other fellow saw, and was going to report to the police?'

'Yes, I saw him running. He was making straight for the nearest farmhouse. They'll have a telephone there.'

'I hope to heaven you're right,' he said.

We sat for a while in silence. He kept sighing, and shaking his head. 'What an experience for you. What a damned awful experience.'

I put my hands in my pockets so that he should not see them shaking. 'Look, Bill,' I said, 'I think I'll go upstairs and lie down. I don't want Vita to know I've even been out. Or Diana either. I want this thing to remain absolutely private between ourselves. There's nothing you or I can do now. I want you to forget it.'

'OK,' he said, 'about not saying anything. But I shan't forget what you've told me. And I'll listen for it on the news. By the way, we shall have to leave after breakfast if we're to catch that plane from Exeter. Is that all right by you?'

'Of course,' I said. 'I'm only sorry to have spoilt your morning.'

'My dear Dick, I'm the one to be sorry, and for you. Yes, I should go upstairs, and try to get some sleep. And look here, don't bother to get up and say goodbye. You can always plead a hangover.' He smiled, and held out his hand. 'We loved yesterday,' he said, 'and a thousand thanks for everything. I only hope nothing else comes up to spoil your holiday. I'll write you from Ireland.'

'Thanks, Bill,' I said, 'thanks a lot.'

I went upstairs, undressed in the dressing-room, then retched violently for about five minutes down the lavatory. The sound must have woken Vita, for I heard her calling from the bedroom.

'Is that you?' she said. 'What's the matter?'

'All that muscadet on top of bourbon,' I said. 'Sorry, I can hardly stand. I'm going to turn in on the divan here. It's still quite early – about half-past six.'

I closed the dressing-room door and threw myself on the divan bed. I was back in the world of today, but God alone knew how long it would stay that way. One thing was certain. As soon as Bill and Diana had gone I should have to telephone Magnus.

The unconscious is a curious thing. I was deeply disturbed over this total confusion of thought that might have made me blab the truth to Bill about the experiment itself; but five minutes or so after I had lain down on the divan I was asleep and dreaming, not, strangely enough, about Bodrugan and his appalling fate, but of a cricket match at Stonyhurst when one of the team got hit on the head with a cricket-ball and died of haemorrhage of the brain twenty-four hours later. I had not thought about the incident for at least twenty-five years.

When I awoke just after nine I was perfectly lucid and clear in the head, apart from a hell of a genuine hangover, and my right eye was more bloodshot than ever. I bathed and shaved, and could hear sounds of movement from our guests in the room next door. I waited until I heard Bill and Diana go downstairs, then I put a call through to Magnus. No luck. He was not at the flat. So I left a message with his secretary at the University saying I wanted to speak to him very urgently, but it might be better if I put the call through to him rather than he to me. Then I stuck my head out of the dressing-room window overlooking the patio and shouted to Teddy to bring me up a cup of coffee. I would appear in the hall to bid our guests godspeed five minutes before departure, and not a moment before.

'What's wrong with your eye? You hit the floor or something?' asked my elder stepson as he brought coffee.

'No,' I told him. 'I think it's a backlash from the wind on Monday.'

'You were up early anyway,' he said. 'I heard you talking to Bill in the kitchen.'

'I was making tea,' I said. 'We both of us had too much to drink at dinner.'

'Guess that's what turned your eye all streaks and not the sea,' he said, looking so like his mother in one of her more perceptive moods that I turned away, and then remembered that his room was above the kitchen and he could conceivably have overheard our conversation.

'Anyway,' I asked before he left the dressing-room, 'what were we talking about?'

'How should I know?' he replied. 'Do you think I'd pull up the floorboards to listen?'

No, I reflected, but his mother might, if she heard a discussion going on between her husband and her guest at 6 a.m.

I finished dressing, drank down my coffee, and appeared at the top of the stairs just in time to help Bill down with the suitcases. He greeted me with a conspiratorial glance of inquiry – the girls were below us in the hall – and murmured, 'Get any sleep?'

'Yes,' I said, 'yes, I'm fine.' I saw him staring at my eye. 'I know,' I said, touching it, 'no explanation for that. Must have been the bourbon. By the way,' I added, 'Teddy heard us talking this morning.'

'I know,' he said, 'I heard him tell Vita. Everything's OK. Don't worry.' He patted me on the shoulder, and we clumped downstairs.

'Heavens!' cried Vita. 'What have you done to your eye?'

'Bourbon allergy,' I said, 'combined with shellfish. It happens to some people.'

Both girls insisted on examining me, suggesting alternative remedies from penicillin ointment to TCP.

'It can't be the bourbon,' said Diana. 'I don't want to be personal, but I noticed it yesterday as soon as we arrived. I said to myself, "Whatever's Dick done to his eye?"'

'You didn't say anything to me,' said Vita.

Enough was enough. I put a hand on each of their shoulders and pushed them through the porch. 'Neither one of you would win a beauty prize this morning,' I said, 'and it wasn't the bourbon that woke me at dawn, but Vita snoring. So shut up.'

We had to install ourselves on the steps for the inevitable picture-taking by Bill, and it was nearly half-past ten before they were finally off. Once again Bill's handclasp was that of a conspirator.

'Hope we get this fine weather in Ireland,' he said. 'I'll watch the papers and listen to the radio forecasts to see what's happening here in Cornwall.' He looked at me, nodding imperceptibly. He meant that his eyes and ears would be alert for the first mention of a dastardly crime.

'Send us postcards,' said Vita, 'Wish we were coming with you.'

'You always can,' I said, 'when you get fed-up here.'

It was not perhaps the most encouraging of remarks, and when we had finished waving and turned back towards the house Vita wore an abstracted air. 'I really believe,' she said, 'you'd be glad if the boys and I had gone off with them. Then you'd have this place to yourself again.'

'Don't talk nonsense,' I said.

'Well, you made your feelings pretty clear last night, flinging off to bed directly we'd finished dinner.'

'I flung off to bed, as you call it, because it bored me stiff to see you lolling about in Bill's arms and Diana waiting to do the same in mine. I'm just no good at party games, and you ought to know it by now.'

'Party games!' she laughed. 'What utter nonsense! Bill and Diana are my oldest friends. Where's your much-vaunted British sense of humour?'

'Not in tune with yours,' I said. 'I've a cruder sense of fun. If I pulled a mat from under your feet and you slipped up, I'd have hysterics.'

We wandered back into the house, and just at that moment the telephone rang. I went into the library to answer it, and Vita followed me. I was afraid it might be Magnus, and it was.

'Yes?' I said guardedly.

'I got your message,' he said, 'but I've a very full day. Is it an awkward moment?'

'Yes,' I said.

'You mean Vita is in the room?'

'Yes.'

'I understand. You can answer yes or no. Anything turned up?'

'Well, we've had visitors. They arrived yesterday, and have just left.'

Vita was lighting up a cigarette. 'If it's your Professor – and I can't think who else it would be – give him my regards.'

'I will. Vita sends her regards,' I told Magnus.

'Return them. Ask her if it would be convenient for me to come for the weekend, arriving Friday evening.'

My heart leapt. Whether with excitement or the reverse I

couldn't say. In any case with relief. Magnus would take over.

'Magnus wants to know if he can come on Friday for the weekend,' I said to her.

'Surely,' she answered. 'It's his house, after all. You'll have more fun entertaining your friend than you had putting up with mine.'

'Vita says of course,' I repeated to Magnus.

'Splendid. I'll let you know the train later. About your urgent call. Does it concern the other world?'

'Yes,' I said.

'You went on a trip?'

'Yes.'

'With ill-effect?'

I paused a moment, with a glance at Vita. She had made no attempt to leave the room. 'As a matter of fact I'm feeling pretty lousy,' I said. 'Something I ate or drank disagreed with me. I've been violently sick and have a peculiar bloodshot eye. It may be due to drinking bourbon before lobster.'

'Combined with taking a trip, you may well be right,' he answered. 'What about confusion?'

'That also. I could hardly think straight when I awoke.'

'I see. Anyone notice?'

I took another glance at Vita. 'Well, we were all pretty high last night,' I said, 'so the males of the party woke early. I had suffered a very vivid nightmare, and told Vita's friend Bill about it over a morning cup of tea.'

'How much did you tell?'

'About the nightmare? Just that. It was very real, you know what nightmares are. I thought I saw someone set on by thugs and drowned.'

'Serves you right,' said Vita. 'And it sounds more like the two helpings of lobster than the bourbon.'

'Was it one of our friends?' asked Magnus.

'Yes,' I answered. 'You know that chap who used to keep a boat years ago over at Chapel Point, and was always sailing round to Par? Well, the nightmare was about him. I dreamt his ship was dismasted in a storm, and when he finally came ashore he was murdered by a jealous husband who thought he was after his wife.'

Vita laughed. 'If you ask me,' she said, 'a dream of that sort means an uneasy conscience. You thought I was getting off with Bill and your vivid nightmare resulted from that. Here, let me talk to your Professor.' She crossed the room and seized the receiver from me. 'How are you, Magnus?' she said, her voice full of calculated charm. 'I shall be delighted to see you here in your own home next weekend. Maybe you'll put Dick in a better temper. He's very sour right now.' She smiled, her eyes on me. 'What's wrong with his eye?' she repeated. 'I haven't the slightest idea. He looks as if he's lost a prize-fight. Yes, of course I'll do my best to keep him quiet until you arrive, but he's very stubborn. Oh, by the way, you'll be able to tell me. My boys adore riding, and Dick says he saw some children on ponies having a lot of fun on Sunday morning when we were in church. I wondered if there were riding-stables somewhere the other side of the village there – what-do-you-call-it – Tywardreath. You don't know? Well, never mind, Mrs Collins might tell me. What? Hold on, I'll ask him . . .' She turned to me. 'He says were the children the two little girls of someone called Oliver Carminowe and his wife? Old friends of his.'

'Yes,' I said. 'I'm almost sure they were. But I don't know where they live.'

She turned back to the telephone. 'Dick thinks yes, though I don't see why he should know if he hasn't met them. Oh well, if the mother is attractive he's probably seen her around some place, and that's how he knows who they were.' She pulled a face at me. 'Yes, you do that,' she added, 'and if you get in touch with them next weekend we might ask them round for drinks, and Dick can get an introduction to her. See you Friday, then.'

She handed the receiver back to me. Magnus was laughing at the other end of the line.

'What's this about getting in touch with Carminowes?' I asked.

'I got out of that rather neatly, don't you think?' he countered. 'In any event, it's what I intend to do, if we can get rid of Vita and the boys. In the meantime I'll get my lad in London to check up on Otto Bodrugan. So he came to a sticky end, and it upset you?'

'Yes,' I said.

'Roger was there, of course? Did he have a hand in it?'

'No.'

'Glad to hear it. Look, Dick, this is important. Absolutely no more trips unless we take one together. No matter how big the temptation. You must sweat it out. Is that agreed?'

'Yes,' I said.

'As I told you before, I shall have the first results from the lab by the time I see you. In the meantime, abstention. Now I must go. Take care of yourself.'

'I'll try,' I said. 'Goodbye.'

It was like cutting off the only link between both worlds.

'Cheer up, darling,' said Vita. 'Less than three days and he'll be here. Won't that be wonderful? Now what about going upstairs to the bathroom and doing something about that eye?'

Later on, the eye bathed and Vita having disappeared into the kitchen to tell Mrs Collins about Magnus coming for the weekend, and doubtless to discuss his gastronomic tastes, I got out my road map and had another look for Tregest. It just was not there. Treesmill was marked, as I knew, and Treverran, Trenadlyn, Trevenna – the last three on the Lay Subsidy Roll as well – but that was all. Perhaps Magnus would find the answer from his London student.

Presently Vita wandered back into the library. 'I asked Mrs Collins about the Carminowes,' she said, 'but she'd never heard of them. Are they very great friends of Magnus's?'

It startled me for a moment to hear her speak the name. I knew I must be careful, or the confusion might start up again.

'I think he's rather lost sight of them,' I replied. 'I doubt if he's seen them for some time. He doesn't get down very often.'

'They're not in the telephone directory – I've looked. What does Oliver Carminowe do?'

'Do?' I repeated. 'I don't really know. I think he used to be in the army. Has some sort of government job. You'll have to ask Magnus.'

'And his wife's very attractive?'

'Well, she was,' I said. 'I've never spoken to her.'

'But you've seen her since you got down here?'

'Only in the distance,' I said. 'She wouldn't know me.'

'Was she around in the old days when you used to stay here as an undergraduate?'

'She could have been,' I said, 'but I never met her, or the husband. I know very little about them.'

'But you knew enough to recognize her children when you saw them the other day?'

I felt myself getting tied up in knots. 'Darling,' I said, 'what is all this? Magnus occasionally mentions names of friends and acquaintances, and the Carminowes were amongst them. That's all there is to it. Oliver Carminowe was married before and Isolda is his second wife, and they have two daughters. Satisfied?'

'Isolda?' she said. 'What a romantic name.'

'No more romantic than Vita,' I replied. 'Can't we give her a rest?'

'It's funny,' she said, 'that Mrs Collins has never heard of them. She's such a mine of information on local affairs. But in any case there's a perfectly good stables up the road from here at Menabilly Barton, she tells me, so I'm going to fix something up with the people there.'

'Thank God for that,' I said. 'Why not fix it right away?'

She stared at me a moment, then turned round and went out of the room. I surreptitiously got out my handkerchief and wiped my forehead, which was sweating again. It was a lucky thing the Carminowes were extinct, or she would have run them to earth somehow and invited a bewildered descendant to lunch next Sunday.

Two, nearly three days to go before Magnus came to my rescue. It was difficult to fob Vita off once her interest was aroused, and it was typical of his malicious sense of fun to have mentioned the name.

The rest of Wednesday passed without incident, and thank heaven I had no return of confusion. It was such a relief to be without our guests that little else mattered. The boys went riding and enjoyed themselves, and, although Vita may have suffered from anti-climax and a normal reaction from a hangover, she had the good sense not to say so, nor did she make any further reference to our party the preceding night. We went to bed early and slept like logs, awaking on Thursday to a day of steady rain. It did not worry me, but Vita and the boys were disappointed, having planned another expedition in the boat.

'I hope it's not going to be a wet weekend,' said Vita. 'What in the world shall I do with the boys if it is? You won't want them hanging about the house all day when the Professor is here.'

'Don't worry about Magnus,' I told her. 'He'll be full of suggestions for them and for us. Anyway, he and I may have work to do.'

'What sort of work? Surely not shutting yourselves up in that peculiar room in the basement?'

She was nearer the truth than she imagined. 'I don't know exactly,' I said vaguely. 'He has a lot of papers tucked away, and he may want to go through them with me. Historical research, and so on. I've told you about this new hobby.'

'Well, Teddy might be interested in that, and so should I,' she said. 'It would be fun if we all took a picnic to some historical site or other. What about Tintagel? Mrs Collins says everyone should see Tintagel.'

'Not exactly Magnus's line of country, and anyway too full of tourists,' I said. 'We'll see what he wants to do when he arrives.'

I wondered how the hell we should be shot of them if Magnus wanted to visit the Gratten. Anyway, it would be his problem, not mine.

Thursday dragged, and a dreary walk along Par sands did little to alleviate it. Magnus had told me to sweat it out, and by the evening I knew what he meant. Sweat was the operative word, and in the physical sense. I had seldom if ever been troubled by this common affliction of mankind. At school, yes, after violent exercise, but not to the extent suffered by some of my companions. Now, after any minor exertion, or even perhaps when sitting still, I would sweat from every pore, the perspiration having a peculiar acid tang to it that I fervently hoped nobody would be aware of but myself.

The first time it happened, after the walk along Par sands, I thought it was merely connected with the exercise I had taken, and I had a bath before dinner, but during the course of the evening, when Vita and the boys were watching television and I was sitting comfortably in the music-room listening to records, it started again. A clammy feeling of sudden chill, then the sweat pouring from my head, neck, armpits, trunk, lasting for perhaps five minutes before it passed, but my shirt was wringing wet by the time the attack was over. Laughable, like seasickness, when it happens to anyone but oneself, this side-effect, which was obviously a new reaction from the drug, threw me into sudden panic. I switched off the gramophone and went upstairs to wash and change for the second time, wondering what on earth would happen if I suffered a further attack later when I was in bed with Vita.

Nervous apprehension did not make for an easy night, and Vita was in one of her conversational moods that lasted through undressing and continued until we were lying side by side. I could not have been more nervous had I been a bridegroom on the first night of honeymoon, and I found myself edging away to my side of the bed, giving vent to prodigious yawns as a sign that excessive fatigue had overtaken me. We turned out the bed-side lights, and I went through a kind of pantomime of heavy breathing on the verge of sleep which may or may not have fooled Vita, but after one or two attempts to coil close – which I ignored – she turned over on her side and was soon asleep.

I lay awake thinking of the hell I would give Magnus when he arrived. Nausea, vertigo, confusion, a bloodshot eye, and now acid sweat, and all for what? A moment in time, long past, that had no bearing on the present, that served no purpose in his life or mine, and could as little benefit the world in which we lived as a scrapbook of forgotten memories lying idle in a dusty drawer. So I argued, up to midnight and beyond, but common sense has a habit of vanishing when the demon of insomnia rides us in the small hours, and as I lay there, counting first two, and then three, on the illuminated face of the travelling clock beside the bed, I remembered how I had walked about that other world with a dreamer's freedom but with a waking man's perception. Roger had been no faded snapshot in time's album; and even now, in this fourth dimension into which I had stumbled inadvertently but Magnus with intent, he lived and moved, ate and slept, beneath me in his house Kylmerth, enacting his living Now which ran side by side with my immediate Present, and so the two merged.

Am I my brother's keeper? Cain's cry of protest against God suddenly had new meaning for me as I watched the hands of the clock move towards ten-past three. Roger was my keeper, I was his. There was no past, no present, no future. Everything living is part of the whole. We are all bound, one to the other, through time and eternity, and, our senses once opened, as mine had been opened by the drug, to a new understanding of his world and mine, fusion would take place, there would be no separation, there would be no death . . . This would be the ultimate meaning of the experiment, surely, that by moving about in time death was destroyed. This was what Magnus so far had not understood. To him, the drug released the complex brew within the brain that served up the savoured past. To me, it proved that the past was living still, that we were all participants, all witnesses. I was Roger, I was Bodrugan, I was Cain; and in being so was more truly myself.

I felt myself on the brink of some tremendous discovery when I fell asleep.

fifteen

I did not wake up until after ten, and when I did Vita was standing by the bed with the breakfast tray of toast and coffee.

'Hullo,' I said. 'I must have overslept.'

'Yes,' she said, and then, looking at me critically, 'Are you feeling all right?'

I sat up in bed and took the tray from her, 'Perfectly,' I said 'Why?'

'You were restless during the night,' she told me, 'and perspired a great deal. Look, your pyjama top is quite damp.'

It was, and I threw it off. 'Extraordinary thing,' I said. 'Be an angel and get me a towel.'

She brought me one from the bathroom, and I rubbed myself down before reaching for the coffee.

'Something to do with all that exercise on Par beach with the boys,' I said.

'I wouldn't have thought so,' she replied, staring at me, puzzled, 'and anyway you took a bath afterwards. I've never known you perspire from exercise before.'

'Well, it happens to people,' I said. 'It's my age-group. The male menopause, perhaps, striking me down in my prime.'

'I hope not,' she said. 'How very unpleasant.'

She wandered over to the dressing-table and surveyed herself in the mirror as if that might hold the answer to the problem. 'It's odd,' she went on, 'but Diana and I remarked on the fact that you weren't looking yourself despite that suntan from sailing.' She wheeled round suddenly, facing me. 'You must admit you're not a hundred per cent,' she went on. 'I don't know what it is, darling, but it worries me. You're moody, distrait, as if you had something on your mind all the time. Then that funny bloodshot eye . . .'

'Oh, for heaven's sake,' I interrupted, 'give it a miss, can't you? I admit I was foul-tempered when Bill and Diana were here, and I apologize. We all had too much to drink, and that was that. Must we do a post-mortem on every hour?'

'There you go again,' she said. 'Always on the defensive. I hope the arrival of your Professor straightens you out.'

'It will,' I answered, 'providing this inquisition on our behaviour doesn't continue through the entire weekend.'

She laughed, or rather her mouth twitched in the way wives' mouths are wont to twitch when they desire to inflict a wound upon the husband. 'I would not dare presume to conduct an inquisition on the Professor. His state of health and his behaviour are no concern of mine, but yours are. I happen to be your wife, and I love you.'

She left the room and went downstairs, and this, I thought, as I buttered my piece of toast, is a good beginning to the day – Vita offended, myself with the sweating sickness, and Magnus due to arrive some time in the evening.

There was a card on the breakfast tray from him, as it happened, hidden by the toast-rack. I wondered if Vita had obscured it deliberately. It said he would be catching the 4.30 from London, arriving at St Austell around ten. This was a relief. It meant that Vita and the boys could go to bed, or at any rate only stay up for the courtesy of greeting the new arrival, and then Magnus and I could talk in comfort on our own. Cheered, I got up, and bathed and dressed with a determination to improve upon the morning's mood and abase myself before Vita and the boys.

'Magnus won't be here until after ten,' I shouted down the stairs, 'so there's no food problem. He'll dine on the train. What does everybody want to do?'

'Go sailing,' cried the boys, who were hanging about in the

hall in the customary aimless fashion of all children who are incapable of organizing their own day.

'No wind,' I said, with a rapid glance out of the window on the stairs.

'Then hire a motor boat,' said Vita, emerging from the direction of the kitchen.

I decided to appease them all, and we set forth from Fowey with a picnic lunch and our skipper Tom in charge, this time not in the sailing-boat but in an ex-lifeboat of his own conversion with an honest chug-chug engine that forged along at about five knots and not a centimetre faster. We went east, out of the harbour, and anchored off Lanlivet Bay, where we picnicked, swam, and took our ease, everybody happy. Half a dozen mackerel caught on the homeward journey proved a further delight for Teddy and Micky, and a sop to Vita's culinary plans for the evening meal. The expedition had proved an unqualified success.

'Oh, do say we can come again tomorrow,' pleaded the boys, but Vita, with a glance at me, told them it would depend upon the Professor. I saw their faces fall, and guessed their feelings. What could be more boring than to have to adjust themselves to this possibly stuffy friend of their stepfather's whom instinct told them their mother did not care for anyway?

'You can go with Tom,' I said, 'even if Magnus and I have other plans.' In any event, I thought, a let-out for us, and Vita would hardly allow them to go alone, even in Tom's charge.

We arrived back at Kilmarth about seven o'clock, Vita going immediately to the kitchen to see about the mackerel, while I had a bath and changed. It was not until about ten to eight that I wandered down the front stairs into the dining-room and saw the piece of paper in Mrs Collins' handwriting propped up against the place where I usually sat. It read: 'Telegram came over the phone to say Professor Lane is catching the 2.30 train from London instead of the 4.30. Arriving St Austell 7.30.'

God! Magnus must have been kicking his heels at St Austell station for the last twenty minutes ... I tore into the kitchen.

'Crisis!' I shouted. 'Look at this! I've only just seen it. Magnus caught an earlier train. Why the hell didn't he telephone? What a bloody mess-up!'

Vita, distraught, looked at the half-fried mackerel. 'He'll be here for dinner, then? Good heavens, I can't give him this! I must say it shows very little consideration for us. Surely . . .'

'Of course Magnus will eat mackerel,' I shouted, already half-way down the back stairs. 'Brought up on it, very probably. And we've cheese and fruit. What are you fussing about?'

I tore out to the car, in half-agreement with her immediate reaction that to change his time of arrival, knowing we could easily be out for the day, showed small consideration for his hosts. But that was Magnus. An earlier train had suited his plans and he had caught it. If I arrived late to meet him he would probably take a taxi and pass me en route with a callous wave of the hand.

Ill-luck dogged me to St Austell. Some fool had driven his car into the side of the road, and there was a long queue of traffic waiting to get past. It was a quarter to nine before I drew up at St Austell station. No sign of Magnus, and I did not blame him. The platform was empty, and everywhere seemed to be shut up. Finally I routed out a porter on the other side of the station. He looked vague, and told me that the seven-thirty had been on time.

'I dare say,' I replied. 'That's not the point. The point is I was meeting someone off it, and he isn't here.'

'Well, sir,' he grinned, 'he probably got tired of waiting and took a taxi.'

'If he'd done that,' I said, 'he would have telephoned, or left a message with the chap in the booking office. Were you here when the train came in?'

'No,' he said. 'The booking office will be open again in time for the next down train, due at a quarter to ten.'

'That's no good to me,' I told him, exasperated. Poor devil, it wasn't his fault.

'I tell you what, sir,' he said, 'I'll open it up and see if your friend left a message.'

We went back to the station and laboriously, or so it seemed to me, he fitted a key in the lock and opened the office door. I followed close behind. The first thing I noticed was a suitcase standing against the wall with the initials M.A.L. upon it.

'That's it,' I said, 'that's his case. But why did he leave it here?'

The porter went to the desk and picked up a piece of paper. 'Suitcase with initials M.A.L. handed in by guard on seven-thirty train,' he read, 'to be delivered to gentleman named Mr Richard Young. You Mr Young?'

'Yes,' I said, 'but where's Professor Lane?'

The porter studied the piece of paper. 'Owner of suitcase, Professor Lane, gave message to guard that he had changed his mind and decided to get out at Par and walk from there. Told guard Mr Young would understand.' He handed me the scrap of paper, and I read it for myself.

'I don't understand,' I said, more exasperated than ever. 'I didn't think the London trains stopped at Par these days.'

'They don't,' replied the porter. 'They stop at Bodmin Road, and anyone wanting Par changes there, and gets the connection. That's what your friend must have done.'

'What a bloody silly thing to do,' I said.

The porter laughed. 'Well, it's a fine evening for a walk,' he said, 'and there's no accounting for tastes.'

I thanked him for his trouble and went back to the car, throwing the suitcase on the back seat. Why the hell Magnus should take it into his head to alter every one of our arrangements beat me. He must be at Kilmarth by this time, sitting down to his mackerel supper, making a joke of the affair to Vita and the boys. I drove back at breakneck speed and arrived home just after half-past nine, furiously angry. Vita, changed into a sleeveless frock and with fresh make-up on, appeared from the music-room as I ran up the steps.

'Whatever happened to you both?' she said, the hostess smile of welcome fading as she saw I was alone. 'Where is he?'

'You mean to say he hasn't turned up yet?' I cried.

'Turned up?' she repeated, bewildered. 'Of course he hasn't turned up. You met the train, didn't you?'

'Oh, Jesus! What the hell is going on? Look,' I said wearily, 'Magnus wasn't at St Austell, only his suitcase. He left a message with the guard on the 7.30 train that he'd be getting out at Par and walking here. Don't ask me why. One of his bloody silly ideas. But he should have been here by now.'

I went into the music-room and poured myself a drink and Vita followed, the boys running down to the car to fetch the suitcase.

'Well really,' she said, 'I expected more consideration from your Professor, I must say. First he changes trains, then he changes connections, and finally he doesn't bother to turn up at all. I expect he found a taxi at Par and has gone off to have dinner somewhere.'

'Maybe,' I said, 'but why not telephone to say so?'

'He's your friend, darling, not mine. You're supposed to know his ways. Well, I'm not going to wait any longer, I'm starving.'

The uncooked mackerel was put aside for Magnus's breakfast, though I was pretty sure orange juice and black coffee would be his choice, and Vita and I sat down to a hasty snack of game pie, which she remembered she had brought down from London and had put at the back of the fridge. Meanwhile Teddy rang, or tried to ring, Par station, with no result. They did not answer.

'You know what,' he said, 'the Professor may have been kidnapped by some organization in search of secret documents.'

'Very likely,' I said. 'I'll give him half an hour longer and then ring Scotland Yard.'

'Or had a heart attack,' suggested Micky, 'flogging up Polmear hill. Mrs Collins told me her grandfather died walking up it thirty years ago when he missed the bus.'

I pushed aside my plate and swallowed the last drop of whisky.

'You're perspiring again, darling,' said Vita. 'I can't say I blame you. But don't you think it might be a good idea if you went up and changed your shirt?'

I took the hint and left the dining-room, pausing at the top of the stairs to glance into the spare-room. Why the hell hadn't Magnus telephoned to say what he was doing, or at least written a note instead of giving the guard a verbal message that had probably been garbled anyway? I drew the curtains and switched on the bedside light, which made the room look more snug. Magnus's suitcase was lying on the chair at the bottom of the bed, and I tried the hasps. To my surprise it opened.

Magnus, unlike myself, was a methodical packer. Sky-blue pyjamas and paisley dressing-gown reposed beneath a top layer of tissue paper, with blue leather bedroom slippers in their own cellophane container alongside. A couple of suits, a change of underwear beneath. Well, it was not an hotel or a stately home; he could do his own unpacking. The only gesture from host to guest – or was it the other way round? – would be to place the pyjamas on the pillow and drape the dressing-gown over the chair.

I took both out of the case, and saw that there was a long, buff-cloured envelope immediately beneath them, and typed upon it the words:

'Otto Bodrugan. Writ and Inquisition, 10 October Edward III (1331)'

The student must have been at work again. I sat down on the edge of the bed and opened the envelope. It was a copy of a document giving the names of the various manors and lands owned by Otto Bodrugan at the time of his death. The manor of Bodrugan was amongst them, but he apparently paid rent for it to Joanna, 'Relict of Henry de Campo Arnulphi' (which must be Champernoune). A further paragraph followed: 'Henry his son, aged twenty-one years and more, was his next heir, who died three weeks after his said father, so that he had no seisin in the inheritance aforesaid, nor did he know of his father's death. William, son of the aforesaid Otto, and brother of the said Henry, aged twenty years on the morrow of the feast of St Giles last, is his next heir.'

It was a strange sensation, sitting there on the bed, reading something I already knew. The monks had done their best, or perhaps their worst, for young Henry at the Priory, and he had never been told of his father's death.

There was another long list of properties which Henry, if he had lived, would have inherited from Otto, and then a further note, taken from the Calendar of Fine Rolls.

'10 October. Westminster. 1331. Order to the escheator on this side Trent to take into the King's hand the lands late of Otto de Bodrugan, deceased, tenant-in-chief.'

The student had scribbled PTO at the bottom of the page, and turning over I found a half-page attached, also taken from the Calendar of Fine Rolls, and dated 14 November 1331, from Windsor.

'Order to the escheator on this side Trent to take into the King's hand the lands late of John de Carminowe, deceased, tenant-in-chief. The like to the same touching the lands of Henry son of Otto de Bodrugan.'

So Sir John must have caught the infection he had so greatly feared and died immediately, and Joanna had lost her choice of a second husband. . . .

I forgot the present, forgot the mix-up at the station, and sat there on the spare-room bed thinking about the other world, wondering what advice, if any, Roger had given to the disappointed Joanna Champernoune. The two Bodrugan deaths, with the successor her nephew and a minor, must have given her every hope of greater power over the Bodrugan lands, and just as the power was within her grasp she found the tables turned, and the Keeper of Restormel and Tremerton Castles gone as well. I felt almost sorry for her. And for Sir John, who, luckless fellow, had held his handkerchief to his mouth in vain. Who would take his place as keeper of castles, woods and parks in the county of Cornwall? Not his brother Oliver, I hoped, the bloody murderer . . .

'What are you going to do?' Vita called up the stairs.

Do? What could I do? Oliver had ridden off with his gang of thugs leaving Roger to take care of Isolda. I still did not know what had happened to Isolda. . . .

I heard Vita coming up the stairs, and instinctively I put the papers back in the envelope and stuffed them in my pocket, closing the suitcase. I must switch myself back to the present. This was not the moment to become confused.

'I was just getting out Magnus's pyjamas and dressing-gown,' I said as she came into the room. 'He'll be pretty well fagged out when he does turn up.'

'Why not run his bath for him as well?' she countered. 'And lay a tray for early morning tea? I didn't notice you being so attentive a host to Bill and Diana.'

I ignored the sarcasm and went along to my dressing-room. The murmur of the television came from the library below. 'Time those boys went to bed,' I said, without conviction.

'I promised them they could wait up for the Professor,' said Vita, 'but really I think you're right, there's not much point in their hanging about any longer. Don't you think you ought to drive down to Par? He might be in some pub getting blind to the world.'

'Magnus isn't the type to hang about in pubs.'

'Well then, he must have come across old friends and has been taking dinner off them instead of us.'

'Very unlikely. And damn rude not to telephone,' I replied. We went together down the stairs and into the hall, and I added, 'Anyway, he doesn't have any local friends, to my knowledge.'

Vita suddenly gave a little cry. 'I know,' she said, 'he's met the Carminowes! They haven't got a telephone. That's what's happened. He must have run into them at Par, and they took him back to dine with them.'

I stared at her, my brain confused. What on earth was she talking about? And suddenly I knew. Suddenly the message from the guard came clear and full of meaning. 'Owner of suitcase, Professor Lane, gave message to guard that he had changed his mind and decided to get out at Par, and walk from there. Told guard Mr Young would understand.'

Magnus had taken the local connection from Bodmin Road to Par because it would travel more slowly through the Treesmill valley than the express. He knew, from my description, that he had only to look left and up, after passing above Treesmill Farm, to see the Gratten. Then, because it was still light when the train arrived at Par, he would have walked up the Tywardreath road and cut across the fields to inspect the site.

'God!' I exclaimed. 'What a fool I've been! It never entered my head. Of course that's it.'

'You mean he's gone to see the Carminowes?' said Vita. I suppose I was tired. I suppose I was excited. I suppose I was relieved. All three in one, and I could not bother to explain or think up some different lie. The most natural thing to say just tripped off my tongue.

'Yes,' I replied. I ran down the steps and across the front path to the car.

'But you don't know where they live!' called Vita.

I did not answer. I waved my hand and leapt into the car, and in a moment I was tearing up the drive and out on to the road.

It was quite dark, with only a waning moon that did not help, but I took the short cut up the lane skirting the village, meeting no one on the way, and parked in the lay-by near the house called Hill Crest. If Magnus found the car before I found him he would recognize it, and wait for me. It was hard going across the field to the Gratten, stumbling about amongst the banks and mounds, and I shouted for him, once I was well out of earshot of the house, but he did not answer. I covered the site thoroughly, but there was no sign of him. I walked along the lower path to the valley itself, and down to Treesmill Farm, but he was not there either. Then I walked up the road to the top of the hill and back to the car. It was as I had left it, empty. I drove down into the village, and walked round the churchyard. The hands on the clock-face said after half-past eleven; I had been searching for Magnus for over an hour.

I went to the telephone-box near the hairdresser and dialled Kilmarth. Vita answered immediately. 'Any luck?' she asked.

My heart sank. I had hoped he might have arrived home. 'No, not a trace of him.'

'What about the Carminowes? Did you find their house?'

'No,' I said, 'no, I think we were on the wrong track there. It was stupid of me. Actually, I've no idea where they live.'

'Well, someone must know,' she said. 'Why don't you ask the police?'

'No,' I said, 'it wouldn't do any good. Look, I'll drive down the village to the station and then come slowly home. There's nothing more I can do.'

But Par station appeared to be closed for the night, and though I circled Par itself twice there was no sign of Magnus.

I began to pray, 'Oh, God let me see him walking up Polmear hill!' I knew just how he would look, my headlights picking him up at the side of the road, the tall angular figure with a loping stride, and I would hoot loudly and he would stop, and I would say to him, 'What the bloody hell ...'

He was not there, though. There was no one there. I turned down the Kilmarth drive, and walked slowly up the steps into the house. Vita was waiting for me by the porch. She looked distressed.

'Something must have happened to him,' she said. 'I do think you ought to ring up the police.'

I brushed past her and went upstairs. 'I'll unpack his things,' I said. 'He may have left a note. I don't know ...'

I took his clothes out of the suitcase and hung them in the wardrobe, and put his shaving tackle in the bathroom. I kept telling myself that any moment I should hear a car coming down the drive, a taxi, and Magnus would jump out of it, laughing, and Vita would call up the stairs to me, 'He's here, he's arrived!'

There was no note. I felt in all the pockets. Nothing. Then I turned to the dressing-gown, which I had unpacked already. My hand closed upon something round in the left-hand pocket, and I drew it out. It was a small bottle, which I recognized at once. It bore a label: B. It was the bottle I had posted to him the week before, and it was empty.

sixteen

I went along to my dressing-room, found my own suitcase, put the bottle in one of the pockets and the documents about Bodrugan as well, locked the case and joined Vita downstairs.

'Did you find anything?' she asked.

I shook my head. She followed me into the music-room and I poured myself a whisky. 'You'd better have one too,' I said.

'I don't feel like it,' she answered. She sat down on the sofa and lit a cigarette. 'I'm quite certain we ought to ring the police.'

'Because Magnus has taken it into his head to roam the countryside?' I queried. 'Nonsense, he knows what he's doing. He must know every inch of the district for miles around.'

The clock in the dining-room struck midnight. If Magnus had left the train at Par, he had been walking for four and a half hours . . .

'You go to bed,' I said. 'You look exhausted. I'll stay down here in case he comes. I can lie on the sofa if I feel like it. Then as soon as it's light, if I'm awake and he hasn't arrived, I'll go out in the car and have another search.'

It was true, she looked all-in: I was not trying to get rid of her. She stood up uncertainly, and wandered towards the door. Then she looked back at me, over her shoulder.

'There's something odd about all this,' she said slowly. 'I have a feeling you know more than you say.' I had no ready answer. 'Well, try and get some sleep,' she went on. 'Something tells me you're going to need it.'

I heard the bedroom door shut, and stretched myself out on the sofa with my hands behind my head, trying to think. There were only two solutions. The first, as I had originally imagined, that Magnus had decided to find the Gratten site, and had either lost his way or ricked his ankle, and so decided to wait where he was until daylight; or the second . . . and the second was the one I feared. Magnus had gone on a trip. He had poured the contents of bottle B into some container that could be carried in a coat pocket, and had got out of the train at Par and walked – to the Gratten, to the church, anywhere in the district, and then swallowed the drug and waited . . . waited for it to take effect. Once this had happened he would not be responsible for his actions. If time took him into that other world that we both knew he would not necessarily witness what I had witnessed, the scene could be different, the point in time earlier or later, but the penalty for touching anyone, as he well knew, would be the same for both of us; nausea, vertigo, confusion. Magnus had not, as far as I knew, touched the drug for at least three or four months; he, the inventor, was not prepared and might not have the stamina to endure it as I, the guinea-pig, could.

I closed my eyes and tried to picture him walking away from the station, up the hill and across the fields to the Gratten, and swallowing the drug, laughing to himself. 'I've stolen a march on Dick!' Then the leap backwards in time, and the estuary below, the walls of the house about him, Roger close at hand – leading him where? To what strange encounter on the hills or beside the strand? To what month, what year? Would he see, as I had seen, the faltering ship, dismasted, enter the creek, the horsemen riding on the opposite hill? Would he see Bodrugan drowned? If so, his actions might not be the same as mine. Knowing his taste for the dramatic, he might have flung himself headlong into the river and struck out for that opposite shore – and there would have been no river, only the smothered valley, the scrub, the marsh, the trees. Magnus could be lying there now, in that impassable wasteland, shouting for help, and none to hear. There was nothing I could do. Nothing until daylight came.

I did sleep, after a fashion, waking with a jerk from some distorted dream that instantly faded, to fall off again once more. A deeper sleep must have come with the first light, for I remember looking at my watch at half-past five and telling myself another twenty minutes would not hurt, and then when I opened my eyes again it was ten past seven.

I made a cup of tea, then crept upstairs and washed and shaved. Vita was already awake. She did not even question me. She knew Magnus had not come.

'I'm going to Par station,' I said. 'They'll know if he handed the ticket in. Then I'll try and trace his movements from there. Somebody must have seen him.'

'It would be so much simpler,' she insisted, 'if you went direct to the police.'

'I will go to them,' I said, 'if no one can tell me anything at the station.'

'If you don't,' she called as I left the room, 'I shall ring them up myself.'

I drew a blank at the station: a chap wandering about told me the booking office would not be open for half an hour. I filled in the time by walking up to the bridge that spanned the railway line and gave a view of the valley. Once this would have been wide estuary; Bodrugan's ship, dismasted by the gale, would have drifted past this very spot, driven by wind and tide, seeking shelter up the creek and finding death instead. Today, part reedy marsh, part scrub, it was still easy to trace the original course of the river from the winding valley itself. A man, sick or in some way hurt, might lie beneath those stubby, close-packed trees for days, for weeks, and no one know of it. Even the marsh ground on which the station stood, the wide, flat expanse between Par and neighbouring St Blazey, was still wasteland to a large extent; even here there were large tracks where no one wandered. Except, perhaps, a traveller in time whose mind trod a vessel's deck upon blue water while his body stumbled amongst scrub and ditch.

I returned to the station and found the booking office open, and for the first time proof that Magnus had arrived. The clerk had not only taken his ticket but remembered the holder of it. Tall, he said, going grey, hatless, wearing a sports jacket and dark trousers, with a pleasant smile, and carrying a stick. No, the clerk had not seen which way he had gone after leaving the station.

I got into the car and drove halfway up the hill, to where a footpath went off to the left. Magnus could have taken it, and I did the same, striking across country to the Gratten. It was warm and misty, foretelling a hot day. The farmer the land belonged to must have opened a gate somewhere since the preceding night, because cows wandered on the hillside now, amongst the gorse-bushes and the mounds, following me in curiosity to the entrance of the overgrown quarry itself.

I searched it thoroughly, every corner, every dip, but found nothing. I looked down into the valley below, across the intervening railway line, to the sweeping mass of trees and bushes covering the one-time river bed. They might have been woven tapestry, coloured with silken threads in every shade of golden green. If Magnus was there, nothing would ever find him but tracker dogs.

Then I knew I must do what I should have done earlier, what I should have done last night. I must go to the police. I must go, as any other man would go whose guest had failed to arrive over twelve hours earlier, though his ticket had been given up at the station at the correct time.

I remembered there was a police station at Tywardreath, and I wound my weary way back again and drove straight there. I felt inadequate, guilty, like all persons who have been lucky enough never to have found themselves involved with the police, beyond minor traffic offences, and my story, as I told it to the sergeant, sounded shamefaced, somehow, irresponsible.

'I want to report a missing person,' I said, and instantly had a vision of a poster with the haunted face of a criminal staring from it, and the words 'WANTED' in enormous letters underneath. I pulled myself together, and told the exact story of all that had happened the preceding day.

The sergeant was helpful, sympathetic and extremely kind. 'I haven't had the pleasure of meeting Professor Lane personally,' he said, 'but we know all about him, of course. You must have had a very anxious night.'

'Yes,' I said.

'There's been no report to us of any accident,' he said, 'but of course I will check with Liskeard and St Austell. Would you like a cup of tea, Mr Young?'

I accepted the offer gratefully, while he got busy on the telephone. I had the sick feeling at the pit of my stomach that people get waiting outside a hospital ward during an emergency operation performed on someone they love. It was out of my hands. There was nothing I could do. Presently he came back.

'There's been no report of any accident,' he said. 'They're alerting the patrol cars in the district, and the other police stations. I think the best thing you can do, sir, is to go back to Kilmarth and wait there until you hear from us. It could be that Professor Lane twisted an ankle and spent the night at one of the farms, but they're mostly on the telephone these days, and it's strange he shouldn't have rung you up to let you know. No previous history of loss of memory, I suppose?'

'No,' I told him, 'never. And he was very fit when I dined with him in London a few weeks ago.'

'Well, don't worry too much, sir,' he said, 'there'll probably be some simple explanation at the end of it.'

I went back to the car, the sick feeling with me still, and drove down to the church. I could hear the organ – they must have been having choir practice. I went and sat on one of the graves near the wall above the orchard – Priory orchard once. Where I sat would have been the monks' dormitory, looking south over the Priory creek; and close at hand was the guest-chamber where young Henry Bodrugan had died of smallpox. In that other time he could be dying still. In that other time the monk, Jean, could be mixing some hell-brew that finished off the business, then sending word to Roger that he must carry the news to the mother and the aunt, Joanna Champernoune. Ill-tidings were all about me, in the other world and in my own. Roger, the monk, young Bodrugan, Magnus; we were all links in an interwoven chain, bound one to the other through the centuries.

'In such a night
Medea gather'd the enchanted herbs
That did renew old Aeson.'

Magnus could have sat here and taken the drug. He could have gone to any of the places where I had been. I drove down to the farm where Julian Polpey had lived six centuries ago, and where the postman had found me a week ago, and walked down the farm-track to Lampetho. If I had traversed the marsh at night, my body in the present, my brain in the past, Magnus could have done the same. Even now, with no water and no tide filling the inlet, only meadow-marsh and reeds, the route was familiar, like some scene from a forgotten dream. The track petered out, though, into marsh, and I could see no way forward, no means of crossing the valley to the other side. How I had done it myself at night, following, in that earlier world, Otto and the other conspirators, God only knew. I retraced my footsteps past Lampetho Farm, and an old man came out of one of the buildings, calling to his dog, who ran towards me, barking. He asked if I had lost my way and I told him no, and apologized for trespassing.

'You didn't by any chance see anyone walking this way last night?' I asked. 'A tall man, grey-haired, carrying a stick?'

He shook his head. 'We don't get many visitors coming here,' he said. 'Doesn't lead anywhere, just to this farm. Visitors stay mostly on Par beach.'

I thanked him and walked back to the car. I was not convinced, though. He could have been indoors between half-past eight and nine; Magnus could be lying in the marsh below his farm . . . But surely someone would have seen him? The effect of the drug, if he had taken it, would have worn off hours ago; if he had taken it at half-past eight, or nine, he would have come to by ten, by eleven, by midnight.

There was a police car drawn up outside the house when I arrived, and as I entered the hall I heard Vita say, 'Here's my husband now.'

She was in the music-room with a police officer and a constable.

'I'm afraid we've no definite news for you, Mr Young,' the Inspector said, 'only a slight clue, which may lead us to something. A man answering to the description of Professor Lane was seen last evening between nine and half-past walking along the Stonybridge lane above Treesmill past Trenadlyn Farm.'

'Trenadlyn Farm?' I repeated, and the surprise must have shown in my face, for he said quickly, 'You know it, then?'

'Why, yes,' I said, 'it's much higher up the valley than Treesmill, it's the small farm right on the lane itself.'

'That's right. Have you any idea why Professor Lane should have been walking in that particular direction, Mr Young?'

'No,' I said with hesitation. 'No . . . There was nothing to take him there. I would have expected him to be walking lower down the valley, nearer to Treesmill.'

'Well,' the Inspector replied, 'our information is that a gentleman was seen walking past Trenadlyn between nine and half-past. Mrs Richards, wife of Mr Richards who owns the farm, saw him from her window, but her brother, who farms Great Treverran, higher up the lane, saw no one. If Professor Lane was walking to Kilmarth it seems a long way round, even for someone who wanted exercise after sitting in a train.'

'Yes, I agree, Inspector,' I went on hesitantly, 'Professor Lane is very interested in historical sites, and this may have been the reason for his walk. I think he was looking for an old manor-house which he believes stood there once. But it couldn't have been either of the farms you mentioned, or he would have called at one of them.'

I knew now why Magnus – and it must have been Magnus, from the woman's description – was walking past Trenadlyn on the Stonybridge lane. It was the route Isolda had taken on horse-back with Robbie, when the two of them had come riding down to Treesmill to the creek, to find Bodrugan murdered, drowned. It was the only route to the unknown Tregest when the ford across Treesmill was impassable through flood or high tide. Magnus, when he passed Trenadlyn farm, was walking in time. He could have been following Roger, and Isolda too.

Vita, unable to contain herself, turned to me impulsively. 'Darling, all this historical business is beside the point. Please don't be angry with me for butting in, but I feel it's essential.' She turned to the Inspector. 'I'm quite sure, and so was my husband last night, that the Professor was going to call on some old friends of his, people called Carminowe. Oliver Carminowe is not on the telephone, but he does live somewhere in that district, where the Professor was last seen. It's quite obvious to me that he was on his way to call on them, and the sooner somebody contacts them the better.'

There was a momentary silence after her outburst. Then the Inspector glanced at me. His expression had changed from concern to surprise, even disapproval.

'Is that so, Mr Young? You said nothing about the possibility of Professor Lane visiting friends.'

I felt my mouth flicker in a weak smile. 'No, Inspector,' I

said, 'of course not. There was no question of the Professor visiting anyone. I'm afraid my wife had her leg pulled over the telephone by the Professor, and I very foolishly did nothing to put her wise, but kept up the joke. There are no such people as Carminowe. They don't exist.'

'Don't exist?' echoed Vita. 'But you saw the children riding ponies on Sunday morning, two little girls with their nurse, you told me so.'

'I know I did,' I said, 'but I can only repeat I was pulling your leg.'

She stared at me in disbelief. I could tell, from the expression in her eyes, that she thought I was lying to get Magnus and myself out of an awkward situation. Then she shrugged her shoulders, flicked a rapid glance at the Inspector and lit a cigarette. 'What a very stupid joke,' she said, and added, 'I beg your pardon, Inspector.'

'Don't apologize, Mrs Young,' he said, rather more stiffly, I thought, than before. 'We all get our legs pulled from time to time, especially in the police force.' He turned again to me. 'You're quite certain about that, Mr Young? You know of no one whom Professor Lane might have been calling upon after he arrived at Par station?'

'Absolutely not,' I said. 'As far as I know we are his only friends here, and he was definitely coming to spend the weekend with us. The house belongs to him, as you know. He's lent it to us for the summer holidays. Quite frankly, Inspector, I was not really concerned about Professor Lane until this morning. He knows the district well, for his father, Commander Lane, had this house before him. I was sure he couldn't lose himself, and that he'd turn up with some plausible explanation of where he had been all night.'

'I see,' said the Inspector.

Nobody said anything for a moment, and I had the impression that he doubted my story, just as Vita did, and that they both thought Magnus had been bound on some doubtful assignation and I was covering up for him. Which, indeed, was true.

'I realize now,' I said, 'that I should have got in touch with you last night. Professor Lane must have twisted his ankle, probably shouted for help, and nobody heard. There wouldn't have been much traffic up that side road once it was dark.'

'No,' the Inspector agreed, 'but the people from Trenadlyn and Trevarran would have been astir early this morning, and should have seen or heard something of him by now, if he had had some mishap on the road. More likely he walked up to the main road, and then he could have taken either direction, on towards Lostwithiel or back to Fowey.'

'The name Tregest doesn't convey anything to you?' I asked cautiously.

'Tregest?' The Inspector thought a moment, then shook his head. 'No, I can't say it does. Is it the name of a place?'

'I believe there was a farm of that name once, somewhere in the district. Professor Lane could have been trying to find it, in connection with his historical research.' Then I suddenly had another idea. 'Trelawn,' I said, 'where exactly is Trelawn?'

'Trelawn?' repeated the Inspector, surprised. 'That's an estate a few miles from Looe. Must be eighteen miles or more from here. Professor Lane would surely not start to try to walk there around nine o'clock at night?'

'No,' I said, 'no, of course not. It's just that I'm trying to think of old houses of historical interest.'

'Yes, but, darling,' interrupted Vita, 'as the Inspector says, Magnus would hardly start looking for something of that sort, miles away, without telephoning us first. That's what I can't understand, why he didn't attempt to telephone.'

'He didn't telephone, Mrs Young,' said the Inspector, 'because he apparently thought Mr Young would know where he was going.'

'Yes,' I said, 'and I didn't know. I don't know now. I only wish to God I did.'

The telephone rang with startling suddenness, like an echo to all our thoughts. 'I'll get it,' said Vita, who was nearest to the door. She crossed the hall to the library, and we stood there in the music-room saying nothing, listening to her voice.

'Yes,' she said briefly, 'he is here. I'll get him.'

She came back into the room and told the Inspector that the call was for him. We waited for what seemed an interminable three or four minutes, while he answered in monosyllables, his voice muffled. I looked at my watch. It was just on half-past twelve. I had not realized it was so late. When he returned he looked directly at me, and I saw from the expression on his face that something had happened.

'I'm very sorry, Mr Young,' he said, 'I'm afraid it's bad news.'

'Yes,' I said, 'tell me.'

One is never prepared. One always believes, in moments of acute stress, that things will turn out all right, that even now, with Magnus missing for so long, it would surely be to say that someone had picked him up with loss of memory and taken him to hospital.

Vita came and stood beside me, her hand in mine.

'That was a message from Liskeard police station,' said the Inspector. 'Word has come through that one of our patrols has found the body of a man resembling Professor Lane near the railway line just this side of Trevarran tunnel. He seems to have received a blow on the head from a passing train, unobserved by the driver or the guard. He managed, apparently, to crawl into a small disused hut just above the line, and then he collapsed. It looks as if he must have been dead for some hours.'

I went on standing there, staring at the Inspector. Shock is a peculiar thing, numbing emotion. It was as though life itself had ebbed away, leaving me a shell, like Magnus. I was only aware of Vita holding my hand.

'I understand,' I said, but it was not my voice. 'What do you want me to do?'

'They are on their way to the mortuary in Fowey now, Mr Young,' he said. 'I hate to trouble you at such a moment, but I think it would be best if we took you there right away to identify the body. I should like to think, for both your sakes, yours and Mrs Young's, that it is not Professor Lane, but in the circumstances I can't offer you much hope.'

'No,' I said, 'no, of course not.'

I let go of Vita's hand and walked towards the door and out of the house into the hot sunlight. Some Scouts were putting up tents in the field beyond the Kilmarth meadow. I could hear them shouting and laughing, and hammering the pegs into the ground.

seventeen

The mortuary was a smallish, red-brick building not far from Fowey station. There was nobody there when we arrived: the second patrol car was still on its way. When I got out of the car the Inspector looked at me a moment, and then he said, 'Mr Young, there may be some delay. I'd like to offer you a cup of coffee and a sandwich at the café just up the road.'

'Thank you,' I said, 'but I'm all right.'

'I can't insist,' he continued, 'but it really would be wise. You'll feel the better for it.'

I gave in, and allowed him to lead me along to the café, and we each had some coffee, and I had a ham sandwich too. As we sat there I thought of the times in the past, as undergraduates, when Magnus and I had travelled down by train to Par to stay with his parents at Kilmarth. The rattle in the darkness and the echo of sound in the tunnel, and suddenly that welcome emergence into the light, with green fields on either side. Magnus must have made that journey every school holiday as a boy. Now he had met his death by the entrance to that same tunnel.

It would make sense to no one. Not to the police, or to his many friends, or to anyone but myself. I should be asked why a man of his intelligence had wandered close to a railway line on a summer's evening at dusk, and I should have to say that I did not know. I did know. Magnus was walking in a time when no railway line existed. He was walking in an age when the hillside was rough pasture, even scrub. There was no gaping tunnel mouth yawning from the hillside in that other world, no metal lines, no track, only the bare grassland, and perhaps a man astride a pony, leading him on . . .

'Yes?' I said.

The Inspector was asking me if Professor Lane had any relatives.

'I'm sorry,' I said, 'I didn't hear what you said. No, Commander and Mrs Lane have been dead for a number of years, and there were no other children. I've never heard him mention cousins or anyone.'

There must be a lawyer somewhere who dealt with his affairs, a bank which managed his finances: now I came to think of it

I did not even know his secretary's name. Our relationship, binding, intimate, did not concern itself with day-to-day matters, with ordinary concerns. There must be someone other than myself who would know about all this.

Presently the constable came to tell the Inspector that the second patrol car had arrived, and the ambulance too, and we walked back to the mortuary. The constable murmured something which I did not hear, and the Inspector turned to me.

'Dr Powell from Fowey happened to be at Tywardreath police station when the message came through from our patrol,' he said, 'and he agreed to make a preliminary examination of the body. Then it will be up to the Coroner's pathologist to conduct the post-mortem.'

'Yes,' I said. Post-mortem . . . inquest . . . the whole paraphernalia of the law.

I went into the mortuary. The first person I saw was the doctor I had met at the lay-by, who had watched me recovering from my attack of vertigo over ten days ago. I saw the instant recognition in his eyes, but he did not let on when the Inspector introduced us.

'I'm sorry about this,' he said, and then, abruptly, 'If you haven't seen anyone before who's been badly smashed up in an accident, let alone a friend, it's not a pleasant sight. This man has had a great gash on the head.'

He took me to the stretcher lying on the long table. It was Magnus, but he looked different – smaller, somehow. There was a sort of cavity caked with blood above his right eye. There was dried blood on his jacket, which was torn, and a tear in one of his trouser legs.

'Yes,' I said, 'yes, that is Professor Lane.'

I turned away, because Magnus himself wasn't there. He was still walking in the fields above the Treesmill valley, or looking about him, in great wonder, in some other undiscovered world.

'If it's any consolation to you,' said the doctor, 'he couldn't have lived very long after receiving a blow like that. God knows how he managed to crawl the few yards to the hut – he wouldn't have been conscious of his movements, he would have died literally a few moments afterwards.'

Nothing was a consolation, but I thanked him all the same.

'You mean,' I said, 'he would not have lain there, wondering why nobody came?'

'No,' he answered, 'definitely not. But I'm sure the Inspector will let you have the full details, as soon as we know the extent of the injuries.'

There was a walking-stick lying at the end of the table. The sergeant pointed it out to the Inspector. 'The stick was lying halfway down the embankment, sir,' he said, 'a short distance from the hut.'

The Inspector looked inquiringly at me, and I nodded. 'Yes,' I said, 'it's one of many he had. His father collected walking-sticks; there are about a dozen in his flat in London.'

'I think the best thing to do now is for us to run you straight back to Kilmarth, Mr Young,' said the Inspector. 'You'll be kept fully informed, of course. You realize that you will be required to give evidence at the inquest.'

'Yes,' I said. I wondered what would happen to Magnus's body after the post-mortem. I wondered if it was going to lie there through the weekend. Not that it mattered. Not that anything mattered.

As the Inspector shook hands he said that they would probably come out on Monday and ask me a few more questions, in case I could add to my original statement. 'You see, Mr Young,' he explained, 'there might be a question of amnesia, or even suicide.'

'Amnesia,' I repeated. 'That's loss of memory, isn't it? Most unlikely. And suicide, definitely no. The Professor was the last man in the world to do such a thing, and he had no cause. He was looking forward to the weekend, and was in very good spirits when I spoke to him on the telephone.'

'Quite so,' said the Inspector. 'Well, that's just the sort of statement the Coroner will want to have from you.'

The constable dropped me at the house, and I walked very slowly through the garden and up the steps. I poured out the equivalent of a triple whisky, and flung myself on the divan bed in the dressing-room. I must have passed out shortly afterwards, for when I woke up it was late afternoon or early evening, and Vita was sitting on the chair nearby with a book in her hands, the last of the sun coming through the western window that gave on to the patio.

'What's the time?' I asked.

'About half-after six,' she said, and came and sat on the bed beside me.

'I thought it wisest to let you lie,' she went on. 'The doctor who saw you at the mortuary telephoned during the afternoon, and asked if you were all right, and I told him you were sleeping. He said to let you sleep as long as possible, it was the best thing that could happen.' She put her hand in mine and it was comforting, like being a child again.

'What did you do with the boys?' I asked. 'The house seems very quiet.'

'Mrs Collins was wonderful,' she said. 'She took them down to Polkerris to spend the day with her. Her husband was going to take them fishing after lunch and bring them back about seven. They'll be home any moment now.'

I was silent a moment, and then I said, 'This mustn't spoil their holiday, Magnus would have hated that.'

'Don't bother about them or me,' she said. 'We can take care of ourselves. What worries me is the shock it's been for you.'

I was thankful she did not pursue the subject, go over the whole business again – why it had happened, what Magnus had been doing, why he did not notice the approaching train, why the driver had not seen him; it would have led us nowhere.

'I ought to get on the telephone,' I said. 'The people at the university should be told.'

'The nice Inspector is taking care of all of that,' she said. 'He came back again, quite soon after you must have gone upstairs. He asked to see Magnus's suitcase. I told him you'd unpacked it last night and hadn't found anything. He didn't either. He left the clothes hanging in the closet.'

I remembered the bottle in my own suitcase, and the papers about Bodrugan. 'What else did he want?'

'Nothing. Just said to leave everything to them, and he'd be in touch with you on Monday.'

I put out my arms and pulled her down to me. 'Thanks for everything, darling,' I said. 'You're a great comfort. I can't really think straight yet.'

'Don't try,' she whispered. 'I wish there was more I could say, or do.'

We heard the boys talking together in their room. They must

have come in by the back entrance. 'I'll go to them,' said Vita, 'they'll want some supper. Would you like me to bring yours up here?'

'No, I'll come down. I'll have to face them some time.'

I went on lying there awhile, watching the last of the sun filtering through the trees. Then I had a bath and changed. Despite the shock and the turmoil of the day my bloodshot eye was back to normal. The trouble may have been coincidental, nothing to do with the drug. In any event it was something, now, that I should never know.

Vita was giving the boys their supper in the kitchen. I could hear what they were saying as I hovered in the hall, bracing myself before I went in.

'Well, I bet you anything you like it turns out to be foul play.' Teddy's rather high-pitched, nasal voice came clearly through the open kitchen door. 'It stands to reason the Professor had some secret scientific information on him, probably to do with germ warfare, and he'd arranged to meet someone near that tunnel, and the man he met was a spy and knocked him on the head. The police down here won't think of that, and they'll have to bring in the Secret Service.'

'Don't be idiotic, Teddy,' said Vita sharply. 'That's just the sort of frightful way rumours spread. It would upset Dick terribly to hear you say things like that. I hope you didn't suggest such a thing to Mr Collins.'

'Mr Collins thought of it first,' chimed in Micky. 'He said you never knew what scientists were up to these days, and the Professor might have been looking for a site for a hush-hush research station up the Treesmill valley.'

This conversation had the instant effect of pulling me together. I thought how Magnus would have loved it, played up to it, too, encouraged every exaggeration. I coughed loudly and went towards the kitchen, hearing Vita say 'Ssh . . .' as I passed through the door.

The boys looked up, their small faces taking on the expression of shy discomfort that children wear when suddenly confronted with what they fear to be an adult plunged in grief.

'Hullo,' I said. 'Had a good day?'

'Not bad,' mumbled Teddy, turning red. 'We went fishing.'

'Catch anything?'

'A few whiting. Mom's cooking them now.'

'Well, if you've any to spare, I'll stand in the queue. I had a cup of coffee and a sandwich in Fowey, and that's been my lot for the day.'

They must have expected me to stand with bowed head and shaking shoulders, for they cheered visibly when I attacked a large wasp on the window with the fly-swatter, saying 'Got him!' with enormous relish as I squashed it flat. Later, when we were eating, I said to them, 'I may be a bit tied up next week because they'll have to hold an inquest on Magnus, and there'll be various things to attend to, but I'll see to it that you go out with Tom in one of his boats from Fowey, engine or sailing, whichever you like best.'

'Oh, thanks awfully,' said Teddy, and Micky, realizing that the subject of Magnus was no longer taboo, paused, his mouth full of whiting, and enquired brightly, 'Will the Professor's life story be on TV tonight?'

'I shouldn't think so,' I replied. 'It's not as if he were a pop-singer or a politician.'

'Bad luck,' he said. 'Still, we'd better watch just in case.'

There was nothing, much to the disappointment of both boys, and secretly, I suspected, of Vita too, but to my own considerable relief. I knew the next few days would bring more than enough in the way of publicity, once the press got hold of the story, and so it proved. The telephone started ringing first thing the following morning, although it was Sunday, and either Vita or I spent most of the day answering it. Finally we left it off the hook and installed ourselves on the patio, where reporters, if they rang the front-door bell, would never find us.

The next morning she took the boys into Par to do some shopping, leaving me to my mail, which I had not opened. The few letters I had were nothing to do with the disaster. Then I picked up the last of the small pile and saw, with a queer stab of the heart, that it was addressed to me in pencil, bore an Exeter postmark, and was in Magnus's handwriting. I tore it open.

'Dear Dick,' I read, 'I'm writing this in the train, and it will probably be illegible. If I find a post-box handy on Exeter station I'll drop it in. There is probably no need to write at all, and by the time you receive it on Saturday morning we shall have had, I trust, an uproarious evening together with many more to come, but I write as a safety-measure, in case I pass out in the carriage from sheer exuberance of spirits. My findings to date are pretty conclusive that we are on to something of prime importance regarding the brain. Briefly, and in layman's language, the chemistry within the brain cells concerned with memory, everything we have done from infancy onwards, is reproducible, returnable, for want of a better term, in these same cells, the exact contents of which depends upon our hereditary make-up, the legacy of parents, grandparents, remoter ancestors back to primeval times. The fact that I am a genius and you are a lay-about depends solely upon the messages transmitted to us from these cells and then distributed through the various other cells and throughout our body, but, our various characteristics apart, the particular cells I have been working upon – which I will call the memory-box – store not only our own memories but habits of the earlier brain pattern we inherit. These habits, if released to consciousness, would enable us to see, hear, become cognoscent of things that happened in the past, not because any particular ancestor witnessed any particular scene, but because with the use of a medium – in this case a drug – the inherited, older brain pattern takes over and becomes dominant. The implications from a historian's point of view don't concern me, but, biologically, the potential uses of the hitherto untapped ancestral brain are of enormous interest, and open immeasurable possibilities.

'As to the drug itself, yes, it's dangerous, and could be lethal if taken to excess, and should it fall into the hands of the unscrupulous it might bring even more havoc upon our already troubled world. So, dear boy, if anything happens to me, destroy what remains in Bluebeard's chamber. My staff – who, however, know nothing of the implications of my discovery, for I have been working on this on my own – have similar instructions here in London, and can be trusted implicitly. As to yourself, if I don't see you again, forget the whole business. If we meet this evening as arranged, and take a walk and perhaps a trip together, as I hope we shall, I intend to have a close look, if I have the luck, at the beautiful Isolda, who, from the evidence in the document at the top of my suitcase, appears to have lost her lover just as you said, and must be in dire need of consolation. Whether Roger Kylmerth can supply it we may discover at the same time. No time to say any more, we are drawing into Exeter. A bientôt, in this world, or the other, or hereafter.
'Magnus'

If we had not gone sailing on the Friday I should have found the telephone message about the earlier train in time . . . If I had made straight for the Gratten after leaving St Austell station, instead of going home. . . . Too many 'ifs', and none of them working out. Even this letter, coming now like a message from the dead, should have reached me on Saturday morning instead of today, Monday. Not that it would have done any good. Nor did it say anything about Magnus's real intentions. Even then, as he posted it, he may not have made up his mind. The letter was a safety-measure, as he said, in case anything went wrong. I read it through again, once, twice, then put my lighter to it and watched it burn.

I went down to the basement and through the old kitchen to the lab. I had not entered it since early Wednesday morning, after returning from the Gratten, when Bill had come downstairs and found me making tea in the kitchen. The rows of jars and bottles, the monkey's head, the embryo kittens and the fungus plants held no menace for me now, nor had they done so since the first experiment. Now, with their magician gone, never to return, they had a wasted, almost a forlorn appearance, like puppets and props from a conjurer's bag of tricks. No ebony wand would bring these things to life, no cunning hand extract the juices, pick the bones and set them fermenting in some bubbling cauldron brew.

I took the jars which held various liquids and poured the contents down the sink. Then I washed the jars out and put them back on the shelf. They could have been used for preserving fruit or jam, for all anybody would ever know; there were no distinctive marks upon them – only labels which I stripped off and pocketed. Then I fetched an old sack which I remembered seeing in the boiler-house, and set about unscrewing the remaining jars and bottles that contained the embryos and the monkey's head. I put them all in the sack, having first poured down the sink the liquid that had preserved them, taking care that none of it touched my hands. I did the same with the various fungi, putting them also in the sack. Only two small bottles remained, bottle A, containing the remains of the drugs I had been using myself to date, and bottle C, untouched. Bottle B I had sent to Magnus, and it was lying empty in my suitcase upstairs. I did not pour the contents of either down the sink. I put them in my pocket. Then I went to the door and listened. Mrs Collins was moving about between the kitchen and the pantry – I could hear her radio going.

I swung the sack over my shoulder and locked the door of the lab. Then I went out through the back door and climbed up to the kitchen garden behind the stable block, and into the wood at the top of the grounds. I went to where the undergrowth was thickest – straggling laurels, rhododendrons that had not bloomed for years, broken branches of dead trees, brambles, nettles, the fallen leaves of successive autumn gales – and I took one of the dead branches and scraped a pit in the wet, dank earth and emptied the sack into it, smashing the monkey's head with a jagged stone so that it no longer bore any resemblance to a living thing, only fragments, only jelly, and the embryos slithered amongst the fragments, unrecognizable, like the stringy entrails flung to a seagull when a fish is gutted. I covered them, and the sack, with the rotting leaves of years, and the brown earth, and a heap of nettles, and the sentence came into my mind, 'Ashes to ashes, dust to dust', and in a sense it was as if I were burying Magnus and his work as well.

I went back into the house, through the basement, and up the little side-stairway to the front, thus avoiding Mrs Collins, but she must have heard me entering the hall, for she called, 'Is that you, Mr Young?'

'Yes,' I said.

'I looked for you everywhere – I couldn't find you. The Inspector from Liskeard was on the telephone.'

'I was in the garden,' I told her. 'I'll ring him back.'

I went upstairs to the dressing-room, and put bottles A and C in my suitcase along with the empty bottle B, locked it once again, put the key on my ring, washed, and went downstairs to the library. Then I put a call through to the police station at St Austell.

'I'm sorry, Inspector,' I said, when they got him on the line. 'I was in the garden when you telephoned.'

'That's all right, Mr Young,' he said. 'I thought you would like to know the news to date. Well, we've made some headway. It was a freight train that caused the accident, that seems to be clearly established. It passed through Treverran tunnel, going up the line, at approximately ten minutes to ten. The driver saw no one near the line as he approached the tunnel, but these freight trains are sometimes of considerable length, and this one carried no guard in the rear, so that once the engine had entered the tunnel there would be no one to observe whether anybody came on to the line and was struck by one of the passing wagons.'

'No,' I said, 'no, I appreciate that. And you think this is what happened?'

'Well, Mr Young, everything points to it. It would seem as though Professor Lane must have continued up the lane past Trenadlyn Farm, but before he got to the main road he turned off into a field they call Higher Gum, well above Treverran, and crossed it in a diagonal direction towards the railway. It is possible, by climbing through the wire and scrambling up a bank, to get on to the line, but anyone doing so could not have failed to notice the freight train. It was dark, of course, but there is a signal just outside the tunnel, and a freight train is far from silent, quite apart from the warning hoot of the diesel engine, which is routine procedure before entering the tunnel.'

Yes, but six centuries ago there were no signals, no wire, no lines, no warning hoots sounding on the air . . .

'You mean,' I said, 'that anyone would have to be blind or stone-deaf not to be aware of a train coming up that valley, even when it is some distance off?'

'Well yes, Mr Young. Of course, it is possible to stand at the side of the line as the train goes by – there is plenty of room on either side of the double tracks – and it would seem that this was what Professor Lane did. We have found marks on the ground where he slipped, and up the bank where he dragged himself to the hut.'

I thought a moment, and then I said, 'Inspector, would it be possible for me to go and see the exact spot myself?'

'As a matter of fact, Mr Young, it was what I was going to suggest, but I was not sure how you would feel about it. It could be helpful, not only to you but to us.'

'Then I'm ready whenever you are.'

'Shall we say eleven-thirty outside the police station at Tywardreath?'

It was already eleven. I was backing my car out of the garage when Vita came down the drive in the Buick with the boys. They scrambled out, clutching baskets filled with provisions.

'Where are you going?' asked Vita.

'The Inspector wants me to see the spot near the tunnel where they found Magnus,' I told her. 'They think they know what did it – a freight train that passed there around ten minutes to ten. The driver would already have been in the tunnel when Magnus walked, or slipped, into one of the rear wagons.'

'Run along,' said Vita sharply to both boys, who were hovering. 'Take those things up to Mrs Collins,' and when they were out of earshot, 'But why should Magnus have been on the line? It makes no sense at all. You know what people are going to say? I heard it in one of the shops, and I felt dreadful . . . That it must have been suicide.'

'Complete and utter drivel,' I said.

'Well, I know. . . . But when anyone is well known, and there is a disaster, there's always such talk. And scientists are supposed to be peculiar anyway, borderline cases.'

'So are we all,' I said, 'ex-publishers, policemen, the lot. Don't wait lunch – I don't know when I'll be back.'

The Inspector took me to the site he had described over the telephone on the lane above Treverran farm. On the way he told me that they had got in touch with the senior man on Magnus's staff, who had been unable to throw any light on the disaster.

'He was very upset, naturally,' the Inspector went on. 'He knew Professor Lane was intending to spend the weekend with you, and was looking forward to it. He concurred with you in stating that the Professor was in perfect health and excellent spirits. Incidentally, he did not seem to be aware of his interest in historical sites, but agreed that it could undoubtedly be a private hobby.'

We took the Treesmill road out of Tywardreath and turned right at the Stonybridge lane, past Trenadlyn and Treverran, and drew up near the top of the lane, parking beside a gate leading into a field.

'What is difficult to understand,' observed the Inspector, 'is why, if Treverran Farm was the place that interested Professor Lane, he did not call there, instead of walking across these fields some distance above the farm.'

I threw a quick glance around me. Treverran was to the left, above the valley but in a dip, with the railway running below it; and beyond the railway line itself the land sloped down again. Centuries ago the contour of the land would have been the same, but a broad stream would have run through the valley below Treverran Farm, more than a stream, a river, which in high autumn spate would flood the low-lying ground before it entered the waters of Treesmill creek.

'Is there a stream there still?' I asked, pointing to the valley base.

'Still?' repeated the Inspector, puzzled. 'There is a ditch at the bottom of the hill, below the railway – you might call it a stream, rather sluggish – and the ground is marshy.'

We walked down the field. The railway was already in sight, and just to the right of us was the ominous tunnel-mouth.

'There might have been a road here once,' I said, 'descending to the valley, and a ford across the stream to the other side.'

'Possibly,' the Inspector said. 'Not much sign of one now, though.'

Magnus wanted to ford the stream. Magnus was following someone on horseback who was going to ford the stream. Therefore he moved swiftly. And it was not a summer's evening at dusk on a clear night: it was autumn, and the wind was blowing, and the rain was coming in gusts across the hills . . .

We descended the field to the railway embankment, close to the tunnel. A short distance to the left there was an archway under the line, forming a passage between one field and another. A number of cattle were standing here, under the arch, seeking shelter from the flies.

'You see,' said the Inspector, 'there's no need for the farmer or anyone to cross the line to get to the opposite field. They can go through the passageway there, where those cattle are standing.'

'Yes,' I said, 'but the Professor might not have noticed it, if he was walking higher up the field. It would be more direct to cross the line itself.'

'What, climb the embankment, get through the wire, and scramble down the bank on to the line?' he said. 'And in the darkness too? I shouldn't care to try it myself.'

In point of fact, it was what we did right then, in broad daylight. He led the way, I followed, and once over the wire he pointed to the disused hut, covered with ivy, a few yards higher up the embankment, just above the line.

'The undergrowth is beaten down because we were here yesterday,' he told me, 'but Professor Lane's tracks were plain enough, where he dragged himself clear of the line and up to the hut; semi-conscious as he must have been, it showed almost superhuman strength and tremendous courage.'

Which world had surrounded Magnus, the present or the

past? Had the freight train rattled towards the tunnel unobserved, as he scrambled down the bank on to the line? With the engine already in the tunnel did he make to cross the line, which in his vision was grass-meadow still, sloping down to the stream below, and so was struck by the swinging wagon? In either world, it was the *coup de grâce*. He could not have known what hit him. The instinct for survival made him crawl towards the hut, and then, please God, merciful oblivion, no sudden loneliness, no knowledge of imminent death.

We stood there, staring into the empty hut, and the Inspector showed me the spot on the earthen floor where Magnus had died. The place was impersonal, without atmosphere, like some forgotten toolshed with the gardener long gone.

'It hasn't been used for years,' he said. 'The gangs working on the line used to brew tea here, and eat their pasties. They use the other hut lower down now, and that not often.'

We turned away, retracing our footsteps along the overgrown bank to the strands of sagging wire through which we had climbed. I looked across to the opposite hills, some of them thickly wooded. There was a farm to the left, with a smaller building above it, and away to the north another cluster of buildings. I asked their names. The farm was Colwith, and the smaller building had been a schoolhouse once. The third, almost out of sight, was another farm, Strickstenton.

'We're on the borders of three parishes here,' the Inspector said, 'Tywardreath, St Sampsons or Golant, and Lanlivery. Mr Kendall of Pelyn is a big landowner hereabouts. Now that's a fine old manor house for you, Pelyn, just down the main road on the way to Lostwithiel. Been in the family for centuries.'

'How many centuries?'

'Well, Mr Young, I'm no expert. Four, maybe?'

Pelyn could not turn itself into Tregest. None of the names fitted Tregest. Somewhere here, though, within walking distance, Magnus had been following Roger to Oliver Carminowe's dwelling, whether it was manor-house or farm.

'Inspector,' I said, 'even now, despite all you've shown me, I believe Professor Lane intended to find the head of the stream somewhere in the valley, and cross it to the other side.'

'With what object, Mr Young?' He looked at me, not unsympathetic but frankly curious, trying to see my point of view.

'If you get bitten by the past,' I said, 'whether you're a historian, or an archaeologist, or even a surveyor, it's like a fever in the blood; you never rest content until you've solved the problem before you. I believe that Professor Lane had one object in mind, and that was why he decided to get off at Par rather than St Austell. He was determined to walk up this valley, for some reason which we shall probably never discover, despite the railway line.'

'And stood there, with the train passing, and then walked into the rear?'

'Inspector, I don't know. His hearing was good, his eyesight was good, he loved life. He didn't walk into the back of the train deliberately.'

'I hope you'll convince the Coroner, Mr Young, for Professor Lane's sake. You almost convince me.'

'Almost?' I asked.

'I'm a policeman, Mr Young, and there's a piece missing somewhere; but I agree with you, we shall probably never find it.'

We retraced our steps up the long field to the gate at the top of the hill. As we drove back I asked him if he had any idea how long it would be before the inquest was held.

'I can't tell you exactly,' he answered. 'A number of factors are involved. The Coroner will do his best to expedite matters, but it may be ten days or a fortnight, especially as the Coroner is bound to sit with a jury, in view of the unusual circumstances of the death. By the way, the pathologist for the area is on holiday, and the Coroner asked Dr Powell if he would perform the autopsy, as he had already examined the body. The doctor agreed. We should have his report some time today.'

I thought of the many times Magnus had dissected animals, birds, plants, bringing to his work a cool detachment which I admired. He suggested once that I should watch him remove the organs of a newly-slaughtered pig. I stood it for five minutes, and then my stomach turned. If anyone had to dissect Magnus now, I was glad it was Dr Powell.

We arrived at the police station just as the constable came down the steps. He said something to the Inspector, who turned to me.

'We've finished the examination of Professor Lane's clothes and effects,' he said. 'We are prepared to hand them over to you if you are willing to accept the responsibility.'

'Certainly,' I replied. 'I doubt if anyone else will claim them. I'm hoping to hear from his lawyer, whoever he may be.'

The constable returned in a few minutes with a brown paper parcel. The wallet was separate, lying on the top, and a paperback he must have bought to read in the train, *Some Experiences of an Irish RM* by Somerville and Ross. Anything less conducive to a sudden brainstorm or attempted suicide I could not imagine.

'I hope,' I said to the Inspector, 'you've noted down the title of the book for the Coroner's attention.'

He assured me gravely that he had already done so. I knew I should never open the paper parcel, but I was glad to have the wallet and the stick.

I drove back to Kilmarth feeling tired, dispirited, no nearer to a conclusion. Before I turned off the main road I stopped on the crown of Polmear hill to let a car pass. I recognized the driver – it was Dr Powell. He pulled in at the side of the road by the grass verge, and I did the same. Then he got out and came to my window.

'Hello,' he said. 'How are you feeling?'

'All right,' I told him. 'I've just been out to Treverran tunnel with the Inspector.'

'Oh, yes,' he said. 'Did he tell you I'd done the post-mortem?'

'Yes,' I said.

'My report goes to the Coroner,' he went on, 'and you'll know about it in due course. But, unofficially, you would probably like to know that it was the blow on the head that killed Professor Lane, causing extensive haemorrhage to the brain. There were other injuries too, due to falling; there's no doubt he must have walked slap into one of the wagons on the freight train.'

'Thank you,' I said. 'It's good of you to tell me personally.'

'Well,' he said, 'you were his friend, and the most directly concerned. Just one other thing. I had to send the contents of the stomach away for analysis. A matter of routine, actually. Just to satisfy the Coroner and jury he wasn't loaded with whisky or anything else at the time.'

'Yes,' I said, 'yes, of course.'

'Well, that's about it,' he said. 'I'll see you in Court.'

He returned to his own car, and I went slowly down the drive to Kilmarth. Magnus drank sparingly in the middle of the day. He could conceivably have had a gin and tonic on the train. Possibly a cup of tea during the afternoon. This much, I supposed, would show up in analysis. What else?

I found Vita and the boys already at lunch. There had been a series of telephone calls throughout the morning, including one from Magnus's lawyer, a man called Dench, and Bill and Diana from Ireland, who had heard the news over the radio.

'It's going to be endless,' said Vita. 'Did the Inspector say anything about the inquest?'

'Probably not for ten days or a fortnight,' I told her.

'Not much holiday for us,' she sighed.

The boys went out of the room to collect their next course and she turned to me, her face anxious. 'I didn't say anything in front of them,' she said in a low voice, 'but Bill was aghast at the news, not just because it was such a tragedy anyway, but because he wondered if there was anything awful behind it. He wasn't specific, but he said you'd know what he meant.'

I laid down my knife and fork. 'Bill said what?'

'He was rather mysterious,' she said, 'but is it true you told him about some gang of thugs in the neighbourhood who were going about attacking people? He hoped you had told the police.'

It only needed that, and Bill's ham-fisted, misplaced efforts to help, to put us all in trouble.

'He's crazy,' I said shortly. 'I never told him anything of the sort.'

'Oh,' she said, 'oh, well ...' and then she added, her face still troubled, 'I do hope you *have* told the Inspector everything you know.'

The boys came back into the dining-room and we finished the meal in silence. Afterwards I took the paper parcel, the wallet and the walking-stick up to the spare-room. Somehow they seemed to belong there, with the rest of the things hanging in the wardrobe. I would use the stick myself; it was the last thing that Magnus had ever held in his hands.

I remembered the collection at the flat. There had been a gun-stick and a sword-stick, a stick with a telescope at one end, and another with a bird's head on the handle. This one was comparatively simple, with the usual silver knob on top, engraved with Commander Lane's initials. He had been the originator of the craze for family walking-sticks, and vaguely I had a recollection of him showing me this particular example, long ago, when I was staying at Kilmarth. It contained some gadget, I had forgotten what, but by pressing the knob down a spring was released. I tried it; nothing happened. I tried it again and then twisted the knob, and something clicked. I unwound the knob and it came away in my hands, and revealed a minute silver-lined measure, just large enough to hold a half-dram of spirit or other liquid. The measure had been wiped clean, probably by a tissue thrown away or buried, when Magnus set off upon his last walk, but I knew now, with absolute certainty, what it must have contained.

eighteen

The lawyer, Herbert Dench, telephoned again during the afternoon, and expressed great shock at his client's sudden death. I told him that the inquest was not likely to be for ten days or a fortnight, and suggested that he should leave the funeral arrangements to me, coming down himself on the morning of the cremation. This suited him, greatly to my relief, for he sounded what Vita called a 'stuffed shirt', and with luck would have the tact to return by an afternoon train, which meant that he wouldn't be on our hands for more than a couple of hours or so.

'I would not trespass upon your time at all, Mr Young,' he said, 'were it not out of respect for the late Professor Lane and the unhappy circumstances of his death, and for the fact that you are a beneficiary under his will.'

'Oh,' I said, rather taken aback, 'I had not realized . . .' and hoped it would be the walking-sticks.

'It is something I would prefer not to discuss over the telephone,' he added.

It was not until I had put down the receiver that I realized I was in a somewhat awkward position, living in Magnus's house rent-free by verbal agreement. It might be the lawyer's intention to kick us out in the shortest possible time, immediately after the inquest, perhaps. The thought stunned me. Surely he would not do such a thing? I would offer to pay rent, of course, but he might bring up some objection, and say the place must be shut up, or handed over to agents prior to a sale. I was depressed and shaken enough, without the prospect of a sudden move to make things worse.

I spent the rest of the afternoon on the telephone, arranging about the funeral, after checking with the police that it was in order to go ahead, and finally ringing back the lawyer to tell him what I had arranged. None of it seemed to have anything to do with Magnus. What the undertaker did, what happened in the meantime to his body, the whole paraphernalia of death before committal to the flames, did not concern the man who had been my friend. It was as though he had become part of that separate world I knew, the world of Roger, of Isolda.

Vita came into the library when I had finished telephoning. I was sitting at Magnus's desk by the window, staring out to sea.

'Darling,' she said, 'I've been thinking,' and she came and stood behind me, putting her hands on my shoulders. 'When the inquest is over, don't you think it would be best if we went away? It would be rather awkward for us to go on staying here, and sad for you, and in a way the whole point of it has gone, hasn't it?'

'What point?' I asked.

'Well, the loan of the house, now Magnus is dead. I can't help feeling an interloper, and that we've really no right to be here. Surely it would be much more sensible if we spent the rest of the holidays somewhere else? It's only the beginning of August. Bill was saying over the telephone how lovely Ireland is; they've found a delightful hotel in Connemara, some old castle or other, with its own private fishing.'

'I bet he has,' I said. 'Twenty guineas a night, and full of your compatriots.'

'Don't be unfair! He was just trying to be helpful. He took it for granted you would want to get away from here.'

'Well, I don't,' I said. 'Not unless the lawyer kicks us out, and that's a different matter.'

I told her that the cremation was fixed for Thursday, and that

Dench would be coming down, and perhaps some of Magnus's staff as well. The prospect of guests for lunch or dinner, or even the night, took her mind off the longer-term suggestion of Ireland, but as it turned out we were spared the worst of it, for Dench and Magnus's senior assistant, John Willis, elected to travel down together through the Wednesday night, attend the cremation, accept our hospitality for lunch, and return to London by a night-train. The boys were sent off for the whole of Thursday for a fishing expedition in charge of the obliging Tom.

I remember little of the cremation service, beyond thinking how Magnus might have devised a simpler method of disposing of the dead by chemicals instead of by fire. Our companions in mourning, Herbert Dench and John Willis, were quite unlike what I had imagined. The lawyer was big, hearty, unpompous, ate an enormous lunch, and regaled us while we consumed our funeral meats with stories of Hindu widows committing suttee on their husbands' pyres. He had been born in India, and swore he had witnessed such a sacrifice as a babe in arms.

John Willis was a little mouse-like man, with intent eyes behind horn-rimmed spectacles, who would not have looked out of place behind a bank's grille; I could not picture him at Magnus's elbow, ministering to live monkeys or dissecting their brain cells. He barely uttered. Not that this signified, for the lawyer spoke enough for all.

Lunch over, we walked through to the library, and Herbert Dench bent to his dispatch case for a formal reading of the will, in which apparently John Willis figured as well as I. Vita, tactfully, was about to withdraw, but the lawyer told her to stay.

'No necessity for that, Mrs Young,' he said cheerfully. It's very short and to the point.'

He was right. Legal language apart, Magnus had left whatever financial assets he possessed at the time of his death to his own college for the advancement of biophysics. His flat in London and his personal effects there were to be sold, and the money given to the same cause, with the exception of his library, which he bequeathed to John Willis in gratitude for ten years of professional cooperation and personal friendship. Kilmarth, with all its contents, he left to me, for my own use or to dispose of, as I wished, in memory of years of friendship dating back to undergraduate days, and because the former occupants of the house would have wished it so. And that was all.

'I take it,' said the lawyer, smiling, 'that by the former occupants he is referring to his parents, Commander and Mrs Lane, whom I believe you knew?'

'Yes,' I said, bewildered, 'yes, I was very fond of them both.'

'Well, there we are. It's a delightful house. I hope you will be very happy here.'

I looked at Vita. She was lighting a cigarette, her usual defence in a moment of sudden shock. 'How . . . how extraordinarily generous of the Professor,' she said. 'I really don't know what to say. Of course it's up to Dick whether he intends to keep it or not. Our future plans are in a state of flux at present.'

There was a moment's awkward silence, as Herbert Dench looked from one to the other of us.

'Naturally,' he said, 'you will have a great deal to discuss together. You realize, of course, that the house and contents will have to be valued for probate. I would appreciate it if I could see over it, by the way, if it wouldn't be too much trouble?'

'Why, of course.'

We all rose to our feet, and Vita said, 'The Professor had a laboratory in the basement, a most alarming place – at least, so my small sons thought. I suppose the things there would hardly go with the house but should be returned to his laboratory in London? Perhaps Mr Willis would know what they are.'

Her face was all innocence, but I had the impression that her mention of the laboratory was deliberate, and she wanted to know what was there.

'A laboratory?' queried the lawyer. 'Did the Professor do any work down here?' He addressed himself to Willis.

The little mouselike man blinked behind his horn-rimmed spectacles. 'I very much doubt it,' he said with diffidence, 'and, if he did, it would be of little scientific importance, and have no connection with his work in London. He may have made a few experiments, just to amuse himself on a rainy day – certainly nothing more, or he would have mentioned it to me.'

Good man. If he knew anything he was not going to commit himself. I could see that Vita was on the point of saying I had told her the contents of the laboratory were of inestimable value, so I suggested that we should inspect the laboratory before visiting the rest of the house.

'Come along,' I said to Willis, 'you're the expert. The room used to be an old laundry in Commander Lane's day, and Magnus kept a lot of bottles and jars in it.'

He looked at me, but said nothing. We all trooped down to the basement, and I opened the door.

'There you are,' I said. 'Nothing very exciting. Just a lot of old jars, as I told you.'

Vita's face was a study as she looked around her. Amazement, disbelief, and then a swift glance of inquiry at me. No monkey's head, no embryo kittens, only the empty rows of bottles. She had the supreme intelligence to remain silent.

'Well, well,' said the lawyer, 'the valuer might put a price of sixpence apiece on the jars. What do you say, Willis?'

The biophysicist ventured a smile. 'I would think,' he said, 'that Professor Lane's mother may have preserved fruit here in former days.'

'A still-room, didn't they call them?' laughed the lawyer. 'The still-room maid would make preserves for the whole year. Look at the hooks in the ceiling! They probably hung the meat here too. Great sides of ham. Well, Mrs Young, this will be your province, not your husband's. I recommend an electric washing-machine in the corner to save your laundry bills. Expensive to install, but it will pay for itself in a couple of years, with a young family.'

He turned, still laughing, back into the passage, and we followed. I locked the door behind me. Willis, who was hovering in the rear, bent to pick up something from the stone floor. It was a label from one of the jars. He gave it to me without a word, and I put it in my pocket. Then we tramped upstairs to inspect the remainder of the house, Herbert Dench making the remarkable suggestion that if we wanted to turn the property into an investment we might split the whole place up into flat-lets for summer visitors, keeping for our own use the bedroom suite with the view of the sea. He was still extolling the idea to Vita as we wandered round the garden. I saw Willis glance at his watch.

'You must have had about enough of us,' he said. 'I told Dench on the way down that we would call in at Divisional Headquarters at Liskeard and answer any questions the police might want to put to us. If you'd telephone for a taxi we could go there straight away, and have dinner in Liskeard later before catching the night train.'

'I'll drive you myself,' I said. 'Hold on, there's something I want to show you.' I went upstairs, and after a few minutes came back with the walking-stick. 'This was near Magnus's body. It belongs with the others in the London flat. Do you think they will let me keep it?'

'Surely,' he said, 'and the other sticks too. I'm so glad you've got this house, by the way, and I hope you won't part with it.'

'I don't intend to.'

Vita and Dench were still a short distance off on the terrace.

'I think,' said Willis quietly, 'we had better tell more or less the same story at the inquest. Magnus was an enthusiastic walker, and if he wanted some exercise after hours in the train it was typical of him.'

'Yes,' I said.

'Incidentally, a young friend of mine, a student, has been looking up historical stuff for Magnus at the BM and the Public Record Office. Do you want him to continue?'

I hesitated. 'It might be useful. Yes . . . If he turns anything up ask him to send it to me here.'

'I'll do that.'

I noticed for the first time an expression of loss, of emptiness, behind the horn-rimmed spectacles.

'What are your own plans?' I asked.

'I shall go on just the same, I suppose,' he said. 'Try to carry on something of Magnus's work. But it will be tough going. As boss and colleague he will be irreplaceable. You probably realize that.'

'I do.'

The others came up, and nothing further was said between Willis and myself. After a cup of tea, which none of us wanted but Vita insisted on getting, Willis suggested the move to Liskeard. I knew now why Magnus had chosen him as senior member of his staff. Professional competence apart, loyalty and discretion were the qualities behind that mouse-like appearance.

Once we were in the car, Dench asked if we might cover part of the route Magnus had taken on the Friday night. I drove them along the Stonybridge lane past Treverran farm and up to the gate near the top of the hill, and pointed across the fields down to the tunnel.

'Incredible,' Dench murmured, 'quite incredible. And dark, too, at the time. I don't like it, you know.'

'How do you mean?' I asked.

'Well, if it doesn't make sense to me it won't to the Coroner, or to the jury. They're bound to see something behind it.'

'What sort of thing?'

'Some sort of compulsion to get to that tunnel. And once he found it we know what happened.'

'I don't agree,' said Willis. 'As you say, it was dark at the time, or nearly dark. The tunnel wouldn't have shown up from here, or the line either. I believe he had the idea to go down into the valley, perhaps take a look at that farmhouse from the other side, and when he got to the bottom of the field the railway viaduct interfered with his view. He scrambled up the bank to find out the lie of the land, and the train hit him.'

'It's possible. But what an extraordinary thing to do.'

'Extraordinary to the legal mind,' said Willis, 'but not to Professor Lane. He was an explorer in every sense of the word.'

After I had landed them safely at the police headquarters I turned back for home. Home . . . The word had a new significance. It was my home now. The place belonged to me, as it had once belonged to Magnus. The strain that had been upon me through the day began to lift, and the weight of depression, too. Magnus was dead; I should never see him again, never hear his voice, rejoice in his company or be aware of his presence in the background of my life, but the link between us would never be broken because the home that had been his was mine. Therefore I could not lose him. Therefore I should not be alone.

I passed the entrance to Boconnoc, which in that other time had been Bockenod, before descending the hill to Lostwithiel, and thought of poor Sir John Carminowe, already infected with the dreaded smallpox, riding beside Joanna Champernoune's clumsy chariot on that windy October night in 1331, to die a month later, having enjoyed his position as Keeper of Restormel and Tremerton Castles for barely seven months. On the other side of Lostwithiel I took the road to Treesmill, so that I could have a closer view of the farms situated on the opposite side of the valley from the railway. Strickstenton was on the left-hand side of the narrow road, and, from the brief glimpse I had from the car, of considerable age, and what a tourist brochure would describe as 'picturesque'. The pasture land belonging to it sloped downwards to a wood.

Once I was out of sight of the house I got out of the car and looked across to the railway on the other side of the valley. The tunnel showed up plainly, and even as I watched a train emerged like a straggling snake, yellow-headed, evil, and wound its way below Treverran Farm and disappeared down to the lower valley. The freight train that had killed Magnus had appeared from the opposite direction, climbing the rising ground and vanishing into the tunnel, a reptile seeking cover in the underworld, as Magnus, who had neither seen nor heard it, dragged himself, dying, to the hut above. I drove on down the twisting lane, noting on my left the turning which, I judged, led past Colwith Farm to the bottom of the valley and what remained of the original river stream. At some time, before the railway cut into the land, there would have been a track leading from Great Treverran across the valley to its smaller neighbour, Little Treverran. Either farm might be the Tregest of the Carminowes.

I went on down to Treesmill, and up the hill to the callbox in Tywardreath. I dialled the Kilmarth number, and Vita answered.

'Darling,' I said, 'it seems rather rude to leave Dench and Willis on their own in Liskeard, so I think I'll hang around until they have finished with the police, and then have dinner with them.'

'Oh well,' she said, 'if you must. But don't be late. No need to wait for the train.'

'Probably not,' I told her. 'It depends how much there is to discuss.'

'All right. I'll expect you when I see you.'

I rang off, and returned to the car. Then I drove back again to Treesmill and up the twisting lane, and this time took the turning that led to Colwith. The lane went on, past the farm, as I had thought it would, becoming steeper, and finally petered out in a small water-splash at the bottom of the hill. To the left, across a cattle-grid, was a narrow entrance to Little Treverran. The buildings themselves were out of sight, but a board with lettering on it said: 'W. P. Kelly. Woodworker.'

I risked the water-splash and parked the car, out of sight of the lane, in the field beyond, close to a line of trees and only a few hundred yards from the railway.

I looked at my watch. It was a little after five. I opened the boot of the car and took out the walking-stick, which I had primed, in the dressing-room, with the last of bottle A, before showing it to John Willis in the library.

nineteen

It was snowing. The soft flakes fell upon my head and my hands, and the world all about me was suddenly white, no lush green summer grass, no line of trees, and the snow fell steadily, blotting the hills from sight. There were no farm-buildings anywhere near me – nothing but the black river, about twenty foot broad where I was standing, and the snow, which had drifted high on either bank, only to slither into the water as the mass caved in from the weight, revealing the muddied earth beneath. It was bitter cold; not the swift, cutting blast that sweeps across high ground, but the dank chill of a valley where winter sunshine does not penetrate, nor cleansing wind. The silence was the more deadly, for the river rippled past me without sound, and the stunted willows and alder growing beside it looked like mutes with outstretched arms, grotesquely shapeless because of the burden of snow they bore upon their limbs. And all the while the soft flakes fell, descending from a pall of sky that merged with the white land beneath.

My mind, usually clear when I had taken the drug, was stupefied, baffled; I had expected something akin to the autumn day that I remembered from the previous time, when Bodrugan had been drowned, and Roger carried the dripping body in his arms towards Isolda. Now I was alone, without a guide; only the river at my feet told me I was in the valley.

I followed its course upstream, groping like a blind man, knowing by instinct that if I kept the river on my left I must be moving north, and that somewhere the strip of water would narrow, the banks would close, and I should find a bridge or ford to take me to the other side. I had never felt more helpless or lost. Time, in this other world, had hitherto been calculated by the height of the sun in the sky, or, as when I traversed the Lampetho valley at night, by the stars overhead; but now, in this silence and beneath the falling snow, there was no means of gauging whether it was morning or afternoon. I was lost, not in the present, with familiar landmarks close at hand, the reassuring presence of the car, but in the past.

The first sound broke the silence, a splash in the river ahead, and moving swiftly I saw an otter dive from the further bank and swim his way upstream. As he did so a dog followed him, and then a second, and immediately there were some half-dozen of them yelping and crying at the river's brink, splashing their way into the water in chase of the otter. Someone shouted, the shout taken up by another, and a group of men came running towards the river through the falling snow, shouting, laughing, encouraging the dogs, and I saw they were coming from a belt of trees just beyond me, where the river curved. Two of them scrambled down the bank into the water, thrashing it with their sticks, and a third, holding a long whip, cracked it in the air, stinging the ear of one of the dogs still crouching on the bank, which plunged after its companions.

I drew nearer, to watch them, and saw how the river narrowed a hundred yards or so beyond, while on the left, at the entrance to a copse of trees, the land fell away and the stream formed a sheet of water like a miniature lake, a film of ice upon its surface.

Somehow the men and the dogs, between them, drove the hunted otter into the gulley that fed the lake, and in a moment they were upon him, the dogs crying, the men thrashing with their sticks. The dogs floundered as the ice cracked, the surface crimsoned, and blood spattered the film of white above black water as the otter, seized between snapping jaws, was dragged from the hole he sought, and torn to pieces where the ice held firm.

The lake can have held little depth, for the men, hallooing and calling to the dogs, strode forward on to it, careless of the crack appearing suddenly from one end to the other. Foremost among them was the man with the long whip, who stood out from his fellows because of his height, and his dress as well, a padded surcoat buttoned to the throat and a high beaver hat upon his head, shaped like a cone.

'Drive them clear,' he shouted, 'to the bank on the further side. I'd as soon lose the lot of you as one of these,' and bending suddenly, amongst the pack of yelping hounds, he lifted what remained of the otter from the midst of them and flung it across the lake to the snow-covered verge. The dogs, baulked of their prey, struggled and slid across the ice to retrieve it where it now lay, while the men, less nimble than the animals, and hampered by their clothing, floundered and splashed in the breaking ice, shouting, cursing, jerkins and hoods caked white with the falling snowflakes.

The scene was part brutal, part macabre, for the man with the conical hat, once he knew his hounds were safe, turned his attention, laughing, to his companions in misfortune. While he himself was wet now to the thigh, he at least had boots to protect his feet, while his attendants, as I supposed they were, had some of them lost their shoes when the ice broke, and were thrashing about with frozen hands in useless search of them. Their master, laughing still, regained the bank, and, lifting his conical hat a moment, shook the snowflakes clear before replacing it once more. I recognized the ruddy face and the long jaw, although he was some twenty feet away. It was Oliver Carminowe.

He was staring hard in my direction, and although reason told me he could not see me, and I had no part in his world, the way he stood there, motionless, his head turned towards me, disregarding his grumbling attendants, gave me a strange feeling of unease, almost of fear.

'If you want to have speech with me, come across and say so,' he called. The shock of what I thought discovery sent me forward to the lake's edge, and then, with relief, I saw Roger standing beside me to become, as it were, my spokesman and my cover. How long he had been there I did not know. He must have walked behind me along the riverbank.

'Greetings to you, Sir Oliver!' he cried. 'The drifts are shoulder-high above Treesmill, and your side of the valley too, so Rob Rosgof's widow told me at the ferry. I wondered how you fared, and the lady Isolda too.'

'We fare well enough,' answered the other, 'with food enough to last a siege of several weeks, which God forbid. The wind may change within a day or two and bring us rain. Then, if the road does not flood, we shall leave for Carminowe. As to my lady, she stays in her chamber half the day sulking, and gives me little of her company.' He spoke contemptuously, watching Roger all the while, who moved nearer to the riverbank. 'Whether she follows me to Carminowe is her concern,' he continued. 'My daughters are obedient to my will, if she is not. Joanna is already promised to John Petyt of Ardeva, and, although a child still, prinks and preens before the glass as if she were already a bride of fourteen years and ripe for her strapping husband. You may tell her godmother Lady Champernoune so, with my respects. She may wish a like fortune for herself before many years have passed.' He burst out laughing, and then, pointing to the hounds scavenging beneath the trees, said, 'If you have no fear of fording the river where the plank has rotted, I will find an otter's paw which you may present to Lady Champernoune with my compliments. It may remind her of her brother Otto, being wet and bloody, and she can nail it on the walls of Trelawn as a memento to his name. The other paw I will deliver to my own lady for a similar purpose, unless the dogs have swallowed it.'

He turned his back and walked towards the trees, calling to his hounds, while Roger, moving forward up the river bank, and I beside him, came to a rough bridge, made out of lengths of log bound together, the whole slippery with the fallen snow, and partly sagging in the water. Oliver Carminowe and his attendants stood watching as Roger set foot upon the rotting bridge, and when it collapsed beneath his weight and he slipped and fell, soaking himself above his thighs, they roared in unison, expecting to see him turn again and claw the bank. But he strode on, the water coming nearly to his waist, and reached the other side, while I, dry-shod, followed in his wake. He walked directly to the edge of the copse where Carminowe stood, whip in hand, and said, 'I will deliver the otter's paw, if you will give it to me.'

I thought he would receive a lash from the whip across his face, and I believe he expected the same himself, but Carminowe, smiling, his whip raised, lashed suddenly amongst the dogs instead, and whipping them from the torn body of the otter took the knife from his belt, and cut off two of the remaining paws.

'You have more stomach than my steward at Carminowe,' he said. 'I respect you for that, if for nothing else. Here, take the paw, and hang it in your kitchen at Kylmerth, amongst the silver pots and platters you have doubtless stolen from the Priory. But first walk up the hill with us and pay your respects to Lady Carminowe in person. She may prefer a man, once in a while, to the tame squirrel she occupies her days with.'

Roger took the paw from him and put it in his pouch, saying nothing, and we entered the copse and began threading our way through the snow-laden trees, walking steadily uphill, but whether to right or left I had no idea, having lost all sense of direction, knowing only that the river was behind us and the snow was falling still.

A track packed high with snow on either side led to a stone-built house, tucked snugly against the hill; and, while Carmi-nowe's attendants still straggled in our rear, he himself kicked open the door before us and we entered a square hall, to be greeted at once by the house-dogs, fawning upon him, and the two children, Joanna and Margaret, whom I had last seen riding their ponies across the Treesmill ford on a summer's afternoon. A third, somewhat older than the others, about sixteen, whom I took for one of Carminowe's daughters by his first marriage, stood smiling by the hearth, nor did she embrace him, but pouted with a sort of petulant grace when she saw he was not alone.

'My ward, Sybell, who seeks to teach my children better man-ners than their mother,' Carminowe said.

The steward bowed and turned to the two children, who, after having kissed their father, came to welcome him. The elder, Joanna, had grown, and showed some sign of dawning self-consciousness, as her father had said, by blushing, and tossing her long hair out of her eyes, and giggling, but the younger, with still some years to go before she too ripened for the mar-riage-market, struck out her small hand to Roger and smote him on the knee.

'You promised me a new pony when last we met,' she said, 'and a whip like your brother Robbie's. I'll have no truck with a man who fails to keep his word.'

'The pony awaits you, and the whip too,' answered Roger gravely, 'if Alice will bring you across the valley when the snow melts.'

'Alice has left us,' replied the child. 'We have her to mind us now,' and she pointed a disdainful finger at the ward Sybell, 'and she's too grand to ride pillion behind you or Robbie.'

She looked so much like her mother as she spoke that I loved her for it, and Roger must have seen the likeness too, for he smiled and touched her hair, but her father, irritated, told the child sharply to hold her tongue or he would send her supperless to bed.

'Here, dry yourself by the fire,' he said abruptly, kicking the dogs out of the way, 'and you, Joanna, warn your mother the steward has crossed the valley from Tywardreath and has a message from his mistress, if she cares to receive him.'

He took the remaining otter's paw from his surcoat and dangled it in front of Sybell. 'Shall we give it to Isolda, or will you wear it to keep you warm?' he teased. 'It will soon dry, furry and soft, inside your kirtle, the nearest thing to a man's hand on a cold night.'

She shrieked in affectation and backed away, while he pursued her, laughing, and I saw by the expression in Roger's eyes that he had fully grasped the relationship between guardian and ward. The snow might remain upon the hills for days or weeks; there was little at the moment to tempt the master of this establishment back to Carminowe.

'My mother will see you, Roger,' said Joanna, returning to the hall, and we crossed a passageway into the room beyond.

Isolda was standing by the window, watching the falling snow, while a small red squirrel, a bell around its neck, squatted upon its haunches at her feet, pawing at her gown. As we entered she turned and stared, and although to my prejudiced eyes she looked as beautiful as ever I realized, shocked, that she had become much thinner, paler, and there was a white streak in the front of her golden hair.

'I am glad to see you, Roger,' she said. 'There have been few encounters between our households of late, and we are seldom here at Tregest these days, as you know well. How is my cousin? You have a message from her?'

Her voice that I remembered, clear and hard, defiant, almost, had become flat, toneless. Then, sensing that Roger wished to speak to her in private, she told her daughter Joanna to leave them alone.

'I bear no message, my lady,' said Roger quietly. 'The family are at Trelawn, or were, when I last had word. I came out of respect for you, Rob Rosgof's widow having told me you were here, and were not well.'

'I'm as well as I ever shall be,' she answered, 'and whether here or at Carminowe the days are much the same.'

'That's ill-spoken, my lady,' said Roger. 'You showed more spirit once.'

'Once, yes,' she replied, 'but I was younger then . . . I came and went as I pleased, for Sir Oliver was more frequently at Westminster. Now, whether from malice through not obtaining Sir John's position as Keeper of the King's forests and parks in Cornwall, as he hoped, he wastes his days keeping women instead. The present fancy is hardly more than a child. You have seen Sybell?'

'I have, my lady.'

'It's true she is his ward. If I should die it would be convenient to both of them, for he could marry her and install her at Carminowe in all legality.'

She stooped to pick up the pet squirrel at her feet, and, smiling for the first time since we had come into the small room, which was as sparsely furnished as a nun's cell, she said, 'This is my confidante now. He takes hazel nuts from my hand and regards me wisely all the while with his bright eyes.' Then, serious once more, she added, 'I am kept prisoner, you know, both here and when we are at Carminowe. I am prevented even from sending word to my brother Sir William Ferrers at Bere, who is told by his wife that I have gone out of my mind and am therefore dangerous. They all believe it. Sick in body, indeed, I have been, and in pain, but so far it has not sent me mad.'

Roger moved silently to the door, opened it, and listened. There was still the sound of laughter from the hall: the otter's paw continued to cause diversion. He closed the door again.

'Whether Sir William believes it or not I cannot say,' he said, 'but talk of your illness there has been, and for some months. That is why I have come, my lady, to prove it a lie for myself, and now I know it to be so.'

Isolda, with the squirrel in her arms, might have been her small daughter Margaret as she looked at the steward steadily, weighing in the balance his trustworthiness.

'I did not like you once,' she said. 'You had too shrewd an

eye, casting about you for your own advantage, and, because it suited you to serve a woman rather than a man, you let my cousin Sir Henry Champernoune die.'

'My lady,' said Roger, 'he was mortally sick. He would have died anyway within a few weeks.'

'Perhaps, but the way he went showed undue haste. It taught me one thing – to beware of potions brewed by a French monk. Sir Oliver will seek to rid himself of me by other methods, a dagger's thrust or strangulation. He won't wait for nature to put an end to me.' She dropped the squirrel on the floor and, moving to the window, looked out once more at the still falling snow. 'Before he does,' she said, 'I'll rather take myself outdoors and perish. With the country covered as it is today I'd freeze the sooner. How about it, Roger? Carry me in a sack upon your back and cast me somewhere at the cliff's edge? I'd thank you for it.'

She meant it as a joke, if somewhat twisted, but crossing to the window beside her he stared up at the pall of sky and pursed his lips in a soundless whistle.

'It could be done, my lady,' he said, 'if you had the courage.'

'I have the courage if you have the means,' she replied.

They stared at one another, an idea suddenly taking root in both their minds, and she said swiftly, 'If I went from here, and thence to my brother's at Bere, Sir Oliver would not dare to follow me, for he could never sustain his lies about my sick mind. But in this weather the roads would be impassable. I could not reach Devon.'

'Not immediately,' he said, 'but once the roads are fit it could be done.'

'Where would you hide me?' she asked. 'He has only to cross the valley to search the Champernoune demesne above Trees-mill.'

'Let him do so,' answered Roger. 'He would find it barred and empty, with my lady at Trelawn. There are other hiding-places, if you cared to trust yourself to me.'

'Such as where?'

'My own house, Kylmerth. Robbie is there, and my sister Bess. It's nothing but a rough farm, but you are welcome to it, until the weather mends.'

She said nothing for a moment, and I could see, by the expression in her eyes, that she still had some lingering doubt of his integrity.

'It's a question of choice,' she said. 'To stay here a prisoner, at the mercy of my husband's whim, who can hardly wait to rid himself of a wife who is a lasting reproach, and an encumbrance too, or throw myself on your hospitality, which you may deny when it pleases you to do so.'

'It will not please me,' he answered, 'nor will it ever be denied, until you say the word yourself.'

She looked out once again at the falling snow and the slowly darkening sky, which foretold not only worsening weather to come but the approach of evening and all the hazards of a winter's night.

'I am ready,' she said, and throwing open a chest against the wall drew out a hooded cloak, a woollen kirtle, and a pair of leather shoes that must surely never have seen service out of doors except thrust into a covering bag when she rode side-saddle.

'My own daughter Joanna, who overtops me now, climbed from this same window a week ago,' she said, 'after a wager with Margaret that she had grown too fat. I am thin enough, in all conscience. What do you say? Do I lack spirit now?'

'You never lacked it, my lady,' he answered, 'only the spur to prick you to endeavour. You know the wood below your pastureland?'

'I should,' she said. 'I rode in it most days when I was free to do so.'

'Then lock your door, after I have left the room, climb from the window, and make your way to it. I will see that the track is deserted and the household all within, and will tell Sir Oliver that you dismissed me and wish to be alone.'

'And the children? Joanna will be aping Sybell, as she has done continually these past weeks, but Margaret . . .' she paused, her courage ebbing. 'Once I lose Margaret, there is nothing left.'

'Only your will to live,' he said. 'If you keep that, you keep all things. And your children too.'

'Go quickly,' she said, 'before I change my mind.'

As we left the room I heard her lock the door, and looking at Roger I wondered if he knew what he had done, urging her to risk her life and her future in an escapade that must surely fail.

The house had grown silent. We walked along the passage to the hall and found it empty, except for the two children and the dogs. Joanna was pirouetting before the looking-glass, her long hair dressed in braids with a ribbon threaded through it which had, a short time before, been on Sybell's head; while Margaret sat astride a bench, her father's conical hat upon her head and his long whip in her hand. She looked at Roger severely when he entered.

'Observe now,' she said, 'I am obliged to make do with a bench for a horse and borrowed plumage for equipment. I'll not remind you of your failings again, my master.'

'Nor shall you have to,' he told her. 'I know my duty. Where is your father?'

'He's above,' answered the child. 'He cut his finger severing the otter's paw, and Sybell is dressing it for him.'

'He'll not thank you to disturb him,' said Joanna. 'He likes to sleep before he dines, and Sybell sings to him. It makes him drop off the sooner and wake with better appetite. Or so he says.'

'I do not doubt it,' replied Roger. 'In that event, please thank Sir Oliver for me and bid him good-night. Your mother is tired and does not wish to see anyone. Perhaps you will tell him so?'

'I may,' said Joanna, 'if I remember.'

'I'll tell him,' said Margaret, 'and wake him too, if he does not descend by six o'clock. Last night we dined at seven, and I can't abide late hours.'

Roger wished them both good-night and, opening the hall-door, stepped outside, closing it softly behind him. He stole round to the back of the house and listened. There were sounds coming from the kitchen-quarters, but windows and doors were fastened tight, and the shutters barred. The hounds were yelping from outbuildings in the rear. It would be dark within half an hour or even less; already the copse below the field was dim, shrouded by the pall of snow, and the opposite hills were bleak and bare under the grey sky. The tracks we had made ascending to the house were almost blotted out by the fresh-fallen snow, but beside them were new prints, closer together, like those of a child who, hurrying for shelter, runs like a dancer upon her toes. Roger covered them with his own long stride, disturbing the ground, kicking the snow in front of him as he walked rapidly downhill towards the copse; and now if anyone should venture forth before darkness came they would see nothing but the tracks he had made himself, and those would be blotted too within the hour.

She was waiting for us by the entrance to the wood, carrying her pet squirrel, her cloak drawn close around her and her hood fastened under her chin. But her long gown, which she had tried to fasten up under the belted cloak, had slipped down again below her ankles and hung about her feet like a dripping valance. She was smiling, the smile her daughter Margaret would have worn had she too set forth on some adventure, with the promise of a pony at the end of it instead of a bleak unknown.

'I dressed my pillow in my night-attire,' she said, 'and heaped the covers over it. It may fool them for a while, should they break down the door.'

'Give me your hand,' he said. 'Disregard your skirts and let them trail. Bess will find warm clothes for you at home.'

She laughed and put her hand in his, and as she did so I felt as if it were in mine as well, and that the pair of us were lifting, dragging her through the fallen snow, and he was no longer a steward bound in the service of another woman and I a phantom from a later world, but both of us were men sharing a common purpose and a common love that neither of us, in his time or mine, would ever dare make plain.

When we came to the river and the rotten bridge that lay half-broken in mid-stream he said to her, 'You must trust me once again and let me carry you across, as I would your daughter.'

'But if you let me fall,' she answered, 'I will not clout you about the head, as Margaret would.'

He laughed, and bore her safely to the other side, once more soaking himself nearly to the waist. We went on walking through the little line of stunted, shrouded trees, the silence all about us no longer ominous, as it had been when I walked alone, but hushed with a sort of magic, and a strange excitement too.

'The snow will be thicker in the valley around Treverran,' he said, 'and if Ric Treverran should see us he might not hold his tongue. Have you breath enough left to strike out into the open and climb the hill to the track above? Robbie awaits me there with the ponies. You shall choose which of us you please to ride behind. I am the more cautious.'

'Then I choose Robbie,' she said. 'Tonight I bid farewell to caution, and for ever.'

We turned left and began to climb the hill out of the valley, the river behind us, the snow reaching above the knees of my companions with every step, making progress laborious and slow.

'Wait,' he said, letting go her hand, 'there may be a drift ahead before we strike the path,' and he plunged upwards, sweeping the snow aside with both his hands, so that for a moment, as he walked on alone to higher ground, I was left with her, and could stare for a brief instant at the small, pale, resolute face beneath the hood.

'All's well,' he called. 'The snow is firmer here. I'll come and fetch you.'

I watched him turn and advance, half-sliding down the slope towards her, and it seemed to me suddenly that two men were moving there, not one, and both of them were holding out their hands to help her climb. It must be Robbie, having heard his brother's voice, who had come down from the track above.

Some instinct warned me not to move, not to climb, but to let her go alone and grasp their hands. She went from me and I lost sight of her, and of Roger, and of the third shadowy figure too, in a sudden great pall of snow that blotted all of them from sight. I stood there, shaking, the strands of wire between me and the line, and it was not snow that blanketed the opposite hills and the high bank, but the grey canvas hangings looped to the wagons of the freight train as it rattled and lumbered through the tunnel.

twenty

Self-preservation is common to all living things, linked perhaps to that older brain which Magnus said forms part of our natural inheritance. Certainly in my own case instinct transmitted a danger signal; had it not done so I should have died as he did, through the same cause. I remember stumbling blindly away from the railway embankment to the protection of the passageway where the cattle had sheltered, and I heard the wagons thunder over my head as they passed down the line into the valley. Then I crossed a hedge and found myself in a field behind Little Treverran, home of the woodworker, and so on to the field where I had left the car.

There was no nausea, no vertigo, the instinct to 'awake' had spared me this as well as my life, but as I sat huddled behind the wheel, still shaking all over, I wondered whether, had Magnus and I ventured forth together on that Friday night, there would have been what the reporters like to term a double tragedy. Or would both of us have survived? It would never now be proved; the opportunity for us to wander together in another time had gone for ever. One thing I knew, which no one else would ever know, and that was why he had died. He had stretched out his hand to help Isolda in the snow. If instinct had warned him otherwise he had disregarded it, unlike myself, and therefore showed the greater courage.

It was after half-past seven when I started the car, and as I drove over the water-splash I still did not know how far I had walked during the excursion to the other world, or which farm or former site had proved to be Tregest. Somehow it no longer mattered. Isolda had escaped, and on that winter's night of 1332, or '33, perhaps even later, had been bound for Kilmarth; whether she reached it or not I might discover. Not now, nor tomorrow, but one day . . . My immediate purpose must be to conserve my strength and mental alertness for the inquest, and above all watch out for the after-effects of the drug. It would not do to appear in Court with a couple of bloodshot eyes and an inexplicable sweating sickness, especially with Dr Powell's experienced eye upon me.

I had no desire for food, and when I arrived home at about half-past eight, having parked the car at the top of the hill to while away the time, I called to Vita that we had all dined early at the hotel in Liskeard, and I was dead-beat and wanted to go to bed. She and the boys were eating in the kitchen, and I went straight upstairs without disturbing them, and put away the walking-stick in the dressing-room cupboard. I knew now, to the fullest extent, what it felt like to lead what is called a 'double life'. The walking-stick, the bottles locked in the suitcase, were like keys to some woman's flat, to be used when opportunity offered; but more tempting still, and more insidious, was the secret knowledge that the woman herself might be under my own roof, even now, tonight, in her own time.

I lay in bed, my hands behind my head, wondering how Robbie and the wild-haired sister Bess received their unexpected visitor. First warm clothes for Isolda, and food before the smoky hearth, the youngsters tongue-tied in her presence, Roger playing host; then groping her way to bed up that ladder to one of the straw-filled mattresses, hearing the cattle moving and stamping in the byre beneath her. Sleep might come early, through exhaustion, but it would more likely be late, because of the strangeness of everything about her, and because she would be thinking about her children, wondering whether she would see them again.

I shut my eyes, trying to picture that dark, cold loft. It would correspond in position, surely, to the small back bedroom above the basement, used in other days by Mrs Lane's unfortunate cook, and filled today with discarded trunks and cardboard boxes. How near to Roger in the kitchen below, how unattainable, both then and now!

'Darling . . .'

It was Vita bending over me, fantasy and confusion combining to make her other than she was, and when I pulled her down beside me it was not the living woman and my wife whom I held but the phantom one I sought and who I knew, in reality and the present, never could respond. Presently, when I opened my eyes – for I must have dozed off for a while – she was sitting on the stool before the dressing-table, smothering her face with cream.

'Well,' she said smiling, looking at me in the glass, 'if that's the way you celebrate your inheritance of this place I'm all for it.'

The towel, wrapped turban-fashion round her head, and the mask of cream gave her a clown-like appearance, and suddenly I felt revolted by the puppet world in which I found myself, and desired no part of it, neither now, nor tomorrow, nor at any time. I wanted to vomit. I got out of bed and said, 'I'm going to sleep in the dressing-room.'

She stared at me, her eyes like holes in the mask. 'What on earth's the matter?' she said. 'What have I done?'

'You've done nothing,' I told her. 'I want to sleep alone.'

I went through the bathroom to the dressing-room and she followed me, the silly shift she wore in bed flouncing round her knees, grotesquely ill-suited to the turban; and it struck me for the first time that the varnish on her fingernails made her hands like claws.

'I don't believe you've been with those men at all,' she said. 'You left them in Liskeard and have been drinking at some pub. That's it, isn't it?'

'No,' I answered.

'Something's happened, all the same. You've been somewhere else, you're not telling me the truth; everything you say and do is one long lie. You lied about the laboratory to the lawyer and that Willis man, you lied to the police about the way the Professor died. For God's sake what's behind it? Did you have some secret pact between you both that he would kill himself, and you knew about it all the time?'

I put my hands on her shoulders and began to push her out of the room. 'I've not been drinking. There was no suicide pact. Magnus died accidentally, walking into a freight train as it was going into a tunnel. I stood by the line an hour ago and nearly did the same. That's the truth, and if you won't accept it it's just too bad. I can't make you.'

She stumbled against the bathroom door, and as she turned to look at me I saw a new expression on her face, not anger, but amazement, and disgust as well.

'You went and stood there again,' she said, 'by the place where he was killed? You deliberately went and stood there and watched a train go by that might have killed you too?'

'Yes.'

'Then I'll tell you what I think. I think it's unhealthy, morbid, crazy, and the worst thing about it is that you were capable, after such an experience, of coming here and making love to me. That I'll never forgive, or forget. So for heaven's sake sleep in the dressing-room. I prefer it that way.'

She slammed the bathroom door, and I knew this time it was not another of her gestures, made on impulse, but something fundamental, springing from the core of innermost feeling shocked beyond measure. I understood, even honoured her for it, and was torn by a strange, inarticulate pity, but there was nothing I could say, nothing I could do.

We met next morning not as husband and wife on edge after yet one more marital tiff, but as strangers who, through force of circumstance, were obliged to share a common roof – dress, eat, walk from room to room, make plans for the day, exchange pleasantries with the children, who were bred of her body and not mine, thus making the division yet more complete. I sensed her profound unhappiness, was aware of every sigh, every dragging step, every weary inflection in her voice, and the boys, sharp like little animals to the atmospheric change of mood, watched both of us with gimlet eyes.

'Is it true,' asked Teddy warily, catching me alone, 'that the Professor has left the house to you?'

'It is,' I answered. 'Unexpected, but very kind of him.'

'Will it mean we shall come here every holidays?'

'I don't know, it depends on Vita,' I said.

He began fiddling with things on tables, picking them up and putting them back again, then kicking aimlessly at the backs of chairs.

'I don't believe Mom likes it here,' he said.

'Do you?' I asked.

'It's all right,' he shrugged.

Yesterday, because of fishing and the genial Tom, enthusiasm. Today, with the adult mood at odds, apathy and insecurity. My fault, of course. Whatever happened in this house had been, would be, my fault. I could not tell him so, or ask forgiveness.

'Don't worry,' I said. 'It will sort itself out. You'll probably spend the Christmas holidays in New York.'

'Whew . . . How super!' he exclaimed, and ran out of the room on to the terrace, calling to Micky, who was outside, 'Dick says we may spend next holidays back home.'

The cheer that echoed from his young brother summed up their joint attitude to Cornwall, England, Europe, doubtless to their stepfather as well.

We got through the weekend somehow, though the weather broke, making it the more difficult, and while the boys played a form of racquets in the basement – I could hear the balls thudding against the walls below – and Vita wrote a ten-page letter to Bill and Diana in Ireland, I made an inspection of all Magnus's books, from the nautical tales of Commander Lane's day to his own more personal choice, touching each one with possessive pride. The third volume of *The Parochial History of the County of Cornwall* (L to N – no sign of the other volumes) was tucked behind *The Story of the Windjammers*, and I pulled it out and ran my eye over the index of parishes. Lanlivery was there, and in the chapter allotted to it pride of place was given to Restormel Castle. Alas for Sir John; his seven months' tenure as Keeper was not mentioned. I was just about to replace the book, with the intention of reading it in full another time, when a line at the top of the page caught my attention.

'The manor of Steckstenton or Strickstenton, originally Tregesteynton, belonged to the Carminowes of Boconnoc, and passed from them to the Courtenays, and eventually to the representatives of the Pitt family. The estate of Strickstenton is the property of N. Kendall, Esq.'

Tregesteynton ... the Carminowes of Boconnoc. I had got it at last, but too late. Had I known ten days ago, had we both known, Magnus could have crossed the valley lower down, at Treesmill, and need not have died. As to the original manor-house, the site of it had surely been below the present farm-house, or, trespassing there in time last Thursday evening, I must have been seen by the present owners.

Strickstenton ... Tregesteynton. One thing was certain: I could bring the name up in Court if the Coroner questioned me.

The date of the inquest was fixed for Friday morning – earlier than had been expected. Dench and Willis would do as they had done before – travel down by a night train and return after it was over. I was congratulating myself, as I was shaving on the day of the inquest, that I had suffered no side-effects from the drugs, no sweats, no bloodshot eyes, and despite the estrangement with Vita had passed the last few days in comparative peace, when suddenly, for no reason, the razor dropped from my hand into the wash-basin. I tried to pick it up, and my fingers would not coordinate; they were numb, with a sort of cramp. There was no feeling in them, no pain – they just did not function. I told myself it was nerves, due to the forthcoming ordeal, yet later at breakfast, as I reached for a cup of coffee without thinking, the cup slipped out of my hand, spilling the contents and smashing itself on the tray.

We were breakfasting in the dining-room to be on time for the inquest, and Vita was sitting opposite me.

'Sorry,' I said. 'What a bloody clumsy thing to do.'

She stared at my hand, which had started to tremble, the tremor seeming to run up the wrist to the elbow. I could not control it. I thrust my hand into my jacket pocket and kept it close to my side, and the tremor eased.

'What's wrong?' she asked. 'Your hand is all shaking.'

'It's cramp,' I said. 'I must have lain on it during the night.'

'Well, blow on it or something,' she said. 'Stretch the fingers, and bring the circulation back.'

She began mopping up the tray, and poured me a fresh cup of coffee. I drank it with my left hand, but appetite had gone. I was wondering how I was going to drive the car, with one hand trembling or useless. I had told Vita that I preferred to attend the inquest alone, for there was no reason for her to come with me, but when the moment drew near to leave my hand was still useless, although the tremor had ceased.

'Look, I think you'll have to take me into St Austell,' I said. 'My right hand has still got this infernal cramp.'

The warm sympathy which would have been hers a week ago was lacking. 'I'll drive you, of course,' she replied, 'but it's rather odd, isn't it, suddenly to have cramp? You've never had it before. You had better keep your hand in your pocket, or the Coroner will think you have been drinking.'

It was not a remark calculated to put me at my ease, and the very business of having to sit as passenger, humped beside Vita as she drove instead of being at the wheel myself, did something to my self-respect. I felt inadequate, frustrated, and began to lose the thread of the answers to the Coroner which I had so carefully rehearsed.

When we arrived at the White Hart and met Dench and Willis Vita, quite unnecessarily, apologized for her presence by saying, 'Dick's disabled. I had to act as chauffeur,' and the whole silly business was then explained. There was little time for talking, and I walked with the others to the building where the inquest was to be held, feeling a marked man, while the Coroner, doubtless a mild enough individual in private life, took on, in my eyes, the semblance of a judge of the Criminal Court, with the jury, one and all, adepts at finding a prisoner guilty.

The proceedings started with the police evidence about the finding of the body. It was straightforward enough, but as I listened to the story I thought how strangely it must fall on other ears, and how suggestive of someone who had temporarily lost his reason and been bent on his own destruction. Dr Powell was then called to give evidence. He read his statement in that clear, no-nonsense-about-it voice which suddenly reminded me of one of the younger Rugger-playing priests at Stonyhurst.

'This was the well-preserved body of a man of about forty-five years of age. When first examined at 1 p.m. on Saturday August 3rd death had occurred about fourteen hours previously. The autopsy, performed the following day, showed superficial bruises and abrasions of the knees and chest, deeper and more severe bruising of the upper arm and shoulder, and extensive laceration of the right side of the scalp. Underlying this was a depressed fracture of the right parietal region of the skull, accompanied by lacerations of the brain and bleeding from the right middle meningeal artery. The stomach was found to contain about one pint of mixed food and fluid, which on subsequent analysis contained nothing abnormal and no alcohol. Blood samples examined were also normal, and the heart, lungs, liver and kidneys were all normal and healthy. In my opinion, death was due to a cerebral haemorrhage following a severe crushing blow on the head.'

I relaxed in my seat, tension momentarily lifted, wondering if John Willis did the same, or whether he had never had cause for concern.

The Coroner then asked Dr Powell if the brain injuries were consistent with what might be expected if the deceased had come into violent contact with a passing vehicle such as the wagon of a freight train.

'Yes, definitely,' was the reply. 'A point of some importance is that death was not instantaneous. He had strength enough to drag himself a few yards to the hut. The head blow was sufficient to cause severe concussion, but actual death from haemorrhage probably took place five to ten minutes afterwards.'

'Thank you, Dr Powell,' said the Coroner, and I heard him

call my name. I stood up, wondering if the fact that my right hand was in my pocket gave me too casual an appearance, or whether, in point of fact, anyone noticed it at all.

'Mr Young,' said the Coroner, 'I have your statement here, and propose reading it to the jury. Stop me if there is anything you wish to correct.'

The statement, as read by him, made me sound callous, as if I had been more preoccupied in missing my dinner than anxious for the safety of my guest. The jury would get the impression of a loafer, spinning away the small hours with a cushion behind his head and a bottle of whisky at his elbow.

'Mr Young,' said the Coroner, when he had finished, 'it did not occur to you to contact the police on the Friday night. Why?'

'I thought it unnecessary,' I replied. 'I kept expecting Professor Lane to turn up.'

'You were not surprised at his getting off the train at Par and taking a walk instead of meeting you at St Austell as arranged?'

'I was surprised, yes, but it was quite in character. If he had some objective in view he followed it through. Time and punctuality meant nothing to him on these occasions.'

'And what do you think was the particular objective Professor Lane had in view on the night in question?' asked the Coroner.

'Well, he had become interested in the historical associations of the district, and the sites of manor-houses. We had planned to visit some of them during the weekend. When he did not turn up I assumed he must have decided to take a walk to some particular site which he had not told me about. Since I made my statement to the police I believe I have located the site he had in mind.'

I thought there might be a stir of interest amongst the jury but they remained unmoved.

'Perhaps you will tell us about it,' said the Coroner.

'Yes, of course,' I answered, self-confidence returning, and inwardly blessing the *Parochial History*. 'I believe now, which I did not know at the time, that he was trying to locate the one-time manor of Strickstenton in Lanlivery parish. This manor belonged at one time to a family called Courtenay' – I was careful not to mention the Carminowes, because of Vita – 'who also used to own Treverran too. The quickest way between these houses, as the crow flies, would be to cross the valley above the present Treverran farm, and walk through the wood to Strick-stenton.'

The Coroner asked for an ordnance map, which he examined carefully. 'I see what you mean, Mr Young,' he said. 'But surely there is a passageway under the railway which Professor Lane would have taken in preference to crossing the line itself?'

'Yes,' I said, 'but he had no map. He might not have known it was there.'

'So he cut across the line, despite the fact that it was by then quite dark, and a freight train was coming up the valley?'

'I don't think the darkness worried him. And obviously he didn't hear the train – he was so intent on his quest.'

'So intent, Mr Young, that he deliberately climbed through the wire and walked down the steep embankment as the train was passing?'

'I don't think he walked down the bank. He slipped and fell. Don't forget it was snowing at the time.'

I saw the Coroner staring at me, and the jury too. 'I beg your pardon, Mr Young,' said the Coroner, 'did I hear you say it was snowing?'

I took a moment or two to recover, and I could feel the sweat breaking out on my forehead. 'I'm sorry,' I said. 'That was mis-leading. The point was that Professor Lane had a particular in-terest in climatic conditions during the Middle Ages; his theory was that winters were much harder in those days than they are now. Before the railway cutting was built through the hillside above the Treesmill valley the ground would have sloped down continuously all the way to the bottom, and drifts would have lain there heavily, making communication between Treverran and Strickstenton virtually impossible. I believe, from a scientific rather than a historical point of view, he was thinking so much about this, and the general incline of the land about him, and how it would be affected by snowfall, that he became oblivious of everything else.'

The incredulous faces went on staring at me, and I saw one man nudge his companion, signifying that either I was a raving lunatic or the Professor had been.

'Thank you, Mr Young, that is all,' said the Coroner and I sat down, pouring with sweat and a tremor shooting down my arm from elbow to wrist.

He called John Willis, who proceeded to give evidence that his late colleague had been in the best of health and spirits when he saw him before the weekend, that he was engaged in work of great importance to the country which he was not at liberty to speak about, but that naturally this work had no connection with his visit to Cornwall, which was in the nature of a private visit and in pursuance of a personal hobby, mainly historical.

'I must add,' he said, 'that I am in complete agreement with Mr Young as to his theory of how Professor Lane met his death. I am not an antiquarian, nor a historian, but certainly Professor Lane held theories about the extent of snowfall in previous centuries,' and he proceeded, for about three minutes, to launch into jargon so incomprehensible and above my head and the heads of everybody present that Magnus himself could not have surpassed it had he been giving an imitation, after a thundering good dinner, of the sort of stuff published in the more obscure scientific journals.

'Thank you, Mr Willis,' murmured the Coroner when he had finished. 'Very interesting. I am sure we are all grateful for your information.'

The evidence was concluded. The Coroner, summing up, directed that, although the circumstances were unusual, he found no reason to suppose that Professor Lane had deliberately walked on to the line as the train approached. The verdict was death by misadventure, with a rider to the effect that British Railways, Western Region, would do well to make a more thorough inspection of the wiring and danger notices along the line.

It was all over. Herbert Dench turned to me with a smile, as we left the building, and said, 'Very satisfactory for all concerned. I suggest we celebrate at the White Hart. I don't mind telling you I was afraid of a very different verdict, and I think we might have had it but for your and Willis's account of Professor Lane's extraordinary preoccupation with winter conditions. I remember hearing of a similar case in the Himalayas . . .' and he proceeded to tell us, as we walked to the hotel, of a scientist who for three weeks lived at some phenomenal altitude in appalling conditions to study the atmospheric effect upon certain bacteria. I did not see the connection but was glad of the respite, and when we reached our destination went straight to the bar and got quietly and very inoffensively drunk. Nobody noticed, and what is more the tremor in my hand ceased immediately. Perhaps after all it had been nerves.

'Well, we mustn't keep you from enjoying your delightful new home,' the lawyer said, when we had consumed a brief but hilarious lunch. 'Willis and I can walk up to the station.'

As we moved towards the door of the hotel I said to Willis, 'I can't thank you enough for your evidence. What Magnus would have called a remarkable performance.'

'It made its impact,' he admitted, 'though you had me somewhat shaken. I wasn't prepared for snow. Still, it goes to prove what my boss always said: the layman will accept anything if it is put forward in an authoritative enough fashion.' He blinked at me behind his spectacles and added quietly, 'You did make a clean sweep of all the jam-jars, I take it? Nothing left that could do you or anyone else any damage?'

'Buried,' I replied, 'under the debris of years.'

'Good,' he said. 'We don't want any more disasters.'

He hesitated, as if he might have been going to say something else, but the lawyer and Vita were waiting for us by the hotel entrance, and the opportunity was lost. Farewells were said, hands shaken, and we all dispersed. As we made our way to the car park Vita remarked in wifely fashion, 'I noticed your hand recovered as soon as you reached the bar. Be that as it may, I intend to drive.'

'You're welcome,' I said, borrowing her country's curious phraseology, and, tilting my hat over my eye as I got into the car, I prepared myself for sleep. My conscience pricked me, though. I had lied to Willis. Bottles A and B were empty, true enough but the contents of bottle C were still intact, and lay in my suitcase in the dressing-room.

twenty-one

The effects of conviviality in the White Hart subsided after a couple of hours, leaving me in a truculent mood and determined to be master in my own house. The inquest was over, and despite my gaffe about the snow, or perhaps because of it, Magnus's good name remained untarnished. The police were satisfied, local interest would die down, and there was nothing more I had to fear except interference from my own wife. This must be dealt with, and speedily. The boys had gone off riding and were not yet home. I went to look for Vita and found her eventually, tape-measure in hand, standing on the landing outside the boys' room.

'You know,' she said, 'that lawyer was perfectly right. You could get half a dozen small apartments into his place – more if you used the basement too. We could borrow the money from Joe.' She flicked the tape-measure back into its case and smiled. 'Have you any better ideas? The Professor didn't leave the money to keep up his house, and you haven't a job, unless you cross the ocean and Joe gives you one. So . . . How about being realistic for a change?'

I turned and walked downstairs to the music-room. I expected her to follow me, and she did. I planted myself before the fireplace, the traditional spot sacrosanct from time immemorial to the master of the house, and said, 'Get this straight. This is my house, and what I do with it is my affair. I don't want suggestions from you, lawyers, friends, or anyone else. I intend to live here, and if you don't care to live here with me you must make your own arrangements.'

She lighted a cigarette and blew a great puff of smoke into the air. She had gone very white. 'This is the showdown, is it?' she asked. 'The ultimatum?'

'Call it what you like,' I told her. 'It's a statement of fact. Magnus has left me this house, and I propose to make a life for myself here, and for you and the boys if you want to share it. I can't speak plainer than that.'

'You mean you have given up all idea of taking the directorship Joe offered you in New York?'

'I never had the idea. You had it for me.'

'And how do you think we are going to live?'

'I haven't the slightest idea,' I said, 'and at the moment I don't care. Having worked in a publishing firm for over twenty years I know something about the game, and might even turn author myself. I could start by writing a history of this house.'

'Good heavens!' She laughed, and extinguished her barely-lighted cigarette in the nearest ashtray. 'Well, it might keep you occupied if nothing else. And what would I do with myself in the meantime? Join the local sewing society or something?'

'You could do what other wives do, adapt.'

'Darling, when I agreed to marry you and live in England you had a perfectly worthwhile job in London. You've thrown it up for no reason at all, and now want to settle down here at the back of beyond, where neither of us knows a soul, hundreds of miles from all our friends. It's just not good enough.'

We had reached an impasse; and I disliked being called darling when we were locked in argument instead of an embrace. Anyway, the situation bored me; I had said my say, and argument led nowhere. Besides, I had an intense desire to go up to dressing-room and examine bottle C. If I remembered rightly, it looked slightly different from bottles A and B. Perhaps I ought to have given it to Willis to try out on his laboratory monkeys; but if I had taken him into my confidence he might never have sent it back.

'Why don't you take your tape-measure,' I suggested, 'and think up some bright ideas for curtains and carpets, and send them to Bill and Diana for their opinion in Ireland?'

I did not mean to be sarcastic. She could do what she liked, within reason, with Magnus's furnishings and bachelor taste. Rearranging rooms was one of her favourite things: it kept her happy for hours.

My effort to appease rebounded. Her eyes filled, and she said, 'You know I'd live anywhere if only I thought you loved me still.'

I can take anger any day and feel justified in returning blow for blow. Not unhappiness, not tears. I held out my arms and she came at once, clinging to me for comfort like a wounded child.

'You've changed so these last weeks,' she told me. 'I hardly recognize you.'

'I haven't changed,' I said. 'I do love you. Of course I love you.'

Truth is the hardest thing to put across, to other people, to oneself as well. I did love Vita, for moments shared during months and years, for all those ups and downs of married life that can be precious, exasperating, monotonous and dear. I had learnt to accept her faults, and she mine. Too often, wrangling, the insults hurled were never meant. Too frequently, used to each other's company, we had left the sweeter things unsaid. The trouble was, some inner core within had been untouched, lain dormant, waiting to be stirred. I could not share with her or anyone the secrets of my dangerous new world. Magnus, yes ... but Magnus was a man, and dead. Vita was no Medea with whom I could gather the enchanted herbs.

'Darling,' I said, 'try and bear with me. It's a moment of transition for me, not a parting of the ways. I just can't see ahead. It's like standing on a spit of shore with an incoming tide, waiting to take the plunge. I can't explain.'

'I'll take any plunge you want, if you'll take me with you,' she answered.

'I know,' I said, 'I know . . .'

She wiped her eyes and blew her nose, the temporarily blotched features oddly touching, making me feel the more inadequate.

'What's the time? I shall have to pick up the boys,' she said.

'No, we'll go together,' I told her, glad of an excuse to prolong the *entente*, to justify myself not only in her eyes but in my own as well. Cheerfulness broke in; the atmosphere, that had been so heavy with resentment and unspoken bitterness, cleared and we were almost normal again. That night I returned, from self-banishment in the dressing-room, not without regret, but I felt it polite; besides, the divan bed was hard.

The weather was fine, and the weekend passed with sailing, swimming, picnics with the boys, and as I resumed my role of husband, stepfather, master of the house, I planned in secret for the week ahead. I must have one day to myself alone. Vita herself, in all innocence, supplied the opportunity.

'Did you know Mrs Collins has a daughter in Bude?' she said on Monday morning. 'I told her we'd take her over there one day this week, drop her off with the daughter, and pick her up again later in the afternoon. So how about it? The boys are keen to go, and so am I.'

I pretended to damp the idea. 'Awful lot of traffic,' I said. 'The roads will be jammed. And Bude packed with tourists.'

'We don't mind that,' said Vita. 'We can make an early start, and it's only about fifty miles.'

I assumed the look of a hard-pressed family man with a backlog of work on hand he was given no time to clear. 'If you don't mind, I'd rather you left me out of it. Bude on a mid-August afternoon is not my idea of a perfect way of life.'

'OK . . . OK . . . We'll have more fun without you.'

We settled for Wednesday. No tradesmen called that day, so it suited me. If they left at half-past ten and picked up Mrs Collins again around five o'clock, they'd be home by seven at the latest.

Wednesday dawned fine, luckily, and I saw the party off in the Buick soon after half-past ten, knowing that I had at least eight hours ahead of me, hours for experiment and recovery too. I went up to the dressing-room and took bottle C out of my suitcase. It was the same stuff all right, or appeared to be, but there was a brownish sediment at the bottom, like cough-mixture put away after the winer and forgotten until the cold weather comes again. I took out the stopper and smelt the contents: they had no more colour and smell than stale water – less, in fact. I poured four measures into the top of the walking-stick, and then decided to screw it up for future use, and pour a fresh dose into the medicine-glass, which was still lying on a shelf with the jars in the old laundry.

It was an odd sensation, standing there once more, knowing that the basement all around me and the house above were empty of their present occupants, Vita, the boys, while waiting in the shadows were possibly the people of my secret world.

When I had swallowed the dose I went and sat in the old kitchen, expectant and alert as a theatregoer who has just slipped into his stall before the curtain rises on the eagerly awaited third act of a play.

In this case either the players were on strike or the management at fault, for the curtain of my private theatre never rose, the scene remained unchanged. I sat down there in the basement for an hour, and nothing happened. I went out on to the patio, thinking the fresh air might do the trick, but time stayed obstinately at Wednesday morning in mid-August; I might have swallowed a draught from the kitchen tap for all the effect bottle C had upon mind or stomach.

At twelve o'clock I returned to the lab and poured a few more drops into the medicine-glass. This had done the trick once before, and without any ill-effect.

I returned to the patio and stayed until after one o'clock, but still nothing happened, so I went upstairs and had some lunch. It must mean that the contents of bottle C had lost their strength, or Magnus had somehow missed out on the special ingredients and bottle C was worthless. If this was so, I had made my last trip. The curtain had risen on my journey across the Treesmill stream in the snow, only to fall by the railway tunnel at the close of the third act. I had come to journey's end.

The realization was so devastating that I felt stunned. I had lost not only Magnus but the other world. It lay here, all around me, but out of reach. The people of that world would travel on in time without me, and I must keep to my own course, fulfilling God only knew what monotonous day by day. The link between the centuries had gone.

I went down to the basement once more and out into the patio, thinking that by walking on the stone flags and touching the walls some force would come through to me, that Roger's face would look out at me from the hatch-door to the boiler-room, or Robbie would emerge from the stables under the loft leading his pony. I knew they must be there, and I could not see them. Isolda too, waiting for the snows to melt. The house was inhabited not by the dead but by the living, and I was the restless wanderer, I was the ghost.

This urge to see, to listen, to move amongst them was so intense that it became intolerable; it was as though my brain had been set alight by some tremendous fire. I could not rest. I could not set myself to any humdrum task in the house or garden; the whole day had gone to waste, and what had promised to be hours of magic were slipping by unused.

I got out the car and drove to Tywardreath, the sight of the solid parish church a mockery to my mood. It had no right to be there in its present form. I wanted to sweep it away, leaving only the south aisle and the Priory chapel, see the Priory walls enclosing the churchyard. I drove aimlessly to the lay-by at the top of the hill beyond the Treesmill turning and parked, thinking that, if I walked down the road and crossed the fields to the Gratten, memory of what I had once seen would fill the vacuum.

I stood by the car, reaching for a cigarette, but it had not touched my lips before a jolt shook me from head to foot, as though I had stepped on a live cable. There was no serene transition from present to past but a sensation of pain, with flashes before my eyes and thunder in my ears. 'This is it,' I thought. 'I'm going to die.' Then the flashes cleared, the thunder died away, and there was a mass of people lining the summit of the hill where I stood, crowding and pressing towards a building across the road. More people came from the direction of Tywardreath, men, women, children, some walking, some running. The building was the magnet, irregular in shape, with leaded windows, and what appeared to be a small chapel beside it. I had seen the village once before, at Martinmas, but that was from the green beyond the Priory walls. Now there were no booths, no travelling musicians, no slaughtered beasts. The air was crisp and cold, the ditches banked with frozen snow that had turned grey and hard from lying during weeks. Small puddles in the road had turned to craters of sheeted ice, and the ploughlands across the ditches were black with frost. Men, women and children alike were wrapped and hooded against the cold, their features sharp like the beaks of birds, and the mood I sensed was neither jocular nor gay but somehow predatory, the mob of people bent upon a spectacle that might turn sour. I drew nearer to the building, and saw that a covered chariot was drawn up by the chapel entrance, with servants standing by the horses' heads. I recognized the Champernoune coat-of-arms, and the servants too, while Roger himself stood within the chapel porch, his arms folded.

The door of the main building was shut, but as I stood there watching it opened, and a man, better dressed than those lining the route, emerged with a companion. I knew them both, for I had seen them last on the night when Otto Bodrugan had urged them to join in his rebellion against the King: they were Julian Polpey and Henry Trefrengy. They came down the pathway, and threading their way through the crowd paused near to where I stood.

'God preserve me from a woman's spite,' said Polpey. 'Roger has held the office for ten years, and now to be dismissed without reason being given, and the stewardship handed to Phil Hornwynk . . .'

'Young William will reinstate him when he comes of age, no doubt of that,' replied Trefrengy. 'He has his father's sense of justice and fair play. But I could smell the change coming these past twelve months or more. The plain truth is that she lacks not only a husband but a man as well, and Roger has had his belly-ful and will oblige no more.'

'He finds his oats elsewhere.'

The last speaker, Geoffrey Lampetho from the valley, had shouldered his way through the crowd to join them. 'Rumour has it there's a woman under his roof. You should know, Tref-rengy, being his neighbour.'

'I know nothing,' answered Trefrengy shortly. 'Roger keeps his counsel, I keep mine. In hard weather such as this wouldn't any Christian give shelter to a stranger on the road?'

Lampetho laughed, digging him with his elbow. 'Neatly said, but you can't deny it,' he said. 'Why else does my Lady Cham-pernoune come here from Trelawn, disregarding the state of the roads, unless to snuff her out? I was in the geld-house here be-fore you to pay my rents, and she sat in the inner room while Hornwynk collected. All the paint in the world couldn't hide the black look on her face: dismissing Roger from his stewardship won't see the end of it. Meantime, sport for the populace of another kind. Will you stay to watch the fun?'

Julian Polpey shook his head in disgust. 'Not I ' he answered. 'Why should we in Tywardreath have some custom foisted upon us from elsewhere, making us barbarians? Lady Champernoune must be sick in mind to think of it. I'm for home.'

He turned and disappeared into the crowd, which was now thick not only upon the summit of the hill where the house and chapel stood, but halfway down the track to Treesmill. One and all wore this curious air of expectancy upon their faces, half-resentful, half-eager, and Geoffrey Lampetho, pointing this out to his companion, laughed again.

'Sick in mind, maybe, but it salves her conscience to have another widow act as scapegoat, and sweetens Quadragessima for us. There's nothing a mob likes more than witnessing public penance.'

He turned his head, like the rest, towards the valley, and Henry Trefrengy edged forward past the Champernoune ser-vants to the chapel entrance where Roger stood, while I followed close behind.

'I'm sorry for what has happened,' he said. 'No gratitude, no recompense. Ten years of your life wasted, gone for nothing.'

'Not wasted,' answered Roger briefly. 'William will come of

age in June and marry. His mother will lose her influence, and the monk as well. You know the Bishop of Exeter has expelled him finally, and he must return to the Abbey at Angers, where he should have gone a year ago?'

'God be praised!' exclaimed Trefrengy. 'The Priory stinks because of him, the parish too. Look at the people yonder . . .'

Roger stared over Trefrengy's head at the gaping crowd. 'I may have acted hard as steward, but to make sport of Rob Rosgof's widow was more than I could stomach,' he said. 'I stood against it, and this was another reason for my dismissal. The monk is responsible for all of this, to satisfy my lady's vanity and lust.'

The entrance to the chapel darkened, and the small, slight figure of Jean de Meral appeared in the open doorway. He put his hand on Roger's shoulder.

'You used not to be so squeamish once,' he said. 'Have you forgotten those evenings in the Priory cellars, and in your own as well? I taught you more than philosophy, my friend, on those occasions.'

'Take your hand off me,' replied Roger curtly. 'I parted company with you and your brethren when you let young Henry Bodrugan die under the Priory roof, and could have saved him.'

The monk smiled. 'And now, to show sympathy with the dead, you harbour an adulterous wife under your own?' he asked. 'We are all hypocrites, my friend. I warn you, my lady knows your wayfarer's identity, and it is partly on her account that she is here in Tywardreath. She has certain proposals to put before the Lady Isolda when this business with Rosgof's widow has been settled.'

'Which business, please God, will be struck from the manor records in years to come, and rebound upon your head instead, to your everlasting shame,' said Trefrengy.

'You forget,' murmured the monk, 'I am a bird of passage, and in a few days' time shall have spread my wings for France.'

There was a sudden stir amongst the crowd, and a man appeared at the door of the adjoining building, which Lampetho had named the geld-house. Stout, florid-faced, he held a document in his hand. Beside him, wrapped in a cloak from head to foot, was Joanna Champernoune.

The man, whom I took to be the new steward Hornwynk, advanced to address the crowd, unrolling the document in his hand.

'Good people of Tywardreath,' he proclaimed, 'whether freeman, customary tenant or serf, those of you who pay rent to the manor-court have done so here today at the geldhouse. And since this manor of Tywardreath was once held by the Lady Isolda Cardinham of Cardinham, who sold it to our late lord's grandfather, it has been decided to introduce here a practice established in the manor of Cardinham since the Conquest.' He paused a moment, the better to impress his words upon his listeners. 'The practice being,' he continued, 'that any widow of a customary tenant, holding lands through her late husband, who has deviated from the path of chastity, shall either forfeit her lands or make due penance for their recovery before the lord of the manor and the steward of the manor-court. Today before the Lady Joanna Champernoune, representing the lord of the manor William, a minor, and myself, Philip Hornwynk, steward, Mary, widow of Robert Rosgof, must make such penance if she desires the restoration of her lands.'

A murmur rose from the crowd, a strange blend of excitement and curiosity, and a sudden sound of shouting came from the road leading down to Treesmill.

'She'll never face them,' said Trefrengy. 'Mary Rosgof has a son at home who would rather surrender his farmland ten times over than have his mother shamed.'

'You are mistaken,' answered the monk. 'He knows her shame will prove his gain in six months' time, when she is brought to bed of a bastard child, and he can turn both out of doors and keep the lands himself.'

'Then you've persuaded him,' said Roger, 'and lined his purse in so doing.'

The shouting and the cries increased, and as the people pressed forward I saw a procession ascend the hill from Treesmill, lumbering towards us at a jog-trot. Two lads raced ahead, brandishing whips, and behind them came five men escorting what at first sight I took to be a small moorland pony with a woman mounted on its back. They drew closer, and the laughter amongst the spectators turned to jeers, as the woman sagged upon her steed and would have fallen, had not one of the men escorting her held her fast, flourishing a hay-fork in his other hand. She was not mounted upon a pony at all but on a great black sheep, his horns beribboned with crêpe, and the two fellows on either side had thrust a halter over his head to lead him, so that, startled and terrified of the crowd about him, he ducked and stumbled in a vain endeavour to throw his passenger from his back. The woman was draped in black to match her steed, with a black veil covering her face, her hands bound in front of her with leather thongs; I could see her fingers clutching at the thick dark wool on the sheep's neck.

The procession came stumbling and lurching to the geld-house, and as it drew to a standstill before Hornwynk and Joanna, the escort jerking the halter, the man with the hayfork dragged off the woman's veil to disclose her features. She could not have been more than thirty-five, her eyes as terror-stricken as the sheep that bore her, while her dark hair, roughly scissored, stood out from her head like a cropped thatch. The jeering turned to silence as the woman, trembling, bowed her head before Joanna.

'Mary Rosgof, do you admit your fault?' called Hornwynk.

'I do in all humility,' she answered, her voice low.

'Speak louder for all to hear, and state its nature,' he cried.

The wretched woman, her pale face flushing, raised her head and looked towards Joanna.

'I lay with another man, my husband not six months dead, thus forfeiting the lands I held in trust for my son. I crave indulgence of my lady and the manor court, and beg for the restoration of my lands, confessing my incontinence. Should I give birth to a base-born child, my son will take possession of the lands and do with me as he pleases.'

Joanna beckoned the new steward to her side, and he bent low as she whispered something in his ear. Then he turned once more and addressed the penitent.

'My gracious lady cannot condone your fault, which is of a nature abhorrent to all people, but since you have admitted it in person, and before the manor court and others of this parish, she will, in great clemency, restore the forfeited lands you rent from her.'

The woman bowed her head and murmured gratitude, then asked with swimming eyes if there was further penance she must do.

'Aye,' returned the steward. 'Descend from the sheep that

carried you in your shame, proceed to the chapel here, crawling on your knees, and confess your sin before the altar. Brother John will hear your confession.'

The two men who held the sheep pulled the woman from its back, forcing her to her knees, and as she dragged herself along the path towards the chapel, hampered by her skirts, a groan arose from the watching crowd, as if this total degradation could in some way appease their own sense of shame. The monk waited until she had crawled to his feet, then turned into the chapel, where she followed him. Her escort, at a sign from Hornwynk, set the sheep free, whereupon it ran in terror amongst the crowd, scattering them to either side, and a great shout of hysterical laughter burst forth, as they drove it back along the road to Treesmill, pelting it with pieces of packed snow, sticks, anything they could find. With the sudden release from tension everyone was in a moment laughing, joking, running, seized by a holiday mood, what was happening making a break between winter and the Lenten season just begun. Soon they had all dispersed, and no one was left before the geld-house but Joanna herself, Hornwynk the steward, and Roger and Trefrengy standing to one side.

'So be it,' said Joanna. 'Tell my servants I am ready to leave. There is nothing further to keep me here in Tywardreath save a certain business which I can attend to on the road home.'

The steward went down the path to prepare for her departure, the servants opening the carriage door in readiness, and Joanna, pausing, looked across the path at Roger.

'The people were well satisfied if you are not,' she said. 'and will pay their rents the sooner for it in the future. The custom has its merits if it inspires fear, and may well spread to other manors.'

'God forbid,' answered Roger.

Geoffrey Lampetho had been right about the paint on her face, or perhaps the atmosphere inside the geld-house had been close. It ran in streaks now on either cheek, which, with increasing weight, were a puffy puce. She seemed to have aged, since I saw her last, a good ten years. The splendour had gone from her brown eyes, turning them hard like agate.

She put out her hand now and touched Roger's arm. 'Come,' she said, 'we have known one another too long for lies and subterfuge. I have a message for the Lady Isolda from her brother

Sir William Ferrers, which I have promised to deliver to her in person. If you bar your door to me now I can summon fifty men from the manor to break it down.'

'And I another fifty between here and Fowey to withstand them,' answered Roger. 'But you may follow me to Kylmerth if you wish, and beg an interview. Whether it will be granted or not I cannot say.'

Joanna smiled. 'It will,' she said, 'it will,' and taking her skirts in her hands she swept down the path towards the carriage, followed by the monk. Once it would have been Roger who helped her mount the steps into the waiting vehicle; today it was the new steward Hornwynk, flushed with self-esteem and bowing low, while Roger, crossing to a gate behind the chapel, where his pony was tethered, leapt upon its back, and kicking his heels into its side rode out into the road. The lumbering chariot rumbled after him, Joanna and the monk inside it, and the few stragglers at the top of the hill stared to watch it pass down the icy road to the village green and the Priory wall beyond. A bell sounded from the Priory chapel and the vehicle began to draw away from me, and Roger too, and I started running, fearing to lose both. Then a pounding in my heart began, and a singing in my ears, and I saw the carriage lurch to a standstill; the window was lowered, and Joanna herself looked out of it, waving her hand and beckoning to me. I stumbled to the window, breathless, the singing increasing to a roar. Then it ceased, absolutely, and I was swaying on my feet, with the clock in St Andrew's church striking seven, and the Buick had drawn up on the road ahead of me, with Vita waving from the window, and the surprised faces of the boys and Mrs Collins looking out.

twenty-two

They were all talking at once, and the boys were laughing. I heard Micky say, 'We saw you running down the hill, you looked so funny . . .' and Teddy chimed in, 'Mom waved and called, but you didn't hear at first, you seemed to look the other way.' Vita was staring at me from the open window by the driving seat. 'You'd best get in,' she said, 'you can hardly stand,' and Mrs Collins, red in the face and flustered, opened the door for me the other side. I obeyed mechanically, forgetting my own car parked in the lay-by, and squeezed in beside Mrs Collins, as we continued along the lane skirting the village towards Polmear.

'A good thing we drove this way,' said Vita. 'Mrs Collins said it was quicker than going down through St Blazey and Par.'

I could not remember where they had been or what they were doing, and although the singing in my ears had stopped my heart was thumping still, and vertigo was not far away.

'Bude was super,' said Teddy. 'We had surf-boards, but Mom wouldn't let us go out of our depth. And the ocean was rolling in, huge great waves, much better than here. You ought to have come with us.'

Bude, that was right. They had gone to spend the day at Bude, leaving me alone in the house. But what was I doing wandering in Tywardreath? As we passed the almshouses at the bottom of Polmear hill and I looked across to Polpey and the Lampetho valley, I remembered how Julian Polpey had not waited for the loathsome spectacle outside the geld-house but had walked home, and Geoffrey Lampetho had been one of those amongst the crowd who had pelted the sheep with stones.

It was over and done with, finished. It was not happening any more. Mrs Collins was saying something to Vita about dropping her at the top of Polkerris hill, and the next thing I knew was that she had disappeared and Vita had drawn up outside Kilmarth.

'Run along in,' she said sharply to the boys. 'Put your swimming-trunks in the hot cupboard and start laying the supper,' and when they had vanished up the steps into the house she turned to me and said, 'Can you make it?'

'Make what?' I was still dazed, and could not follow her.

'Make the steps,' she said. 'You were rocking on your feet when we came on you just now. I felt terrible in front of Mrs Collins and the boys. However much have you had to drink?'

'Drink?' I repeated. 'I haven't drunk a thing.'

'Oh, for heaven's sake,' she said, 'don't start lying. It's been a long day, and I'm tired. Come on, I'll help you into the house.'

Perhaps this was the answer. Perhaps it was best she should

think I had been sitting in some pub. I got out of the car, and she was right – I was still rocking on my feet, and I was glad of her arm to steady me up the garden and into the house.

'I'll be all right,' I said. 'I'll go and sit in the library.'

'I'd rather you went straight to bed,' she said. 'The boys have never seen you like this. They're bound to notice.'

'I don't want to go to bed. I'll just sit in the library and shut the door. They needn't come in.'

'Oh well, if you insist on being obstinate . . .' She shrugged in exasperation. 'I'll tell them we'll eat in the kitchen. For heaven's sake don't join us – I'll bring you something later.'

I heard her walk through the hall to the kitchen, and slam the door. I flopped on a chair in the library and closed my eyes. A strange lethargy crept over me; I wanted to sleep. Vita was right, I should have gone to bed, but I hadn't the energy even to get up out of the chair. If I stayed here quietly, in the stillness and the silence, the feeling of exhaustion, of being drained, would pass away. Tough luck on the boys, if there was some programme they hoped to watch on TV, but I would make it up to them tomorrow, take them sailing, go to Chapel Point. I must make up to Vita too; this business would set us back again, the sweat of reconciliation would have to start all over again.

I awoke with a sudden jerk, to find the room in darkness. I glanced at my watch, and it was almost half-past nine. I had slept for nearly two hours. I felt quite normal, hungry too. I went through the dining-room into the hall, and heard the sound of the gramophone coming from the music-room, but the door was shut. They must have finished eating ages ago, for the lights were turned out in the kitchen. I rummaged in the fridge to find eggs and bacon to fry, and I had just put the frying-pan on the stove when I heard someone moving about in the basement. I went to the top of the back stairs and called, thinking it was one of the boys, who might report to me on Vita's mood. Nobody answered.

'Teddy?' I shouted. 'Micky?'

The footsteps were quite definite, passing across the old kitchen and then on towards the boiler-room. I went down the stairs, fumbling for the lights, but they were not in the right place, I couldn't find the switch, and I had to grope my way to the old kitchen by feeling for the walls. Whoever it was ahead of me had passed through the boiler-room on to the patio, for I could hear him stamping about there, and he was drawing water from the well that lay in the near corner and was covered up and never used. And now there were further footsteps, but not from the patio, from the stairs, and turning round I saw the stairs had gone and the footsteps were coming from the ladder leading to the floor above. It was no longer dark, but the murky grey of a winter afternoon, and a woman was coming down the ladder, bearing a lighted candle in her hands. The singing started in my ears, the bursting thunder-clap of sound, and the drug was taking effect all over again *without having been renewed*. I did not want it now, I was afraid, for it meant that past and present were merging, and Vita and the boys were with me, in my own time, in the front part of the house.

The woman brushed past me, shielding the candle's flame from the draught. It was Isolda. I flattened myself against the wall, holding my breath, for surely she must dissolve if I as much as moved, and what I was seeing was a figment of the imagination, an aftermath of what had been that afternoon. She set the candle down on a bench, lighting another that stood beside it, and began humming under her breath, an odd sweet snatch of song, and all the time I could hear the distant throbbing of the radiogram from the music-room on the ground floor of the house.

'Robbie,' she called softly. 'Robbie, are you there?'

The boy came in from the yard through the low arched doorway, setting his pail of water on the kitchen floor.

'Is it freezing still?' she asked.

'Aye,' he said, 'and will do until full moon is past. You must stay a few days yet, if you can bear with us.'

'Bear with you?' she smiled. 'Rejoice in you, rather, and willingly. I wish my daughters were as well-mannered as you and Bess, and minded what I tell them as you mind your brother Roger.'

'If we do it's from respect for you,' he answered. 'We got hard words from him, and a belting too, before you came.' He laughed, shaking the thick hair out of his eyes, and lifting the pail poured the water into a pitcher on the trestle table. 'We eat well, too,' he added. 'Meat every day instead of salted fish, and the pig I slaughtered yesterday would have stayed in his sty until Quadragessima was done had you not graced our table. Bess and I would have you live with us for ever and not leave us when the weather mends.'

'Ah, I understand,' said Isolda, mocking. 'It isn't for myself you like me here but for the ease of living.'

He frowned, uncertain what she meant, then his face cleared, and he smiled again. 'Nay, that's untrue,' he said. 'We feared when you first came that you'd play the lady and we couldn't please you. It's not so now, you could be one of us. Bess loves you, and so do I. As for Roger, God knows he has sung your praises to us these past two years or more.'

He flushed, suddenly awkward, as if he had said too much, and she put out her hand to him and touched his arm.

'Dear Robbie,' she said gently, 'I love you too, and Bess, and the warm welcome you have given me these past weeks. I shall never forget it.'

The sound of footsteps made me raise my head to the loft above, but it was only the girl descending the ladder, certainly cleaner than when I saw her last, her long hair combed and smooth, her face well scrubbed.

'I can hear Roger riding through the copse,' she called. 'See to the pony, Robbie, when he comes, while I set the table.'

The boy went out into the yard and his sister heaped fresh turf upon the hearth, and furze as well. The furze flickered and caught, throwing great tongues of flame upon the smoky walls, and as Bess looked over her shoulder, smiling at Isolda, I knew how it must have been here for the four of them, night after night, during the time of frost, seated at the trestle table with the candles set amongst the pewter plates.

'Here's your brother now,' said Isolda, and she went and stood by the open door as he rode into the yard and flung himself off the pony, throwing the reins to Robbie. It was not yet dark, and the yard, so much wider than the patio I knew, stretched to the wall above the fields, so that through the open gate I could see the fields sloping to the sea beyond and the wide expanse of bay. The mud in the yard was frosted hard, the air was sharply cold, and the small trees in the copse stood black and naked against the sky. Robbie led the pony to his shed beside the byre, as Roger crossed the yard towards Isolda.

'You bring bad news,' said Isolda. 'I can tell it from your face.'

'My lady knows you are here,' said Roger. 'She is on her way to see you, with a message from your brother. If you wish it I can turn the chariot back from the top of the hill. Robbie and I will have no trouble with her servants.'

'No trouble now, perhaps,' she answered, 'but later she could do harm to you, to Robbie and Bess, to this whole place. I would not have that happen for the world.'

'I would sooner she razed the house to the ground than cause you suffering,' he said.

He stood there, looking down at her, and I knew instinctively that they had reached a point in their relationship, through proximity and sympathy during the past days, when his love for her could no longer smoulder and be contained, but must burn up and reach the sky, or else be quenched.

'I know you would, Roger,' she said, 'but any further suffering that may come my way I can bear alone. If I have brought dishonour on two houses, my husband's and Otto Bodrugan's, which doubtless will be said about me down the years, I'll not do the same to yours.'

'Dishonour?' He spread out his hands and looked about him at the low walls encircling the yard, the narrow thatched dwelling where the ponies and the cows were housed. 'This was my father's farm and will be Robbie's when I die, and had you sheltered here for one night only and not fifteen, you would have lent it grace enough to last through centuries.'

She must have sensed the depth of feeling in his voice, and possibly the passion too, for a sudden shadow came across her face, a wariness, as if prompted by an inner voice that murmured, 'Thus far, and no further.' Moving to the open gate she put her hand upon it, and looked out over the fields to the bay beyond.

'Fifteen nights,' she repeated, 'and on each one of them, since I have been with you, and in the daytime too, I have stood looking out across the sea to Chapel Point, remembering that his ship would anchor there, below Bodrugan, and this was the bay he sailed when he came to find me in the Treesmill creek. Part of me died with him, Roger, the day they drowned him, and I think you know it.'

I wondered what Roger's dream had been, and whether, as we all do, he had created a fantasy that their lives would somehow fuse; not in marriage, not as lovers, even, but in some sort of drifting intimacy, intuitive and silent, that no one else would ever share. Whether it were so or not, the dream was shattered; by speaking Bodrugan's name she had made this plain.

'Yes,' he said, 'I have always known it. If I have given you cause to believe otherwise, forgive me.'

He lifted his head and listened. She did the same, and beyond the dark copse above the farm came the sound of voices and tramping of feet, and then the figures of three of the Champernoune servants emerged through the naked trees.

'Roger Kylmerth?' one of them called. 'Your road is too rough to drive the chariot down to your dwelling, and my lady waits within it on the hill.'

'Then she must stay there,' answered Roger, 'or come on foot, with your assistance. It's one and the same to us.'

The men hesitated a moment, conferring under the trees, and Isolda, at a sign from Roger, turned quickly and passed across the yard into the house. Roger whistled, and Robbie came out of the door where the ponies were stabled.

'Lady Champernoune is above, and some of her servants,' said Roger quietly. 'She could have summoned others between here and Tywardreath, and we may have trouble. Stay within call should I need you.'

Robbie nodded, and went back into the stables. It was growing darker every moment, colder, too, the trees in the copse etched more sharply against the sky. Presently I saw the lights of the first flares on the crest of the hill; Joanna was descending, three of the servants with her, and the monk as well. They came slowly and in silence, Joanna's dark cloak and the monk's habit blending as though the two were one; and standing beside Roger, watching their progress, it seemed to me that the group had something sinister about it; the hooded figures could have been walking in procession through a churchyard to a waiting grave.

When they arrived at the open gate Joanna paused and looked about her, then she said to Roger, 'In all the ten years you served my household you never thought to bid me welcome here.'

'No, my lady,' he replied, 'you neither asked for refuge nor desired it. Consolation was ever ready for you under your own roof.'

The irony did not touch her, or if it did she chose to ignore it, and Roger led the way towards the house.

'Where must my servants wait?' she asked. 'Have the courtesy to direct them to your kitchen.'

'We ourselves live in the kitchen,' he told her, 'and Lady Carminowe will receive you there. Your men will find it warm enough in the byre amongst the cows, or with the ponies, which ever they please.'

He stood aside to let her pass with the monk, and followed after, and as we crossed the threshold I saw that the trestle table had been pulled close to the hearth, the tallow candles set upon it, and Isolda sat alone at the head of the table. Bess must have gone to the room above.

Joanna stared about her, at a loss, I think, to find herself in such surroundings. God knows what she had expected – some greater attempt at comfort, perhaps, with furnishings pilfered from her own abandoned manor house.

'So . . .' she said at last, 'this is the retreat, and snug enough, no doubt, on a winter's night, apart from the smell of beasts across the yard. How do you do, Isolda?'

'I do very well, as you see,' Isolda answered. 'I have lived better here, and had more kindness, in two weeks than in as many months or years spent at Tregesteynton or Carminowe.'

'I don't doubt it,' said Joanna. 'Contrast ever whetted appetite grown stale. You had a fancy for Bodrugan Castle once, but had Otto lived you would have become as weary there and of him as you have of other properties and other men, including your own husband. Well, this is a rich reward. Tell me, do both brothers share you here before the hearth?'

I heard Roger draw in his breath, and he moved forward, as though to place himself between the two women, but Isolda, her small face pale in the flickering light of two candles, only smiled.

'Not as yet,' she said. 'The elder is too proud, the younger too shy. My protestations of affection fall upon deaf ears. What do you want with me, Joanna? Have you brought a message from William? If so, speak plainly and have done with it.'

The monk, who was still standing by the door, took a letter from his habit to give to Joanna, but she waved it aside.

'Read it to Lady Carminowe,' she said. 'I have no desire to strain my eyes in this dim light. And you may leave us,' she added to Roger. 'Family matters are no longer your concern. You meddled with them enough when you were my steward.'

'This is his house, and he has the right to be here,' said Isolda. 'Besides, he is my friend, and I prefer him to stay.'

Joanna shrugged, and sat down at the lower end of the table opposite Isolda.

'If Lady Carminowe permits,' said the monk smoothly, 'this is the letter from her brother, Sir William Ferrers, which came to Trelawn a few days since, Sir William thinking his messenger would find her there with Lady Champernoune. It reads thus:

' "Dearest Sister, the news of your flight from Tregesteynton has only reached us here at Bere within the past week, because of the hard weather and the state of the roads, I am at a loss to understand either your action or your great imprudence. You must know that by deserting your husband and your children you forfeit all claims on his and their affection, and, I am bound to say, on mine as well. Whether Oliver, in Christian charity, will receive you at Carminowe again I cannot say, but I misdoubt it, fearing your pernicious influence upon his daughters, and for my own part I could not offer you protection at Bere, for Matilda, as Oliver's sister, has too much sympathy for her brother to offer hospitality to his erring wife. Indeed, she is in so sore a state since hearing you have deserted him that she could not countenance your presence amongst us with our five sons. It seems, therefore, there is only one course upon to you, which is to seek refuge in the nunnery of Cornworthy here in Devon, the Prioress being known to me, and to remain there in seclusion until such time as Oliver, or some other member of the family, may be willing to receive you. I have every confidence that our kinswoman, Joanna, will permit her servants to escort you to Cornworthy.

' "Farewell, in the power of Christ,
  ' "Your sorrowful brother,
    ' "William Ferrers" '

The monk folded the letter and passed it across the table to Isolda. 'You may see for yourself, my lady,' he murmured, 'that the letter is in Sir William's own handwriting, and bears his signature. There is no deception.'

She barely glanced at it. 'You are very right,' she said, 'there is no deception.'

Joanna smiled. 'If William had known you were here and not at Trelawn, I doubt if he would have written so generously, nor would the Prioress at Cornworthy be willing to open her convent doors. However, you may count on me to keep it secret, and arrange your escort into Devon. Two days under my roof to make the necessary preparations, a change of attire, which I can see you need, and you can be on the road.' She leant back in her chair, a look of triumph on her face. 'I am told the air is mild at Cornworthy,' she added. 'The nuns there live to a great age.'

'Then let us dwell behind convent walls together,' replied Isolda. 'Widows, when their sons marry, as your William does next year, must needs find new shelter, along with erring wives. We will be sisters in misfortune.'

Proud and defiant, she stared at Joanna down the length of the trestle table, and the candlelight, throwing shadows on the wall, distorted both their figures, turning Joanna, because of her hooded cloak and widow's veil, to the likeness of some monstrous crab.

'You forget,' she said, playing with her multitude of rings, slipping them from one finger to another, 'I have a licence to remarry, and can do so whenever I choose to pick a new husband from a chain of suitors. You are still bound to Oliver, and furthermore disgraced. There is a second course open to you other than the nunnery at Cornworthy, if you prefer it, and that is to remain as drab here to my one-time steward, but I warn you the parish might serve you as they served my tenant this day in Tywardreath, and have you riding to do penance in the manor chapel on the back of a black ram.'

She broke into a peal of laughter, and, turning to the monk who was standing behind her chair, she said, 'What do you say, Frère Jean? We could mount the one on a ram and the other on a ewe, and have them jog-trot together or forfeit the Kylmerth land.'

I knew it must happen, and it did. Roger seized the monk and threw him back against the wall. Then, bending to Joanna, he jerked her to her feet.

'Insult me as you please, not Lady Carminowe,' he said. 'This is my house, and you shall leave it.'

'I will do so,' she replied, 'when she has made her choice. I have three servants only in your cow-house in the yard, but a score or more waiting by my carriage on the hill, only too willing to pay off ancient grudges.'

'Then summon them,' said Roger, freeing her. 'Robbie and I can defend our home against every one of your tenants, the whole parish if you will.'

His voice, raised in anger, had penetrated to the sleeping-room above, and Bess came running down the ladder, pale and anxious, to take her stand behind Isolda's bench.

'Who's this?' asked Joanna. 'A third for the sheepfold? How many other slatterns do you harbour in your loft?'

'Bess is Roger's sister, and so my own,' answered Isolda, putting her arm round the frightened girl. 'And now, Joanna, call your servants so that this household can be rid of you. God knows we've borne your insults long enough.'

'We?' queried Joanna. 'Then you count yourself one of them?'

'Yes, while I receive their hospitality,' said Isolda.

'So you do not intend to travel with me to Trelawn?'

Isolda hesitated, glancing first at Roger, then at Bess. But before she could reply the monk stepped out of the shadows on the wall and stood beside them.

'There is a third choice yet for Lady Carminowe,' he murmured. 'I sail from Fowey, within twenty-four hours, to the parent house of St Sergius and Bacchus at Angers. If she and the girl care to accompany me to France, I know very well I could find asylum for them there. No one would molest them, and they would be safe from all pursuit. Their very existence would be forgotten once they were in France, and Lady Carminowe herself be at liberty to start life anew in pleasanter surroundings than behind convent walls.'

The proposal was so obvious a trick to get both Bess and Isolda out of Roger's care and into his own charge, to dispose of them as he wished, that I expected even his patroness to round upon him. Instead, she smiled, and shrugged her shoulders.

'Upon my word, Frère Jean, you show true Christian feeling,' she said. 'What do you say, Isolda? Now you have three alternatives: seclusion at Cornworthy, life in a pigsty at Kylmerth, or the protection of a Benedictine monk across the water. I know which I would choose.'

She glanced about her as she had first done when she entered the house, and moving round the room touched the smoke-grimed walls, grimacing, then examined her fingers, wiping them with the handkerchief she carried, and finally paused by the ladder leading to the loft above, her foot upon one rung.

'One pallet amongst four, and louse-ridden?' she asked. 'If you travel into Devon or to France, Isolda, I'll thank you to sprinkle your gown with vinegar first.'

The singing started in my ears, and the thunder. Their figures began to fade. All but Joanna's, standing there at the foot of the ladder. She stared towards me, her eyes opening wide, and I did not care what happened afterwards, I wanted to put my hands round her throat and choke her before she vanished, like the others, out of sight. I crossed the room and stood beside her, and she did not fade. She began to scream, as I shook her backwards and forwards, my hands round her plump, white neck.

'Damn you,' I shouted, 'damn you . . . damn you . . .' and the screaming was all around me, and above as well. I loosened my grip and looked up, and the boys were crouching there on the landing at the top of the back stairs, and Vita had fallen against the banister beside me, and was staring at me, white-faced, terrified, her hands to her throat.

'Oh, my God!' I said. 'Vita . . . darling . . . Oh, my God . . .'

I fell forwards on to the banister rail beside her, retching, seized by the uncontrollable, blasted vertigo, and she dragged herself away up the stairs to safety beside the boys, and they all started screaming once again.

twenty-three

There was nothing I could do. I lay there on the stairs, clinging to the handrail, arms and legs splayed out grotesquely, with walls and ceiling reeling above my head. If I shut my eyes the vertigo increased, with streaks of golden light stabbing the darkness. Presently the screaming stopped; the boys were crying, and I could hear the crying die away as they ran into the kitchen overhead, slamming both the doors.

Blinded by dizziness and nausea, I started to crawl upstairs, step by step, and when I had reached the top stood upright, swaying, and felt my way across the kitchen to the hall. The lights were on, the doors were open. Vita and the boys must have run up to the bedroom and locked themselves in. I staggered into the lobby and reached for the telephone, floor and ceiling blurring to become one. I sat there, holding the receiver in my hand, until the floor steadied, and the telephone directory, instead of being a jumble of black dots, straightened into words. I found Dr Powell's number at last and dialled it, and when he answered the tension inside me broke, and I felt the sweat pouring down my face.

'It's Richard Young from Kilmarth,' I said. 'You remember, the friend of Professor Lane.'

'Oh yes?' He sounded surprised. After all, I was not one of his patients, and I must only be a face amongst hundreds of summer visitors.

'The most frightful thing has happened,' I said. 'I had a sort of black-out and tried to strangle my wife. I may have hurt her, I don't know.'

My voice was calm, without emotion, yet all the time my heart was pounding, and the realization of what had happened was clear and strong. There was no confusion. No merging of two worlds.

'Is she unconscious?' he asked.

'No,' I said, 'no, I don't think so. She's upstairs, with the boys. They must have locked themselves in the bedroom. I'm speaking to you from the lobby downstairs.'

He was silent, and for one terrible moment I was afraid he was going to tell me it was none of his business and I had better call the police. Then, 'All right, I'll be along straight away,' he said, and rang off.

I put down the receiver and wiped the sweat off my face. The vertigo had subsided, and I was able to stand without swaying. I walked slowly upstairs and through the dressing-room to the bathroom door. It was locked.

'Darling,' I called, 'don't worry, it's OK. I've just telephoned the doctor. He's coming out at once. Stay there with the boys until you hear his car.' She did not answer, and I called louder. 'Vita,' I shouted, 'Teddy, Micky, don't be frightened, the doctor's coming. Everything's going to be all right.'

I went back downstairs and opened the front door, and stood

waiting there on the steps. It was a fine night, the sky ablaze with stars. There was no sound anywhere; the campers in the field across the Polkerris road must have turned in. I looked at my watch. It was twenty to eleven. Then I heard the sound of the doctor's car coming along the main road from Fowey, and I began to sweat again, not from fear but from relief. He turned down the drive and came to a standstill in the sweep before the house. I went through the garden to meet him.

'Thank God you've come,' I said.

We went into the house together, and I pointed up the stairs. 'First room at the top, on the right. That's my dressing-room, but she's locked the bathroom beyond. Tell them who you are. I'll wait for you down here.'

He ran upstairs, two steps at a time, and I kept thinking that the silence from above meant that Vita was dying, that she was lying on the bed, and the boys were crouching beside her, too terrified to move. I went into the music-room and sat down, wondering what would happen if he told me Vita was dead. All of it was happening. All of it was true.

He was up there a long time, and presently I heard the sound of shifting furniture; they must be dragging the divan bed through the bathroom to the bedroom, and I could hear the doctor talking, and Teddy too. I wondered what the hell they were doing. I went and listened at the foot of the stairs, but they had gone through to the bedroom again and shut the door. I sat on in the music-room, waiting.

He came down just after the clock in the hall struck eleven. 'Everything's under control,' he said. 'No panic stations. Your wife's all right, and so are your stepsons. Now what about you?'

I tried to stand up, but he pushed me back into the chair.

'Have I hurt her?' I asked.

'Slight bruising on the neck, nothing more,' he said. 'It may look a bit blue tomorrow, but it won't show if she wears a scarf.'

'Did she tell you what happened?'

'Supposing you tell me?'

'I'd rather hear her version first,' I said.

He took a cigarette out of a packet and lighted it. 'Well,' he said, 'I gather you didn't want any dinner, for reasons known best to yourself, and she spent the evening in here with the boys, while you were in the library. Then they decided to go to bed, and she found you had gone to the kitchen and switched on the lights. There was bacon on the stove burnt to a frazzle, the stove still on, but nobody there. So she went down to the basement. It seems you were standing there, near the old kitchen, so she said, waiting for her to come downstairs, and as soon as you saw her you went straight across to the foot of the stairs and began swearing at her, and then you put your hands round her throat and tried to throttle her.'

'That's right,' I said.

He looked at me sharply. Perhaps he thought I would deny it. 'She insists you were fighting drunk and didn't know what you were doing,' he said, 'but it was a pretty grim experience for all of them, and she and those boys were scared out of their wits. More so, as I gather you're not a drinking type.'

'No,' I said, 'I'm not. And I wasn't drunk.'

He did not answer for a moment. Then he came and stood in front of me, and taking some sort of flash thing from the bag he had with him he examined my eyes. Afterwards he felt my pulse.

'What are you on?' he asked abruptly.

'On?'

'Yes, what drug. Tell me straight, and I'll know how to treat you.'

'That's just it,' I said. 'I don't know.'

'Was it something Professor Lane gave you?'

'Yes,' I replied.

He sat down on the arm of the sofa beside my chair. 'By mouth or by injection?'

'By mouth.'

'Was he treating you for something specific?'

'He wasn't treating me for anything. It was an experiment. Something I volunteered to do for him. I've never taken drugs in my life before I came down here.'

He went on looking at me with his shrewd eyes, and I knew there was nothing for it but to tell him everything.

'Was Professor Lane on the same drug when he walked into that freight train?' he asked.

'Yes.'

He got off the sofa and began walking up and down the room, fiddling with things on tables, picking them up and putting them down again, as Magnus himself used to do when coming to a decision.

'I ought to get you into hospital for observation,' he said.

'No,' I said, 'for God's sake . . .' I got up from my chair. 'Look,' I said, 'I've got the stuff in a bottle upstairs. It's all there is left. One bottle. He told me to destroy everything I found here in his lab, and I did – it's all buried in the wood above the garden. I only kept the one bottle, and I used some of it today. It must be different in some way – stronger, I don't know – but you take it away, have it analysed, anything. Surely you realize, after what has happened tonight, I couldn't touch the stuff again? Christ! I might have killed my wife.'

'I know,' he said. 'That's why you ought to be in hospital.'

He did not know. He did not understand. How could he understand?

'Look,' I said, 'I never saw Vita, my wife, standing at the foot of the stairs. It wasn't her I tried to strangle. It was another woman.'

'What woman?' he asked.

'A woman called Joanna,' I said. 'She lived six hundred years ago. She was down there, in the old farmhouse kitchen, and the others were with her too. Isolda Carminowe, and the monk Jean de Meral, and the man the farm belonged to, who used to be her steward, Roger Kylmerth.'

He put out his hand and held my arm. 'All right,' he said, 'steady on, I follow you. You took the drug, and then you went downstairs and saw these people in the basement?'

'Yes,' I said, 'but not only here. I've seen them in Tywardreath as well, at the old manor-house below the Gratten, and at the Priory too. That's what the drug does. It takes you back into the past, straight into an older world.'

I could hear my voice rising in excitement, and he kept a firm grip on my arm. 'You don't believe me?' I persisted. 'How can you possibly believe me? But I swear to you I've seen them, heard them talking, watched them moving, I've even seen a man, Isolda's lover Otto Bodrugan, murdered down in Treesmill creek.'

'I believe you all right,' he said. 'Now supposing we go together and you hand over that remaining bottle?'

I led him upstairs to the dressing-room, and took the bottle out of the locked suitcase. He did not examine it, he just put it in his bag.

'Now I'll tell you what I'm going to do,' he said. 'I'm going to give you a pretty hefty sedative that will put you out until tomorrow morning. Is there some other room than this where you can sleep?'

'Yes,' I said. 'There's the spare-room along the landing here.'

'Right,' he said. 'Collect a pair of pyjamas and let's go.'

We went together into the spare-room, and I undressed and got into bed, feeling suddenly humble and subdued, like a child without responsibility.

'I'll do anything you say,' I told the doctor. 'Put me right out, if you like, so that I never wake again.'

'I shan't do that,' he answered, and for the first time smiled. 'When you open your eyes tomorrow I shall probably be the first object you see.'

'Then you won't pack me off to hospital?'

'Probably not. We'll talk about it in the morning.'

He was getting a syringe out of his bag. 'I don't mind what you tell my wife,' I said, 'as long as you don't tell her about the drug. Let her go on thinking I was crazy drunk. Whatever happens she mustn't know about the drug. She disliked Magnus – Professor Lane – and if she knew about this she'd dislike his memory even more.'

'I dare say she would,' he answered, wiping my arm with spirit before plunging his needle in, 'and you could hardly blame her.'

'The thing was,' I said, 'she was jealous. We'd known one another for so many years, he and I; we were at Cambridge together. I used to come and stay here in the old days, and Magnus seemed to take charge. We were always together, the same things intrigued us, the same things made us laugh, Magnus and I ... Magnus and I ...'

The depth of an abyss or the long sweet sleep of death, I did not mind. Five hours, five months, five years ... in point of fact, so I learnt later, it was five days. The doctor always seemed to be there, when I opened my eyes, giving me another jab, or else sitting at the end of the bed swinging his legs, listening while I talked. Sometimes Vita looked in at the door with an uncertain smile, then disappeared. She and Mrs Collins between them must have made my bed, washed me, fed me – though I have no recollection of eating anything at all. Memory of those days is blotted out. I could have cursed, raved, torn the bedding, or merely slept. I understand I slept, and also talked. Not to Mrs Collins, but to the doctor. However many sessions it took between jabs I have no idea, nor do I know just what I said, but I gather I spilt, as the saying goes, the beans from start to finish, with the consequence that in the middle of the following week, when I was more or less back to normal and sitting around in a chair upstairs instead of lying in bed, body and mind felt not only rested but completely purged.

I told him so, over coffee which Vita had brought and left with us, and he laughed, saying a thorough clear-out never did any harm, and it was amazing the amount of stuff people locked away in attics and cellars they had forgotten about, which would be all the better if the light got through to it.

'Mind you,' he added, 'purging the soul comes easier to you than to others, because of your Catholic background.'

I stared. 'How did you know I was a Catholic?' I asked.

'It all came out in the wash,' he said.

I felt strangely shocked. I had imagined that I had told him everything from start to finish about the experiment with the drug, and had described to him, in detail, the happenings of the other world. The fact that I had been born and bred a Catholic had no bearing on this at all.

'I'm a very bad Catholic,' I said. 'I couldn't wait to get away from Stonyhurst, and I haven't been to Mass for years. As to Confession . . .'

'I know,' he said, 'all in the attic or underground. Along with your dislike of monks, stepfathers, widows who remarry, and other little things along the same line.'

I poured myself another cup of coffee, and one for him as well, throwing in too much sugar and stirring furiously.

'Look here,' I said, 'you're talking nonsense. I never give a thought to monks, widows or stepfathers – with the exception of myself – in my ordinary present-day life. The fact that these people existed in the fourteenth century, and I was able to see them, was entirely due to the drug.'

'Yes,' he said, 'entirely due to the drug.' He did his abrupt thing of getting up and walking round the room. 'That bottle you gave me, I did what you ought to have done after the inquest. I sent it up to Lane's chief assistant, John Willis, with a brief word that you had been in trouble with it, and could I have a report as soon as possible? He was good enough to ring me up on the telephone as soon as he had my letter.'

'Well?' I asked.

'Well, you're a very lucky man to be alive, and not only alive but here in this house and not in a loony-bin. The stuff in that bottle contained probably the most potent hallucinogen that has ever been discovered, and other substances as well which he isn't even sure of yet. Professor Lane was apparently working on this alone: he never took Willis fully into his confidence.'

A lucky man to be alive, possibly. Lucky not to be in a loony-bin, agreed. But much of this I had told myself already, when I first started the experiment.

'Are you trying to tell me,' I asked, 'that everything I've seen has been hallucination, dug up from the murky waste of my own unconscious?'

'No, I'm not,' he said. 'I think Professor Lane was on to something that might have proved extraordinarily significant about the workings of the brain, and he chose you as guinea-pig because he knew you would do whatever he told you, and that you were a highly suggestible subject into the bargain.' He wandered over to the table and finished his cup of coffee. 'Incidentally, everything you've told me is just as secret as if you had spilt it into the Confessional. I had an initial struggle with your wife to keep you here, instead of sending you in an ambulance to some top chap in Harley Street who would have bunged you straight into a psychiatric home for six months. I think she trusts me now.'

'What did you tell her?' I asked.

'I said you had been on the verge of a nervous breakdown, and suffering from strain and delayed shock owing to the sudden death of Professor Lane. Which, you may agree, is perfectly true.'

I got up rather gingerly from my chair and walked over to the window. The campers had gone from the field across the way, and the cattle were grazing once again. I could hear our own boys playing cricket by the orchard.

'You may say what you like,' I said slowly, 'suggestibility, breakdown, Catholic conscience, the lot, but the fact remains that I've been in that other world, seen it, known it. It was cruel, hard, and very often bloody, and so were the people in it, except Isolda, and latterly Roger, but, my God, it held a fascination for me which is lacking in my own world of today.'

He came and stood beside me at the window. He gave me a cigarette, and we both smoked awhile in silence.

'The other world,' he said at last. 'I suppose we all carry one inside us, in our various ways. You, Professor Lane, your wife, myself, and we'd see it differently if we all made the experiment together – which God forbid!' He smiled, and flicked his cigarette out of the window. 'I have a feeling my own wife might take a dim view of an Isolda if I took to wandering about the Treesmill valley looking for her. Which is not to say I haven't done so through the years, but I'm too down to earth to go back six centuries on the off-chance that I might meet her.'

'My Isolda lived,' I said stubbornly, 'I've seen actual pedigrees and historical documents to prove it. They all lived. I've got papers downstairs in the library that don't lie.'

'Of course she lived,' he agreed, 'and what is more had two small girls called Joanna and Margaret, you told me about them. Little girls are more fascinating sometimes than small boys, and you have a couple of stepsons.'

'And what the hell is that supposed to mean?'

'Nothing,' he said, 'just an observation. The world we carry inside us produces answers, sometimes. A way of escape. A flight from reality. You didn't want to live either in London or in New York. The fourteenth century made an exciting, if somewhat gruesome, antidote to both. The trouble is that day-dreams, like hallucinogenic drugs, become addictive; the more we indulge, the deeper we plunge, and then, as I said before, we end in the loony-bin.'

I had the impression that everything he said was leading up to something else, to some practical proposition that I must take a grip on myself, get a job, sit in an office, sleep with Vita, breed daughters, look forward contentedly to middle-age, when I might grow cacti in a greenhouse.

'What do you want me to do?' I asked. 'Come on, out with it.'

He turned round from the window and looked me straight in the face.

'Frankly, I don't mind what you do,' he said. 'It's not my problem. As your medical adviser and father confessor for less than a week, I'd be glad to see you around for several years to come. And I'll be delighted to prescribe the usual antibiotics when you catch the flu. But for the immediate future I suggest that you get out of this house pretty quick before you have another urge to visit the basement.'

I drew a deep breath. 'I thought so,' I said. 'You've been talking to Vita.'

'Naturally I've talked to your wife,' he agreed, 'and apart from a few feminine quirks she's a very sensible woman. When I say get out of the house I don't mean for ever. But for the next few weeks at least you'd be better away from it. You must see the force of that.'

I did see it, but like a cornered rat I struggled for survival and played for time.

'All right,' I said. 'Where do you suggest we go? We've got those boys on our hands.'

'Well, they don't worry you, do they?'

'No . . . No, I'm very fond of them.'

'It doesn't matter where, providing it's out of the pull of Roger Kylmerth.'

'My alter ego?' I queried. 'He and I are not a scrap alike, you know.'

'Alter egos never are,' he said. 'Mine is a long-haired poet who faints at the sight of blood. He's dogged me ever since I left medical school.'

I laughed, in spite of myself. He made everything seem so simple. 'I wish you had known Magnus,' I said. 'You remind me of him in an odd sort of way.'

'I wish I had. Seriously, though, I mean what I say about your getting away. Your wife suggested Ireland. Good walking country, fishing, crocks of gold buried under the hills . . .'

'Yes,' I said, 'and two of her compatriots who are touring around in the best hotels.'

'She mentioned them,' he said, 'but I gather they've gone — got fed up with the weather and flown to sunny Spain instead. So that needn't worry you. I thought Ireland a good idea because it only means a three-hour drive from here to Exeter, and then you can fly direct. Hire a car the other side, and you're away.'

He and Vita had the whole thing taped. I was trapped; there was no way out. I must put a brave face on it and admit defeat.

'Supposing I refuse?' I asked. 'Get back into bed and pull the sheet over my head?'

'I'd send for an ambulance and cart you off to hospital. I thought Ireland was a better idea, but it's up to you.'

Five minutes later he had gone, and I heard his car roaring up the drive. The sense of anti-climax was absolute: the purge had been very thorough. And I still did not know how much I had told him. Doubtless a hotch-potch of everything I had ever thought or done since the age of three, and, like all doctors with leanings towards psychoanalysis, he had put it together and summed me up as the usual sort of misfit with homosexual leanings who had suffered from birth with a mother complex, a stepfather complex, an aversion to copulation with my widowed wife, and a repressed desire to hit the hay with a blonde who had never existed except in my own imagination.

It all fitted, naturally. The Priory was Stonyhurst, Brother Jean was that silken bastard who taught me history, Joanna was my mother and poor Vita rolled into one, and Otto Bodrugan the handsome, gay adventurer I really longed to be. The fact that they all had lived, and could be proved to have lived, had not impressed Dr Powell. It was a pity he had not tried the drug himself, instead of sending bottle C to John Willis. Then he might have thought again.

Well, it was over now. I must go along with his diagnosis, and his holiday plans as well. God knows it was the least that I could do, after nearly killing Vita.

Funny he hadn't said anything about side-effects, or delayed action. Perhaps he had discussed this with John Willis, and John Willis had given the OK. But then Willis didn't know about the bloodshot eye, the sweats, the nausea and the vertigo. Nobody did, though Powell may have guessed, especially after our first encounter. Anyway, I felt normal enough now. Too normal, if the truth be told. Like a small boy spanked who had promised to amend his ways.

I opened the door and called for Vita. She came running up the stairs at once, and I realized, with a sense of shame and guilt, what she must have been through during the past week. Her face was drained of colour and she had lost weight. Her hair, usually immaculate, was swept back with a hasty comb behind her ears, and there was a strained, unhappy look in her eyes that I had never seen before.

'He told me you had agreed to come away,' she said. 'It was his idea, not mine, I promise you. I only want to do what's best for you.'

'I know that,' I said. 'He's absolutely right.'

'You're not angry, then? I was so afraid you'd be angry.'

She came and sat beside me on the bed, and I put my arm round her.

'You must promise me one thing,' I said, 'and that is to forget everything that's happened up to now. I know it's practically impossible, but I do ask you.'

'You've been ill. I know why, the doctor explained it all,' she said. 'He told the boys too, and they understand. We none of us blame you for anything, darling. We just want you to get well and to be happy.'

'They're not frightened of me?'

'Heavens, no. They were very sensible about it. They've both been so good and helpful, Teddy especially. They're devoted to you, darling, I don't think you realize that.'

'Oh, yes, I do,' I said, 'which makes it all the worse. But never mind that now. When are we supposed to be off?'

She hesitated. 'Dr Powell said you'd be fit to travel by Friday, and he told me to go ahead and get the tickets.'

Friday . . . The day after tomorrow.

'OK,' I said, 'if that's what he says. I suppose I'd better move about a bit to get myself in trim. Sort out some things to pack.'

'As long as you don't overdo it. I'll send Teddy up to help you.' She left me with the best part of a week's mail, and by the time I'd been through it, and chucked most of it into the wastepaper basket, Teddy had appeared at the door.

'Mom said you might like some help with your packing,' he said shyly.

'Good lad, I would. I hear you've been head of the house for the past week, and doing a fine job.'

He flushed with pleasure. 'Oh, I don't know. I haven't done much. Answered the phone a few times. There was a man called up yesterday, asked if you were better and sent his regards. A Mr Willis. He left his number, in case you wanted to ring him. And he left another number too. I wrote them both down.'

He brought out a shiny black notebook and tore out a page. I recognized the first number – it was Magnus's lab – but the other one baffled me.

'Is this second one his home number, or didn't he say?' I asked.

'Yes, he did say. It's someone called Davies, who works at the British Museum. He thought you might like to get in touch with Mr Davies before he went on holiday.'

I put the torn page in my pocket, and went along with Teddy to the dressing-room. The divan bed had gone, and I realized what the dragging sound had signified the night the doctor came: the bed had been moved into the double room and put under the window.

'Micky and I have been sleeping in here with Mom,' said Teddy. 'She felt she wanted company.'

It was a delicate way of putting that she wanted protection. I left him in the dressing-room pulling things out of the wardrobe, and picked up the telephone receiver beside the bed.

The voice that answered me, precise and rather reserved, assured me the owner's name was Davies.

'I'm Richard Young,' I told him, 'a friend of the late Professor Lane. You know all about me, I believe.'

'Yes, indeed, Mr Young, I hope you are better. I heard through John Willis that you'd been laid up.'

'That's right. Nothing serious. But I'm going away, and I gather you are too, so I wondered if you had anything for me.'

'Unfortunately nothing very much, I'm afraid. If you'll excuse me a moment, I'll just get my notes and read them out to you.'

I waited, while he put down the receiver. I had the uncomfortable feeling that I was cheating, and that Dr Powell would have disapproved.

'Are you there, Mr Young?'

'Yes, I'm here.'

'I hope you won't be disappointed. They are only extracts from the Registers of Bishop Grandisson of Exeter, one dated 1334, the second 1335. The first relates to Tywardreath Priory, and the second to Oliver Carminowe. The first is a letter from the Bishop at Exeter to the Abbot of the sister-house at Angers, and reads as follows:

'John, etc., Bishop of Exeter, sends greeting with true kindness of thought in the Lord. Inasmuch as we expel from our fold the diseased sheep which is wont to spread its disorder, lest it should infect our other healthy sheep, so in the case of Brother Jean, called Meral, a monk of your monastery at present living in the Priory of Tywardwreath in our diocease, which is ruled by a Prior of the Order of St Benedict, on account of his outrageous abandonment of all shame and decent behaviour, in spite of frequent kindly admonitions – and because, alas, as I am ashamed to say (not to mention his other notorious offences), he has nevertheless become more hardened in his wickedness – we have therefore, with all zeal and reverence for your order and for yourself, arranged to send him back to you to be subjected to the discipline of the monastery for this evil behaviour. May God Himself maintain you in the rule of this flock in length of days and health.'

He cleared his throat. 'The original is in Latin, you understand. This is my translation. I couldn't help thinking, as I copied it out, how the phrasing would have appealed to Professor Lane.'

'Yes,' I said, 'it would.'

He cleared his throat again. 'The second piece is very short, and may not interest you. It is only that on 21 April, 1335, Bishop Grandisson received Sir Oliver Carminowe and his wife Sybell, who had been clandestinely married without banns or licence. They confirmed that they had erred through ignorance. The Bishop relaxed the sentences imposed upon them and confirmed the marriage, which seems to have taken place at some previous date, not stated, in Sir Oliver's private chapel at Carminowe, in the parish of Mawgan-in-Meneage. Proceedings were taken against the priest who married them. That's all.'

'Does it say what had happened to the previous wife, Isolda?'

'No. I presume she died, possibly a short while before, and this other marriage was clandestine because it took place so soon after her death. Perhaps Sybell was pregnant, and a private ceremony seemed necessary to save face. I'm sorry, Mr Young, but I haven't been able to turn up anything else.'

'Don't worry,' I said. 'What you've told me is very valuable. Have a good holiday.'

'Thank you. The same to you.'

I put down the receiver. Teddy was calling to me from the dressing-room.

'Dick?'

'Yes?'

He came through from the bathroom with Magnus's walking-stick in his hands.

'Will you be taking this with you?' he asked. 'It's too long to fit into your suitcase.'

I had not seen the stick since I had poured into it the colourless liquid from bottle C nearly a week ago. I had forgotten all about it.

'If you don't want it,' said Teddy, 'I'll put it back in the cupboard where I found it.'

'No,' I said, 'give it to me. I do want it.'

He pretended to take aim at me, smiling, holding it balanced like a spear, then lobbed it gently in the air. I caught it and held it fast.

twenty-four

We sat in the lounge at Exeter airport waiting for our flight to be called. Take-off was twelve-thirty. The Buick was parked behind the airport, to remain there until our return, whenever that should be. I got sandwiches for all of us, and while we ate them cast an eye over our fellow-travellers. There were flights that afternoon for the Channel Isles as well as Dublin, and the lounge facing the airfield was filled with people. There were a number of priests returning from some convocation, a party of schoolchildren, family parties such as our own, and the usual sprinkling of holiday types. There was also a hilarious sextet who, from their conversation, were on their way to, or from, a riotous wedding.

'I hope,' said Vita, 'we aren't going to find ourselves beside that lot on the plane.'

The boys were already doubled up with laughter, for one of the group had donned a false nose and a moustache, which he kept dipping into his glass of Guinness, to emerge beaded with froth.

'The thing to do,' I said, 'is to leap to our feet as soon as our flight is called, so that we can get right up to the front, well away from them.'

'If that man with the false nose tries to sit beside me, I shall scream,' said Vita.

Her remark set the boys off again, and I congratulated myself on having ordered generous rations of cider for the boys and brandy and soda – our holiday drink – for Vita and myself, because it was that, more than the wedding party, which was making the boys giggle and causing Vita to squint as she peered in her powder-compact. I kept a close watch on the plane on the runway, until I saw that it was loaded. They were pulling the baggage trucks away, and a hostess was walking across the tarmac to our door.

'Damn!' I said. 'I knew it was a mistake to swill all that coffee and brandy. Look, darling, I must rush to the gents. If they call the flight go ahead and get seats in front, as I said. If I'm caught up in the mob I'll find myself a seat at the back and change places after take-off. As long as you three are together you'll be all right. Here – you take your boarding cards and I'll hang on to mine, just in case.'

'Oh, Dick, honestly!' exclaimed Vita. 'You might have gone before. How typical of you!'

'Sorry,' I said: 'Nature calls . . .'

I walked rapidly across the lounge as I saw the hostess enter the door, and waited inside the gents. I heard the flight number called over the loudspeaker, and after a few minutes, when I came out again, our party was walking with the hostess across to the aircraft, Vita and the boys in the van. As I watched, they disappeared into the plane, followed by the school-children and the priests. It was now or never. I went rapidly out of the main door of the airport building, and crossed over to the car park. In a moment I had started the Buick and pulled out of the airport entrance. Then I drew into the side of the road and listened. I could hear the sound of the engines before the plane taxied to the start, which must mean that everyone was aboard. If the engines ceased it would mean my plan had gone for nothing, and the hostess had discovered that I was missing. It was twelve thirty-five exactly. Then I heard the engines increase in pitch and in a few minutes, unbelievably, my heart pounding, I saw the silver streak of the aircraft speeding along the runway and take off, gain height and flatten out, and then it was away amongst the clouds and out of sight, and I was sitting there, at the wheel of the Buick, on my own.

They were due to touch down at Dublin at one-fifty. I knew exactly what Vita would do. She would put through a call from the airport to Dr Powell in Fowey, and find him out. He would be out because it was his half-day. He had told me so, when I had rung up after breakfast to say goodbye. He had said that, if it was fine, he was going to take his family over to the north coast to surf, and he would be thinking about us, and would I please send him a postcard from Ireland saying 'Wish you were here.'

I started to sing, as I turned into the main road and touched seventy. This was how a criminal must feel when he had just robbed a bank and got away with the loot in a stolen van. A pity I had not the whole day before me to explore at leisure, drive over to Bere and look up Sir William Ferrers and his wife Matilda, perhaps. I had found the spot on the map – it was only just across the Tamar in Devon – and I wondered if their house was standing still. Probably not, or, if it had turned itself into a farm like Carminowe. I had located Carminowe on my map at the same time, when Teddy was up in my dressing-room packing my case, and had also found the reference to it in the old volume of *Parochial History* that had given me Tregesteynton. Carminowe was in Mawgan-in-Meneage, near the Loe Pool, and the writer said that the ancient mansion and chapel had fallen into decay in the reign of James I, along with the old burial ground.

I took the Launceston road after leaving Okehampton, for it was faster than the way we had come, and as I crossed from Devon into Cornwall, heading for Bodmin moor like a homing pigeon, I sang louder still, for even if Vita had beaten me to it, and was about to land in Dublin, I was safe from pursuit; she could not reach me now. This was my last trip, my final fling; and whatever became of me in the process I could not hurt either her or the boys, for they would be safe on Irish soil.

'In such a night
Stood Dido with a willow in her hand
Upon the wild sea-banks, and wav'd her love
To come again to Carthage.'

The trouble was, Isolda's lover had died in Treesmill creek upon the strand, and I doubted if either the threat of convent walls, or Joanna's taunts, or the monk's promise of safe passage to some doubtful refuge in Angers would have made her turn to Roger in the end. The future was bleak, six hundred years ago, for wives who left their husbands, especially when the husband had an eye to a third bride. It would have suited Oliver Carminowe, and the Ferrers family too, if Isolda had simply disappeared, which she might well have done had she entrusted herself to Joanna's care; but to remain under Roger's roof was at best only a stop-gap measure, and could not have continued long.

As I drove across Bodmin moor, rejoicing that each mile brought me nearer home, exhilaration was tempered by the knowledge that not only must this be the last trip to the other world, but that when I entered it I had no choice of date or season. The thaw could have come and Lent be over, high summer have taken its place, Isolda herself, having made her choice, be languishing behind those convent walls somewhere in Devon, in which case she would have moved out of Roger's life, and mine as well. I wondered, had Magnus lived, whether he could have perfected the timing factor, thus leaving the awakening from present to past to the participant's own choice; so that today, by some infinitesimal alteration of the dose, I could have summoned up at will those figures in the basement where I had left them last. Never, in the few weeks of experiment, had it happened that way. There had always been a jump in time. Joanna's carriage would no longer be waiting on the top of the hill above Kylmerth; Roger, Isolda and Bess would have left the farmhouse kitchen. That single draught in the walking-stick could guarantee re-entry to my world, but not what I should find there when I did.

The halt-sign brought me up with a jerk on to the main Lost-withiel-St Blazey road. I had driven the last twenty miles like an automaton, and I remembered the side turning that would take me past Tregesteynton to the Treesmill valley. I drove down it with a strange nostalgic sense, and as I passed the present farm-house of Strickstenton, and a black-and-white collie darted out on to the road barking, I thought of small Margaret, Isolda's younger child, who had wanted a riding-whip like Robbie's, and Joanna, the elder, preening in the looking-glass while her father chased Sybell up the stairs with the otter's paw.

I came down into the valley, and so intense was my identification with the past that I had forgotten, momentarily, that the river would no longer be there, and I looked for Rosgof's cottage by the side of the ford opposite the mill; but of course there was no river and no ford, only the road turning left and a few cows grazing in the marshy field.

I wished I was in the Triumph, for the Buick was too big and conspicuous. On sudden impulse I parked by the bridge below the mill, and, walking a short way up the lane, climbed over the gate into the field leading to the Gratten. I knew I must stand there once more amongst the mounds before returning home, for once back at Kilmarth the future would be uncertain; the last experiment might land me in some trouble unforeseen. I wanted to carry in my mind the image of the Treesmill valley as it looked today under the late August sun, letting imagination and memory do the rest, bringing back the winding river and the creek, and the anchorage below the long-vanished house. They had been harvesting in the Chapel Park fields behind the Gratten, but here where I walked beneath the hedge it was all grass, and cows were grazing. I came to the first of the gorse-bushes, climbing to the top of the high bank surrounding the site, and then looked down to the apron of grass which had once been a path under the hallway window, where Isolda and Bodrugan had sat holding hands.

A man was lying there, smoking a cigarette, his coat propped under his head as pillow. I stared hard, unbelieving, thinking that guilt and an uneasy conscience must have conjured his image out of the air; but I was not mistaken. The man who was lying there was very real, and it was Dr Powell.

I stood there a moment watching him, then deliberately, without malice but with total resolution, I unscrewed the top of Magnus's stick and took out the little measure. I swallowed my last dose, and replaced the measure once again inside the stick. Then I walked down the mound and joined him.

'I thought,' I said, 'you had gone surfing on the north coast?'

He sat up instantly, and I experienced, for the first time since knowing him, the immensely satisfying feeling that I had caught him unawares and at a disadvantage.

He recovered quickly, the look of astonishment giving place

to an engaging smile. 'I changed my mind,' he said calmly, 'and let the family go off without me. You seem to have done the same.'

'So Vita beat me to it after all. She didn't lose much time,' I told him.

'What's your wife got to do with it?'

'Well, she telephoned you from Dublin, didn't she?'

'No,' he said.

Now it was my turn to look astonished and stare at him. 'Then what the hell are you doing here waiting for me?'

'I wasn't waiting for you. Rather than brave the Atlantic breakers I decided to explore your piece of territory. A hunch that has apparently paid off. You can show me round.'

My one-upmanship began to fade, my self-confidence desert me. He seemed to be playing my own game and getting away with it.

'Look,' I said, ' don't you want to know what happened at the airport?'

'Not particularly,' he replied. 'The plane took off, I know, because I rang through to Exeter and checked. Whether you were on it or not they couldn't tell me, but I knew that if you weren't you would head back for Kilmarth, and if I turned up there for a cup of tea I'd find you in the basement. Meanwhile, burning curiosity drove me to while away half an hour or so down here.'

His cocksure attitude infuriated me, but I was even more angry with myself. If I had taken the other road, if I had not come through the Treesmill valley and allowed momentary sentiment to sway me, I should have been safely back at Kilmarth with at least half an hour or more in hand before he breezed in to take possession.

'All right,' I said, 'I know I've played a dirty trick on Vita and the boys, and she's probably ringing you from Dublin airport now and getting no reply. What staggers me is that you let me go knowing what might happen. It's almost as much your fault as mine.'

'Oh, I agree,' he answered. 'I'm equally to blame, and we'll both apologize when we get her on the telephone. But I wanted to give you a chance, just to see if you could make it, instead of going by the rules.'

'And what do the rules say?'

'Put your addict inside, once he's well and truly hooked.'

I looked at him thoughtfully, and leant on Magnus's walking-stick for support. 'You know very well,' I said, 'I gave bottle C to you, and that was the last; and you must have given the house a pretty thorough search when I was lying prone upstairs all the week.'

'I did,' he replied, 'and searched it again today. I told Mrs Collins I was looking for buried treasure, and I think she believed me. Suspicious sort of chap, aren't I?'

'Yes. And you found nothing, because there was nothing there.'

'Well, you may count yourself damn lucky that there wasn't. I've got Willis's final report in my pocket.'

'What does it say?'

'Only that the drug contains a substance of some toxicity that could seriously affect the central nervous system, possibly leading to paralysis. No need to elaborate.'

'Show it to me now.'

He shook his head, and suddenly he was not there any more, and the walls were all around me, and I was standing in the hall of the Champernoune manor-house looking out of the casement window at the rain. Panic gripped me, for it was not meant to happen, at least not yet; I had counted on being home, behind my own four walls, with Roger acting as my usual guide-protector. He was not here, and the hall was empty, and had been altered since I had seen it last. There seemed to be more furniture, more hangings, and the curtain masking the doorway to the stair above was drawn aside. Someone was crying in the bedroom overhead, and I could hear the sound of heavy footsteps pacing the floor. I looked out of the casement window once again, and saw through the falling rain that it must be autumn, for the clump of trees on the opposite hill where Oliver Carminowe had concealed himself and his men, as they lay in ambush waiting for Bodrugan, was golden brown as it had been then. But today no wind blew, tossing the leaves on to the ground below; the steady mizzle made them hang dispirited, and a shroud of mist clung above Lanescot and the river's mouth.

The crying turned to a high-pitched laugh, and down the stairs came a cup and ball, rolling one behind the other, until they reached the floor of the hall itself, when the ball rolled slowly under the table. I heard a man's voice call anxiously, 'Mind how you go, Elizabeth!' as someone, still laughing, came clumping down the stairs in search of the toy. She stood a moment, her hands clasped in front of her, her long dress trailing, an absurd little bonnet askew on her auburn hair. Her likeness to Joanna Champernoune was startling, then tragic, for this was an idiot girl, about twelve years old, with a full loose mouth, and eyes set high in her head. She nodded, laughing, then picked up the ball and cup and began to throw them in the air, screaming with delight. Suddenly, tiring of the game, she tossed them aside and started to spin around in circles until she became giddy, when she fell on to the floor and sat there motionless, staring at her shoes.

The man's voice from above called out again, 'Elizabeth ... Elizabeth', and the girl struggled clumsily to her feet and smiled, gazing at the ceiling. Footsteps came slowly down the stairs and the man appeared, wearing a long, loose robe to his ankles, and a night-cap. I thought, for a moment, I had travelled back in time and it was Henry Champernoune who stood there, weak and pale in his final illness, but it was Henry's son William, an adolescent when I saw him last, squaring up to take his place as head of the family when Roger broke the news of his father's death. Now he looked thirty-five or even more, and I realized, with a shock of dismay, that time had leapt ahead of me at least twelve years, and all the intervening months and years were buried in a past I should never know. The frozen winter of 1335 meant nothing to this William, who had been a minor and unmarried then. He was now master of his own house, although battling, it would seem, against sickness, and enmeshed as well in the inescapable net of some family flaw.

'Come, daughter, come, love,' he said gently, holding out his arms, and she put her finger in her mouth and sucked it, shaking her shoulders, then, with a sudden change of mind, darted to the floor and picked up her cup and ball again and gave it to him.

'I'll toss it for you above, but not down here,' he said. 'Katie has been sick as well, and I must not leave her.'

'She'll not have my toy, I won't let her,' said Elizabeth, nodding her head up and down, and she put out her hand and tried to snatch it back.

'What? Not let your sister share it when she gave it to you? That's not my Lizzie speaking, surely? Lizzie's flown up the chimney and a bad girl has taken her place.'

He clicked his tongue in reproof, and at the sound of it her full mouth drooped, her eyes filled with tears, and she flung her arms about him, crying bitterly, clinging to his long robe.

'There, there,' he said. 'Father did not mean it, Father loves his Liz, but she must not tease him, he is still weak and sick, and poor Katie too. Come, now, upstairs, and she can watch us from her bed, and when you toss the ball high she'll be the better for it, and maybe smile.'

He took her hand and led her towards the stairs, and as he did so someone came through the door leading to the kitchen quarters. William heard the footsteps and turned his head.

'See that all the doors are fastened before you go,' he said, 'and bid the servants keep them so, and open them to no one. God knows I hate to give the order, but I daren't do otherwise. Sick stragglers bide their time, and wait for darkness before they walk abroad and knock on men's doors.'

'I know it. There have been many so in Tywardreath, and death has spread because of it.'

There was no doubt about the speaker who stood at the open door. It was Robbie, a taller, broader Robbie than the lad I knew, and his chin was bearded now like his brother's.

'Watch how you go upon the road, then,' answered William. 'The same poor demented wanderers might attempt to strike you down, thinking, because you ride, you have some magic property of health denied to them.'

'I'll ride with care, Sir William, have no fear. I would not leave you for the night except for Roger. Five days since I was home, and he's alone.'

'I know, I know. God keep you both, and watch over all of us this night.'

He led his daughter up the stairs to the room above, and I followed Robbie to the kitchen-quarters. Three servants sat there in dejected fashion, hugging the hearth, one with his eyes closed and his head resting against the wall. Robbie gave him William's message, and he echoed, 'God be with us' without opening his eyes.

Robbie shut the door behind him and walked across the

stable-court. His pony was tied to the stall inside the shed. He mounted and began riding slowly up the hill through the mizzling rain, passing the small cottages that formed part of the demesne, lining the muddied track. All the doors were fastened tight, and smoke came from the roofs of only two, the others seeming deserted. We reached the brow of the hill, and Robbie, instead of turning to the right on the road to the village, paused by the geld-house on the left, and, dismounting, tied his pony to the gate and walked up the path to the chapel alongside. He opened the door and entered, I following after. The chapel was small, hardly more than twenty feet in length and fifteen broad, with a single window facing east behind the altar. Robbie, making the sign of the Cross, knelt down before it, and bowed his head in prayer. There was an inscription in Latin beneath the window, which I read:

'Matilda Champernoune built this chapel in memory of her husband William Champernoune, who died in 1304.'

A stone before the chancel steps was inscribed with her own initials and the date of her death, which I could not decipher. A similar stone, to the left, bore the initials H.C. There were no stained glass windows, no effigies or tombs built against the walls: this was an oratory, a memorial chapel.

When Robbie rose from his knees and turned away, I saw another stone before the chancel steps. The lettering read I.C.; the date was 1335. As I followed Robbie out into the rain and down towards the village, I knew of only one name that would fit, and it was not Champernoune.

Desolation was all about me, here by the geld-house and in the village too. No people on the green, no animals, no barking dogs. The doors of the small dwellings huddled close around the green were closed, like those on the demesne itself. A single goat, half-starved by its appearance, with ribs protruding from its lean body, was tethered by a chain near to the well, cropping the rough grass.

We climbed the hill-track above the Priory, and looking down on to the enclosure I could see no sign of life from behind the walls. No smoke came from the monks' quarters, nor from the chapter-house; the whole place seemed abandoned, and the ripening apples in the orchard had been left to cluster on the trees unplucked. And when we passed the ploughlands on the high ground I saw that the soil had not been turned, and some of the corn was not even harvested but lay rotting on the earth, as if some cyclone in the night had swept it down. As we came to the pastureland on the lower slopes the Priory cattle, roaming loose, came lowing after us in desperation, as though in hope that Robbie, on his pony, might drive them home.

We crossed the ford with ease, for the tide was ebbing fast and the sands lay uncovered, flat and dirty brown under the rain. A thin wreath of smoke came from Julian Polpey's roof – he at least must have survived calamity – but Geoffrey Lampetho's dwelling in the valley looked as bare and deserted as those on the village green. This was not the world I knew, the world I had come to love and long for because of its magic quality of love and hate, its separation from a drab monotony; this was a place resembling, in its barren desolation, all the most hideous features of a twentieth-century landscape after disaster, suggesting a total abandonment of hope, the aftertaste of atomic doom.

Robbie rode uphill above the ford, and passing through the copse of straggling trees came down to the wall encircling Kylmerth yard. No smoke curled up from the chimney. He flung himself from his pony, leaving it to wander loose towards the byre, and running across the yard he opened the door.

'Roger!' I heard him call, and 'Roger!' once again. The kitchen was empty, the turf no longer smouldered on the hearth. The remains of food lay untouched upon the trestle table, and as Robbie climbed the ladder to the sleeping-loft I saw a rat scurry across the floor and disappear.

There can have been no one in the loft, for Robbie came down the ladder instantly, and opened the door beneath it which gave access to the byre, revealing at the same time a narrow passage ending in a store-room and a cellar. Slits in the thickness of the wall allowed streaks of light to penetrate the gloom, and this was the only source of air as well. There was little draught to cleanse the atmosphere of sweet mustiness pervading, due to the rotting apples laid in rows against the wall. An iron cauldron, unsteady on three legs, and rusted from disuse, stood in the far corner, and beside it pitchers, jars, a three-pronged fork, a pair of bellows. This store-room was a strange choice for a sick man to make his bed. He must have dragged his pallet from the sleeping-loft and placed it here beside the slit in the wall, and then, from increasing weakness or lack of will, lain through the days and nights until today.

'Roger . . .' whispered Robbie, 'Roger!'

Roger opened his eyes. I did not recognize him. His hair was white, his eyes sunk deep in his head, his features thin and drawn; and under the white furze that formed his beard the flesh was discoloured, bruised, with the same discoloured swellings behind his ears. He murmured something, water, I think it was, and Robbie rose from his side and ran into the kitchen, but I went on kneeling there beside him, staring down at the man I had last seen confident and strong.

Robbie returned with a pitcher of water, and, putting his arms round his brother, helped him to drink. But after two mouthfuls Roger choked, and lay back again on his pallet, gasping.

'No remedy,' he said. 'The swelling's spread to my throat and blocked the windpipe. Moisten my lips only, that's comfort enough.'

'How long have you lain here?' asked Robbie.

'I cannot tell. Four days and nights, maybe. Not long after you went I knew it had me, and I brought my bed to the cellar so that you could sleep easy above when you returned. How is Sir William?'

'Recovered, thanks be to God, and young Katherine too. Elizabeth still escapes infection, and the servants. More than sixty died this week in Tywardreath. The Priory is closed, as you know, and the Prior and brethren gone to Minster.'

'No loss,' murmured Roger. 'We can do without them. Did you visit the chapel?'

'I did, and said the usual prayer.'

He moistened his brother's lips with water once again, and in rough but tender fashion tried to soften the swellings beneath his ears.

'I tell you, there's no remedy,' said Roger. 'This is the end. No parish priest to shrive me, no communal grave amongst the rest. Bury me at the cliff's edge, Robbie, where my bones will smell the sea.'

'I'll go to Polpey and fetch Bess,' said Robbie. 'She and I can nurse you through this together.'

'No,' said Roger, 'she has her own children to care for now, and Julian too. Hear my confession, Robbie. There's been something on my conscience now these thirteen years.'

He struggled to sit up but had not strength enough, and Robbie, the tears running down his cheeks, smoothed the matted hair out of his brother's eyes.

'If it concerns you and Lady Carminowe, I don't need to hear it, Roger,' he said. 'Bess and I knew you loved her, and love her still. So did we. There was no sin in that for any of us.'

'No sin in loving, but in murder, yes,' said Roger.

'Murder?'

Robbie, kneeling by his brother's side, stared down at him, bewildered, then shook his head. 'You're wandering, Roger,' he said softly. 'We all know how she died. She had been sick for weeks before she came here, and hid it from us; and then when they tried to carry her away by force she gave her promise she would follow in a week, and so they let her stay.'

'And would have gone, but I prevented it.'

'How did you prevent it? She died before the week had passed, here, in the room above, with Bess's arms about her, and yours too.'

'She died because I would not let her suffer pain,' said Roger. 'She died because, had she kept her bargain and travelled to Trelawn and thence into Devon, there would have been weeks of agony ahead, even months, agony that our own mother knew and endured when we were young. So I let her go from us in sleep, knowing nothing of what I had done, and you and Bess in the same ignorance.'

He put out his hands and felt for Robbie's, holding it tight. 'Did you never wonder, Robbie, when in the old days I stayed at the Priory late at night, or on occasion brought de Meral here to the cellar, what it was I did?'

'I knew the French ships landed merchandise,' said Robbie, 'and you conveyed it to the Priory. Wine and other goods which the Prior lacked. And the monks lived well because of it.'

'They taught me their secrets too,' said Roger. 'How to make men dream and conjure visions, rather than pray. How to seek a paradise on earth that would last for a few hours only. How to make men die. It was only after young Bodrugan perished in de Meral's care that I sickened of the game, taking no further part in it. But I had learnt the secret well, and so made use of it, when the time came. I gave her something to ease pain and let her slip away. It was murder, Robbie, and a mortal sin. And no one knows of it but you.'

The effort of speaking had drained him of all strength, and Robbie, lost and frightened suddenly in the presence of death, let go his hand, and, stumbling to his feet, went blindly along the passage to the kitchen, in search, I think, of some additional covering to draw over his brother. I went on kneeling there, in the cellar, and Roger opened his eyes for the last time and stared at me. I think he asked for absolution, but there was no one there, in his own time, to grant it, and I wondered if, because of this, he had travelled through the years in search of it. Like Robbie, I was helpless, and six centuries too late.

'Go forth, O Christian soul, out of this world, in the name of God the Father Almighty, who created thee; in the name of Jesus Christ, the Son of the living God, who suffered for thee; in the name of the Holy Ghost, who sanctified thee . . .'

I could not remember any more, and it did not matter, because he had already gone. The light was coming through the chinks of the shuttered window in the old laundry, and I was kneeling there, on the stone floor of the lab, amongst the empty bottles and the jars. There was no nausea, no vertigo, no singing in my ears. Only a great silence, and a sense of peace.

I raised my head and saw that the doctor was standing by the wall and watching me.

'It's finished,' I said. 'Roger's dead, he's free. It's all over.'

The doctor put out his hand and took my arm. He led me out of the room and up the stairs, and through to the front part of the house and into the library. We sat down together on the window-seat, staring out across the sea.

'Tell me about it,' he said.

'Don't you know?'

I had thought, seeing him in the lab, that he must have shared the experience with me, then I realized it was impossible.

'I waited with you on the site,' he told me, 'then walked with you up the hill, and followed behind you in the car. You stopped for a moment in a field above Tywardreath, near where the two roads join, then down through the village and along the side-lane to Polmear, and so back here. You were walking quite normally, rather faster, perhaps, than I would have cared to do myself. Then you struck to the right through the wood, and I came down the drive. I knew I should find you below.'

I got up from the window-seat and went to the bookshelf, and took down one of the volumes of the *Encyclopaedia Britannica.*

'What are you looking for?' he asked.

I turned the pages until I found the reference I sought.

'The date of the Black Death,' I said, '1348. Thirteen years after Isolda died.' I put the book back upon the shelf.

'Bubonic plague,' he observed. 'Endemic in the Far East — they've had a number of cases in Vietnam.'

'Have they?' I said. 'Well, I've just seen what it did in Tywardreath six hundred years ago.'

I went back to the window-seat and picked up the walking-stick. 'You must have wondered how I managed that last trip,' I said. 'This is how.' I. unscrewed the top and showed him the small measure. He took it from me and held it upside down. It was fully drained.

'I'm sorry,' I said, 'but when I saw you sitting there below the Gratten I knew I had to do it. It was my last chance. And I'm glad I did, because now the whole thing is done with, finished. No more temptation. No more desire to lose myself in the other world. I told you Roger was free, and so am I.'

He did not answer. He was still staring at the empty measure.

'Now,' I said, 'before we put through a call to Dublin airport and ask if Vita is there, supposing you tell me what else was written in that report John Willis sent you?'

He picked up the stick, and replacing the measure screwed on the top and gave it back to me.

'I burnt it,' he said, 'with the flame from my lighter, when you were on your knees in the basement reciting that prayer for the dying. Somehow it seemed to me the right moment, and I preferred to destroy it rather than have it lying in the surgery amongst my files.'

'That's no answer,' I told him.

'It's all you're going to get,' he replied.

The telephone started ringing from the lobby in the hall. I wondered how many times it had rung before.

'That will be Vita,' I said. 'Now for the count-down. I'd better get on my knees again. Shall I tell her I got locked in the gents and I'll join her tomorrow?'

'It would be wiser,' he said slowly, 'if you told her you hoped to join her later, perhaps in a few weeks' time.'

'But that's absurd,' I frowned. 'There's nothing to hold me back. I've told you it's all over and I'm free.'

He did not say anything. He just sat there staring at me.

The telephone went on ringing, and I crossed the room to answer it, but a silly thing happened as I picked up the receiver. I couldn't hold it properly; my fingers and the palm of my hand went numb, and it slipped out of my grasp and crashed to the floor.